1906

1906

A NOVEL

JAMES DALESSANDRO

CHRONICLE BOOKS
SAN FRANCISCO

Library of Congress Cataloging-in-Publication Data available.

ISBN 0-8118-4313-0

Manufactured in the United States of America

Book and cover design by Tracy Sunrize Johnson
Cover photo used with permission of the California Historical Society Collection,
    USC Specialized Libraries and Archival Collections
Back flap photo by J.B. Monaco, courtesy of Richard Monaco

Distributed in Canada by Raincoast Books
9050 Shaughnessy Street
Vancouver, British Columbia V6P 6E5

10 9 8 7 6 5 4 3 2

Chronicle Books LLC
85 Second Street
San Francisco, California 94105
www.chroniclebooks.com

TO

KATIE DALESSANDRO
GLADYS HANSEN.
KEN KESEY

PROLOGUE

---∞---

THE UNOFFICIAL STORY

——◆·◇◦·◆——

TELEGRAPH HILL

MAY 30, 1906. 8:00 A.M.

It was a month ago that I finally managed to convince myself I was still alive. That day—a week after the inferno burned out—the fire clap had faded from my ears enough that I was able to hear a knock on the door of our baked Victorian.

I arose from a seated position on the floor where I had been typewriting day and night on the Remington, and shuffled through inch-deep ash, little clouds erupting with every step. I jerked open the brittle front door to discover an overdressed man waiting on the soot-covered stoop.

He asked for Annalisa Passarelli, opera and theater critic for the *Evening Bulletin*, cringing at the sight of me. When I said I was she, he lowered the handkerchief he had been clutching to his nose to ward off the acrid smell of burnt everything and introduced himself as Mr. Charles Appleby. He stated he had been sent by the California State Historian at Sacramento, removed his bowler hat as if preparing for a benediction, and began to recite a litany of statistics.

Three hundred miles of California coastline reconfigured. Santa Rosa, Palo Alto, San Jose, and several dozen other small towns reduced to rubble from Humboldt County to Monterey. Nearly a half million people sent running for their lives, more than thirty thousand buildings incinerated, including thirty-seven national banks, the Pacific Stock Exchange, two opera houses; hundreds of millions of dollars in smoke and ash.

I interrupted to explain that I was aware of the physical losses, having witnessed much of it with my own eyes.

He then mentioned an honorarium that sounded like one thousand dollars, offering me a position as one of six writers chosen by the State Historian's office to report the events of April 18, 1906, and the three terrible days that followed. After aiming one blistered ear, then the other, straining for detail, I had my cracked lips parted and my swollen tongue dislodged and was about to accept when he mentioned the phrase "Official Story." He looked up, braving the sight of me as chivalrously as his horror permitted, stating that all of the required fodder for the effort would be provided by the office of our Mayor, the ever-grinning marionette Eugene Schmitz.

The six writers would be encouraged to add "little dashes of color" and "some inspiring bits of human interest" that would then be reviewed by the Official Information and Oversight Committee. For some reason that portion of Mr. Appleby's tale came through quite clearly.

The undulating crimson veil that had colored my field of vision had also subsided, enough so that I was able to examine the written proffer. After further Appleby emphasis of just how keen everyone was to perpetrate the official fraud—his voice filtered through the metal-on-metal shriek that had replaced the fire's throb—I returned his document and gave a shake of my frazzled head, sending a faint halo of ash floating down on him.

He returned to his carriage with the half-skipping gait usually seen on tourists who inadvertently wander—or once wandered—into the Barbary Coast after dark. The dappled mare tethered to the black runabout was as anxious to leave as queasy Mr. Appleby.

Had I accepted, I would have been, at twenty-two, the youngest of the deceitful six and the only woman. Add that I was the opera and theater critic for Mr. Fremont Older's *Evening Bulletin*, a crusading journal that appeared to have soundly lost the crusade, and I was easily the group's most unlikely candidate. A thousand dollars was an attractive sum in a city living in Army tents, standing in soup lines or spearing rodents for sustenance, but I was content with my decision as I was not prepared to enter the whoring profession just yet.

I had my own version of the story, much of it collected and composed before the horror struck; a version that would do nicely without assistance from City Hall.

But I have gotten ahead of myself, a dangerous state of affairs for a writer.

The city of San Francisco is no more. The Paris of the Pacific, the wealthiest and wickedest of American cities, is now ash and memories. All that remains are blackened wharves, the iron puddle of a church bell, a mound of cinders where a school once stood, hilly graveyards of charred bricks and melted iron skeletons, an endless scorch mark that was once the grandest boulevard in the West. A city of four hundred and fifty thousand frenetic souls; shaken from its moorings, burnt to a crisp, vanished from the face of the earth.

The fire stopped a block below us, here at the crown of Telegraph Hill, sparing seven houses where once were thousands, seven sullied teeth in the mouth of a black-gummed giant. Seven houses where once sat a raucous Barbary Coast, a majestic Market Street, a teeming Chinatown, seven houses for all of North Beach and Russian Hill and Cow Hollow and the Embarcadero.

I write my story, still floating in a sea of ash. Ash that was once the city of San Francisco: once someone's mansion, someone's opera house, someone's tenement, someone's bakery. Someone's someone. My cough sends a fluffy tail snaking across the feathery surface of something that was once precious to someone.

I cringe at the further horror wrought by the lies that Mayor Schmitz and his minions attempt to foist upon us. Let me tell you what really happened here, before deception triumphs and the truth is lost forever. Let me paint for you the Imperial City of San Francisco: part Paris, part Dodge City; literate and boorish, libertine and feudal, a soiled Mecca, a beacon for those who had grown weary of the broken promises. San Francisco had invigorated the dream and become the new America.

I offer my own version of this extraordinary tale, one that began well before the holocaust. It is a personal observation; part history and part memoir, an attempt to add a human face to a most inhumane series of events.

I complete my version of the story, cross-legged in a barren Victorian on roasted Telegraph Hill while the unholy trinity of Mayor Eugene Schmitz and Boss Adam Rolf and Napoleonic General Frederick Funston are meeting at a bakery on Fillmore Street in the Western Addition, just past the fire line, to concoct their account. Their objectives are quite simple: to protect themselves from the hangman's noose, minimize the totality of the horror lest the sane world recoil from our restoration, and defraud history by convincing us this was all God's will and not their folly.

The newspapers, printed daily in Oakland, barrage us with tales of their heroics: of the steely resolve of Mayor Schmitz and the unflinching courage of Funston's square-jawed troops and of the brilliant plans of Boss Rolf to engineer our resurrection. Four hundred and seventy-eight dead, they report. Four hundred and seventy-eight. There were that many bodies in the twisted tenements South of Market, on Howard Street alone. The true number is in the thousands.

I must offer a shifting mosaic of characters and events as no one story could ever render up the heart of this great matter, of a wondrous and dangerous city that is no more. I rely upon a bit of hearsay, tales retold, on points of view disparate and even contradictory. I have used diaries and letters, from both the living and the dead, to construct my story. I must fictionalize, on some accounts, the words and actions of characters whom neither I nor my legion of observers could record firsthand. Those instances are quite small in number. The liberties I take are minor.

What transpired here was a war for a city's heart that merely climaxed on April 18, 1906, at 5:13 A.M., a moment etched in the memories of all who survived. But if earthquake and fire is all that is remembered, then all is lost, for what we truly witnessed was a battle between good and evil the likes of which we have not seen outside of war itself.

Schmitz, Rolf, and Funston will no doubt twist any truth to convince you our demise was merely fate unavoidable, and whatever bad things this noble trio might have done, they did so with our welfare at the fore. Do not believe it. It did not have to happen. Good men and women, the unlikeliest of heroes, might have stopped it. The warning signs were everywhere.

The die was cast, not by the great earthquake but three days earlier, when the true heroes began to assemble. They were an unlikely lot: a runaway Kansas farm girl, a Chinese slave girl, a martyred fire chief, and a group of fearless young cops they called The Brotherhood. Lest anyone question the inspired significance of the cast, God, who loves a wild yarn as much as anyone, sent His voice, the great Enrico Caruso, to preside.

Most of all, there were the Fallons: Byron, a man whose belief in justice consumed him; Christian, his elder son, a man at war with his own soul; and Hunter, the younger son, who found greatness before our eyes.

The story began, not on April 18, the day the Devil called, but three days earlier, when a remarkable young man named Hunter Fallon came home from Stanford University.

Remarkable indeed, for Hunter alone might have saved us.

—ANNALISA PASSARELLI

PART ONE

THE FALLONS

San Francisco, since the earliest years . . . has always been a money town. When John Jacob Astor was clipping dimes in the trade in New York Real Estate and Commodore Vanderbilt was ferrying passengers to Staten Island for a shilling, the wife of San Francisco's mayor . . . was pouring tea from a solid gold service, the first such in America . . . and the town's first jeweler was advertising silver watches that weighed a full honest pound, since no miner could be found who would carry one that weighed less.

—LUCIUS BEEBE, HISTORIAN

Chapter 1

STANFORD UNIVERSITY

APRIL 15, 1906. 5:30 A.M.

The horses woke Hunter Fallon that Easter morning, neighing and kick-ing in the stalls beneath him. He opened his eyes to a sight as discom-forting as the sound: an empty loft that until the day before had been crammed with graphs and charts, measuring devices, Bunsen burners and Petri dishes, microscopes, boxing gloves, leather football helmets, and sporting trophies of every shape and size. Gone, all of it crated and shipped by rail to his father's house in San Francisco.

Hunter lay there a minute, the rolling emptiness inducing a sort of vertigo. He dismissed the fractiousness of his four-legged companions as some sort of equine melancholy, convinced they were as saddened as he was over his departure.

The loft where he slept, above the palatial stables on the edge of the campus, had been his home since the recently deceased Jane Stanford, angel of the university, had awarded him a scholarship in the fall of 1900. Exercising and tending Jane's prized thoroughbreds and trotters had pro-vided loft and board. He had described those years, in a constant stream of letters to his father, as more a miracle than an education. But that was over now. The adventures just ahead would be unlike any he had ever dreamed.

A golden beam of sunlight appeared on the redwood ceiling high above him, growing quickly from band to square to rhomboid. Hunter rose and stretched to his full six-foot height, and descended the ladder to the rough mahogany floor, where he quickly offered his good-byes.

"Mr. Whitman," he told a chestnut colt, "don't tell the others, but I loved you best." He scratched Mr. Lincoln, nuzzled Mr. Twain, accepted a pink and soggy good-bye kiss from Miss Woodhull, Miss Duncan, Mr. Edison, Mr. Roosevelt, Mr. Caruso. Hunter was, as were his charges, sturdy, handsome, and noble of stock.

A decade earlier, when we were both near the age of twelve, I had developed a schoolgirl infatuation with him, and was not alone among the young girls in North Beach, San Francisco's Latin Quarter. He was, even then, more an element of nature than an adolescent, restless and unyielding as the tide and fog that move through the Golden Gate. He was often seen tearing about on a bicycle he had built from spare parts, stopping to engage even casual acquaintances with dissertations on emerging developments in the telephone or new steering mechanisms in the automobile. His precocity was tolerated by most, as he was the offspring of legends.

His grandfather Malachi and granduncle Arthur founded San Francisco's police department during the Gold Rush, their primary qualification a willingness to battle a gang of former Australian convicts, the Sydney Ducks. As sons and nephews and grandsons followed them, the Fallon/Fagen/Rinaldi clan, more than a dozen of them, earned a city's reverence as the department's most honest and fearless officers.

The last I had seen of Hunter, his father was marching him home, dragging the pieces of a homemade glider constructed according to diagrams in Chanute's *Progress in Flying Machines*. Byron had caught Hunter near Sutro Baths just as he was about to launch himself and the contraption off the ocean cliffs. He was fourteen at the time and earned a considerable tarring for his efforts. Age, I was to discover, only enhanced Hunter's considerable gifts.

On that momentous Easter morning, now nearly twenty-three, Hunter sported the dark eyebrows, flawless olive complexion, and impassioned intellect of his Italian mother Isabella. From his Irish father he inherited a square-set jaw, haunting blue eyes, and unflinching determination. Summers in construction work and years of athletics provided a frame straining with muscle.

The ache of his bittersweet departure was tinged with apprehension. After all, it is not often that a young man's final college examination runs the risk of killing him.

Hunter donned faded Levi blue jeans, a gray woolen shirt, black leather engineer's boots, and a Pittsburgh Pirates cap signed by the great shortstop Honus Wagner, twisting the brim backward on his head. Moments later, he pushed a gleaming black and chrome Waltham out onto Stanford Lane. With an engine shaped like an enormous V, the motorcycle had arrived the previous winter in several hundred pieces and taken Hunter six months to assemble.

A quarter-mile away, a crowd of fifty had gathered for his benediction: fresh-faced young men in brown tweed suits and bowler hats, rosy-cheeked coeds in long skirts, square-shouldered jackets, and broad-brimmed bonnets plumed with Easter orchids.

Hunter lowered a pair of jockey's goggles over his Pirates cap and kicked the starter pedal. Three, four, five times, adjusting valves and levers. On the sixth try, the Waltham roared to life. He engaged the gear lever and rode in ever-widening circles, listening for signs the whole thing might explode between his legs.

As he circled, staring out at the lush green valley and the creek swollen with spring runoff, he thought of his mother Isabella, who had died a month before he entered the University. It made him tearful that she was not present to witness his finest moment.

On Stanford Lane, his friend and mentor, the patrician Director of Graduate Engineering studies, fretful and asthmatic Professor Rudy Durand, raised a small red flag. Hunter stopped the Waltham at a white chalk mark and gunned the engine several times. The flag dropped.

The motorcycle lurched, throwing the front wheel skyward, spitting a puff of ebony smoke, and slammed back onto the ground, the rear wheel blasting sand and pebbles down the lane. The howling machine gasped, bucked, and bolted forward.

In fifty yards, he had it up to thirty. Thirty-five, forty, forty-five. Hunter's heart pounded as he roared down the quarter-mile stretch, the wind ripping at his leather jacket, flattening the goggles against his eyes. The umbrella of eucalyptus funneled and amplified the sound across the valley. Above fifty, the road threatened to tear the tires from their steel rims. Hunter pushed the throttle lever to the bottom of its transit, fighting desperately for control as he charged toward Professor Durand. Fifty, fifty-five, sixty.

Half on and half off, Hunter crossed the finish line as Professor Durand clicked the watch. The gallery cheered and spun like tops as the blast of wind sent hats and bonnets flying.

"Sixty-four and one-half miles per hour," the professor shouted. "That beats the California motorized record of sixty-three miles per hour."

Hunter circled the crowd, pumping his fist like a victorious gladiator, and offered a good-bye wave. He charged across the picturesque quadrangle, past the majestic sandstone buildings, and through the stone Arch of Triumph, slowing briefly to capture a melancholy glimpse of the campus. He was struck by an eerie feeling, a disturbing sense that he might never see his beloved Stanford again. The feeling was so keen that he abruptly turned the Waltham in a wide circle, fixing in his mind the buildings and the great arch, the towering barn and golden poppy–dotted hills, finally offering a pained salute to the memory of Jane Stanford.

North he flew, onto majestic El Camino Real, weaving through belching Fords ferrying churchgoers and over-laden wagons hauling the spring harvest from the lush Santa Clara Valley.

His thoughts turned to his father's home, and the apprehension did not ease. He had rarely returned during those six years, unable to leave his stablemates; a plan that Byron had secretly arranged, an attempt to dampen Hunter's interest in the family's bloody business.

On the evening before his son's return, I suggested to Byron that after a six-year absence Hunter might scarcely recognize the City.

Both Hunter and I had been born in 1883, into a dark and silent world poised for transformation by a flurry of technological wonders such as the world had never seen. In just over two decades the world had changed more than in a millennium. We witnessed the coming of the telephone, electric light, aero plane, automobile, phonograph, antiseptic surgery, the moving picture, and the X-ray machine.

At the turn of the century, the head of the U.S. Patent Office was reported to have declared that all of the world's great inventions had already been discovered. If all of the world's great marvels had already been invented, Hunter wrote, how could he invent them? In the six years since he had last lived on Telegraph Hill, those once-wondrous things had become staples in the public diet. San Francisco was bursting at the seams with change.

Byron had taken to sharing his son's frequent letters with me, until I felt I knew him almost as well as his father did. Hunter's musings included a hodgepodge of ideas: the enhancement of police work by scientific applications, his zeal for the progressive/conservationist politics of Teddy Roosevelt, theories on wireless communication, fund-raising activities for the defense of I.W.W. lion Big Bill Haywood for his trial in the bombing death of Idaho Governor Steunenberg, fervent support for the clarification of English via the Simplified Language movement, and Hunter's personal guarantee that the aero plane would soon replace the railroad as the principal transporter of people and goods.

In one missive received a week before his return, Hunter argued that Thomas Edison had become more influential than Queen Victoria in the five years since her death; ragtime and a new music called jazz would soon liberate the common spirit, replacing opera and helping to bring equality for Negroes; he finished with a timetable for the triumph of Suffrage and Industrial Unionism (less than ten years).

Byron was exhausted when he finished reading this letter aloud. I, on the other hand, though dubious about Hunter's technological predictions as I considered the march of progress a dehumanizing lockstep toward sooty oblivion, was touched by his impassioned belief in social progress, a commonality of spirit that, I must admit, awakened my former schoolgirl interest.

That Sunday, April 15, as he powered north through the once-rustic Peninsula, Hunter fretted over the proliferation of gabled mansions rapidly replacing the blinds and lodges where he and his father and brother Christian had hunted boar and pheasant. The astonishing wealth of San Francisco, fountainhead of the West, was spilling over, and the Peninsula, the puddle beneath the spout, was in danger of becoming an amorphous suburban lump stretching from San José to San Francisco.

Hunter motored onto the final stretch, the Bayshore Highway, the imperial city towering just ahead of him. He reached back to check the two documents inside his saddlebag.

The first was a letter from the San Francisco Police Department, confirming his acceptance. He would be the first college graduate to join the department, provided his father did not kill him.

The second was the engineering survey he had prepared for San Francisco Fire Chief Dennis Sullivan, entitled "An Independent Survey of Tectonic Movement along the San Andreas Fault and Its Effect on Subterranean Water Systems in San Francisco."

In the days that followed, we would realize how those two documents might have changed the fate of nearly half a million souls.

Chapter 2

TELEGRAPH HILL

APRIL 15, 1906. 5:45 A.M.

The San Francisco Police Department was the only life Byron Fallon had ever known. He had joined at age seventeen, believing it God's calling that he help end violence and corruption in the lawless city. He was a devout Catholic, blessed with a fearlessness and natural intelligence that earned him the rank of detective by age twenty-five. He bore two distinct physical traits that were of significance to his line of work: a set of cornflower blue eyes so soothing that they sometimes coaxed confessions from reluctant miscreants, and a pair of enormous hands that often worked where the former did not.

The fact that the dozen members of the Fallon/Fagen/Rinaldi clan had never taken a dirty dime had long ceased to bother—at least openly— other, less scrupulous police officers. It simply left a larger pot, and fewer hands to be divided among.

In 1895 Byron had been promoted to Chief of Detectives for his work in solving the sensational Belfry Murders at the Emmanuel Baptist Church. A church acolyte with a predilection for bathing in chicken blood while engaging Barbary Coast prostitutes had murdered two young girls and left their bodies in the church steeple, a case that became front-page news in all five of the town's papers.

As sunrise approached Easter morning, the bald, thick-limbed, fifty-three-year-old patriarch of the Fallon clan arose after another restless night. He paced his bedroom in the highest house atop Telegraph Hill, a two-story Italianate Victorian with modest dormers and white fish-scale siding. He paused at a window and gazed across San Francisco Bay as the water turned a shimmering pink, and a golden crown appeared atop Mount Tamalpais twenty miles away. He lifted a photo taken during vows at Mission Dolores: Isabella in a white lace dress and black velvet choker, silk flowers woven through her upswept hair, and he sporting a gray pin-stripe morning coat, red cravat, and well-waxed handlebar.

"*La luce splendida*," he muttered, as he had every morning since she died of pneumonia.

Above the faded cherry chiffonier an electric light suddenly burned. Byron had it installed two years earlier, when he had the house elec-trified, so that his Cantonese housekeeper, Mr. Lee, could signal his arrival and not be shot as an intruder. Byron took his Colt revolver from beneath the pillow—it is doubtful he had taken a step in more than thirty years without it—and padded across his bedroom on feet akin to bony flapjacks. His hips tilted left, his shoulders twisted right, and his right hand, the one that clutched the Colt, dangled lower than the other. Tattooed by scars and divots, he moved like a broken puppet repaired by a drunken craftsman.

"I make Hunter room with fresh blanket for him," Mr. Lee said, as he poured hot water into the basin before hurrying back to the kitchen.

Byron stared through the tiny bathroom window to Mount Tamalpais across the bay.

"How's the miracle this morning?" Isabella's voice. It had happened often lately: her voice, the rustle of her skirt, the waft of her familiar scent.

"Fine," he answered.

He washed and shaved and slid into a boiled shirt, brown bow tie, tan leather galluses, and a brown wool suit, purchased at the Emporium the previous week for the rather indulgent sum of nine dollars. He placed the Colt in a holster on his right hip, slipped a .32 caliber derringer into his right front pocket and a razor-sharp pocket knife in his left. Then he pinned a seven-pointed detective's golden star to the pocket of his vest.

In the kitchen, Byron toyed with his liver and eggs, a breakfast that had once caused normally taciturn Mr. Lee to ask him how white men could eat the things they do. The clanging of the Filbert Street cable car, his morning signal, sent Byron toward the door, his breakfast barely touched.

"Hunter make policeman like you, Lootenant Byron?" Mr. Lee asked as Byron headed for the door.

"No, Mr. Lee. We won't be needing him. By tomorrow, things will be different here."

Byron donned his bowler hat and stepped outside, inhaling the fragrant spring air that San Franciscans believe God created especially for them. Twelve blocks south, the lights of Market Street's hulking skyscrapers, some as high as eighteen stories, glowed carnival green against the violet light of morning. The jangle of forced laughter and tired fandangos drifted from the Barbary Coast saloons just below Telegraph Hill. He had heard but a few scattered gunshots the night before, the Coast almost tame compared to when he walked its streets as a patrolman years before.

He stared east, along the piers of the Embarcadero, a thousand masts waving back like an enormous field of wheat. Past and present jockeyed for position as stodgy, steam-powered tugs and graceful wind-powered clippers plowed against a meandering riptide. A paddle-wheel ferry and a tiny Whitehall boat crossed paths, the latter having deposited the latest shanghaied victims from the Barbary Coast at one of the barks or whalers anchored offshore.

Byron boarded the cable car for the steep three-block ride to Montgomery Street.

"Happy Easter, Lieutenant Fallon. I was down to Molinari's yesterday mornin' buyin' some strained tomatoes and Gino tol' me Hunter's comin' home from college." The city's only Negro gripman eased the brake lever and ratcheted up the hook that snagged the heavy cable underground. The six-ton car lurched forward, jerking and rumbling past the Victorian row houses.

"Yes, he does, Pericles. He comes home today."

"That will be one fine Easter present, Lieutenant Fallon."

"Yes, it will. And a Happy Easter to you too." Within seconds, the rising sun illuminated the entire bay and filled the cable car with blinding amber light.

It was the brilliant beginning to what Byron expected to be his most glorious day. Before the sun rose again over Telegraph Hill, he planned to arrest the mayor, city attorney, police chief, and all eighteen members of San Francisco's Board of Supervisors. It would be the greatest political coup and launch the biggest corruption trial in American history. President Roosevelt himself would issue a statement from Washington, announcing that San Francisco would serve as the model for a national crusade against graft.

The heinous crimes of shanghaiing unwitting men and slave trading in helpless Chinese girls would finally end. Honest businessmen would no longer suffer the official extortions of City Hall. The blight of urban America, the rule of city "Bosses" and their political puppets would hear its death knell. If Roosevelt's grand scheme succeeded, Byron believed it would usher in a new era in democracy, one safe from the pervasive power of Big Business and Boss Rule to control every aspect of modern life.

By April 17, two days later, the appearance of the great Caruso at our Grand Opera House would be a coronation of virtue over evil, of good men replacing bad. Byron Fallon would wield the scalpel that excised the cancer eating at the heart of our beloved San Francisco, and the ripple would affect an entire nation.

What he did not know that morning was that the final task would not be his.

That duty would soon fall to another member of the Fallon clan.

Chapter 3

APRIL 15, 1906. 6:00 A.M.

Christian Fallon's nightmare had begun a year earlier. At first it was a chorus of sounds: dogs howling, horses nickering, the tinkling of chandeliers, people whimpering, followed by the ghastly wrenching of post and beams, roofs and floors collapsing. Within weeks of the first dream, the unnerving sounds were joined by terrible sights: cascading torrents of mortar and brick, plumes of smoke and flame billowing from a vast sea of wreckage, all finally joined by the noxious scent of burning paint and varnish, wood and flesh.

That Sunday morning, five hours after Christian, elder of Byron's two sons, returned from foot patrol on the Barbary Coast, was the seventh day in a row the nightmare had raged full fury. He began to twitch, his thoughts a nickelodeon of horror: buildings ablaze, writhing victims and torn bodies scattered among the collapsed walls and chimneys, people dashing about bloodied and tear-streaked, naked or in nightclothes as dazed firemen watched helplessly near their fallen horses and shattered hydrants.

"Christian! Christian! Wake up! Christian!"

He opened his eyes to his wife Elizabeth staring down at him. At twenty-nine her delicate Welsh features were lined with fear and worry, her thick red hair sporting streaks of gray.

"Christian. Please. You have to tell somebody."

He squirmed in the creaking brass bed until the images faded and he could catch a breath. "Who should I tell, Elizabeth? My father? Chief Donen? So they can take my badge and send me down to Agnews with the other loonies? They already think I'm crazy." He slipped from beneath the patchwork quilt, retrieved his gray woolen trousers and a navy-blue sweater, and tugged them over his knotted frame.

At five feet nine and a hundred and sixty-five pounds, he was the greatest bare-knuckle boxer on the Barbary Coast, where such matters are routinely determined. He had Byron's square jaw, Isabella's deep-set eyes, and a face so chiseled it created its own shadows. Police work was the only profession he could follow. Fishing made him seasick and the numbers on a carpenter's rule appeared oddly backward. Bartending would have presented an even greater peril.

He was also the co-leader of a fearless group of five young Irish and Italian cops whom the *Bulletin* had dubbed "The Brotherhood" for both their familial relationship and devotion to the reformist rhetoric of the expatriate Irish priest, Father Peter Yorke. Along with his four cousins, Francis and Patrick Fagen, and Max and Carlo Rinaldi, they supplied the muscle and fire-power for Byron Fallon's burgeoning war on shanghaiers and slave traders.

"I'll be back in time to take the kids to church," he said as he kissed her. Then he trudged down the dark, narrow stairway into the cool morning.

He paused briefly, staring down Union Street at the one-story shops and cheap two-story tenements, cluttered plumbing stores and faded blacksmith stables and grimy machine repair shops. Scattered among them were scores of taverns that served free lunches, saloons where working men drank ten cent shots of whiskey until dawn.

Christian tried to banish the nightmare from his foggy mind and shuffled down the heavy concrete sidewalk, everything padlocked and sleepy in a still morning air thick with salt from the bay marshes two blocks away. He arrived at the corner of Webster Street where a light burned in the Hartford Insurance office.

A tinkling bell announced his arrival.

Ian Senzon peered up through wire-rim glasses permanently embedded in his fleshy cheeks.

"Ian. I had a hunch you might be the only man on Union Street working Easter."

"Sunday morning, only time I get to catch up on my paperwork. You up early or getting home late?"

"Wasn't sleepin' too well. I was thinking maybe I should go ahead and take out that policy."

Ian dug through the clutter on his desk and found a blank application form. "Just fill in your name and sign it."

"This will protect everything?" Christian inquired.

"Since you don't own the building, there's no coverage on that. But all your possessions, your clothes, your furnishings, anything in case of fire. It's two policies actually. If anything happens to you, God forbid, Elizabeth will receive three thousand dollars. Something a cop should have, to my thinking."

Christian signed his name and slid over a dollar and twenty-three cents, two months' premium. He wished Ian a Happy Easter, then boarded the cable car as it made the morning's maiden journey to North Beach.

Christian loved few things—his family, Elizabeth and little Katie and young Byron—and after them, fighting and Irish whiskey. He was quick to rile and in a confrontation that required fists or firearms, there were few more capable. His temperament was so unlike Hunter's that Byron had sometimes wondered how they could be siblings.

A change had come over Christian that year, a pained and distant look that, coupled with a burgeoning indulgence in strong drink, worried his wife and his father to no end.

Christian stood on the rear platform of the Union Street cable car as it climbed the steep western slope of Russian Hill. He inhaled the chill spring air, staring out through the Golden Gate as the surface of the dark blue Pacific ignited with the shimmering gold and crimson sunrise. It was a sight that often comforted him, though on that morning it did not.

According to Elizabeth Fallon, Christian returned later that morning and handed her the insurance policy he had purchased from Ian Senzon. He also swore that on his day off, Wednesday the eighteenth, he would visit the fire chief, Dennis Sullivan, a family friend, and tell him of his nightmares.

It was a promise Christian would not keep.

———••⧜••———

Chapter 4

SOUTH OF MARKET STREET

APRIL 15, 1906. 6:20 A.M.

I should use this opportunity to better introduce myself. Jack London once told me—before I rejected his opium-glazed advances at Poppa Coppa's bohemian café in North Beach—that a reader must have a precise image of his subject or else be lost.

My mother named me Annalisa after her elder sister, who had died en route from Rome to San Francisco when her ship sunk while rounding Cape Horn. I was a bookish and artistic child who grew up immersed in the writings of Jane Austen, Susan B. Anthony, and Nellie Bly—the latter became a personal icon when she defied convention and offered first-person observations of the stories she reported, a technique I have emulated from the moment I took up the pen. I graduated valedictorian, class of 1904, from the University of California in Berkeley. I am also tall and athletic; the latter a result of years pedaling a bicycle over San Francisco's imposing hills. I have the arched eyebrows, aquiline nose, and obsidian eyes of my mother. A mass of black curly hair seems to boil about my shoulders.

After college, I attempted to join Fremont Older's journalistic campaign against our city's corruption. Learning of my fluency in French and Italian, and perusing my theater reviews for the college newspaper, Mr. Older instead assigned me to cover the opera and theater, replacing the male critic who had been shot and wounded, albeit non-fatally, by a disgruntled actor who had taken umbrage over a scathing review. Muckraking, Mr. Older informs me whenever the subject is revisited, is a distinctly male occupation.

I am also a Suffragist, reform Catholic, and Progressive Socialist, and pray these admissions not deter you from my story.

Shortly after sunrise—the last Easter sunrise over the city of San Francisco as we knew her—I was absorbed in the newest phonograph recordings of Enrico Caruso, records that were as yet unreleased and sent by a friend, a music and theater reporter for one of the New York newspapers.

I listened attentively to two arias Caruso would perform at our Grand Opera House, "*Che Gelida Manina*" (What a Frozen Little Hand) from *La Bohème* and "*Il Fior Che Avevi a Me Tu Dato*" (The Flower That You Gave Me) from his opening night's *Carmen*. I was grateful for the near-deafness of my Polish neighbor lady, as I played them over and over, twirling rapturously about my tiny room.

As a young girl visiting New York with my parents, I attended the Metropolitan Opera to hear both Italo Campanini and the legendary Jean de Reske, and was at the Tivoli in San Francisco when our own Luisa Tetrazzini first leapt into the opera firmament. Those memories paled in comparison to the sound resonating from the brass horn of my Victor, a voice of seemingly incongruous elements; thunderous and sweet, profound and joyous, so impassioned and precise that I listened in disbelief.

I left my cramped tenement building South of Market—South of the Slot, the cable car slot, the only area I could afford on a reporter's salary—and dodged the clanging trolley cars and clomping horses and honking automobiles on Market Street. I scarcely heard the clatter, still dizzy with Caruso in my ears.

At Bush Street near the gateway to Chinatown, I ducked inside the entrance of the *Evening Bulletin* just as Fire Chief Dennis Sullivan and his men returned to Central Station across the street. Sullivan and his men struggled with their spent horses and ornate brass pumpers after battling an all-night blaze at a paint and solvent factory out near Hunter's Point Shipyard at the city's southeastern edge.

When I reached the top floor of the *Bulletin* offices, I dropped my review of Caruso's new recording, which I headlined "The Voice of God," on the cluttered oak desk of my editor, Mr. Fremont Older, and hurried back downtown.

At approximately seven twenty, I passed Union Square on its southern border, crossing behind the Powell Street cable car as the rhythmic clanging of its brass bell resounded off the massive granite face of the St. Francis Hotel. At the corner of Geary and Powell, I stopped to observe a red and green Ocean Beach Railroad car, already jammed with people. If New Yorkers are the country's most refined city dwellers, we are certainly the most vigorous, a people obsessed with recreation and outdoor frivolity.

Though a few clinging to the running boards were dressed in Easter finest for services at St. Ignatius and St. Mary's, most of the energetic contingent carried towels and bathing suits for Sutro Baths or the waterslides at Chutes on Haight Street. Some sported knickers for bicycling excursions, others toted Hawkeye cameras to photograph the Arboretum or giant water lilies at Golden Gate Park. A lone woman on the running board of the rear dummy car carried a banner emblazoned with the likeness of Suffragist Susan B. Anthony, who had died the previous Thursday, and for whom services were being conducted in the park.

When the trolley passed, I crossed and headed South of the Slot, toward the Grand Opera House.

Meanwhile, in keeping with the city's singular reputation for irreverence, three of San Francisco's most powerful men began arriving at a whorehouse, on Easter Sunday no less, for a meeting that would forever seal our fate.

The infamous Poodle Dog, a five-story Victorian at the corner of Mason and Eddy Streets, sat a block from our famed Palace Hotel; a great convenience for many of the latter's male guests. From six until eleven every evening, well-turned residents and visitors dined on the Poodle Dog's sumptuous fare at the chandeliered first-floor restaurant. After witching hour, the male elite retired to other diversions via a private elevator to the penthouse suites, where "dining French" meant ordering the specialty of the house, the black-stockinged *Femme du Jour*.

"Handsome" Eugene Schmitz, the city's mayor, arrived first, following Mass at St. Mary's, still dressed in his pious suit and sporting a red Easter carnation in his lapel. The former conductor of the Columbia Theater Orchestra and past President of the Musicians' Union, he had recently been re-elected to his third term as the titular head of the Union Labor Party—a fabrication of Adam Rolf designed to capitalize on the burgeoning Progressive movement—a party that was neither pro-Union nor pro-Labor. Schmitz was a perfect icon of the city at large: attractive, buoyant, corrupt, and hollow as a drum.

He was soon joined by his master and benefactor, Boss Adam Rolf, a uniquely San Francisco version of the traditional urban power broker: a champagne-and-opera-loving alternative to the beer-swilling, bawdy house brawlers such as New York's William Tweed, Boston's Martin Lomasney, and the recently deposed Ed Butler of St. Louis. A brilliant attorney, fluent in French and Latin, Rolf had executed one of the shrewdest maneuvers in American politics when he created the Union Labor Party five years earlier to fill the vacuum left when public outrage drove the corrupt Democratic potentate, "Blind" Chris Buckley, into exile.

In search of a candidate long on charm, short on morals, and bereft of a spinal column, Rolf plucked popular Eugene Schmitz out of the Columbia's orchestra pit and anointed him puppet-mayor.

According to a Poodle Dog waiter who provided information in exchange for opera tickets or a cash gratuity, Rolf had spent the previous night in the fifth-floor penthouse, resplendent with Persian carpets, Tiffany lamps, mahogany-paneled walls, and a Turkish sitz bath, where he dined on baked abalone, potatoes *au gratin*, leg of lamb *au jus* with mint sauce, a double magnum of *Château Lafite* '79, plus *apéritif* of peroxide blonde, a head taller than he, with a garnish of red-headed Jewish girl from Boston. Rolf was a slight man, barely five feet two with watery gray eyes, a proboscis ample enough to gaff steelhead, and the conscience of a famished rodent.

The trio was completed by the arrival of one of their principal adversaries, the rugged Fire Chief, Dennis Sullivan, still red-eyed from the fire he had battled past sunrise. The Poodle Dog was otherwise empty save for the cleaning and preparatory staff, including the aforementioned waiter.

Sullivan quenched his parched throat from a crystal goblet that had been poured for Handsome Eugene, and then pulled a report from inside his gray tunic. He donned his wire-rim glasses and read aloud, his voice hoarse from shouting orders until dawn.

"The fact that the city of San Francisco has not burned to the ground *yet again* can only be attributed to the diligence of the fire department and the will of the Divine. Nowhere have we seen a city that so violates every rule of modern construction and common sense. Virtually every building is made of wood and there is insufficient space between them to slip a fire hose. One-quarter of the buildings in the Financial District, one-half of those on the waterfront, and every building south of Market Street is built on filled land. In lieu of any effort at self-preservation by the current city administration of San Francisco, a conflagration of epic proportions is inevitable.

"That is not my opinion," Sullivan concluded. "That is the report of the Fire Underwriters Association of America." Dennis Sullivan had long been the most revered man in San Francisco, a legend from the days when volunteer companies raced to arrive first at a blaze, dragging their ornate pumpers as hundreds of citizens rose from their beds to chase after them. He was strong-willed, intolerant of corruption and sloth, and bore the leathery skin of a man who had spent his life too close to fire. Both Schmitz and Rolf knew he was not a man to be taken lightly.

Sullivan stared as Schmitz licked coffee from his well-waxed mustache, smiling throughout.

"My conclusions, gentlemen, are much harsher than those of the Fire Underwriters," Sullivan added.

"Were your conclusions anything less than harsh, Chief Sullivan," Adam Rolf replied, "we would be gravely disappointed."

Sullivan's singed face flushed a deeper shade of crimson. "I have here," he continued, summoning the document that Hunter Fallon had delivered earlier that morning, "a report on the condition of the water system, compiled by the College of Engineering at Stanford University. All three of the main conduits running from the Spring Valley Water Company run over a major earthquake fault, the one they are calling the San Andreas. Two of the feeder lines pass through filled ground. The entire system could not be more fragile if it lay across the cable car tracks. I have said it time and again. This city needs a supplemental salt water system, a renovation of the cisterns beneath the streets, a new set of enforceable building codes and enough honest men to enforce them!"

Schmitz rose and cleared his throat. "Splendid work, Chief Sullivan. You will have to excuse us. We must attend to final preparations for the arrival of Enrico Caruso. We certainly don't want to embarrass our great city by being unprepared, do we? Therefore, I declare, as Mayor of San Francisco, that no flaming holocaust shall occur until *after* Maestro Caruso has made his curtain call."

"And what should I do with these reports, Your Honor? Tack them up at Lotta's Fountain so the people who pay our salaries can see how concerned you are about their lives? Three years now, I've been pleading to deaf ears, and every time that bell rings, I wonder if it's going to be the one that gets away from us."

"Have the reports sent to Mr. Rolf's office tomorrow, Chief Sullivan. He will give them his immediate attention."

Rolf tugged at his collar, fuming at Schmitz assigning him chores.

"And how much of a bribe should I pay Mr. Rolf to read the damn things?" Sullivan thundered, his chair scraping the polished floor. Before he could strangle them, Schmitz and Rolf were gone.

Schmitz' long, graceful stride carried him out into the warm spring morning. The symphony of rumbling trolleys and clanging cable cars, the bobbing, colorful sway of bowler hats and feathered *chapeaux* swirled about him. He breathed that special air, struggling to calm the tempest boiling beneath the painted smile.

With his short choppy steps, Rolf walked purposefully past Schmitz. Tommy Biggs, Rolf's cauliflower-faced goon and driver, had the Phaeton's leather top down and was polishing the brass headlights when his boss arrived. Tommy dutifully set the spark, turned the starter crank, and climbed behind the wheel as the Rolls belched to life.

With Rolf and Schmitz on the pleated black leather seat behind him, Tommy spun a dizzying turn onto Market Street, posters of Caruso dressed as *La Bohème*'s impoverished poet Rodolfo or *Carmen*'s Spanish corporal Don José swaying from the spiderweb of telephone and electric lines above. The sidewalk cafés were crowded with the nattily attired breakfast crowd, and Caruso's voice seemed to blare from every window on a boulevard that rivaled Paris' splendid *St. Germaine*.

Despite his flippant dismissal of Dennis Sullivan's demands, Eugene Schmitz was troubled. He loved his city and his job more than any other man alive. His city had risen, in a single lifetime, from a sand dune village of eight hundred to one of astonishing wealth and influence. Schmitz' San Francisco was built on money, wave after wave of it: gold, silver, shipping, transcontinental railroad, Coast redwood, Sierra lumber, Napa wine, and the Green Gold Rush of the Santa Clara and San Joaquin valleys. The Jewel of the Pacific, a freewheeling city unfettered by the Brahmin pretensions of the East had spawned an artistic revolution virtually unmatched: Mark Twain, Jack London, Isadora Duncan, Lincoln Steffens, Frank Norris, Ambrose Bierce. A half-century of progress and profit that had not merely transformed San Francisco, but an entire nation. No city anywhere on Earth had ever grown so wealthy or so powerful so quickly, and Eugene Schmitz was paper lord of it all.

Schmitz' euphoria had dimmed in recent weeks, thanks to the mounting vitriol of Fremont Older's anti-corruption editorials and Dennis Sullivan's apocalyptic warnings.

"I don't know how long we can put Chief Sullivan off like this, Adam," Schmitz said. "God knows what would happen if another earthquake strikes like the one in '68. They would nail our charred hides to City Hall."

"Dennis Sullivan is the least of your worries. The new Federal Prosecutor, Charles Feeney? He's not really here to count pork rations at the Presidio. After schemin' Joe Folk brought down Ed Butler in St. Louis, that meddler Roosevelt got his powder primed. He sent Feeney to nail us in our coffins. Be proud, Eugene. Your name is atop the gallows, right next to mine."

Tommy gazed casually over his shoulder as Schmitz' throat tightened and his face flushed. Despite the throbbing of the Rolls' engine, Tommy overheard it all. Handsome Eugene gripped the polished door handle with both hands: a moving Rolls Royce made an inconvenient place to vomit.

From a doorway across from the Grand Opera House on Mission Street, where I had been waiting impatiently for their arrival, I watched Tommy jump down and help a visibly wobbly Schmitz to the ground, whereupon he followed Boss Rolf inside.

Once he was assured that Rolf was out of sight, Tommy returned to the Rolls and produced a small leather-bound book from inside his chauffeur's tunic. He began to scribble the details of the conversation between his boss and His Honor, for unbeknownst to them, Tommy had recently gained a second master. Byron Fallon.

I hiked the ankle-length black dress that covered my jodhpur pants and sprinted down Market Street to the Financial District, where I jumped onto the rear platform of the California Street cable car.

It was not the brief run that made my heart pound wildly.

———•⚬•———

Chapter 5

HALL OF JUSTICE

APRIL 15, 1906. 9:30 A.M.

After leaving Easter services at St. Peter and Paul Church at Dupont and Filbert, Byron Fallon worked his way down teeming Montgomery Street, the cobblestone canyon that separates Telegraph Hill and Russian Hill. The streets were choked with rumbling Berlins and wobbling Broughams filled with churchgoers, and the popular Lieutenant nodded frequently to the tipped brim and raised cane.

He arrived at the side entrance of the red brick Hall of Justice, across from Portsmouth Square, where the six-member Chinatown Squad waited with two Chinese girls, the older no more than twelve. Both were clad in flour-streaked green silk blouses, the trademark dress of Chinatown's most powerful madam, Ah Toy.

Byron stopped next to Charlie McBride, the most honest of the Chinatown Squad by virtue of taking bribes only from gamblers and opium dealers. Jack rollers and slavers were off limit, making him only half the department outcast that Byron was. "You had a good night, Charlie?"

Charlie moved a Cuban victory cigar to the corner of his mouth, rippling the edges of his drooping moustache. "We hit 'em this mornin' Lieutenant," he answered in the voice of County Cork. "When the pigtail bastards was sleepin'. Pulled these two little twists from a flour barrel where they made 'em sleep 'cause they didn't make their pokey last night. Miss Cameron will be along to take 'em to the Mission. Tried ta' bribe 'em with a sweet to come inside but the Tongs tell 'em there's a monster inside bites little girls' heads off."

"You get any of them?"

"Got a couple a' the hatchet swingin' bastards gettin' Bertillon'd upstairs."

Byron gazed toward Chinatown, to the alley where he and Charlie had investigated the murder of "Little Pete," Chinatown's leading gangster, gunned down while having his queue braided and forehead shaved in high-brow style.

"Good work, Charlie." It was a halfhearted gesture. Two girls rescued from among a thousand held in the fetid catacombs below Chinatown, the whole sordid business protected by Police Chief Donen and his patrons at City Hall.

"Heard y'r boy come home ta'day, Lieutenant."

Byron nodded and forced a smile. He entered the Hall of Justice and promptly took the elevator to the sixth floor.

The elevator doors opened to his nephew, Anthony Fallon, a gangly, simpleminded rookie dressed in a thick blue tunic and busy measuring the hat size of a defiant Tong who sat naked on a wooden stool. "Six and a quarter," Anthony called.

Sergeant Whiskey Willy Tate scribbled an illegible number next to "Crown Size" on the Bertillon sheet.

"You sure you're doing it right this time, Anthony?" Byron called out.

"Yes, sir, Uncle Byron, Lieutenant, sir. Done it three times, like it says on the chart." Anthony pointed to the wall where dozens of charts on eye color and ear shapes hung under the banner "Bertillon System of Criminal Identification."

"Where's the other one?"

"That Chinese lady, Ah Toy, come by and made bail for 'im. Soon's I'm finished with this one, he's sprung too."

A rill of acid bubbled in Byron's throat.

"Uncle Byron. I mean Lieutenant Fallon, sir. Father Yorke is waiting in your office."

Byron bolted through the fire door, his footsteps clanking on the iron steps as he scampered to the Detective Bureau a floor below. He burst through the back door and skipped across the heavily stained floor.

Four detectives were scattered among the forty wooden desks, a long leather belt flapped softly as it turned the ceiling fans overhead. He spotted Father Yorke through the glass window that separated his office from the detectives' squad room. The last time Father Yorke had shown up on a Sunday, Christian had been stabbed while on patrol.

"Peter. What the hell are you doing here?"

Peter Yorke, the Warrior Priest, a stout man with thinning hair and a raspy baritone, had been a leading figure in the Irish revolt until the British sent him packing under threat of death. His ministry now included the San Francisco waterfront and the souls who were quarry to shanghaiers and boardinghouse owners. Father Yorke turned to the man sitting next to him, a human scarecrow shivering and wet inside a gray woolen blanket.

Jessie Fallon cast his sunken eyes up at Byron and sent a jolt through his uncle's heart.

"My Lord, what the hell happened, Jessie? We tore the city apart looking for you and Elliot! Almost six months you've been gone."

It took a moment for Jessie to find his voice. "Kelly. Shanghaied us an hour after we pinched two of his men. Six of 'em jumped us. The Whale, Scarface, didn't get a look at the rest. Never had a chance to draw our revolvers. Belaying pins, busted us up real good."

"I'd tried ta' take 'im to Doc Genovese," Father Yorke intoned. "He insisted on seein' you first."

Jessie struggled, his voice reed thin and trembling. "They shipped us on a British bark, the *Liverpool*. Twelve of us shanghaied. Limey captain laughed when Elliot told him we were cops. Elliot liked to have a fit, demandin' they take us back to San Francisco. Captain tied him to the boom, made the crew take turns floggin' 'im. I tried to stop it. When I come to again, my head was split, my ribs was busted. Elliot looked half-dead, ain't never seen a man beat so bad." Jessie chewed a piece of biscuit, his stare a thousand yards away. "Near the end, they give us two tablespoons of rancid beans, half a cup of water. Men was eatin' their leather belts, drinkin' their own piss. Elliot . . ."

"Take your time, Jessie," Byron told his nephew.

"Elliot. Elliot stole a crust of stale bread. They give him forty lashes. Captain tied him naked to the anchor chain, above the water line so's the salt water would lick his wounds. They locked me in the fo'c'sle so I couldn't get to him. It was freezing. I could hear Elliot screaming, banging against the bow, then he got real hoarse, his voice gave out. They up and left him there for the birds to pick at."

Jessie's lip trembled, his skin translucent, the blue veins around his eyes twitching with his spiny jaw. Byron produced a flask of brandy and Jessie sipped.

"Half the lot of them jumped ship as soon as they hit harbor," Father Yorke added. "Once they abandoned ship, the captain kept their wages. Three of the poor souls drowned. The Sausalito ferry fished Jessie and two others out of the bay."

"When I get my strength back," Jessie said, "I'll put a bullet in Kelly's kneecaps and one in his skull. Three bullets, one for Elliot, one for me, and one for the rest of the men."

Through the glass partition, Byron spotted the desk sergeant pointing Hunter toward his office. "Father, take Jessie to Doc Genovese. Don't feed him too much or his belly will burst. I'll get a signed statement from him later."

"I want to be there, Byron. When Kelly gets his bloody due and an honest man can walk the waterfront."

"You can give him last rites at the hanging, Father."

Father Yorke took Jessie by the arm and helped raise him from the chair.

Hunter was so anxious to see his father he failed to recognize his cousin Jessie as he squeezed past him at the door.

"Hello, dad."

"Hunter. Welcome home, son. You're all finished then?"

"Graduation isn't until May, but I finished my last examination this morning. I put a motorcycle together. A proto-type they call it, not even in production. Broke the state speed record."

"You graduated first in your class, did you?"

"Yes, sir. I did two graduate projects instead of one, the motorcycle and a water survey for Chief Sullivan. I used to take the train up in the morning, after chores, and do the surveying. I dropped it off at the fire station a little while ago. The Chief looked like he aged some. All that fire and worry."

Hunter offered an uncertain smile, dismayed at how old and tired his father looked.

"I imagine you're going on some interviews with engineering firms. Last I looked, nobody's built that bridge across the Golden Gate you were always talking about."

"I'm going to have to put off bridge building for a time. I have a job already."

Byron stared at him uneasily. "And what might that be?"

"I joined the Department."

"I'm sorry, son. I thought I heard you say you joined the Department."

"Yes, sir. That's what I said."

"Ahh, so I'm not deaf. No. The answer's no."

"I thought maybe you had to take a test or go through some kind of training or something. Six years into the twentieth century and all you have to do to be a San Francisco cop is fill out a piece of paper and sign your name on it."

"No one told me about it."

"I asked the recruiting sergeant not to say anything. It was a surprise."

"I'll have a word with him. The answer's no."

"Dad, I'm almost twenty-three. I'm a grown man. I earned my own way through Stanford, never asked anyone for a dime. I didn't do it out of disrespect."

"Don't play possum with me, Hunter. How many times have we had this conversation?"

"It was more like a monologue, dad."

"And don't patronize me. I had this conversation with your mother a few days before she died. She made me swear on the Holy Book. Six years of college, a master's degree, all those awards. For what? To walk the Barbary Coast and risk your life for twenty-two dollars a week?"

"The waiters have a union, the housepainters have a union, even the piano polishers have one. Maybe if the men in the department got organized like everyone else in this city, they wouldn't have to settle for pitiful wages and take bribes from shanghaiers and opium dealers so they can feed their families."

Byron walked over and made sure the door was tightly closed. "Watch what you say between these walls, Hunter. The manure shovelers will have a union before we do."

"I'm sorry, dad. I have ideas eating me up inside. Last month the New York City cops won a murder case using fingerprints. Fingerprints! What do we have, the stupid Bertillon system? Measuring someone's hat size? 'Yeah, officer, the guy who robbed me had a distended ear lobe and a black spot on his iris. His hat size was seven, maybe seven and a quarter.' Fingerprints, dad. We could solve half the unsolved murders in San Fran-cisco with fingerprints, evidence collection, crime scene photographs."

"I got this sinking feeling nothing I say is going to matter to you."

"If Christian can cut it, so can I."

"The only thing you two have in common is stubbornness."

Byron looked at the clock. It was not half over yet and the finest day of his long career was dying before it was half over.

"You chose your life, dad. All I'm doing is choosing mine. If you would rather, I can get my badge and weapon from the desk sergeant."

"The Fallons hang their own dogs, son." Byron walked behind his battered desk and pulled a shiny patrolman's star from a drawer.

Hunter held his hand out. Byron ignored it and pinned the star to the pocket of Hunter's shirt. "You could walk a beat on the Coast ten years before you make it up here to the Bureau, Hunter. That's hoping you live that long."

"Nobody kills the Fallons, dad. It's the Irish in 'em."

"You keep talking malarkey like that and I'll have to do what no man ever wants to do. Bury his own child. From now on, as long as you work here, I'm your boss, not your father. Understood?"

"Yes."

"Yes, *sir*."

"Yessir."

"Come with me. I'll get you your weapon."

He led his self-conscious son across the squad room as the detectives stared.

"They hate us," Byron said quietly. "Get used to it."

Christian arrived at the top of the stairs, still sweating from a workout at the police gym that included six rounds of boxing with his burly cousin, Max Rinaldi. Christian moved deliberately across the room, stopping to return the hostile stares of the few detectives scattered about the room. He stopped when he got close to his father and was about to speak when he noticed Hunter's shirt.

"Jesus Christ, dad, tell me that ain't a star he's wearin'."

"It's Easter Sunday, Christian, try to show the Lord a little respect one day a year."

Byron left Christian stewing and joined Hunter in the corner of the room.

He pointed Hunter to a dusty desk with foot-high stacks of paper. Wagon wheels thundered, horses whinnied frantically in the street below.

"These animals have been crazed for a week now," Byron said, waiting for the ruckus to diminish. He had difficulty looking at Hunter. "Can you use a typing machine like this?"

"Yes, sir. I bought Jack London's old one from him when we were at University Prep. Remington Number Seven. We boxed some, him and me. Hell of a sailor, good street fighter but not much with the gloves on. All that dissipation and what not."

Byron stifled an unwelcome grin. Since childhood, Hunter had instinctively offered twelve answers for every question he had been asked. "Then this is your weapon. Get done what you can, then get your camera and all the film you can muster up. Meet me at Digli's on Montgomery at noon."

Hunter started to protest but thought the better of it. Beginning his career with an act of insubordination might not do wonders for his tenure. He looked down at the desk and thumbed the edge of the ragged pile.

The reports were handwritten, barely legible, and bore dark brown stains that were either coffee or blood. He scanned the top page; a complaint from a prostitute named Susie Starr who claimed her pimp Antoine owed her two hundred dollars and gave her a runny dose. Hunter's enthusiasm for police work suffered its first setback.

Byron gazed over at Christian, who smirked nearby, then turned back to Hunter. "Tonight you can go visit Jessie and see how he's doing. I have work to do."

"Jessie? Jessie who?"

"Your cousin. That was him you passed on the way in."

"What happened to him?"

"He tried to arrest Shanghai Kelly's men," Byron said, lingering to see it register with his son.

Byron took a few steps toward the center of the room, where he spoke softly to Christian. "Meet me at Meigg's Wharf at seven o'clock tonight. And don't be late this time or I'll have your badge and your hide."

"What's going on at Meigg's Wharf?"

"You'll find out when you get there. When you leave the wharf, I'll have warrants for you and The Brotherhood to serve on John Kelly and his men."

"Easter Sunday?"

"Father Yorke brought in Jessie this morning. He and Elliot got shanghaied aboard a British bark by Kelly's men. Scarface, the Whale, probably Chicken Devine, that dirty lot always sticks together."

"Where's Elliot?"

"The English captain flogged him to death, left his bones for the birds to pick at." Byron could see the fury rising in his elder son, his jaws working so intently Christian could not have spoken had he cared to.

"And stay out of the bars. I want no tomfoolery when we pinch them up tonight, understood?"

Christian offered a pained nod, and then waited until his father was out of earshot.

He eased himself enough to reclaim his smirk and sauntered over to his brother. "You know, Hunter, a career as the department secretary ain't that bad. Really."

"Go to Hell, Christian. I can fight and shoot as well as any man in here." He looked toward his father, his braggadocio fading to concern. "What's dad up to that he's working Easter Sunday? He looks worried."

"Don't know. He's probably just a little daft his favorite son decided to chuck all that learnin' and make flatfoot like the rest of his sorry kin."

"There's something else."

"See there, Hunter. You made detective already."

"Just like I can tell you don't have a clue what he's up to, and it riles you."

"Maybe we can just stop beatin' on guys, let you read their minds for us."

Hunter smiled and stared intently at Christian. His older brother looked like he had shrunk in those six years, the cocky grin unable to mask a troubled spirit.

Christian examined him like a shepherd dog cocking his head from side to side. "I don't know what dad's up to. But you're right. It must be something if he's working on Easter."

Chapter 6

—·◆◇◆·—

NOB HILL

APRIL 15, 1906. 11:00 A.M.

I share the controversial notion that the imperial throne of America lies—
or did so until recently—not on Pennsylvania Avenue or upper Broadway,
but three thousand miles away, on a four-block area of San Francisco
known as Nob Hill, so named for the British slang for wealthy: Nabob, or
Nob. The American West may not have been built from the Atlantic
Ocean outward, as generally assumed, but from the Pacific Ocean
inward.

Several decades ago, the mansions along our eastern waterfront sank
through the paddy-shoveled sand into the muck of Rincon Swamp. Soon
after, a Scottish wire-rope manufacturer named Andrew Hallidie invented
the cable car. Leland Stanford, the principal force behind the western
stretch of the transcontinental railroad, financed a cable line up California
Street where Nob Hill, once the domain of goats and fresh-air enthusiasts,
was quickly parceled like a giant chessboard.

Stanford and his partners, Collis Huntington, Charles Crocker, and
Mark Hopkins, the infamous Big Four, fled to the high ground. They
began a chess match of architectural excesses that was described as "an
orgy of gingerbread and ignorance."

The Great Fixer, politician-buying Collis Huntington, struck first,
erecting a French château containing enough forged artwork, overstuffed
furnishings, funereal drapery, and maudlin décor to earn the moniker
"The Big Embalming House."

A block east, Stanford—who proclaimed while driving the gold spike
at Promontory Point, Utah, in 1869 that he had "annexed America," turn-

ing the most ambitious construction project in history into the most corrupting influence in American life—soon topped him. The Giant of California built a fifty-room palace whose entrance boasted a seventy-foot-high vestibule with the twelve signs of the zodiac done in black marble. Castle Stanford offered a hothouse conservatory, indoor Corinthian pillars of red Aberdeen granite, mechanical singing birds, a music room where a servant changed cylinders every few minutes so that a continual stream of classical music was piped throughout the house, a miniature railroad, and enough gilded mirrors to make escape nearly impossible.

Stanford had once introduced his newborn son, Leland Jr., to his well-heeled pals by presenting the infant on a silver tray, naked amidst a bed of orchids and chrysanthemums.

On the adjacent parcel, while eccentric Mark Hopkins was riding about town on a mule selling homegrown tomatoes, his wife Mary built a Norman castle with a Palace of Doges drawing room, velvet-upholstered doors, and a cavernous bedroom replete with angels in precious stone, beneath which she devoured wanton novels whose virginal heroines were prone to bouts of sexual delirium. A relieved Mark Hopkins died before the mansion was completed: the building then became the Hopkins Art Institute.

Next, Charles Crocker built a French château across from Huntington, turning fifty wood-carvers loose on a patchwork of plinths, cornices, over-wrought wainscots, fluted corners, and dizzying curlicues that resembled a cuckoo clock factory constructed by a cloistered madman.

It was these same Railroad Barons, whose wealth and power corrupted every facet of modern American life, who inspired Frank Norris, in *The Octopus*, and Ambrose "Bitter" Bierce to take up pen against them, raising a national outcry.

I had plenty of time to reacquaint myself with Nob Hill. For several hours that Easter morning, I waited at the as-yet-unopened Fairmont Hotel at California and Mason, directly across from where interloper Adam Rolf—whose obsession with being included in the nefarious club had earned him the title of "The Half in the Big 4½"—had finalized the competition with a Mediterranean-style behemoth of two-ton Connecticut brownstone slabs. The house made Alcatraz seem flimsy by comparison.

As I watched from a fourth-floor window of the Fairmont, scheduled to open that Wednesday, April 18, a parade of painters, plumbers, masons, and upholsterers wove their way through dozens of San Francisco's newest landmarks. Pickets. Pickets seeking higher wages for chambermaids, Industrial Unionism, shorter hours for carpenters, Suffrage for women, jobs for Negroes, vegetarianism, enforced temperance, recruits for Socialism, an end to Imperialism, and a return to God. The Prevent Premature Burial consortium and the short-lived Committee for Improved Mastication ("32 Chews to a Healthier You") appeared to have lost steam to the point of near-extinction, as had the Back to Africa outfits. A roller skater headed for the frightening plunge down Mason Street almost took one of the Temperance women with him.

A few minutes later, Rolf's assistant chef—a German named Hans or Franz—and two helpers emerged from the mansion and loaded wicker baskets and iced champagne buckets into Rolf's Phaeton. They climbed in and motored off with Tommy at the wheel.

As soon as they were out of sight, a slender white hand raised the embroidered green velvet shade in Rolf's study.

Too impatient for the elevator, I hurried down the iron stairway, wove through the Fairmont lobby and out onto Mason Street.

I slowed my gait to avoid being crushed between two furniture delivery wagons and crossed Mason to the circular cobblestone driveway near the sprawling garage of the Rolf mansion.

As I shuffled up the granite steps to the servant's entrance, the rear door opened in front of me.

I stepped inside and slammed the door behind me. "You alone, Pierre?"

"I can't do this, Annalisa. Mr. Rolf will kill me. He'll have Tommy and Shanghai Kelly's goons take me out and torture me. Oh, God."

Pierre was thin, hawk-nosed, and effeminate. A limp *soufflé* set him aquiver. The thought of crossing Adam Rolf had him tipping toward hysteria.

I slapped an envelope against his chest and left him thumbing the stack of fifty-dollar notes as I entered the massive, chandeliered hallway, and trudged past the gleaming suits of armor and leaden Renaissance paintings offering joyless Annunciations and desultory Resurrections, my heart pounding so intensely I thought it would break through my ribs.

I stepped into Rolf's office, which, as was in vogue, appeared to be more stuffed than decorated. Ivory tusks, zebra-skin chairs, Napoleon's pearl inlaid writing table and credenza, Egyptian tapestries, chintz draperies, ubiquitous civic awards and proclamations, enormous Ming vases, and a collection of Dutch paintings so grim they could swallow the light from a forest fire.

I found the imposing brass and steel Diebold safe amidst the posh debris, tucked between rows of leather-bound law books.

Pierre entered behind me. "Did you hear what I said, Annalisa? I can't do this."

"Where are the numbers?"

"Before you get the numbers, I get my pictures."

I handed him a pack of photographs, taken clandestinely by an employee in a homosexual brothel who had been bribed by Byron Fallon. Each one depicted Pierre with opium-glazed City Works Director Walter Berman, San Francisco's premier voice for evangelical purity.

Pierre examined the set of four and gasped out loud.

"The numbers, Pierre, give me the numbers."

"*I'll* do it." He produced a slip of paper, his hand shaking so badly he could barely grasp the dial.

I snatched the paper from his hand and shoved him from the light. "Oh, God, they are going to kill me, they're going to rip me to shreds."

"We're just borrowing it, Pierre. He won't even know it's missing."

I turned the numbers until the tumbler clicked in place. A twist of the nickel handle and the massive door swung open. I extracted a red accounting ledger, marked the spot where it had stood with a slip of paper, and stuffed the thick volume into my shoulder bag. I closed the massive door and carefully spun the dial back to the number on which I had found it.

I ignored Pierre's whimpering, slipped out the back door and walked down steep California Street, where I hopped aboard the Powell Street cable car, frightened and jubilant.

Chapter 7

——◆◇◆——

APRIL 15, 1906. 12:40 P.M.

By the time I settled into the Powell Street cable car for its tortoise-like journey toward Chinatown, Hunter Fallon was leaving Central Fire Station, where Fire Chief Sullivan had conveyed the results of the morning's contentious meeting with Boss Rolf and Mayor Schmitz.

Hunter crossed Broadway, leaving behind the foul smells and garishness of the Barbary Coast for the bakeries and bohemian charm of North Beach. He reached Digli's Luncheonette—the thick black exhaust driving off passersby—and chained the motorcycle to a lamp post.

His father exited Digli's to join him, waving his hand to ward off the lingering stench. They strolled calmly past the colorful delicatessens and coffee shops, all closed for the Sabbath.

"I just saw Chief Sullivan. You know what he said, dad? Mayor Schmitz and Adam Rolf laughed in his face when he showed them our report on the water system. You ever read Lincoln Steffens? It used to be Emperors and Popes dictating people's lives, now it's Big Business and dirty politicians and political bosses like Rolf. A round of applause for the forward march of Democracy. How long can they keep doing this, lining their pockets and ignoring the fire chief?"

"Until the place burns to the ground or somebody throws them in jail. Now hush, I have more immediate things to worry about."

Hunter's silence lasted four or five paces. "They can't pay for a supplemental water system or rebuild the cisterns because they spent it all on that monstrosity they call City Hall. This is like Boss Tweed building that

New York courthouse with eighty-thousand-dollar windows and fifteen-hundred-dollar dust brooms. Our boodlers spent eight million dollars for a building that was supposed to cost a million. You know how many times this city has burned to the ground? Six. Six, that's how many. Because they keep stealing all the money that should go to saving the place."

Byron was quickly reacquainted with Hunter's proclivity for asking and answering his own questions, scarcely drawing a breath between. "You have to slow down, Hunter. You drive a church-going man to drink. Save it for when I'm done doing what I'm doing."

"What *are* you doing, dad?"

"How many pictures can you take?"

Hunter patted the black leather satchel slung over his shoulder. "These Hawkeyes are as smart as anything. You just slide a roll of film in the back and shoot. Not like the old stuff that had to be loaded one by one. And the emulsion's fast, you can use a quicker shutter speed, you don't have to hold so steady."

Byron stared at Hunter until he relented.

"A dozen rolls, a dozen frames a roll. A hundred and forty-four frames. What are we shooting?"

"A book, handwritten. Now, I had a man lined up to do this work but he took ill. Tell me you can do this, Hunter, I have no time to waste."

"If I can get enough light. Handwriting gets a little thin in spots." Hunter finally resigned himself to silence. This time it lasted almost a dozen steps. "Since I don't have a gun, maybe I should have brought my typewriter. I could bash them with it if something goes wrong."

"Your marksmanship skills are well noted, son. A man is not a turkey or a wild boar. When you prove to me you know when *not* to use it, you'll get one."

While father and son debated whether the coming Socialist Revolution or a return to Catholic values was panacea for society's ills, I jumped off the cable car a few blocks away and headed through Chinatown.

Throngs of women in silk pajamas and rocker shoes, men in black skullcaps and braided hip-length queues picked through bins of vegetables, writhing eels, sea slugs, and lotus root. Scarcely anyone stopped to examine the Occidental woman passing through their midst.

I slowed at the alley named Virtue and Harmony, fixing the frightful sight of a fawn-eyed "Daughter of Joy," perhaps eleven, hawking her sexual wares, her nose pressed between the barred windows of a heavy wooden door. Through the door on the right, another girl climbed on a wooden crate to expose her bare buttocks and pubes.

I wanted to yell out the Cantonese phrases I had learned on rescue efforts with Dolly Cameron: "freedom is here," "your suffering is over," "we have come to give you a home with food, where no one will hurt you." Phrases we had repeated hundreds of times in the sanctuary of the Presbyterian Mission just five blocks away.

"*Vi torniamo presto.*" *We return for you soon,* I uttered softly.

The crowds had thinned dramatically since the morning church rush. I crossed Broadway, a half block from the old jail, and slowed to a cautious pace until I reached Molinari's Italian Grocery on Montgomery.

I stopped at the front door and knocked soundly. Gino Molinari, a rotund Genovese, stepped from behind the door, startling me. He quickly re-locked the deadbolt and lowered the tan shade.

From beneath the awning of a bakery across the street, Byron watched me enter, waiting for a full minute to see if someone were following. He slid his .32 caliber derringer into the pocket of his son's leather jacket, an act that heightened Hunter's already eager attention.

"Be careful with that thing, Hunter, and don't say a blessed word unless it's 'duck,' you understand me? Now, just walk slow, keep your eyes open, a nice friendly father and son reunion, understood?"

"Yes, sir."

"Good. You're learning."

They stepped onto the cobblestone surface of Montgomery, their feet deftly avoiding piles of fresh manure. The warm spring sun had begun to bake the ubiquitous equine offerings, blending it with the aroma of half-burned gasoline.

"You go in the front door, Hunter; I'll meet you inside. If anyone tries to force their way in, which I doubt, I give you permission to shoot them. Make sure that person is not me or your Uncle Gino or the young lady who just entered. And if you ask me one more question before the sun goes down, I'll fire you and take your badge away."

"You wouldn't do that, would you?"

While Byron turned up Vallejo Street, Hunter walked to the front door, knocked, and was permitted entry by Gino.

Once inside, he breathed in the damp air, scented with buffalo mozzarella and provolone and sharp cheddar, Genovese salami, thyme, marjoram,

and tarragon tied up in bunches and hanging along the back wall in front
of the canned peas and carrots and strained tomatoes. Crates of fresh
broccoli, cauliflower, and brussel sprouts from the winter crop of the San
Joaquin Valley crammed the sawdust floor. He realized he was home.

He followed Gino into the back room, where a chopping block lay
covered in crisp white butcher paper.

Byron made his way up the alley behind the store and knocked briskly
on the heavy wooden door that led to the basement.

I quickly unbolted it, handing Byron an oil lantern. I followed him back
through a dank brick passageway lined with wooden barrels guarded by
gleaming-eyed felines smug in their rodent-hunting skills.

"Where's Rolf?" Byron asked me.

"He's at the Opera House. They just took lunch over to them, right on
the dot, like Tommy told you. Rolf's been meeting there all week with his
cronies. A smart cover. It looks like they are just dropping in to watch
rehearsals."

"He must suspect someone is on to him. I hope you were careful,
Annalisa."

I handed Byron a thick sheaf of papers covered in brown leather and
bound with a black silk cord. "I typed up everything, all my notes, sixteen
months' worth. Over a hundred pages: dates, times, locations. Who said
what to whom. Everything I overheard from Rolf and his drunken friends
and their drunken wives, with my signed affidavits for all of it. Just like
Mr. Feeney requested."

Byron thumbed quickly through the pages, checking dates. "This should
make quite a story, Annalisa," he said.

"I've already written quite a bit of it. I think I'll call it the 'The
Champagne Confessionals.'"

"I'll get you a photograph of Rolf and Schmitz in wrist manacles for the
cover. I think we'll pinch them up Wednesday morning, after Caruso's
opening night, when they've been up all night guzzling champagne and
telling each other how wonderful they are."

"Get them in their tuxedos," I said, managing a smile. "The latest fashion statement; top hats and iron bracelets."

I pulled the red leather accounting ledger loose from my bag and
handed it over. "The twisted dealings of Adam Rolf. In his own hand. I
paged through on the cable car. The dates and figures match my notes
perfectly."

"Hunter's upstairs. Perhaps you should wait here."

My heart leapt unexpectedly. "He's the photographer?"

"He joined the force, much to my displeasure. That may change first thing in the morning."

"I would like to see him."

Byron hesitated, and then took my arm and led me up the steep, dusty steps to the storeroom.

As we squeezed through a leather curtain separating the stairs from the storage room, Hunter looked up, easing his hand out from his pocket.

"Good, son. You didn't shoot your Lieutenant. Always a good sign."

Byron stepped aside and ushered me into the room.

In the stark light of the bare overhead bulb, Hunter looked at me, his brow furrowing in a struggle for recognition. Even in the garish light, I was struck by his chiseled appearance, the deep, intelligent eyes. His was a disarming presence. I realized that through the letters his father had shared, and my conversations with Byron, I knew much about Hunter. He knew nothing of me, as his father had carefully shielded my work from all but two men: Byron's nephew, Francis Fagen—The Brotherhood's co-leader—and Prosecutor Charles Feeney.

"What's the matter, son, you don't recognize Annalisa?"

Even then he struggled. "Annalisa? Annalisa Passarelli? Not that skinny little girl who used to come into mom's spaghetti shop?"

I smiled self-consciously, embarrassed at the reference.

"The one who is now doing the opera and theater column in the *Bulletin*?"

"That's a good guess, son, now step to it. We have to get Annalisa out of here as fast as possible."

Hunter's stare lingered a second before he reached into a large leather bag to remove a collapsible tripod. It was hand-fashioned from what appeared to be the legs of old oak crutches and small brass window hinges. He quickly set the camera atop and began focusing.

"I need more light."

He spotted an old bureau mirror in the corner, dusted and placed it carefully on the edge of the chopping block to reflect the light of the single Edison bulb.

Byron utilized the short delay to page through the ledger. Under "Accounts Receivable" he found "PT&T," for Pacific State Telephone and Telegraph, with a monthly retainer of $12,000 from "T. H.," Theodore Halsey, their General Agent. From PT&T's rival, Home Telephone Company, payments totaling $125,000. United Railroads, $200,000. Under Pacific Gas & Electric, several payments including one for $35,000 two days before city supervisors voted a large increase in county rates.

Payments from Tessie Wall, the city's premier madam, were listed at $5,000 per month. Jerome Bassity, proprietor of several posh brothels, including an establishment where mask-wearing society women were reportedly serviced by handsome young men, showed a $5,000 monthly retainer as well. Under Parkside Real Estate, developers of the Sunset and Richmond Districts bordering Golden Gate Park, were bribes amounting to $400,000. There were payoffs from boxing promoters, ferry boat operators, and City Hall maintenance contractors.

I thought Byron would swallow his moustache at the page listing Bay Cities Water, rivals of the Spring Valley system, with a payment to Rolf of $1,000,000.

In the section marked "Accounts Payable" were hundreds of payments to Police Chief Jessie Donen, Mayor Eugene Schmitz, and members of the Board of Supervisors, funneled through Rolf's head lackey, Board President James L. Gallagher.

But it was the final entry, dated for two days later, Tuesday, April 17, that produced the greatest start yet. Next to the name "Payton," as in Senator Payton, was a $100,000 payoff.

Byron placed the book down on the butcher paper, securing it with two weights. "Do you need me to change pages for you, Hunter?"

"No, dad, I can do it faster myself."

Byron pulled me into the storage area so that Hunter could work unfettered. I took out a fountain pen and asked Byron to recount the day's events from the moment he arose. The imminent arrests of Rolf and Schmitz and their minions would be of great significance, not just in San Francisco. I was determined to write a full account, including as much personal detail as Byron would permit.

When Hunter finished, we returned to the storage room.

"All right," Byron said, "we have to move. Hunter, you go back to the house and start developing the film. All your equipment and supplies are in the cellar near the wine barrels. I'll escort Annalisa to return the ledger."

"I'm not sure that's the best plan, dad," Hunter said. "I think it might be better if I took Annalisa to Adam Rolf's house so she can tuck this back in his safe. I doubt anyone will recognize me after all the years I've been gone. We'll be two young people on an outing."

Rolf's name had not been mentioned, nor had it appeared anywhere in the ledger. Byron and I were speechless. Hunter was not.

"Judging by the musty, metallic smell of this book, plus the indentations where it was crammed in a shelf, this thing had to come from someone's safe. Since there were probably only five men in San Francisco who could muster graft of this scope, and Stanford, Huntington, Crocker, and Hopkins are all dead, this has to be Adam Rolf's ledger."

He fought off a self-assured grin, a wise decision given the mounting consternation of his father.

"The word 'retainer' appeared on several pages. Adam Rolf is the only lawyer among the bunch. It's obvious he's claiming all these bribes as legal fees. I read Annalisa's column periodically. She has probably been using her access to Rolf's opera box to do more than report on diamonds and divas."

I was not sure whether to laugh or weep. A plan we had carefully concocted over many long, hard months had been deduced by Hunter in minutes.

"If everything were ready," Hunter added, less cocksure, "I could have these photos developed in an hour."

Minutes later, after a stern admonition from his father not to speak a word of our efforts to anyone, Hunter and I boarded the Powell Street cable car for the return to Nob Hill. We moved to the back of the dummy car, where the rumble of wheels and clanking of the underground cable helped mask our conversation from two well-dressed couples seated near the grip car.

Hunter leaned close, smiling, almost flirtatious. "He's going to arrest Adam Rolf tonight, isn't he? It's perfect. Rolf will never expect it on Easter Sunday. Who else is he pinching up?"

I took his arm and leaned in close, smiling as though we were courting. "Whatever your father wants to tell you, he will tell you. I tend to follow his instructions. That's how I made it this far."

"Then tell me about you. How long have you been helping him?"

I had to smile at his persistence. "Very clever, Hunter. I'll tell you my story, and that's it. A year and a half ago, I was at a supper at the Palace's

Garden Room when I overheard the drunken wife of a PG&E executive complain about the bribe her husband had to pay to get a gas rate increase passed by the supervisors. Then the owners of several French restaurants chimed in about Rolf extorting more and more money for liquor licenses. I was about to pass the information to my editor, Mr. Older, when I spotted your father at Lone Mountain Cemetery, where my aunt is buried. I found out from the attendant that Byron visits your mother's site every other Sunday. I waited for him one morning and offered to collect information on Rolf and his cronies. Your father refused. He said it was too dangerous. I came back several times with new information until finally he relented. Now, how did you figure all that out so quickly back there?"

"There were other clues. When you arrived, the pleats on the back of your dress, behind your thighs and hips, were squashed down, only a hard wooden bench would do that. Not just pressed, but mashed: it's warm out, your body heat, a little perspiration."

"Your intellect is only rivaled by your tact."

He smiled. "But the pleats on the back of your torso were perfectly fresh, intact, which meant you were leaning forward during the ride. You rode the cable car down a steep hill, leaning forward. The California Street line, down Nob Hill, was my guess. The rest was pretty elementary. It didn't take Scotland Yard to figure that ledger was Adam Rolf's."

"Elementary. That's right, you wrote about Sherlock Holmes in one of your letters." No sooner had the words left my tongue than I regretted it.

"That would mean that dad has been sharing my letters with you for a year, at least," Hunter countered. "The only time I made a Holmes reference was last year. A day or so after I helped the San Mateo County Coroner solve the murder of a minister's wife. That would have been early March, probably the ninth or tenth that I wrote that letter."

I was impressed by his skills of memory and deduction. I'm sure it showed.

His boyish smile was self-satisfied, without being bold or arrogant. It appeared that it was the challenge, not any sense of conquest or superiority, that invigorated him. As a man accustomed to charming others by force of intellect, he was succeeding nicely.

"He was lonely, your father," I explained. "He was proud of you and he had no one to whom he could sing your praises. Sharing your letters with me was not meant as an intrusion. It was the only thing he ever did that approached showing off. That's how proud he was of you. Now, you tell me something. Do you ever find it a damper on conversation when you do the thinking for both parties?"

He smiled, teasingly. "I'm sorry I did not recognize you."

"I'm pleased you didn't. I'd hate to think that timid, bony thing was still me."

We rode in silence for the next few minutes, as though it were indeed an outing. We transferred to the California Street line for the climb up Nob Hill.

After we settled in, he asked about my family. I explained that my parents had returned to Italy when I was fifteen, where they died in the great influenza epidemic of 1898. He offered his sympathies and then asked how I wound up on the "diamonds and divas" beat at the *Bulletin*.

"I wanted to be a muckraker, like Lincoln Steffens and Nellie Bly. Jack London. The only paper that would hire a woman with no professional experience was the *Bulletin*. My editor, Mr. Older, is adamant that sort of thing is not for women. That's one of the reasons I turned to your father. Ironic, isn't it? Mr. Older is leading the public crusade against Rolf and Schmitz, and I'm sitting there right under his nose, collecting information he's never dreamt of, and turning it over to one of his corruption hunters."

Hunter watched me intently, with a gaze both pleasant and piercing, suggesting something more than friendly or flirtatious interest. It appeared he was reading me, probing for some meaning beneath my words. I was intrigued but said nothing. The exchange had helped calm my uneasiness over the day's activities.

The bell of St. Mary's, several blocks away in Chinatown, pealed twice as we neared Nob Hill. I pressed a key into Hunter's calloused hand. "Room 434, go up the back stairwell of the hotel, your father has been using it for surveillance. I'll be in the first floor office, the section that juts out closest to you. I'll be wearing a white scarf if things are well. If I remove it, things are not."

Hunter was about to ask another question, thought better of it, and hopped off the moving cable car as we approached the Fairmont. I watched him dash toward the rear entrance, threading a path through the frantic workmen before he disappeared into the iron stairwell.

I got off the cable car in front of Adam Rolf's mansion, the anxiousness returning as I walked purposefully up the front steps, donning the white scarf.

The moment the door opened, Pierre plunged into panic.

"Oh, God, hurry! He just called on the telephone, he's on his way home!"

I bolted down the long hallway and into the office, where I grasped the thick nickel dial on the safe, hand and mind trembling so that twice I dialed past the first number. I wiped my damp fingers on my dress and forced myself to turn the dial as slowly as I could until the numbers began to align. After two more failed attempts, I managed to execute three of the numbers properly before dialing past the fourth and final one. I looked up at the clock: two fourteen.

Hidden in the shadows of the fourth-floor Fairmont room across the street, Hunter checked his pocket watch, briefly examining his mother's sepia photograph inside the silver casing. He offered a hasty apology for joining the department against her wishes, and then went back to watching the windows of Rolf's mansion.

I finally managed to align the numbers, breathing a sigh of relief as the safe sprung open. I fumbled the red ledger from my bag and placed the book next to the paper I had used to mark its position on the upper shelf. I closed the enormous steel door so quickly it trapped the air inside and I was forced to ease it back. I turned the enormous handle and spun the dial to forty-two, the number it was on when I first saw it.

I had barely taken two steps when Adam Rolf strode into the room, reading his mail. I stopped in my tracks as he looked up.

"Annalisa! To what do I owe this surprise?"

Pierre slipped into the room behind Rolf, holding his hand to his mouth.

I forced a smile and reached inside my purse, Rolf's eyes flaring as my hand re-appeared, wrapped about a dark object. I stepped forward and pressed the small, hand-carved mahogany box into his hand.

While he opened it, I inched toward the window facing the Fairmont.

In the velvet interior of the mahogany box, Rolf found a silver watch chain, anchored by a cursive sterling "AR." He opened a small, hand-written card tucked against the lining as I managed a nervous smile. He smiled back and stroked his salt-and-pepper goatee.

"*Please accept this as a modest acknowledgment of all the things you have done for me. And for all of San Francisco,*" he read aloud. "*Fondly, Annalisa.*" When he lowered the note, he was beaming.

"It is such a tiny gesture, I was too embarrassed to hand it to you directly. I pleaded with Pierre to allow me to leave it on your desk."

Rolf pivoted and cast a quick look at Pierre, who managed to conceal a felonious heart with a smile of simple trespass.

"Pierre. I think we have some chilled champagne in the cold box."

He practically sprinted from the room.

"With my initials in silver yet! I'm flattered," Rolf beamed.

I started breathing again.

He removed his watch from his fob pocket and started disconnecting the chain. "My father gave me this old chain when I went to school at Berkeley. Made from a nugget he found in the American River. The only nugget he found, I might add. You noticed how fragile it has become. How thoughtful and observant of you, Annalisa." At his most charming, Rolf exuded a paralyzing warmth, thick and cloying as it enveloped friend and foe.

He held the watch and chain aloft, nearly misty-eyed, possibly the only gift anyone had ever given him that was not the product of extortion.

I toyed with the white scarf, turning my profile to the window and smiling broadly in hopes of assuaging Hunter's concerns. I looked up and caught a quick glimpse of him. It offered further comfort.

I turned. "I'm glad you like it, Mr. Rolf. I wasn't sure what to give a man who has obtained all he wanted in life."

I hoped my next present would be a noose to match his collar size.

Chapter 8

UNION SQUARE

APRIL 15, 1906. 6:15 P.M.

Several hours after my precarious encounter with Adam Rolf, Christian Fallon held court among the sweaty denizens of McGinty's, a tubercular tavern out on Union Street, a block from Washerwoman's Lake.

"Kelly's main crew, Scarface and the Whale, they had bartenders serving Mickey Finns at half the slop holes and blind pigs on the Barbary Coast. Them they didn't drug they set on with these oak dowels, three feet long, smooth as a baby's ass. By the end of the night they were all brown and sticky from the blood. Shanghaied nineteen of the poor bastards, took two big dump wagons just to collect them all."

Christian paused to down a shot of Bushmills. Most of his wobbly companions had heard the story a dozen times, yet no one seemed to care.

"But they promised these *Portugee* whalers they'd have 'em twenty men. One of the crimps notices a guy floatin' facedown near Mission Wharf. We find ten, twenty a year like that on the Coast. Scarface and the Whale, they ain't about to pass on another ninety dollars. So they fish 'im out and now they got twenty."

A guffaw made the rounds as Phil the Bartender refilled Christian's shot glass. Even his wife called him Phil the Bartender, a sodden lump who last bathed on his wedding day.

Christian tipped it up and the Bushmills went down warm and soothing as the salty breeze blowing from the marshy bay nearby. "Next day, the *Portugee* captain has a problem wakin' his new deck hand. Now Scarface, he's smarter than the Whale, but so is a stump. Scarface knows the captain will dump the stiff before they haul anchor. So they fish him out and mix him in with another lot. 'Throw some cold water on him, he'll be fine in the morning,' they tell the next dumb bastard captain. They sell a bloody corpse three times before the smell gives them away." His words brought a low roar from the bleary-eyed crowd, a melody of forced laughs and hacking howls.

Christian looked up at the grandfather clock behind the cluttered bar: six twenty-five. Time for two more shots of Bushmills before the rendezvous with his father.

Meanwhile, in the wine cellar of the Fallon house atop Telegraph Hill, Hunter fished the last of sixty photographs from the pungent fixer bath and hung it on a clothesline. The smell made his eyes run and his head swampy.

Byron entered the dank cellar and stopped at the sight of the perfect images. His face bore a mixture of foreboding and pride.

"Do you realize what you have here, dad? This is the Holy Grail."

"Son, I know you're smart, but sometimes you make people feel like they were bred from a turnip seed. How long have I been working on this?"

"I know, dad, but just look at these," Hunter continued unabated, snatching down several photographs, flapping them to speed the drying process. "A million dollars from the Bay Cities Water Company. Twice Congress turned down that abomination to dam up the Hetch Hetchy Valley and ship the water to San Francisco. When I was working on the water survey, the Bay Cities Company was drafting an alternative plan, to use the American River instead and get the city to foot the bill. Ten million dollars, the bastards are asking. They're going to pay Rolf a million dollar bribe to get his toadies on the board to vote for it."

Byron stepped forward and began to examine the photographs.

"Here's another beauty. Home Telephone. Home Telephone has a system where you dial some numbers—like the combination on a safe— and the call goes directly to the party without an operator. I took one of them apart last semester; it's ingenious the time and money it would save. They want a franchise to compete with Pacific State Telephone, so Rolf collected bribes from both of them."

Byron shuffled slowly through one photo, then another, a pained resignation in deep set eyes, a look not lost on his son.

"See this payment from the United Railway, dad? Those are the guys who want to tear out the cable cars and replace them with overhead

trolley lines so the city looks like one big web. Look at this photo here."
He took a photo from his father's hand and handed him another. "Rolf
collected $200,000 from W. H., that's William Herrin, chief lobbyist
of the Union Pacific Railroad, the parent company of United Railway.
Now, look at this one here," he said, replacing it with still another.
"Two days later, Rolf doles out the two hundred grand. He keeps fifty
for himself, gives Eugene Schmitz fifty, and gives the other hundred
grand to J. G., James Gallagher, President of the Board of Supervisors.
Gallagher splits the money among seventeen supervisors. There's a
check mark beside each name, dated the day before the vote. Only
problem is, there are eighteen supervisors."

Hunter pulled down several more photographs, hastily paging
through. "One supervisor, Louis Rea: no check marks anywhere in the
ledger. Rea refuses the bribes every time! He's the key, the only honest
one on the board. Rolf's ledger exonerates him. If you can get to Rea, he
will give up Gallagher, and Gallagher will save his behind by testifying
against Schmitz and Rolf. Then *they* give you Calhoun and Herrin and
when the dust clears, there's E. H. Harriman, most powerful railroad man
in America, butt naked in the middle of it."

Byron's head was reeling. Hunter was almost breathless.

"Dad, this is more than Rolf and Schmitz, this is the whole corrupt
system. The railroad, the utility companies, every politician-buying, boss-
making, worker-exploiting corporate trust in America is connected to this
book in one way or another. Mr. Feeney will have to build a wing onto
San Quentin."

"Who told you about Feeney?"

"Last year, he put away a senator from Oregon for massive land fraud.
Then he tours the country giving lectures on how Big Business is killing
democracy. He didn't move to San Francisco because he likes the salt
water soak at Sutro Baths."

"Then go to law school, son, become a prosecutor or a judge. Stop this
cop nonsense."

"Maybe later. Nothing changes unless somebody's willing to do the
dirty work. It's my turn now."

The look on Byron's face said it all. He knew his son was right, much
as it pained him. Evil was now the province of men in ascots and automobiles. It would take someone like Hunter, as smart as they were, to
defeat them.

It was a new war, unlike any seen before. The standard was passed, from father to son, old warrior to young, in the dusty wine cellar of the Fallon house that Easter Sunday.

"Let's put this stuff in my leather valise, Hunter. All the prints, the film, everything. We have to get to Meigg's Wharf. Looks like a blow is coming."

They exited the house atop Telegraph Hill as the fog began rolling through the Golden Gate, the sinking sun illuminating the billowing puffs in palettes of rose and violet. The cable car was nowhere to be seen; the cable had jumped its guides, as it did often on the steep line.

"Damn it. All right, Hunter, get that motorized thing of yours."

Hunter bolted into the garage and reappeared pushing the Waltham. He primed the coil and kicked the pedal and the engine roared to life. Byron climbed onto the long, flat leather seat behind Hunter and stared anxiously at the whitecaps rising on the surface of the bay.

They roared off with Byron clutching his portfolio and holding onto Hunter, the cobblestones chattering beneath them. Hunter took the curve at the top of Filbert so quickly he almost spilled his father.

At McGinty's Tavern on Union Street, Christian looked again at the grandfather clock. Six forty. Then he noticed the plumber next to him checking his pocket watch. He grabbed the man's wrist: a bolt shot through Christian as the minute hand came into focus. Six fifty-three.

"Goddamn it," he shouted, draining his glass.

He hit the wooden sidewalk at full stride, cut left through the dirt lot behind D'Egidio Die-Makers and down Laguna, weaving amongst the cars and carriages. It was twenty blocks to the waterfront, all of it flat or downhill.

Hunter and Byron rumbled over the rough timbers of Meigg's Wharf, the rusty iron fastenings jangling as the wind whistled between the boarded-up souvenir shops and food stands.

The sun touched the edge of the Pacific and a sheet of crimson spread across the dark blue surface. A steam launch waited at the end tie, its shifting white plume aglow with sunset.

Hunter killed the engine, rolling to a stop next to the launch.

"Where's Christian?" Byron bellowed to his nephew Anthony.

"I dunno, Uncle Byron. Lieutenant, sir. I been here about twenty minutes and I ain't seen no hide of him yet."

"He's in a Goddamn bar somewhere. I swear, I'll suspend him a month without pay. After I wring his miserable neck." Byron gazed at the churning, mile-wide mouth of the Golden Gate. On the other side of the bay, a fresh breeze fanned the spindly grass of the Marin Headlands.

In the fading light, both Byron and Hunter spotted the riptide, the massive collision of flood and ebb tides. The rip's telltale ribbon stretched through the Golden Gate, into the bay and past Alcatraz, winding south toward San José.

"Dad, let me go with you. You can't go, just you and Anthony."

"No. The fog's coming in, the shanghaiers will be out in force. You go to Fort Gunnybags, tell Max and Francis and the rest of The Brotherhood to get out after Kelly's men for what they did to Elliot and Jessie. Then go home and wait for me. You can help me serve the warrants on Rolf and Schmitz tomorrow."

Byron pulled his Colt and handed it to Hunter, taking back his derringer. "Be careful when you head to Fort Gunnybags, that's the Barbary Coast, you ain't used to that."

He turned toward the launch, struggling to contain his anger. "Anthony," he yelled above the noise of the boiler, "can you handle this thing?"

"I never steered one this big, Uncle Byron, but I think I can handle it. We better get a move on, it's gettin' rowdy out there."

"Dad, please. If you won't let me help you, at least let me help The Brotherhood. I can fight as well as any of them."

"You don't know what you're asking, son. Now, deliver the message to The Brotherhood and go home. We'll talk over breakfast." Then he did something he had not done since Isabella's funeral. He hugged his son.

In the pilothouse above deck, Anthony readied the throttle while Byron cast the bow and spring lines. Byron looked back at Hunter, offering a terse salute as they drifted away.

Hunter returned a half-hearted salute, seething with anger at his brother. He fired the Waltham and roared off down the wharf.

"Belvedere," Byron shouted in the stiffening wind. "Get me to Belvedere as fast as you can!"

Anthony pointed the launch northward, opening the throttle. The wind howled and sent a rainbow of spray over the deck.

Outside the Golden Gate, the sun sank in an explosion of red and orange, a fantail of eerie mauve igniting the cloudy heavens above.

They slipped into the ebb tide, Anthony angling the launch slightly eastward to keep them from being pushed out past the Marin Headlands and into the Pacific. Before them, Belvedere Island was disappearing beneath a wispy tail of fog meandering through the Golden Gate toward Raccoon Straits and Richardson Bay.

Christian arrived on the wharf to see the lights of Byron's launch growing smaller as it headed into deep water. He cursed and stomped as the launch pushed out past the cliffs at Fort Point, to the full expanse of the gaping Golden Gate.

On board, a gust hit them like a sledgehammer. The wind and waves lifted the bow clear, slamming the launch on its starboard side. A wave breached the deck, sending Byron sliding toward the stern.

Anthony stumbled to his knees, still clutching the wheel.

Then they entered the rip.

Chapter 9

BELVEDERE ISLAND

APRIL 15, 1906. 7:25 P.M.

Just north of the Golden Gate, at the Spreckels weekend mansion on Belvedere Island, six men waited anxiously for the arrival of Byron Fallon. Three of the men would soon be known by a common name: the Graft Hunters.

The financial leader of the group, Rudolph Spreckels, paced about the room, periodically raising a brass telescope to his eye, his efforts to spot Byron's launch impeded by the fog blanketing San Francisco Bay. At age thirty-eight, Spreckels was medium of height and build, long on courage and integrity. His father, Claus, had been a penniless German who became the sugar magnate of America by developing a process to extract sugar from beets.

Rudolph had made millions on his own. He was a yachtsman, opera lover, and zealot for clean government. He developed a simmering hatred for Rolf when the Boss tried to coax him into buying $15 million in city bonds at half their value, offering to trigger their devaluation with a punishing city rail strike. Rolf demanded half the profits once the strike was settled and the bonds regained their value.

Spreckels had stormed off, too furious to reply. The two had been enemies ever since.

Seated behind Spreckels was *Evening Bulletin* editor Fremont Older, who had launched the crusade in the spring of 1905. Older had traveled to the White House and enlisted the aid of President Theodore Roosevelt in combating the tidal wave of corruption that followed Rolf's Union Labor Party sweeping the Mayor's and Supervisors' offices. Roosevelt, who had failed to end graft while Police Commissioner of New York, offered the services of his finest prosecutor, Charles Feeney, but had no money in the Federal treasury to support the effort.

When he returned to San Francisco, Older engaged the help of his friend Rudolph Spreckels, who offered the astonishing sum of $100,000, plus the use of his homes for planning sessions.

"It's getting darker by the second," Spreckels reported, looking glumly down at Older, who was fiddling with his notes and gulping buttermilk in a vain attempt to pacify his ulcerous stomach.

Next to Older sat the worried Fire Chief, Dennis Sullivan. Next to him was James D. Phelan, the reformist Mayor who had been ousted by Eugene Schmitz five years before.

Apart from the group sat mustachioed Federal Prosecutor Charles Feeney, who clutched indictments for half the members of the city administration, from Rolf and Schmitz to the county dogcatcher.

"I'm curious," Older inquired, "as to the presence of a military commander in a domestic affair. Are we expecting another Civil War?" His question was directed to the group's newest and least welcome addition, added that very day at Spreckels' behest: Brigadier General "Fearless" Frederick Funston, Deputy Commander of the Presidio and Medal of Honor winner for his heroics during the Philippine Insurrection.

"We weren't expecting the last one, Mr. Older," Funston answered, failing to conceal his contempt for newspapermen, even one who shared his loathing for the Rolf/Schmitz machine.

The level of tension and uncertainty at the Spreckels house could not match that unfolding on San Francisco Bay.

The wind and waves tossed the launch about like a toy boat. With the fog shrouding them, Byron and Anthony suffered a terrifying, undulating form of vertigo. And they were caught in the riptide.

Anthony battled desperately at the helm, freeing the launch from one swirling eddy, only to be gripped by another. The wind tore at his clothes and torrents of water poured over the bow, slamming against the cabin house and soaking the pilot's roost above. He had vomited a half-dozen times already.

He looked at the deck below, where Byron clung precariously to the railing. A wave crested the bow and swamped the deck, washing him halfway overboard. He dangled by the crook of his left arm, refusing to surrender the leather portfolio he clutched with his right.

Anthony tethered the wheel and slid down the slippery steps, scrambling desperately toward his uncle. He seized Byron by the britches and pulled him back aboard, the pair collapsing on the deck. Anthony thought to take him below, but dismissed the idea for fear Byron might slide into the boiler.

"Hold on, sir! You gotta hold on!"

Anthony grabbed the stern line and tied it to the railing with a double bowline. He pulled the other end of the line around Byron's waist and tied it firmly, anchoring him with five feet of slack.

"Get us out of this damn rip and get us to Belvedere, Anthony. Now!"

Anthony pulled himself back up to the pilothouse. He reached for the wheel as a wave hit the bow and knocked him backward. His foot caught the top of the steps, preventing him from plummeting headfirst to the deck below. He dangled painfully, his foot wedged between the steps, his ankle crushed, until he could muster the strength to grab the rail and pull himself up. He crawled to the wheel, trembling with pain and weeping from exhaustion.

Seconds later, he saw a torrent of water hit Byron in the chest, pushing him toward the stern until the rope jerked him to a wrenching halt. Anthony sobbed, too weak to cry out.

At the mansion on Belvedere, Spreckels scanned the bay through the telescope. "Nothing. It's as black as I've ever seen it."

Dennis Sullivan returned from his fourth trip to the telephone closet. "The conditions are so bad the Life Saving Station can't send anyone out after them," he said, his face a deathly pallor.

Somewhere south of Belvedere, Anthony rode the lip of a whirlpool, gunned the throttle, and vaulted free. He worked the wheel to a heading of approximately twenty degrees northeast and attached the tethers. He staggered down the steps on his one good foot and sloshed his way along the lower deck, grasping the rail for support.

He spotted the rope hanging over the side.

"Uncle Byron! Uncle Byron!"

The boat tossed and knocked him to the seat of his sopping pants. Gasping, he crawled on bruised and bloodied knees through stinging salt water until he reached the rail. From his knees, he jerked the line with all his strength.

The effort sent him reeling backward, clutching an empty rope.

Chapter 10

━━━◦∞◦━━━

THE TENDERLOIN

APRIL 15, 1906. 7:40 P.M.

Oblivious to the terror on San Francisco Bay, I was seated in the luxurious Delmonico Restaurant on O'Farrell Street, enduring what seemed, at the time, a horror of my own. A steady stream of Mumm's champagne had loosened Adam Rolf's tongue and swollen his self-importance. He was singing a wearisome tune that had lasted for hours, making me question if a sudden death for trespassing in his office would not have been a less painful affair.

"The bloody railroad, the curse of the great Leland Stanford. No man will ever obtain real power in this country until he buries the Stanford blight. That's why I let them build the Fairmont Hotel—it blocks my view of his onion-domed monstrosity."

The rant against Stanford had become the chorus of Rolf's verbal memoirs. It had begun, over cheese toast and lobster *bisque*, with a detailed recollection of his father, Warren, buying up ships in Yerba Buena Cove after their crews abandoned them for the gold mines in '49. Between mouthfuls of baked oysters, candied yams, and *Chateaubriand*, he explained how the Rolf proprietorship of the waterfront created "the true Gold Rush. The one that never runs dry."

It left me wondering which component in alcohol encourages a man to hold the floor for hours, reciting *ad nauseam* the minutiae of his life as though it were some missing biblical text. I am not a temperant woman, but I could well become one.

"Once a man obtains his worldly deserts, Annalisa, he thinks of a legacy. The future. How he'll be remembered. He asks himself, 'What can I do for future generations? What can I do to see that able men, men like myself, continue to dictate the course of human affairs? How does one preserve the state of things, ensure proper selection, and keep the unwashed and unworthy from destroying what we men of destiny have built?'"

Cross-eyed and beaming with delight over his personal rendition of Social Darwinism, he reached across the Irish linen to stroke the back of my wrist with his index finger.

With the thumb of my other hand, I caressed the razor-sharp tines of my silver dessert fork and fought the urge to pin his hand to the table. "My goodness," I muttered instead. "We're going to be late for the theater. I doubt Mr. Barrymore will go on without us!"

Forcing a smile, Rolf reached for my arm and led me across Delmonico's thickly carpeted dining room, nodding to all who proffered the slightest genuflection.

Morning, and his arrest, could not come soon enough.

We climbed into the back seat of his newest prize, a gleaming, onyx, block-long Thomas Flyer, for the trip to the California Theater. Tommy cranked the lever and jumped into the driver's seat, and soon had the Flyer at twenty-five miles per hour, scattering horses and angry pedestrians. I squirmed on the tucked-and-rolled red leather seat while Rolf shouted over the noise.

"Fifty horsepower, nineteen precision bearings, same number as there are jewels in a fine Swiss watch. About four thousand, a reasonable price with the leather bonnet. Much less than I paid for the Rolls Royce. And she's faster."

The bumping of the Flyer, the unavoidable bouquet of horse manure and half-burned petroleum sent my stomach reeling. We motored past Union Square, spun a dizzying turn up Bush and in three blocks jerked to a stop at the California Hotel, next door to Central Fire Station.

Overhead, on a wire stretched between the California Hotel and the *Bulletin* across the street, hung banners featuring Caruso in costume for *Carmen* and *La Bohème*.

Tommy jumped from the driver's seat and opened the rear door, extending a calloused hand, a leer across his cratered face.

I entered the theater on the arm of my reptilian host as the fog began pouring down Bush Street, raising my concern for Byron Fallon.

Ten blocks away on the Barbary Coast—in a warehouse dubbed Fort Gunnybags by the Committee of Vigilance, from which they had lynched a half-dozen murderers decades earlier—The Brotherhood prepared for battle. They were minus their principal warrior, Christian Fallon, and none too happy for it.

"Alright," Francis Fagen said, spreading a map onto the planked floor, "we're going to proceed as we are. The Merchant Seamen's Office has requests for seventy able-bodied seamen. They don't have ten available. With the fog coming in, the shanghaiers will be out in force." At age twenty-seven, six feet three inches tall, Francis was the tallest man in the department. He was a tee-totaling Catholic with a missionary's zeal and a natural instinct for guiding men that made him, along with Christian, shared leader of The Brotherhood.

"Damn Christian, that bastard," Max Rinaldi raged, "leaving the Lieutenant with his ass hanging out like that. I'll kill him when I find him." At five feet ten, two hundred and twenty pounds, with fists like Christmas hams, Max was easily the department's strongest man. He showed more hair on his upper lip than on his head, where a single curl pointed toward a bony brow. He was the only member of The Brotherhood fool enough to do physical battle with Christian Fallon.

Next to Max stood his younger brother, Carlo, stout as a whiskey barrel, with arms and hands that could crush a boulder. A lifelong stutter rendered him painfully shy in everything save physical confrontation.

Steadying a lantern above Francis' head was his younger brother, Patrick, at twenty the youngest of The Brotherhood, whip thin and nearly as tall as his sibling. He was blue-eyed and slight of physique, as quick with a Bible quote as he was with a nightstick or revolver.

Hunter, the last to arrive, had delivered the news of Christian's failure to arrive at Meigg's Wharf.

"And you're tryin' to tell us your father said you could take Christian's place?" Max inquired.

"That's what he said."

"Strange," Max countered, "seein' he'd never stand for you bein' a cop."

"Right now," Francis said, "we can use every man we got. Hunter can work with me and Patrick. Now, Scarface and the Whale, they work Pacific and Jackson, workin' the slop holes to pay off the bartenders for slippin' Mickey Finns. We'll start on the north side."

The heavy oak door behind them banged open, a silhouette burst in, fingers pointed like six-shooters.

"Bang! You blue bastards are all dead!"

Max was about to pump a slug into the silhouette when Christian stepped into the flickering light cast by the lantern, shouting, "What's the matter, you guys jumpy?"

Christian's boot heels echoed through the cavernous room, halting only as Max holstered his revolver and lunged for him. Before he could wrap his hands around Christian's throat, Patrick and Francis managed to dive for the big man, pinning his arms to his sides.

"I'll kill you, Christian, leaving your father hanging like that. Who's with him, Anthony, that damn idiot?"

Hunter stepped in front of Christian to keep him from counter-attacking.

"What are you going to do, Max, hang me for being two minutes late? It's a boat ride, not a gunfight. Save the piss and vinegar for Shanghai Kelly's men." Then he turned to Hunter. "Why didn't you go with dad?"

"He wouldn't let me. He told me to get The Brotherhood after Kelly's men for what they did to Jessie and Elliot."

"He told you to go with us?"

"Since you're too busy slugging down booze to give a damn about your own father, somebody had to do it."

Christian seethed.

Max made another attempt to free himself from the grip of the Fagen brothers.

"Enough of this," Francis ordered. "We got a war going on, the Lieutenant will settle this matter when it's over. Understood?"

Max calmed himself enough that Francis and Patrick let him loose, though they maintained positions between him and Christian.

"All right," Francis continued, "let's get on with it. If Hunter wants to go, he can deal with the Lieutenant later. Divide into two three-man teams."

"We'll divide into three two-man teams," Christian argued, "that way we cover more of the Coast."

"That's not smart, Christian," Patrick said. "Kelly's men work four to a crew. It's risky, just two of us."

"Three men, too easy to spot," Christian said. "Half of them recognize us a block away as it is. Two-man teams. Let's put the hurt on 'em for what they did to Jessie and Elliot."

Though Francis held the superior rank of Sergeant, power on the Barbary Coast lay in the fist and the revolver, where Christian reigned. At one time or another, he had rescued every one of them.

"Brothers with brothers," Christian said. "Max, you and Carlo start from the south, work Clay Street to the piers. Francis, you and Patrick start north on Broadway. Hunter and I will take Pacific Avenue in the middle and meet up with everyone at the Tiburon ferry slip."

"You're gonna take a green rookie ain't never been on the Coast through Murderers' Triangle?" argued Max. "Who you trying to get killed, you or him?"

"My kid brother can handle anything. Right, Hunter? What were you, middleweight champ down at Stanford two years running?"

"Three. Undefeated. I won every amateur contest in San Mateo and Santa Clara County from middle to heavyweight."

"See?" Christian said, grinning broadly. "If we run into any opium-crazed fraternity boys, Hunter can handle 'em."

Christian extended a hand toward Francis, who passed over a sawed-off, double-barreled Remington and a handful of shells. Christian hung the shotgun upside down from the leather strap inside his coat, trapping the stock beneath his armpit.

They stepped outside and walked silently up Jackson Street, careful to keep Max away from Christian, passing the night crew and the day crew at Hotaling's Whiskey as they traded shifts.

On Montgomery, Hunter peered up at the banner strung between two Edison light poles that read BENVENUTO ENRICO CARUSO, and in smaller, cursive print, *I CUGINI NAPOLITANI.* The whole city had succumbed to Caruso fever. Victors and Gramophones blared from apartment windows, smiling schoolgirls twirled their hips, mimicking *Carmen*'s saucy dance. Restaurants and theaters were full, Broughams glistened more brightly, and even the whores on the Barbary Coast appeared better dressed.

Four whiskey-emboldened college boys in Berkeley sweaters stumbled by, jabbering about Dr. Jordan's Museum of Horrors several blocks away, where they had paid four bits apiece to examine an embalmed five-legged cow, a two-headed rattlesnake, and the floating head of the Gold Rush bandit Joaquín Murietta. They staggered down Jackson Street, bound for the deadfalls and brothels.

"Enjoy it, lads," Christian called out, "for tomorrow you'll be suckin' hind wind to Shanghai."

"We keep in touch by call box," Francis said. "You spot the Whale or Scarface, call for backup. No bloody heroes, understood?"

"Yes, sir," Christian replied with a mocking salute.

"I'm just glad the tenderfoot is covering your ass and not mine," Max growled.

"Let's have a minute here," Patrick said. He bowed his head and held his hand out. All but Hunter followed suit. "Christian told us you were one of those bloody Socialists," Patrick said. "If you are, you do it on your own time. This is His work we're doing here."

Hunter reluctantly put his hand atop the pile.

"Protect us, Father," Patrick intoned. "Guide us with faith and righteousness. Give us the courage and steadfastness to wipe this evil from our hearts and our home."

"A-a-a-men," added Carlo.

All but Hunter echoed "amen."

"What's the matter, Hunter, the Lord abandon you? Or you abandon him?" Patrick asked.

"I'm a Freethinker. You believe what you want, Patrick."

"Let's go," Christian ordered. "They'll have nabbed half their lot by the time we get moving."

Max gave Christian a final angry stare and headed downhill toward Clay Street, his brother Carlo close behind. Francis and Patrick headed uphill toward Broadway.

Christian looked at his younger brother. "What do you have for weapons? Some little bean shooter?"

"Dad's Colt revolver. He gave it to me at the docks, before he took off. Just him and Anthony."

Christian ignored the dig and produced a two-foot length of iron pipe from inside his coat. He lifted Hunter's left wrist, slid the pipe inside his sleeve along the underside of his forearm, and tied his cuff with a piece of dark cord.

"Pay attention, Hunter. Kelly's men like to slash at you with those long hara-kiri knives. Cut a cop, you drink for a week free anywhere on the Barbary Coast. He loses an eye or a limb, you drink a month. Kill him and you can stay drunk 'til Kingdom come. Block with your left arm, the pipe will save you from needin' a hook for a hand. Pull the slipknot and the pipe drops in your hand for a weapon."

"You should have been there, Christian, you should never have let dad go off alone."

Despite the odor of Irish whiskey, Christian's gaze was unflinching.

"Dad's been wearing a star his whole life. He don't need me. He don't need you. He don't need anybody. Keep your ass below your elbows and do like I tell you. And don't make me daft by asking all those damn questions like you used to."

Hunter followed Christian toward shadowy Pacific Street, craning his neck skyward as fog threatened to blanket the entire city. It did nothing to ease his worry over his father.

They entered Pacific Street at the tip of Murderers' Triangle, a pie-shaped six-block section bordered by Broadway, Kearny, and Montgomery, packed with rancid bars and stall-like cribs where women of indeterminate age and origin did anything for any price, depending on their state of inebriation. It was the battles of the brothers' granduncle Arthur and grandfather Malachi with the Sydney Ducks that helped give Murderers' Triangle its name.

The first thing that hit Hunter was the noise of blaring trumpets, flatulent tubas, tinkling pianos, and screeching non-sopranos that spilled from every door of the crowded saloons and dance halls. His gait slowed when the smell hit, a nose-curdling meld of stale booze, dried sweat, perfumed sex, cheap tobacco, and manure, garnished by a pungent lilt of burning opium. Still, the teeming streets offered up a darkly festive atmosphere.

Hunter and Christian picked through hop heads, weary prostitutes, tottering sailors, slumming college boys, razor-eyed gamblers, and leering thugs. The brothers squeezed past the Bear Café where a chained black bear bummed opium-spiked drinks from the surging crowd. Three Cockney sailing men swayed beneath the Café's dull red light, negotiating with an ill-favored crib girl who applied her makeup with a ladle.

Christian took a long pull from a pocket flask, then tapped Hunter under the jaw until his mouth closed.

"What's the big attraction down here?" Hunter asked. "Getting drugged and shanghaied? I've been in outhouses that smelled better than this place."

"Cheap whiskey, three thousand whores, anything you want for a price. Got a crib on the next block, four hundred fifty stalls, smaller than jail cells. The crib girls and the hostesses at the Melodeons are the worst. Give you a dose make your willy wilt. The French restaurants on Jackson Street, that's where they keep most of the fine tail. You still cherry, or one of those college girls do the job for free?"

Hunter was distracted by raucous laughter pouring from the Bella Union, its doors wide open to ease the heat. He walked close and peered inside.

On a battered, garishly lit stage, Big Bertha and Oofty Goofty performed a distinctly San Franciscan form of Shakespeare. "What light through filthy window barely shines?" bellowed three-hundred-pound Bertha. Too fat to climb the parapet, she played Romeo in leather breeches that cost several cows their lives.

"That's no light, you blubbery slut! That's my stinkin' arse!" cried the troll-like Oofty Goofty from the parapet, where he stood clad in the gown and wig of Juliet.

A stagehand jumped from the wings and struck Oofty Goofty with a pool cue, sending him over the rail. He crashed to the floor to a roar of hoots and laughter.

"Oofty Goofty," Christian offered. "The painless man. For a quarter you can kick him. Four bits, you can hit him with a stick. Supposed to be good luck. Ain't a businessman in town doesn't have a whack at him before he makes a deal."

Hunter spotted two shadowy figures leading a disoriented man from the alley entrance of the Bella Union. The taller of the two men struck the tottering victim with a club; his partner caught the limp body in one swift movement and tossed him into a nearby wagon.

"Let's move on them, Christian."

"No. We're after Scarface and the Whale."

"They're going to shanghai that guy."

"The minute we pinch somebody, the word will spread like wildfire. It's Easter Sunday, ain't nobody expecting us to be out."

"What the hell is going to happen to him?"

"He's going to wind up starved, beaten, buggered, and worked to death. Probably never see San Francisco again. Remember that when it comes time to stomp the bastards."

The crimps led the wagon away, struggling with their unruly horses.

At the end of Pacific Avenue, several blocks ahead, the waterfront was disappearing beneath scarves of fog that grew thicker by the minute, shrouding the bay as dirge-like horns sounded their ominous warnings.

Hunter thought of his father, and a shiver of fear went through him.

Chapter 11

———◆◆◆◆———

APRIL 15, 1906. 8:10 P.M.

While The Brotherhood trolled the Barbary Coast in search of Shanghai Kelly's men, I assisted Adam Rolf in holding court at the California Theater. I did so with all the enthusiasm one feels when waltzing with a rattlesnake.

"Mrs. Flood. Mrs. Herrin. Mrs. Gallagher," I called as the cream of San Francisco's Social Register sashayed by, decked out in a blinding display of baubles. In most cities, madams and courtesans aspire to the dress and decorum of women of means. San Francisco's storied elite owed all things cultural, fashionable, and even culinary to the influence of whores, mostly French.

During our Gold Rush, Napoleon's petulant nephew, Louis, spared himself a trip to the guillotine by distracting his subjects with a national lottery. The prize was fourteen million francs in freshly plucked California bullion; the profits, Louis claimed, would send five thousand of France's poor to our gilded shores. The French went mad for the idea, gobbling up every ticket.

Surprisingly, Louis lined his pockets, ignoring the poor and choosing instead to unclog Paris' crowded boulevards by sending hundreds of the soiled doves to our marshy shores. The brave *femmes de joie*, more cultured than their Ohio and Missouri cousins, disembarked nineteen thousand miles later to a filthy enclave lined with lonely men whose pockets were bulging with gold.

Overnight, lonely miners traded mule shanks and *crème de bark* for a taste of French cuisine. Wooden sidewalks appeared to protect hemlines, public baths sprang up, and former swine farmers suddenly developed an appreciation for Molière. Enterprising unions between the women and suddenly rich merchants and miners created theater and opera guilds, a lavish stream of entertainment, a flourishing fashion industry, a *bon vivant* spirit that nurtured a uniquely sophisticated bacchanalia. They begat mansions, public gardens, opera houses, grand boulevards, and gaslight cafés, with a boisterous *joie de vivre* unmatched in the East.

It was their lascivious heirs, the whores and madams of our day, who fired the first salvo in the next great social revolution.

Margaritte Jensen—seated in the box adjacent to Rolf's, and dressed in a pale silver gown and enough black pearls to cover a barrel—had been complaining for weeks about Boss Rolf's mounting extortion of her Jackson Street French restaurant, nicknamed "The Municipal Crib" for the number of city officials who dallied there. Margaritte and the owner of Marchand's, Pierre, had contacted Fremont Older after Rolf had raised the tariff for each ninety-day liquor license renewal to $10,000. They offered to testify before a grand jury. And so the war began.

We settled in for *The Dictator*, featuring the emerging legend in American theater, John Barrymore. The door opened behind us and the light from the hallway caught my attention. A tree stump of a man moved next to Adam Rolf, close enough that I could hear his labored breathing.

"Annalisa, I'm not sure you've ever met Mr. John Kelly," Rolf said.

The broken-nosed thug plunged into the seat next to Rolf, looking as though meat packers had stuffed him into his tuxedo.

"Mr. Kelly here represents our interests along the waterfront. I'm about to announce his candidacy for a supervisor's seat next election."

"Miss Passarelli," he growled with whiskey breath.

"Mr. Kelly. Excuse my ignorance, but are you the one they call Shanghai Kelly?"

"We try not to use that nickname," Rolf laughed.

I was gratefully distracted when Barrymore arrived on stage to a thunderous reception.

From the corner of my eye, I noticed Rolf click open his pocket watch and offer a peek to Kelly, who smiled. The seemingly innocuous gesture disturbed me greatly. The room seemed to tilt and the chair wavered beneath me.

The end could not come soon enough.

Chapter 12

BARBARY COAST

APRIL 15, 1906. 9:40 P.M.

As John Barrymore roamed the stage to repeated outbursts of applause, I scribbled notes, oblivious to the drama unfolding outside the confines of the theater.

Hunter and Christian approached Lime Juice Corner, at the dark end of Pacific Avenue, where British captains prowled in search of reluctant sailors. It was nearly ten o'clock when Christian jerked Hunter into a doorway and pointed toward the cellar door of Henderson's Melodeon, where a giant figure emerged.

"See that ugly mound of blubber?" Christian warned. "The Whale. When he's not out shanghaiing, he bounces at Kelly's place. Likes to get you in a bear hug and bite your nose off. Got twenty of 'em pressed under the glass on Kelly's bar. He even looks at you cross-eyed, shoot him."

The Whale was quickly joined by a dapper little man with a waxed mustache and flattened nose.

Christian grinned and took a celebratory pull from his flask. "This is getting good. Chicken Devine. See his left hand?"

The light streaming through Henderson's cellar doors illuminated Chicken's metal hook as he reached up to adjust his porkpie hat.

"The Chicken had a run-in with another shanghaier and one of those hara-kiri knives. Took his hand off with one swing. Likes to tell people a dog snatched it. Packs an Army Colt and a Bowie knife so sharp you could shave with it. Keep an eye on that one good hand of his."

A limp body was shoved upward into the waiting arms of the Whale and Chicken Devine. The Whale gave him a kick. Nothing. A second body was passed up.

"That looks like a kid, Christian."

"Charlie Tate. He was at the station yesterday asking for food. He's fourteen, ran away from somewhere in South Dakota. Farm boy. I gave him a dime for lunch and told him stay away from the Barbary Coast. Didn't listen, like a lot of people I know."

Hunter ignored the slight. He could see a large purple bruise on the side of Charlie Tate's face.

"They'll get ten dollars extra from some toothless captain who likes 'em young," Christian said. "Two days at sea, the kid will be cursing his mother for having him." Christian grabbed Hunter's arm to keep him from charging forward. "Easy there, big fella. It ain't shanghaiing until they load 'em in a boat."

"They're not taking that kid, Christian, if I have to kill every one of them myself."

"Listen to you. One day on the job and startin' to sound like a cop."

"They ain't takin' that kid."

After shoving another victim from the basement, a third shanghaier emerged, gaunt-faced and hawk-nosed, a patch over his left eye and a pearl-handled knife in his belt.

Even Christian got his blood up. "Now, there's one I got personal business with. Zipper. Slices a man so fast all you hear is 'zip.' Been lookin' for him since he put an ice pick between my ribs. Yeah, this is gonna be a real good night."

A shallow dump wagon rumbled around the corner. At the reins was a tall, broad-shouldered man, a jagged scar wending from his left ear to his jaw.

"And there's Scarface, Kelly's chief lieutenant. Only one of 'em who ain't dumber than an anvil. The gang's all here."

"Let's move on them. That kid needs a doctor."

Christian was halfway through a good pull from the flask. "We wait." This time he offered a taste to Hunter, who waved it off.

"You keep drinkin' that stuff, maybe I should paint my name on the back of my coat so you don't shoot me."

"I ain't shot you yet."

"We've been partners two hours. You have time."

After Kelly's crew had loaded their prey aboard the dump wagon, Scarface snapped the reins and headed toward the waterfront, his cronies walking close behind.

Christian waited until they were a full block away. "Keep your eyes peeled, watch our backs. These guys use a trailer, some rummy to lag behind in case they're being followed."

The trolling gang crossed through the circle of yellow light illuminating the intersection at Washington Street. Two doors behind them, a burly Negro dressed in plumber's bibs staggered from the door of the Ivy, a raucous colored cabaret. A bartender stepped through the door behind him and whistled, alerting Scarface and the Whale to the presence of a potential victim.

Christian pulled Hunter into the shadows of a dry goods store as the shanghaiers circled back.

"Hey you, young man, you a sailor?" the Whale called.

The man stumbled forward, oblivious to the peril, as the waiting crew tipped their hats in welcome.

"They didn't put enough laudanum in his drink. He's so big he muscled through it," Christian whispered.

The Whale was quickly out of patience. "Hey, you! You a seafarin' man?"

"Wha'sat?"

The crimps surrounded him, hyena-like.

"You lookin' for work?" Scarface asked. "We got us a ship lookin' for crew. Payin' top dollar."

The man slowed, wobbly. "Sailor? Hell no. I got me a job. I'm a plumbin' over ta' Fairmont. Got two colored plumbers workin' there."

The Whale launched a gnarled fist that looked like it would drop an ox.

But the man had begun to turn his head, reducing the effort to a glancing blow. Thick-limbed and broad-shouldered, he raised his fists in defense.

"Sober, he might have a chance," Christian said.

Clumsily, the man struck back at the Whale.

Chicken jabbed at the man's ribs with brass knuckles, while Zipper laid a two-foot length of maple across the man's ear, the crack echoing down the street.

Still, he fought back, shoving Chicken aside and landing a clumsy punch to the middle of the Whale's face.

The Whale cursed, produced a belaying pin, and struck a blow to the man's knee that sent him crashing to the ground. They pummeled him furiously, his howls mixing with the raucous laughter and music drifting through the Barbary Coast.

Hunter pulled his pistol and began to move. Christian shoved him back into the shadows.

"They're going to kill that guy," Hunter said.

"And lose ninety dollars? If we grab 'em now, they'll say he picked a fight. Desk sergeant won't even book 'em."

Hunter stared as the crimps took turns beating their prostrate victim, the spray of blood visible in the yellow streetlight.

The Whale straddled the man and began pounding his face until the howling stopped. Scarface brought the wagon close, and they heaved the man inside, laughing when his body banged on the wooden bed.

Christian pulled the flask from his jacket and took a healthy swig.

"What the hell is that you're drinking?"

"Your guess is good as mine. Sure you don't want a little bracer? Makes it easier to put a slug in a man, especially your first time."

"We're going to arrest them and watch them hang for what they did to Elliot and Jessie. That's the law. We only shoot if they resist," Hunter said.

"Try selling that to Elliot or Jessie." Christian took a final pull at his flask. "Rule Number One. Kill a cop, you die. Save the courts a lot of time and bother."

Scarface eased the brake and started off, his crew walking beside and watching warily. They turned onto Jackson Street, disappearing around The Other Eye Pub.

"Let me have your call box key and I'll sound the others," Hunter said.

"Not yet."

"What do you mean, not yet? They're taking these guys to the wharf on Jackson, that's a block away."

"Christ, Hunter, don't go soft on me. You want, I'll take these guys myself."

At the Jackson Street Pier, the wagon stopped near a small skiff bobbing in the water. Scarface and Zipper shoved the colored plumber from the wagon and laughed hysterically when he landed face first on the wooden pier. They rolled him into the boat, which nearly capsized.

The Whale lifted the unconscious boy like a sack of flour and flung him atop the bleeding, unconscious man.

"All right, Hunter, let's move. And don't get too close to each other. Make them have to turn to see both of us."

Hunter drew his revolver and sprinted forward, blood rushing in his ears, as the third and fourth victims landed in the boat.

"Remember," Christian said. "If you kill 'em, it's a lot less paperwork."

"I'll remember that."

Christian screamed, "Halt! Police!"

Hunter tried to yell the same but his voice failed.

Christian shot a disgusted look at his brother and yelled, "I want to see eight hands!"

"What's this, some kind of shakedown?" the Whale spat. "You boys didn't get your cut from the night shift?"

Christian cursed. "Eight hands. Let me see eight hands or somebody dies!" When Chicken raised a hand and a stump, Christian relented. "Okay. Seven hands and a hook."

Hunter fought the trembling in his hands.

"You know," Scarface offered, "you're interfering with the flow of commerce. These docks dry up for lack 'a crew, ain't a pot to piss in for nobody. You can make a month's pay doin' right here. Just take a little walk."

"Raise your hands, higher!" Hunter yelled, his voice cracking. His adversaries cackled.

"What are you going to do?" the Whale snickered. "Two of you gonna shoot all four of us?"

Zipper, shoulder hidden in the shadows, moved his left hand imperceptibly to his coat pocket. It reappeared with lightning speed, clutching a revolver.

A slug from Christian's Colt shattered Zipper's collarbone and sent him crashing into the water. The water sloshed as Zipper groaned and a dark stain spread around him.

"My math must be bad," Christian shouted. "I only count three of you."

Hunter's mouth grew dry and the rushing in his ears grew louder.

The Whale, Scarface, and Chicken Devine grabbed for their weapons, diving toward the shadows.

As Hunter turned, Scarface put a shot through the fabric of his billowing pea coat, missing his flesh by an inch. Hunter stumbled forward and dropped his revolver, kicking it halfway to the water.

Christian whipped the sawed-off shotgun from his coat as the Whale aimed at Hunter. Christian fired first, and blasted a gaping hole in the Whale's chest that sent him crashing into the boat, dumping the unconscious victims into the bay.

Chicken Devine's shot sliced through the tip of Christian's ear. Christian spun to his right and pointed the Remington.

Chicken dropped his gun and raised his hands in surrender. "I give up, don't sho . . ."

A blast from Christian's shotgun almost cut Chicken's wiry frame in half.

Hunter scrambled toward his revolver as Scarface fired a shot between Christian's legs, just below disaster.

Christian raised his revolver and fired, missing Scarface, who dove beneath the dock, disappearing into the murky water. Christian popped open the shotgun, dumped the two spent shells and reloaded. Despite the blood trickling from his ear, he looked as calm as a man about to order breakfast.

"How you like police work so far, Hunter?"

Hunter retrieved his revolver and ran toward the men floating in the bay, whipping off his shoes and jacket.

"Christ, Hunter, you know how cold that water is?"

He found out instantly, yelping as he hit the surface. He quickly shoved the boy to the dock's edge.

Christian pulled the boy onto the dock with one hand, cradling the shotgun in the other. "You got downright charitable instincts, Hunter. Real valuable in this line of work."

While Hunter maneuvered the Negro's body toward the dock, he looked up and caught Christian gazing toward the fog-shrouded bay. A worried look spread across Christian's face.

"You decide to start worrying about dad? Little late for that, isn't it? He should be on his way back by now."

Then Hunter noticed what had distracted his brother. The dogs were howling, from one end of the Barbary Coast to the other.

This time, Christian was not dreaming.

Chapter 13

———◦∞◦———

BUSH STREET

APRIL 15, 1906. 10:00 P.M.

The week that began on Easter Sunday, 1906, may well go down as the finest week of theater and music the city has ever seen, a cultural ascendance of the grand city of the American West. Those who have awaited the arrival of the world's most famous personality, Enrico Caruso, yet missed the extraordinary performance of John Barrymore in *The Dictator,* have deprived themselves of witnessing a star whose luminance may someday rival that of the great tenor himself. John Barrymore, rapidly gaining fame for his winsome looks and distinctive profile, has affirmed himself as an actor whose dramatic and comedic talent surpasses even his engaging presence. The youngest of "The Royal Acting Family of America"—with the Drews on his mother's side, and siblings Lionel and Ethel—his blossoming impact on the theater and the new medium of moving pictures appears limitless.

Indeed, he may elevate the Barrymores to the stature of the Booth clan, the original "First Family of the Theater," Junius, Edwin, and the infamous John Wilkes, who once ignited San Francisco stages with their naturalistic approach to acting. We may well have witnessed the very future of American dramatic acting.

I scrawled my review as the final curtain approached, eager to switch my attention to more meaningful concerns. The door opened behind me and again the light swept across the box.

Adam Rolf removed the arm he had left lying across the back of my chair as Tommy knelt to whisper in his boss's ear.

When Tommy left a minute later, Rolf leaned over and whispered to Shanghai Kelly, whose face curled in muted anger and disgust. As Boss Rolf whispered on, Kelly's eyebrows arched and his eyes sparkled in triumph, his smile revealing a single gold tooth.

I did not notice the presence of an usher until he tapped me on the shoulder. I almost jumped out of my chair.

"Miss Passarelli. You have a telephone call. They said it's important."

"Excuse me, Mr. Rolf, Mr. Kelly. It must be my editor."

I hiked my dress and hastened to the telephone station on the mezzanine, fighting a mounting sense of dread. I grabbed the ivory-handled receiver from the cord where the usher had left it hanging and closed the cabinet door around me.

"Hello?" The anxiety in my own voice unnerved me.

"Miss Passarelli, are you alone?"

"Who is this?"

"This is Prosecutor Charles Feeney. You know who I am?"

"What say you, sir?"

"Gioia."

My heart leapt into my throat. It was my mother's name, the password Byron Fallon arranged for Mr. Feeney or Francis Fagen to use should any of our plans unravel.

"We have a problem, Miss Passarelli. The boat carrying our friend failed to arrive for the meeting in Belvedere."

I sagged against the wall.

"Miss Passarelli?"

"Yes."

"I'm told the boat is about to dock at Mission Pier. We have reason to believe our friend is not aboard."

"Where is he? Do you know?"

"All we know is that he is missing. The weather changed so quickly we were unable to go out after him. But it's breaking now and we're leaving this moment. I thought it important to warn you. He was carrying some papers, was he not?"

My only response was the receiver banging against the wall where I had dropped it. I tried to gather myself lest I draw attention, walking purposefully down the marble steps.

At the curb outside, I summoned a leather-bonneted Hansom from the block-long cue.

"Mission Pier!"

"Well, now that's near the Barbary Coast, ma'am, not the friendliest 'a places. 'Specially this time 'a night." His lip curled upward, a glint in his eye as he looked me up and down.

"I am not a parlor girl, and I don't need an escort. Now, do you want to get paid? Just get me there as fast as you can!"

He turned and cracked his whip.

At the Hall of Justice, Hunter Fallon sat before the Remington, typewriting his report as Christian stood behind him with a cloth pressed to his bloody ear.

"You going to leave me with all this paperwork?"

"You're a college boy, you should be used to it by now." Christian reached over Hunter and pulled a pen from the desk well. He signed several blank forms.

"You don't even want to know what I'm going to write?"

"Who's gonna fuss about it? The Whale?"

Hunter looked about the squad room, his breathing still labored, his clothes dripping onto the wooden floor. He noticed the desk sergeant staring in his direction. "You didn't tell anyone, did you?"

"Tell 'em what?"

"That I dropped my gun!"

"They hate us enough already. Be sure to have someone fix that bullet hole in your coat so you don't have to answer a lot of questions. See you tomorrow night."

"That's it, you're finished?"

"Kill somebody, get the night off. They figure you might be a little jumpy and shoot your partner. Just make it clear they drew on us first."

"I should leave out the part about the Chicken having his hands up when you shot him."

"One hand, one stump. If you had hung onto your gun, I wouldn't have had to shoot him. And Scarface wouldn't be out there shanghaiing somebody else. Think about that while you're filling out all these stupid forms. You could have got us both killed."

Christian was halfway across the squad room before Hunter noticed he was gone.

Hunter struggled to roll a form into the typing machine, the sound of gunfire still ringing in his ears. His fingers hit one wrong letter, then another. He looked over his shoulder and saw the desk sergeant still staring at him. Hunter stared back until the sergeant lost interest. He tore the first form out and crumpled it up, missing the nearby waste can. A second form suffered the same fate.

The telephone rang on the sergeant's desk, the tinny sound echoing across the hardwood floors and vacant desks.

"Officer Fallon." At first it didn't register. "Officer Fallon!"

"Yes, sir?"

"Telephone call."

Hunter walked quickly across the squad room, uncertain who might call him at the Detective Bureau. The sergeant had left the receiver dangling, departing in the direction of the patrolmen's duty room.

Hunter raised it cautiously to his ear. "Hello?"

"Christian?"

"No. This is his brother, Hunter."

"Hunter? This is Fire Chief Sullivan. There's no graceful way to tell you. Your father never arrived at Belvedere. Was Christian with him?"

"It was just Anthony and my father."

"The Harbor Police spotted the launch headed toward Mission Pier. You better get down there as fast as you can."

Hunter bolted down the steps to the sidewalk and sprinted four blocks to the livery. In seconds, he was roaring down scruffy Clay Street, sending drunks and revelers diving from his path.

At Mission Pier, he spotted a man crawling toward him on hands and knees. He jammed the brake, jumped off and seized the kneeling figure by his sopping jacket.

Anthony looked up, vomiting a mouthful of brackish water and gasping for breath.

"Where is he, Anthony? Where's my father, dammit?"

Anthony sobbed convulsively. "I tied him to the rail . . . there was just the two of us . . . me and him . . . Christian was supposed to be there . . . where the hell was Christian . . . then he was gone . . . I tied him to the rail . . . I pulled the rope up, there was no one there . . . it was so dark . . . it was so dark I couldn't see nothing." Anthony retched again.

Hunter raised the motorcycle and charged down the quarter-mile pier.

At the end tie, the launch bobbed and banged against the pilings. In one move Hunter dismounted and leapt five feet to the heaving deck.

"Dad, Dad!" Hunter slipped on the wet surface and crashed to his knees, still yelling for his father. He scrambled above to the pilot's roost. Nothing. He grasped the brass rail and slid quickly back to the deck.

He ripped open the passage door to the engine room and went below. The door banged shut, plunging him into darkness. Hunter took two steps and tripped over a coil of heavy line. As he tried to untangle himself, he heard soft footsteps on the deck above. He crouched behind the passageway, drawing his revolver as the steps approached.

The door slid open and a silhouette appeared. Hunter seized an upturned collar and shoved the Colt in the intruder's face. "Don't move."

I stared back at him, trembling, mouth agape.

It took a moment for him to recognize me. "Annalisa? What the hell are you doing here?"

"Where's Byron? Where's your father? Please don't tell me something happened to him."

Hunter's face only mirrored my pain. He struggled to respond. "All I know is he's missing. How did you find out, Annalisa? Who told you to come here?"

"An ally of your father," I gasped. Then another horror dawned on me. "The black portfolio. The one with the affidavits and the photographs. Where is it?"

Before Hunter could reply, a police whistle sounded in the distance. Without another word, I scrambled from the engine room, leaving the door to slam behind me.

I spotted men in uniform running toward the launch. I scrambled low across the dock to a dinghy two slips away and crawled beneath a filthy canvas tarpaulin.

Moments later, I peeked from beneath the canvas.

Police Chief Jessie Donen, in civilian clothes and rumpled hair, arrived with a dozen officers. "What the hell is going on here, Hunter?"

"My father is missing, Chief Donen."

"Tell me somethin' I don't already know. Tell me why he was out on the bloody bay in the middle of the Goddamn night!"

"What does that matter? He's missing."

"All right, men, let's search every inch of this thing."

I could see the blue-coated officers jump aboard and scatter in every direction.

"They're trampling the crime scene, sir!" Hunter pleaded.

"Crime scene, what the hell are ya' talkin' about, crime scene? Bloody college boy. Arrest the bloody riptide would you? One day on the force and tellin' me how to do my job. You wanna help yer father? Find yer drunken brother and get every man on the night shift out searchin' the bloody bay."

Hunter watched painfully as Donen's men ran about the boat. "That's an order, *Officer* Fallon. Get everyone out on the bay. Now!"

I pulled the tiny opening closed as Hunter went running down the wooden pier.

The Waltham roared to life and quickly faded in the distance.

I lay there in the cramped and musty enclosure, wondering if my heart could actually explode.

"All right, lads, anybody find anything worth findin'?"

"Nothin', Chief. Ain't no one here."

"Let's be done with it, then. The dumb bastard finally got what's comin' to him. As chief of this fine department, it's my sacred duty to stand a few jolts of cheap Irish down at Kelly's in honor of our departed comrade."

A chorus of laughter mingled with the sound of departing footsteps and the howling of the wind.

I lay shivering beneath my fetid cover for twenty minutes, weeping softly for Byron Fallon. I felt like everything had come crashing down.

But like the Phoenix, the official symbol of the City herself, another hero would soon emerge.

PART TWO

---⌘---

THE VOICE OF GOD

It is an odd thing, but every one who disappears is said to be seen at San Francisco.

—OSCAR WILDE

Chapter 14

APRIL 16, 1906. 12:05 A.M.

My footsteps had been reverberating amongst the empty desks and file cabinets of the *Evening Bulletin*'s editorial offices for more than an hour, every imaginable scenario for the fate of Byron Fallon skipping through my mind. The sudden jolt of electric lights made me jump.

I turned to find Fremont Older striding toward me, his face contorted in anguish.

The shrill voice of Mary McDermitt, sent from the Midwest by Prince Benjamin of the Flying Rollers of the House of David to warn us of the disaster he was about to unleash upon us, rose above the honking horns and rumbling wheels six stories below. "Pride precedeth the fall. Hence did Babylon and Rome reap their vain glory in fiery doom!"

Older stormed to the window and slammed it shut. "Every day, it's a different lunatic. Last month, it was the nuts waving Zadkiel's Almanac, screaming that Mars was in cahoots with Saturn or some nonsense and an earthquake was going to bring everything down on top of us."

He looked at me sternly, as if just noticing my presence.

"If you are filing your Barrymore review, Annalisa, it will have to wait."

"I've already done that, sir. Do you have news of Byron Fallon?"

"Byron Fallon? How did you hear about Byron Fallon?"

I hesitated. "Mr. Feeney telephoned me at the Opera House."

He dropped his brown fedora onto a nearby desk, and might have asked, "And why would he do that?" but the look did it for him.

I breathed a long, pained sigh. The only two men who knew my identity as Byron's informant, Francis Fagen and Charles Feeney, were nowhere to be found, and I was as frightened as I could remember. That left Mr. Older as the only one in whom I could confide, as he had initiated the entire graft hunt. If my fears were realized, the oath of secrecy I had taken to the good Lieutenant was now meaningless.

"I've been his secret informant for almost a year and a half now."

"If this is a joke, Annalisa, I've heard better."

"Not much of a joking matter, sir."

I proceeded to summarize, in a strained, halting voice, my activities: reporting my findings to Byron Fallon, purloining Rolf's ledger, delivering my affidavits.

Older's breathing quickened, his face reddened and collar tightened as the veins strained in his neck. I was afraid his head might explode.

I steadied myself. "Rolf's fawning pals do a lot less fawning and a lot more complaining after a little Mumm's. The only man boorish enough to serve champagne in his opera box. That might actually be his undoing."

Older stammered several times before he managed to get the words out. "I'm so flabbergasted, Annalisa, I'm having trouble being angry. All these months. Working right here under my own nose. You know how this looks? It looks like I sent you in as a spy, like I used you as bait to entice Rolf's pals to turn against him."

"I was only following instructions, sir. Lieutenant Fallon and Mr. Feeney demanded that I report to no one but them."

"I should fire you on the spot."

"I'm sure the city editor at the *Examiner* would be more understanding."

"You would do that to me, Annalisa?"

"The question is, Mr. Older, would you do that to me? Byron Fallon may be dead and God knows who has my signed affidavits. At the moment, my employment is the least of my concerns."

He gazed toward the Ferry Building as a gaff-rigged schooner, its sails illuminated by the ghostly waterfront lights, reached toward the Washington Street Pier.

"Another boatload of those wretched little Chinese girls," he said. "This was supposed to be the day we put an end to this God-forsaken nightmare. Maybe these lunatics are right; we ought to burn in Hell for this madness."

His shoulders slumped; he put his hat back on his head and shuffled painfully toward his office. He stood there in the doorway, unable to move, teetering so that I feared he might collapse.

No one knew the fear of challenging the entrenched evil in San Francisco more than Fremont Older, who inherited the *Bulletin*'s mantle not long after its founding editor, James King of William, was gunned down by a corrupt city supervisor following a series of blistering *exposés*. Older had survived lawsuits, attacks on his employees, labor strikes orchestrated by Adam Rolf, physical assaults, death threats, and editorial ridicule from the *Examiner*'s William Randolph Hearst and the *Chronicle*'s Michael de Young to become the principal voice of the City's reform.

The previous year, Older had devoted the majority of the *Bulletin*'s editorials to defeating Eugene Schmitz' bid for re-election. The effort had little effect on a populace seduced by Schmitz' charm and Rolf's money. Schmitz and his entire ticket, all eighteen of Rolf's hand-picked candidates for supervisor's seats, were swept into office, a triumph that stunned even the victors.

A disbelieving Fremont Older and his wife Cora left the newspaper offices after receiving the election results, only to encounter a jeering mob organized by a vindictive Rolf. The mob followed the couple, hurling debris and insults, all the way to the Palace Hotel where the Olders maintained a suite.

Now, even that pain seemed minor. That his crusade may have cost the life of the bravest police officer in San Francisco pushed Older's spirit to the breaking point.

I sagged into the stiff-backed chair at my cluttered desk, unsure of anything. I let my head drift to the worn surface, too numb and enraged to weep.

Out on San Francisco Bay, the mood was no less pained. The fog and churning sea had delayed the efforts of The Brotherhood by precious hours. Aboard the roiling deck of the steam launch *Alcatrice*, Hunter examined a nautical map as his cousin Francis struggled to steady the bulky Eveready on it.

Hunter pointed to a spot on the map halfway between the Golden Gate and Alcatraz. "If dad went overboard on the San Francisco side of the rip, the ebb tide pulls him out through the Golden Gate. With a six, seven knot current he'd be halfway to the Farallon Islands unless he got lucky and drifted ashore at China Beach or Point Lobos."

Though he was the newest member of The Brotherhood, Hunter was easily the finest sailor, having spent many childhood hours studying nautical maps and tide charts, carefully marking out the locations of the more than two hundred shipwrecks that had occurred around the treacherous bay.

"China Beach, the rocks along there, that's about a man's only chance," Francis said, his normally calm tone now pained and raspy.

A few feet behind them, Max was vomiting over the stern, brother Carlo lying across his ankles, holding him aboard in the chop.

"Then we have to pray he made it over the rip to the flood tide," Hunter shouted as a bow beater soaked them, coating the deck an inch deep in water. "I say we hit Alcatraz, Angel Island, then through Raccoon Straits to Belvedere. If he's at China Beach or on the rocks, he'd probably be safe for awhile."

Throughout, Christian said nothing. Only Max was more seasick than he.

"All right," Francis said, "Hunter's right. I've seen it a dozen times on rescues with the Harbor Police. We hit the islands. Let's move."

Patrick kissed his St. Christopher medal and mumbled a seaman's prayer. He looked over at his brother Francis, whose face reaffirmed his doubt.

It would be a long, cold, painful night, with Max and Christian so ill from the turbulent waters that they were unable to come to blows.

Chapter 15

APRIL 16, 1906. 12:25 A.M.

Several hundred miles east, near moonlit Lake Tahoe, the *Overland Limited* of the Southern Pacific Railroad gasped and wheezed through its final ascent, up the treacherous eastern slope of the High Sierra. It was pulling four mail cars, twenty-three passenger compartments with 478 passengers, including Kaitlin Staley, the newly anointed "Belle of the Pullman."

In a crowded coach halfway between the engine and caboose, Jeremy Darling watched as Kaitlin sketched her ideas for women's "elegant but inexpensive gowns." Most of the passengers were fast asleep, chortling a disparate melody of familiar snores as Jeremy rubbed his sandy eyes, feigning interest in Kaitlin's deft drawings. Fashion meant nothing to him. His true interest was Kaitlin.

"You're sure you're only eighteen? You draw like someone who is— much older."

Jeremy had been making inane comments since she boarded the train in Kansas City and chose him as the most harmless-looking man on board. She had been wearing, at the time of boarding, a tailored shirtwaist with hand-stitched *gigot* sleeves, lace collar, and bodice under a wasp-waisted *bolero* jacket. The black *bolero* melded with a pleated ankle-length skirt that partially covered a pair of battered and misshapen leather high-low boots, the one item she had not been able to fashion for herself.

She had plunked down next to Jeremy, pointed her high bosom and flashed her pale blue eyes and gleaming white teeth straight into his heart.

"Kaitlin Staley. Some people call me Kate but my name is really Kaitlin. With a K. It was the doctor's mistake. Makes you wonder what kind of doctor can't even spell a kid's name. This seat isn't taken, is it?" Jeremy shook his head, speechless, as she squeezed in next to him. "I am going to San Francisco. I have never been there before. Have you?"

"Jeremy Darling," he croaked. "I'm assistant professor of geology at the University of California. That's in Berkeley, which is just across San Francisco Bay."

"Geology. How fascinating, Professor Darling."

"Geology and seismology."

"I'm somewhat of a size-mologist myself. I can just look at you and tell you're a hat size six and three-quarters."

"Seismology. The subterranean movements of the earth's giant plates. That's what causes earthquakes. I study them. If one studies earthquakes, one ought to be in San Francisco or at least nearby."

"Do they really have earthquakes in San Francisco?"

"We had one two years ago this month. Two of them, actually. The last really big one was in '68."

"Well, I'm not having any earthquakes while I'm there. Especially not any really big ones."

"I'm just returning from England, from seeing a man named John Milne. He has built seismograph stations all over the world, so we can measure and record them when they strike. San Francisco is on an earthquake fault they call the San Andreas."

"I'm going to San Francisco to design clothes for the opera and the theater. Clothes that look very expensive but aren't, so women who don't have a lot of money can afford to go nice places."

By the second day, Kaitlin was on her third outfit and fourth or fifth hat. Jeremy was in too much discomfort to keep track. His *derriere* had died outside of Denver. The entire westbound passenger contingent twitched and slithered, displaying the pained waddle dubbed "towing the iron caboose."

Kaitlin scarcely noticed. To her, it had been the "Journey of a Thousand Moments," as she had read repeatedly, through the endless Plains and majestic Rockies, over Promontory Point, past the Great Salt Lake, winding through the Wasatch Range and across the broad Nevada desert into their final leg.

Halfway up the eastern slope of the High Sierra, Jeremy excused himself and headed toward the toilet compartments, discreetly trying to massage life back into his wounded posterior.

Antoine Dugay slid into the vacant seat. He had bribed the conductor with a Parisian Kiss from one of his three female cousins to glean that Kaitlin had boarded alone and was en route to San Francisco.

"You are very beautiful girl," Antoine said, showing a little pink tongue and harelip camouflaged by a greasy mustache. "I can make you mow-nee in San Francisco, lots of mow-nee."

"Oh, yeah, how is that?"

"The melodeons, you can sing, maybe you dance, you tell some joke, some-sing like zat. Men give you mow-nee, lots of mow-nee."

She knew little of melodeons but a lot about manure. "I don't sing, I don't dance, and they didn't make many jokes where I grew up."

"My cousins, they make lots of mow-nee, they no sing, dance so good."

She looked over at his cousins. One was a Jewish girl who sported a dented silver Star of David, a Polish accent, and flaming red hair. The second was an Indian with black circles under her eyes, and the third a waif-like blonde with the hundred-yard stare and slow nod of the opium chum.

Kaitlin had observed the women leaving their seats with gamblers who had slid a coin into Antoine's pocket. Their activities had since been restricted to the baggage stalls, after travelers who actually used the sleeping compartments for sleeping complained about the moaning and banging at all hours of the night.

"Your cousins, they look about as much alike as two stray dogs and a hickory stump."

"What?"

"Hickory stump, dogs, you know, little dogs? Rrr-uff, rrr-uff."

Antoine thought she meant his girls were dogs; that dogs would not have them. "Antoine has no dogs. Antoine has fine bitches," he said, one watery eye twitching steadily.

"Maybe you should slide back on over and join those fine bitches."

Antoine's face showed a mild flush, his jaw clenching. Kaitlin noticed his hand slide into the pocket of his vest.

She tensed. With her hands folded, she began to slide free the long, thick hat pin she had embedded in her left coat sleeve, a trick her father had taught her years before.

"Excuse me," Jeremy interrupted. "I have been sitting in that seat since Chicago," and had the pickled posterior to match the upholstery indent to prove it.

Antoine offered Kaitlin a final flash of the lazy pink tongue. "May-hay-be we see each other some time again in San Francisco, *ma chérie*." He limped away.

Within the hour, the train reached the summit of the High Sierra as Kaitlin dozed. The hacking snore of the apothecary's wife in the seat across the row awakened her. She listened to the rhythmic clacking of the steel wheels and gazed down the aisle.

Four seats away, Antoine's eyes were staring at the ceiling, his thin moustache drawn about his oval, sucking mouth. Protruding from the bottom of the blanket on his lap were the soles of a woman's shoes. The blanket bobbed up and down near Antoine's lap, his pant legs bunched about his ankles. Antoine shivered and shook. In a final gasp, the air rushed past the uneven gold teeth, setting his bountiful nose hairs aflutter.

The Indian cousin emerged from beneath the blanket, dabbing her lips with a handkerchief.

Kaitlin, flushed and startled, suddenly understood what the men who had approached Antoine meant by the "Parisian Kiss." She turned to avoid Antoine's wink, staring out the window as the train entered Summit Tunnel, longest in the High Sierra.

She braced herself as the rocking and swaying increased, the *Overland* rolling toward Donner Pass and the heady descent toward Dutch Flat and Whiskey Ridge.

They emerged from the tunnel; the moonlight illuminated a sign that read WELCOME TO CALIFORNIA—THE 31ST STATE, above an advertisement for men's hair tonic.

Kaitlin pulled her diary from her bag and began to record the evening's events, unaware of how important her highly detailed observations would soon become. She entered a simple phrase.

At least my father will never find me.

Chapter 16

APRIL 16, 1906. 5:20 A.M.

Lincoln Staley, a lean and rugged forty-eight, arrived at the farm of Harvey Poggendorf, ten miles outside Lawrence, at sunrise. Harvey was surrounded by so much debris Lincoln might not have noticed him in the porch hammock were it not for the whiff of stale tobacco smoke.

"Harvey, is Rusty home?"

Harvey didn't get an answer out before Lincoln stomped to Rusty's bedroom, where he jerked the snoring nineteen-year-old behemoth from his filthy bed. Lincoln quickly frog-marched him out the front door and toward the barn while Harvey struggled to keep pace on his Union Army peg leg.

"Pa, what's he doin' to me? Pa!"

Once inside the barn, Lincoln manacled the bellowing Rusty, attached a bailing hook, and hoisted his arms up until his toes barely touched the ground.

Harvey was having a rough time trying to get his pipe relit.

"Pa, he's crazy, Pa, what the hell's he doin'?" Rusty was six feet three, two hundred and forty pounds, and dumb as mud. "Pa. Goddamn it, Pa!"

"I got this new tobacco, Lincoln, might as well be tryin' to light a turd," Harvey said. He was not sure what Rusty had done, but whatever it was, he was sure he had done it.

Lincoln found a broken rake handle and whacked Rusty hard across the rump.

"Ahhh, ahhh, damn it, Pa, I ain't done nothin'. Tell him, Pa, I ain't done nothin'."

Lincoln showed Rusty the newspaper clipping he had found behind the doorframe in Kaitlin's room, and then remembered he could not read. Still, Rusty turned his face away when he saw the drawing of Caruso.

"Enrico Caruso and the Metropolitan Opera Company Travel to San Francisco. Cream of Blueblood Society to Attend. Any of this sound familiar to you, Rusty?"

Lincoln had caught Kaitlin three weeks earlier on the banks of Lawrence Creek, showing Rusty her bare breast in exchange for a silver dollar.

"If this is about Kaitlin, Sheriff, I don't know where she went. I swear to God," Rusty bawled.

Even Harvey winced as Lincoln whacked his son across his ample backside.

"Owwww . . . owwww . . . wooowwww," Rusty blubbered, tears and snot streaming down his cheeks and into his mouth.

"Better tell the man what he wants to know, son. I think Lincoln's gonna last a lot longer than you are." Harvey pissed against a post, adding to the already foul smell. "Son, if he kills you I can't afford to hire no help. Now you tell the man what he wants to know, damn it."

Lincoln prepared to hit him again.

"I took her in the buggy," Rusty blurted. "She said if I didn't take her she'd never talk to me again. I bought her a ticket for San Francisco."

Lincoln cut the rope and let Rusty collapse in a whimpering heap.

Lincoln rode straight home. An hour later, he slid $200 in gold and silver coins into the pockets of his blue jeans, and then kissed Stella and their three sleeping sons good-bye.

He rode south across the Kansas plains, stopping momentarily at the cemetery where 164 gravestones, including those of his father and grandfather, all bore the same date of passing. August 21, 1863.

He rode the line of carefully tended graves, jarred by the memories, the sounds and sights flooding back to him. William Quantrill and Frank James shooting his father in the back, just steps from five-year-old Lincoln's outstretched arms. The crack of gunshots. The smell of burnt powder. The agonized screams and pleas for mercy as bodies piled up and the dusty streets turned red with streams of blood.

He turned and rode away, looking over his shoulder at his farm disappearing in the distance.

Lincoln had raised Kaitlin like he had the boys, to be strong and fearless and independent. She had shown skill at riding, shooting, and even fighting that had surpassed her brothers. By the time she was twelve she was fast becoming a woman, one of such disarming beauty that men everywhere could little help but stare at her.

He spurred his mount as a feeling of dread swept over him.

He arrived in Kansas City as the sun bathed Union Station in sepia light. Lincoln handed a small photograph of Kaitlin, dressed in choir robe, to the ticket master.

The tiny man perused the photo, his plastered hair smelling of chicken fat. "She a busty thing, kinda tall with a lotta teeth?" He held his hands out to indicate the size of Kaitlin's breasts. "Big old set of knockers on her?"

Lincoln quashed an urge to reach through the cage and throttle him. A whistle sounded. "I asked you a question."

"I seen her day 'fore yesterday, some farm boy, size of a mule, bought her a one-way to San Francisco."

"Give me a round-trip, second class, and make it snappy." Lincoln slid over twenty-eight dollars and sixty cents in gold eagles and silver coins, collected his ticket, and slung his saddlebags over his shoulder.

He made the middle of the train and leapt aboard.

He drew his duster closed to cover the star and sidearm and settled into a leather seat near the window, drawing the stares of fellow travelers. The train was barely outside the city limits when his thoughts drifted to his headstrong daughter alone in San Francisco.

He pulled a journal and a fountain pen from inside his coat and began to write. It was a habit he had practiced almost daily since childhood, starting on the return train from Springfield, Illinois, where his widowed mother had taken him to observe the body of his namesake, the great Abraham Lincoln. A habit that Kaitlin had copied from her earliest childhood.

A muffled gunshot shook him from his introspection. No one else seemed to notice. He heard another shot, and then a third.

Lincoln hastily made his way through a dozen Pullman cars, jumping from platform to platform. A group of faro players in a baggage car showed no reaction as he headed in the direction of the gunshots.

After crossing through the empty caboose, he entered a car paneled in mahogany, the floor covered in Moroccan carpets. On the left, a row of sleeping compartments, dressed in Irish lace, stretched from floor to ceiling. On the right, a small kitchen and pantry sat adjacent to a brass bathtub.

A gunshot sounded from the rear platform. Lincoln eased his right hand onto the butt of his single-action Colt. With his left hand, he slid open the door to the platform.

Three men stood with their backs to him. The shortest went through a series of gunfighter-like contortions, wriggling his hand and shoulder before grabbing for the revolver strapped around his waist. An ear-splitting shot grazed the toe of his boot and splintered the wooden deck.

"No! No," said the tall, angular man to the left. "You must pull the pistol from the holster, then squeeze. Pull, *then* squeeze, not squeeze and pull."

Lincoln was examining the two-dozen bullet holes that gave the platform the appearance of Swiss cheese when they noticed him.

They turned in unison to stare at his Stetson hat, long brown duster, and long-barreled Colt. The short man's eyes grew big and a smile crossed his face when he spotted Lincoln's star.

"*Lui è un vigile rustico,*" the shorter man said.

"Yes, I am an old country sheriff."

"*Lei parla l'italiano?*" the short man replied, his eyes growing wider.

"Not Italian. Latin, actually. It was a requirement at the university in Lawrence."

"Allow me to introduce myself, Sheriff," the tall man said. "My name is Alfred Hertz, conductor of the New York Metropolitan Opera. This is our valet, Martino. And this is *Maestro* Enrico Caruso."

"I recognize Mr. Caruso from his photographs. Lincoln Staley, Sheriff of Douglas County, Kansas. Pleased to meet you all."

Caruso shook Lincoln's hand vigorously, his eyes darting between badge and gun. "You are some times use thees *pistola*? I am hear there are many *ladri, banditos,* in San Francisco."

Lincoln eyed Caruso's bullet-frayed pant cuffs and boots. "Sometimes," he said, doing his best not to smile.

Caruso raised a bushy eyebrow. "You can maybe show me thees, *per favore*? You can make 'ow you say? *Dimostrazione.*"

"I'm not sure that would be appropriate, Mr. Caruso."

"Please, Sheriff. I'd be most grateful," Hertz pleaded, sweeping his hand to emphasize the jeopardy to the great tenor's toes.

Lincoln hesitated, then stepped onto the platform and slid the duster to one side. As the train drew abreast of an abandoned buckboard thirty yards from the track, Lincoln whipped the Colt out and fanned the hammer. Five shots thundered forth, four of them splintering the left front wheel. Lincoln spun the Colt by the trigger guard and dropped it nimbly into the holster. The whole display required less than two seconds. He stood quietly amid three slack jaws and the smell of gun smoke.

"*Madre del Dio.* Sheriff Lin-cone. You can please to join us for supper? My butler, Martino, is a *capocuoco magnifico*. We 'ave some nice *vitello*. Veals. And some *San Giovese favoloso*."

"Please do, Sheriff Staley, we would welcome your company," said Hertz, "and I have a proposition for you."

Chapter 17

SAN FRANCISCO BAY

APRIL 16, 1906. 5:45 A.M.

In the cargo hold of the schooner *Falmouth*, twelve-year-old Ting Leo was awakened by footsteps on the gang ladder, the rattling of keys, and the soft unlocking of the gate. "Smy-yays," she said softly, recognizing the silhouette of Smiles, the skinny sailor with the broken teeth.

The one called "Gimpy" grasped the smooth brass rails and slid to the bottom, landing softly behind Smiles. She smelled them, even above the stench of the hold after forty-three days on the Pacific.

Smiles approached. She stiffened as he reached inside her filthy shift and stroked her breasts. With the other hand, he reached inside his rancid linen pants, his hand bobbing up and down. She gritted her teeth and clenched her fists.

But Gimpy said, "Go on," and shoved him away. At least the men had not touched her between her legs.

"Gwo wan," she muttered softly, practicing until she could almost say "go on." She knew Gimpy was telling him to go forward. "Go wan."

She had never seen a white man until she boarded the ship, after her father stripped her naked and sold her for two gold pieces with eagles etched into the shiny metal, bragging that the broker had paid twice his normal price.

"Sam Fransco," she heard the sailors say. She knew that it was Gum Saan, the Golden Mountain she had heard about in her village in Kwangtung.

"Go won," she said, repeating their words: "captain," "evenin'," "aye," and "nay" and all the variations of "bastard," including "Limey bastard," "Yankee bastard," "Chinese bastard," and the like.

Ting Leo watched as Smiles and Gimpy unlocked the brig at the end of the cargo hold. Inside were the two homely girls the captain rented to the crew at a dollar a visit. At first their shrieks had terrified the other girls. Now, after too many visits for anyone to count, their cries had faded to muffled whimpers.

On the wooden slats where she lay, the strongest of the girls in the hold of the *Falmouth*, Ting Leo remembered the talk she heard in her village of a peasants' revolution. The other girls had asked many times if Gum Saan was as evil as their home, if the fathers there killed their infant daughters or sold them to strangers. She answered that a revolution was nearing, and soon a man would come and free them. It was all she could think of to comfort the frightened girls.

When Smiles and Gimpy had finished grunting atop the homely girls, they climbed the stairs and locked the gate behind them. The Captain bellowed on the wooden deck above.

"Hove to!"

Ting Leo sprang to her knees and scurried to a porthole left open by the crew to ease the heat and smell. She gazed at the tallest trees she had ever seen, towering over a rocky coastline.

She hurried to a porthole on the other side, squeezing between two sleeping girls. Her eyes filled with a stirring sight. Dozens of hills covered with houses, their lights glowing in the morning mist, smoke billowing from the chimneys. Hundreds of ships, their masts waving, lay at anchor along a vast harbor. Behind them, rows of stone buildings touched the sky. "Gum Saan," she cried.

Within seconds, the girls around her stirred from sleep, pushing each other aside to peer through the open portholes.

"Gum Saan! Gum Saan!"

The *Falmouth* rode the flood tide through the mile-wide opening of the bay. They passed a white boat with white smoke pouring from its middle, so close Ting Leo thought she could touch it.

On the white boat, men with pained looks on their faces held beams of light in their hands, running them over the surface of the water.

Ting Leo squinted, shading her eyes as one of the young men shone his light on her face.

Amidst the pained expression on his face, she saw eyes of kindness. He raised a hand and wiggled his fingers at her.

"Hunter," someone called to him. "Hunter!"

Slowly, he lowered his hand and moved to the other side of the boat, joining his beam of light with those of two other men.

"Hun-ner", she said aloud. "Hunn-ner." She watched the cloud of steam thicken and the boat pull away. In the glowing sunrise, she saw Hunter look back, again playing his light over the porthole where she stood. She wondered if he was the great man people in her village had talked about. The one who would save them from the hated emperor. This man who held light in his hand and found her in this Gum Saan.

Aboard the *Alcatrice*, the six young members of The Brotherhood were cold and spent from battling the turbulent bay, their batteries and hope nearly exhausted. They were making their second trip around Angel Island, aided now by the amber sunrise.

"There's something over there, tangled in the thickets," Francis shouted over the rattle and wheeze of the boiler. "Looks like a body, floating facedown."

Christian ran to the bow and threw out a weighted line, sounding for the bottom. "You still got a good twenty feet here," he yelled at Nick Hazifotis in the pilot's roost above, his voice strained from a night of vomiting.

"Is too rocky, Christian—is get shallow very fast!"

Hunter peeled down to his wool briefs and dove into the icy water, disappearing beneath the chop. He surfaced thirty yards away and quickly turned the body over.

His father's eyes, clouded by the immersion in salt water, stared blankly skyward.

Christian jumped into the frigid water and swam to them.

The Fallon brothers struggled against the surging water to tow him toward the boat. When they got close enough, Hunter took the rope still tied to his father's waist and threw the end to Francis.

With Francis, Patrick, Max, and Carlo pulling, they raised Byron's body over the rail and onto the slippery deck. Hunter and Christian were pulled aboard.

Hunter crawled to his father's cold, rigid body, cradled his head, and rocked slowly, tears mixing with salt water. The grieving son let out a gasp and the quiver in his lip spread across his face, which he buried in his father's sodden vest.

Max Rinaldi glared at Christian, who had slumped to the deck, his head in his hands. Only his wobbly legs and heaving stomach prevented Max from trying to kill him.

A swirling mass of seagulls erupted off Alcatraz, screeching in frenzy, several of them colliding in midair.

"Ai-ain' n-never seen them do-do that be-before," Carlo said quietly to Francis. "Bad o-omen to a s-sa-sailin' man."

Chapter 18

————◇————

APRIL 16, 1906. 7:00 A.M.

I had retreated to Fremont Older's glass-enclosed inner sanctum to answer the ever-ringing telephone. Across the editorial room, Older tried his best to fend off a mounting stream of people desperate for information.

I had just hung up after explaining our lack of information to Mrs. Older for the third time. The phone rang instantly.

"This is Mr. Feeney. Is Mr. Older in?"

"This is Annalisa Passarelli."

"Annalisa. Lieutenant Fallon's sons have found his body near Angel Island. They should be bringing him to the Ferry Building within the half-hour. They're aboard the *Alcatrice*, a small fishing steamer."

I replaced the receiver and slipped from the room, past Mr. Older who was surrounded by a dozen people, all asking the same questions they had been asking all night. I feared that announcing the news about Byron would start a stampede.

Once I reached Bush Street, I broke into a dead run, weaving through the morning traffic. I ran eight blocks or so to the wharf.

I arrived, breathless, at the cable car turnaround in the Ferry Plaza. In front of me was a crowd of perhaps three hundred people who had assembled to protest the arrival of the Chinese girls. Standing before them were the protest's leaders, Donaldina Cameron, from the Presbyterian Mission, and Father Peter Yorke.

I took my opera glasses from my bag, struggled with the ill-working adjustment, and scanned the piers for signs of the *Alcatrice*. I spotted it offshore, jockeying in the still-rough seas with the ferries and schooners waiting for a place to dock.

A hundred yards away, in the hold of the *Falmouth*, Ting Leo jostled at a porthole with the other girls as the Ferry Building loomed. She caught a glimpse of the boat she had seen upon entering the harbor, straining to see the young man with light in his hand.

Aboard the *Alcatrice*, Hunter and Christian stood with their father's blanket-covered body, the *Falmouth* inching a few yards ahead of them toward the Jackson Street Pier just north of the Ferry Building. The dual tragedy was not lost on Hunter. The man who might have saved the girls from their terrible plight lay cold at his feet.

The *Falmouth* docked. A foul-looking crewman secured the gangplank, and a Chinese girl, her head barely above his waist, took her first wobbly steps forward. When she recoiled, fearful of the crowd below, the sailor shoved her.

A howl went up from the demonstrators. Several girls appeared on deck, tears streaming down their dirty faces.

"Excuse me, can you tell me what's going on here?" a female voice inquired from behind me.

I turned and looked up into sky blue eyes and a sunny face beneath a broad-brimmed hat.

"Chinese slave girls," I replied.

"What?"

"They bring these girls from China, pretending they are going to find work as domestic servants or marry Chinese men. Then they sell them to brothels and businessmen who like them as young as they can get them."

"How can they do that? That's what the whole Civil War was about. You can't just sell human beings."

"My thoughts precisely." I pulled out a notebook and hastily scribbled notes, my hand barely able to function.

"You're a reporter?"

"From the *Bulletin*. Annalisa Passarelli."

"Oh, my gosh. Annalisa Passarelli! The opera writer! Sometimes they print your stories in the *Kansas City Star*! I don't believe it!"

I smiled politely, in no mood for chatter.

"I'm Kaitlin Staley. I just arrived on the train."

"Enjoy your stay, Kaitlin, and be careful," I muttered, moving toward the protestors, who had begun sitting at the foot of the gangplank to block the path of the Chinese girls.

Several paddy wagons stopped at the edge of the crowd, disgorging forty men in blue uniforms.

With his men in tow, Police Chief Donen strode forward. "All right, ladies. I'm gonna say this one time only. You can all avoid a trip to the pokey by coming to your senses and clearin' a path."

Father Yorke and Donaldina Cameron stepped into Donen's path.

"Mornin', Peter. Miss Cameron," the burly Chief said. "Perhaps you two ought to confine your meddlin' to matters of the soul and leave police matters where they belong."

"You surprise me, Jessie," Father Yorke seethed. "You talk about matters of the soul as though you had one."

"You've been warned, Father." Donen stepped back and blew a shrill blast from his whistle.

Two mustachioed officers stepped forward to grab the ankles of a seated female demonstrator, her dress flying above her waist as they dragged her, screaming, toward the paddy wagons. A roar of laughter swept through Donen's men.

"All right, lads," he bellowed, "let's haul 'em off!"

Donen's men waded into the crowd, jabbing their billy clubs at several demonstrators, whose screams mingled with the shrieks of the Chinese girls.

Enraged, I had to fight the urge to join the demonstrators. Instead, I raised the battered opera glasses and gazed toward the *Alcatrice*, which had veered off to dock south of the Ferry piers, where a blanket-covered body was being passed to Hunter and Christian. My insides churning, I cast one last look at the demonstrators, raised the hem of my dress, and sprinted toward the piers.

Hunter and Christian loaded the body of their father into the coroner's wagon. Hunter produced his pocket knife and sliced through the rope Anthony had used to secure his father to the rail of the launch. "You see this, Christian?"

"A piece of wet rope?"

"Do you see the nice clean cut at the end of it?"

"Maybe dad cut it himself, he carries a knife."

"Sever his own lifeline? Why would he do that?"

"It was just him and Anthony on board, remember? Finish your first week on the job before you promote yourself to detective."

Herb Szymanski, the coroner's driver, poked his head around the wagon. "Christian, you both riding with your father?"

"Give us a damn minute here, will you Herbie?"

Herb meekly retreated.

"You believe what you want, Christian. It makes you feel better. Just don't let his body out of your sight. I'll see you at the morgue."

From behind a pile of cargo pallets a hundred feet away, I could see the pain in Hunter's face. I watched him sling a leather bag over his shoulder, unchain his motorcycle from a dock piling, and speed away.

Christian climbed in next to Szymanski, who snapped the reins. The bony gray mare reared her head and lumbered off, the wagon wobbling from side to side as the cries of the demonstrators and the sobs of the Chinese girls drifted through the morning air.

After a breakneck ride along the waterfront, Hunter arrived at Meigg's Wharf. He jumped aboard his father's launch and hurried aft.

He fitted the five-foot length of rope he had removed from Byron's body to the foot-long piece still hanging from the rail. Even if Byron had wanted to cut his own rope, Hunter surmised, he could not have been dangling at the end of it and reached the point where it was cut.

Hunter climbed to the pilot's roost and surveyed the deck below. In the thick fog and rolling seas, he reasoned, it was more than likely Anthony could not see what transpired behind and below him.

Hunter climbed back to the deck and made his way to the boiler room.

He struck a match and lit a candle taken from his shoulder bag. On the jagged iron cage surrounding the boiler, he spotted a sticky, reddish brown substance. Producing two clean glass slides, he collected the blood on one slide, covered it with the other, and tied them together with a string.

On the sharp corner of the angle iron, he noticed a rubbery black substance, apparently soaked with blood. He scraped it into a test tube and corked it firmly.

A trail of blood drops led him back to the passageway. On the smooth brass handle of the door were two bloody fingerprints and a bloody thumbprint. Below them, a bloody hand and palm print. Carefully, he pressed a white paper onto the handprint, repeating the effort with the finger and thumbprint on the brass handle.

He tensed as footsteps approached the passageway. He blew out the candle, unsure whether to hide or accost his visitor.

The door creaked open and a figure entered the dark compartment.

I screamed when he grabbed my shoulder.

"Annalisa? What are you doing here?" He stowed his revolver. "You can't keep sneaking up on me like this."

"I was merely being cautious."

"Look. Annalisa. I want to know what is going on. Everything."

The pale light streaming through the half-opened door illuminated his anguished face.

I stopped, my mouth half open, struck by the familiarity of the gaze: the inquisitive cock of the head, the disarming blue eyes, the steady tone of the voice. They were not the characteristics of the impetuous young man I had encountered the previous day.

They were his father's eyes, his father's mannerisms, Byron's measured and resolute tone.

"Annalisa?"

The fear and horror I felt over his father's death were replaced by an eerie sensation, simultaneously warm and disconcerting: the unearthly feeling that Byron's spirit had passed to his son.

Chapter 19

PACIFIC HEIGHTS

APRIL 16, 1906. 8:00 A.M.

As Hunter gathered evidence aboard the ill-fated launch, I conveyed what I knew of his father's activities in the days and hours prior to his death. I gradually realized Hunter was crafting his entreaties to elicit any hint that I might have tipped off someone to his father's activities. I had been tortured by the possibility since I learned of Byron's disappearance. Nothing terrified me more than the notion I might somehow be responsible. Hunter's insinuations did nothing to ease my distress.

While Hunter and I searched the launch, Mayor Eugene Schmitz was leaving his house on Fillmore Street in Pacific Heights. Sporting his trademark slouch brim hat, he climbed into the red Model N Ford driven by Chief Jessie Donen, who had just left the Ferry Plaza, where his men were still arresting demonstrators.

"His idiot sons found him floatin' facedown near Angel Island," Donen offered. To the Pacific Heights residents they passed, the burly chief seemed almost jubilant, clear-eyed and cocksure beneath his blue cap, the brass buttons on his whipcord uniform glowing in the morning light.

Schmitz, in contrast, appeared tired and wan as they putted up Union Street, dodging milk wagons and bakery drays. "So, Chief, what do I tell reporters when they ask me?"

"Tell 'em you don't know nothin' from nothin'. Just like you always do when things get dicey."

Donen had never been fond of Eugene Schmitz, and the Mayor had always chafed at Donen's abrasiveness. That morning, it was the least of

Schmitz' worries. The Mayor was scheduled to meet that morning with Daniel Burnham, famed designer of the Chicago World's Fair, to discuss his sweeping plans to remake the entire city of San Francisco.

Burnham's plan, delivered months earlier, was to paddle-shovel the city into oblivion and re-create it on the order of Paris. It called for *arrondisements* arranged in concentric circles, neighborhoods wrapped around neighborhoods, transforming the hills into bulls-eyes of boulevards and gardens. Schmitz had hated the idea since inception, but Boss Rolf insisted it be their legacy to make the city more than just a symbolic "Paris of the West," not to mention reaping millions in construction contracts, building permits, and franchise fees.

Donen turned south on Van Ness, stopping at Clay Street for cross-traffic. He idled in the shadows of a French-empire mansion with towering parapets and tiled mansard roof, the home of Rudolph Spreckels, sworn enemy of their regime.

A folded newspaper hit Schmitz in the chest and nearly sent him out of his gray English tweeds. As the Ford jerked forward, he pulled a nickel from his watch pocket and flipped it toward the curb, where the dirty-faced newsboy caught it in his apple hat.

Schmitz opened the *Bulletin* to the front page and scanned the story on Byron Fallon's disappearance. It offered scant information but substantial speculation, finishing with "if foul play is proven, then let those responsible find themselves dancing at the end of a noose."

On the second page, Schmitz located Fremont Older's latest editorial invective, written prior to the awful events.

THE PAINT EATERS

A sane populace would soundly defeat the ridiculous Burnham Plan if put to a moratorium. Only another conflagration of Jerichon proportions could make its implementation anything but corrupt folly. His Honor, Mayor Eugene Schmitz, who once described his greedy minions at City Hall as 'so desperate for boodle they would eat the paint off a house,' is now prepared to start eating the houses.

The Ford stopped on Larkin Street near the side entrance to City Hall, beneath the shadow of the massive bronze *Goddess of Progress* that sat astride the towering Beaux Arts dome, her nose upturned as if to avoid the scent of things below.

Donen sped off the moment the Mayor's feet touched ground.

Schmitz crossed the wide street in spasmodic jumps, cursing the tardiness of the manure trucks. An onslaught of journalists in shapeless suits started huffing in his direction, shouting questions.

"Mr. Mayor. What about the rumors Byron Fallon's own men did him in?" While Schmitz scanned his sparse imagination for a suitable response, more shells were lobbed.

"The Tongs are fumin' about the brothel raids. Is Chief Donen plannin' to haul the hatchet-swingin' bastards in?"

"Shanghai Kelly has been kicking up dust about the war on the crimps and boardinghouse keepers. Is he a suspect?"

Schmitz gazed over their heads, losing himself in the spring explosion of poppies in the planter boxes around City Hall Plaza. He had become adept at sidestepping every challenge to his administration, but that morning fear had left him without defense. "Chief Donen is heading a thorough investigation of this tragic accident. He has requested that all responses come from his office. Lieutenant Fallon was a dedicated public servant who will be greatly missed."

Schmitz found reprieve when Adam Rolf's Phaeton turned the corner from Market Street onto Larkin.

Immediately the reporters flocked in Rolf's direction, leaving His Honor a chance to slip inside his ostentatious palace. Tommy's scowl informed all that City Attorney Rolf had no comment.

Schmitz' heels resounded off the marble portico and echoed into the hollow dome seven stories above. He and Rolf, with Tommy trailing, reached the elevator and stepped into the polished mahogany interior.

"Eugene. You look positively frightened."

"Excuse me, Adam, it's not often I'm the *entrée* at a lynch party. Every damn reporter from every damn newspaper wants to know what we're going to do about the death of the most popular police officer in the whole damn city!"

"And the profanity, so uncharacteristic. Perhaps when Caruso leaves, you might consider a trip to Monterey. Play a little golf at Del Monte, have a mineral bath."

The elevator stopped at the second floor. Schmitz strode quickly ahead of Rolf, bursting into the anteroom of his office.

Before he was halfway through the room, the mayor's secretary intercepted him with a stack of messages.

"Not now, Bertrand. Tell everyone I'm holed up in my office with a bout of apoplexy."

Bertrand slunk back to his desk as Schmitz and Rolf barreled into the Mayor's office, leaving Tommy outside standing watchdog.

Tommy managed to leave the inner door ajar, a fraction of an inch, as per Rolf's standard order.

"Tell me you know nothing about this, Adam. Tell me Byron Fallon just happened to fall off his boat the same night Shanghai Kelly decided to attend the theater."

"You know, Eugene, I'm a small man. No one listens to a small man, regardless of how brilliant his ideas. You, you are magnificent; imposing, attractive, an empty vessel into which I pour these grand ideas. I can make a governor, a senator, maybe even a president of you. Or, you can defy me, start pretending you are not party to all this, and God's wrath will seem a minor inconvenience compared to mine."

Bertrand squeezed past Tommy and stuck his head inside the door, just far enough to remove it quickly if circumstance demanded. "Mayor Schmitz, sir. Mr. Daniel Burnham is on the phone. He insisted I interrupt you."

"Tell Mr. Burnham that we won't be razing and rebuilding the city of San Francisco for at least a few more days. And don't bother me again!"

Bertrand slid out, closing the door until Tommy caught it and motioned him back to his desk. The burly goon stood with his back to the door, his ear turned toward the thin opening.

"Wonderful speech, Adam. The sword and the olive branch, Heaven and Purgatory as simple alternatives. Now. Tell me. What happened to Inspector Fallon? And try not to leave anything out."

Chapter 20

APRIL 16, 1906. 9:05 A.M.

"So that's how you got into Rolf's safe? You had an informant inside his mansion?" Hunter asked me.

"The chef, Pierre. Your father staked out an all-male brothel in the Tenderloin where Pierre was moonlighting as a party boy, very popular with city officials. A waiter drilled a small hole from a pantry next door and took some rather compromising photos. Pierre liked to give cooking tips in the middle of *fellatio*."

Hunter seemed shocked, then amused, that I would use such a word.

"I figured the Latin term was the most civil approach," I said.

"All manners of perversion seem more appealing in Latin," he laughed. "Only in San Francisco do you get culinary insight with your jollies."

Hunter packed away his slides and instruments as we spoke, concluding the search for evidence on his father's launch. We had found no trace of the ledger photographs or my affidavits.

"Actually, we have two informants in Rolf's little circle," I said.

Hunter looked at me, staring again into my eyes as I spoke.

"Tommy Biggs, Rolf's bodyguard. He did a three-year stretch in San Quentin, developed a predilection for male companionship. Pierre started taking him to the Lonely Eye."

"My father told you all this?"

"It was our arrangement. Except for the names of the men involved in the corruption probe, he couldn't keep anything from me, regardless of how salacious. Tommy also has a morphine and opium habit, compliments of San Quentin. When he gets a snoot full, he likes to wander over to the Lonely Eye, dress in frilly garments, and wrestle with the biggest bull in the place while some of the city's more esteemed citizenry lounge in satin chairs and—how shall I put this—amuse themselves."

Hunter seemed thoroughly captivated by my unlady-like candor. Even I had to smile. Byron had hemmed and stuttered when I pressed him for the details, searching for the most genteel words he could find. It was the first I had ever spoken to anyone of such matters, and I was surprised at how easy it was.

"He must cut quite a figure in a whalebone corset," Hunter replied. "Tommy and Pierre, did either of them know the other was working for my father?"

"No. Your father was adamant about that, and both of them are too frightened of Rolf to risk confiding in anyone else. Tommy is by far the most valuable. He kept Byron informed of Rolf's whereabouts. Never leaves his boss's side in public. Your father made Tommy write things down, he gave Tommy a small ledger book. Every few days, Tommy would tear out the pages and leave them at Molinari's deli where your father picked them up."

We left the launch and approached the end of the dock.

"You can ride with me," he said.

I stared with uncertainty at the motorcycle, gleaming black, trimmed with shiny chromed elements, a not unappealing sight, though I am little enamored of machinery. It had wide, sweeping handlebars, levers and cables and handles attached everywhere, and a long, flat leather seat, unlike the bicycle seats I had seen on several others.

"I built that seat special," Hunter said. "Had the saddle maker down at Stanford upholster it for me so I could take someone along if I had to. I've seen similar ones in photographs. It's plenty strong."

After Hunter started the contraption, I held my breath and gingerly climbed on behind him, dismissing the inclination to ride sidesaddle out of fear for my life. I squeezed close, arranged my skirt to keep it from being entangled in the spokes and, at his urging, wrapped my arms around him. It was more intimate than I cared to be, more intimate than I had been with the several men who had courted me, but survival seemed more important than social etiquette.

Within seconds, we began a hair-raising ride along the Embarcadero, weaving in and out between drays and honking automobiles.

We charged up Broadway, then up even steeper Kearny, up, up the southern slope of Telegraph Hill, as I clung to Hunter for dear life, frightened that the whole thing was going to flip over on us like a bucking horse.

We skidded to a stop in front of the Fallon house, where I staggered off, coughing up a tot of soot.

"You'll get used to the smell, Annalisa. You just have to outrun it sometimes."

"Great. If the fumes don't kill you, you can always use your face for a braking mechanism."

We entered the front door, neither of us prepared for the surfeit of calm and emptiness. Hunter gamely forced a smile, trying to ease my distress.

"My mother loved this house, she said it reminded her of the Almafi Coast just below Naples. There isn't a hill in the world too steep for the Italians to build a house on. She and I used to walk up to Pioneer Park just above and identify the boats coming through the Golden Gate: brigantines, clippers, yawls, junks, Whitehalls. Have you been here before?"

"It was the only place we could work without the fear of someone seeing us together. He became almost a substitute father to me. I have no kitchen in my place; I used to cook for him sometimes. He made me feel safe."

Referring to Byron in the past dismayed me. "I know that's inappropriate, Hunter, a single woman visiting a widowed man like that."

"He was a caring man, my father. He would never admit it, but I could tell he was lonely with my mother gone and Christian and me away. I'm thankful he had someone to talk to. I would feel much worse if he had spent his last days alone."

I dabbed at my eyes. "I did not know all the men involved in the corruption probe, but I knew they were going to reinstate James Phelan as Mayor. He was going to appoint your father Chief of Police once Donen was taken off." I had to pause again.

Hunter stared, and I stared back. Despite the heartbreak, I felt a comfort and attraction developing between us. It helped ease the pain.

"There were several times that we worked until the sun came up," I said. "Your father always walked over to the window and muttered something in Italian."

"*La luce splendida*. The splendid light. My mother's favorite time of day. She used to say it every morning. He took to saying it for her after she died. He had started hearing her voice sometimes. Always in the morning, as though she was calling him home."

Hunter paused and composed himself. "He promised to protect you if something went wrong, didn't he?"

I nodded, finding it difficult to speak.

"Then I want you to stay here so I can protect you now. I'll take my father's room and you can have my old one. I'm not interested in social convention, Annalisa. You'll be safer here. If we can prove he was murdered the whole city will rise up in arms."

"You believe someone murdered him? Rolf or someone had him killed?"

"As sure as I'm an orphan in my parents' house. Now we have to prove it."

He squeezed my arm, gently, and I rested my hand on his. I fought the urge to hug him.

"I need your help, Annalisa. We have to move before evidence starts disappearing. My books and microscope are in the wine cellar in boxes. I need them set up."

"I'll let Mr. Lee know we won't need his services for a while." I hesitated and looked at Hunter. "I'll do anything I have to, Hunter. Anything to put away the men who murdered your father. But there can be no secrets, no matter how repulsive or dangerous. You tell me everything. I'm going to finish this story and see that it gets printed."

"You will have plenty to write about before we're done."

He handed me the test tubes and slides from his leather bag and exited quickly, leaving me alone in the unnervingly silent house.

Chapter 21

—••❦••—

APRIL 16, 1906. 10:25 A.M.

While I was busy unpacking and setting up his laboratory instruments in the wine cellar of the Fallon house, Hunter drove through the crowded streets of North Beach. He chained the motorcycle to a telephone pole on Kearny and dashed into the Hall of Justice, avoiding the pack of reporters loitering outside.

He ran down the granite steps to the basement, through the door marked "San Francisco County Coroner," pushing through a second door marked "Official Entry Only—All Others Prohibited" into a dank brick corridor, pungent with the smell of formaldehyde and carbolic acid.

He entered the autopsy room and stopped abruptly at the sight of his father on the table, a white sheet covering all but his very pale feet and head. The overhead light cast a yellowish glow on the bald pate, dusty traces of dried salt glowing faintly on his thick eyebrows and mustache.

On the other side of the table, Christian stared blankly, a sweat magnifying his pallor.

"Where's the coroner, Christian?"

"He left a half-hour ago."

"What did he do, spend all of ten minutes with dad?"

"He drowned. When we turned him over the water came pouring out of him."

"That means he was still breathing when someone cut his life line." Hunter plopped his leather bag onto a small metal table. "Did he photograph the body or take any samples?"

"No."

"Then he didn't do his job."

"It was him and Anthony, remember? Unless somebody just happened to swim by and shove him overboard."

Hunter used a scalpel to probe beneath his father's fingernails, scraping a sticky black substance onto a slide. "You Catholic still, Christian? Come Judgment Day, maybe you can explain how you traded his life for another shot of whiskey."

"Like that story about him sending you on patrol on the Barbary Coast, damn near getting both of us killed? Six years humping little college girls and staring at test tubes while me and Francis and Max are out getting stabbed and shot at every day."

"Good, Christian. Whenever you can't argue the issue, change the subject and trot out the martyr speech. Whatever you did, dad did ten times over without being drunk. Or leaving a good man without covering his back side. Dante says the Ninth Circle of Hell, that's the bottom one, is reserved for the betrayers. Maybe they'll save you a seat."

Christian seethed and Hunter glared across at him, neither brother willing to leap over their father's body to strike the first blow.

"What's the matter, Christian? You think with dad gone there was going to be nobody around to tell you the truth?" After storing the slide, Hunter pressed Byron's rigid fingers onto an inkpad, rolling each one carefully onto a sheet of paper.

"Fingerprinting your own father. You think he killed himself?"

"Process of elimination. I collected bloody fingerprints in the engine room. I'll wager they don't belong to dad or Anthony. Speaking of Anthony."

"You won't get a lot out of him. Chief Donen had Francis and Max take him down to Agnews asylum, out of his head, screaming it wasn't his fault."

"I doubt it was his fault." Hunter placed the fingerprint samples in his bag and produced a long syringe. "Hold his arm steady for me."

Christian used two fingers to gingerly support his father's wrist as the needle slid into a bluish vein. The coagulated blood would not draw. Hunter pushed the tip deeper until a few drops trickled into the syringe.

"What do you think, Christian? Dad just happened to fall off a boat the night before he was going to throw a net over those bastards?"

"What the hell you talking about?"

"You don't know anything about what he was doing, do you?"

"Only thing he ever said was 'Christian, you drink too much.'"

"I wonder where he got that idea."

Christian's breath came in short, labored bursts. "He drowned. And all your fancy Sherlock Holmes stuff ain't going to change that."

"You believe what you want, Christian. Someone killed him, and I swear on my father, lying in front me, I will find the bastards."

"You find out someone did this, they'll answer to me."

"No. The vigilante days are over. If someone killed him, I'll be there at San Quentin to see them hang for it." Hunter abruptly ripped the sheet off, startling Christian with the sight of the naked corpse.

"Now, help me position him so I can get some photographs."

Christian stared, ill at ease over Hunter's tone. The impulsive young man had all but disappeared, replaced by someone frank and unflinching.

Chapter 22

APRIL 16, 1906. NOON

Kaitlin Staley sat in the window of Hoffman's Grill on Market Street, reveling in the fashionable crowd and clanking trolleys outside and enjoying a new avocation, counting cars. She had lost interest in the Ford A's and N's when the numbers reached nearly one hundred, joyously turning her attention to the cape-topped Pierce Arrow and the jet black Orient, spotting a rare Winton and a front-engined Locomobile, a Pope Toledo and an Anderson Steamer, three different models of Rolls Royce and the grandest of them all, a black Mercedes. She noted the preponderance of steering wheels over tillers and the newest innovation, attached luggage compartments behind the seats.

During her survey, she savored a hearty amalgam of eggs scrambled with oysters and bacon, a distinctly San Francisco breakfast named the Hangtown Fry due to its popularity with San Quentin's condemned prisoners. With a side of pickled salmon, toasted sourdough with blackberry jam, orange juice, green Ceylon tea, and a coal-black espresso, it was an indulgent twenty-five-cent fare she had decided upon weeks earlier after reading an article about Hoffman's in *Sunset Magazine*.

Kaitlin walked out in the mid-day sun and stopped to let it warm her face. She wrestled her bulky carpetbag through the jostling crowd, navigating back and forth across Market Street at the distinctive herringbone crossing lanes.

She set the bag down at Market and Sansome, staring up at the towering Occidental Building as the City enveloped her: clanging bells, honking horns, rumbling trolley wheels, dizzying spires and massive domes and mansard roofs viewed through the spiderweb of telephone and electric wires crisscrossing the impossibly blue sky. She had read hundreds of stories of San Francisco, but nothing prepared her for the overwhelming effect of it.

She gazed at the row of skyscrapers stretching the length of Market Street, her treasure trove of photographs springing to life: the wedge-shaped Crocker Building and the onion-domed *Chronicle* Building, the brownstone Spreckels Building, the angular Academy of Sciences, and the towering, eighteen-story Call Building.

Then she saw it. The Palace Hotel. She stared and hundreds of gleaming bay windows stared back. She stepped forward unconsciously: a clanging trolley shook her from her reverie seconds before she would have stumbled into its path. She shrieked as the burly gripman clanged the gleaming brass bell above his head and doffed his bulky cap.

Kaitlin picked her way back across Market Street amidst honking cars and thundering wagons, crossing the four cable and horse-drawn trolley lines.

Turning in a daze down New Montgomery, she froze at the sight of the Palace's massive circular carriage entrance, the gleaming cars and bonneted Landaus bathed in a kaleidoscope of light from the enormous stained glass dome perched above the seven tiers of balconies.

"Excuse me, ma'am, but you look like a princess in a fairy tale."

She wheeled to face a thin young man, his black hair plastered against his head, the practiced smile of hotel courtesy etched across his face.

"No. I, I . . . I just got off the train a few hours ago."

"First time at the Palace, I take it?"

"I have seen pictures and read most everything, but this . . ."

"Does she live up to her billing?"

"Oh, my, yes. It is a palace. I read that there are rooms here that cost a hundred dollars for one night."

"Some more than that. Suites we call 'em. More like a fancy apartment than a hotel room. Some have their own parlors, with a piano and a butler and two bathrooms with hot running water."

"Like the one where Enrico Caruso will be staying. I read about it in the *Kansas City Star*."

"Like that, yes. But, if you're looking for a room here, I'm afraid you're a bit out of luck. Ain't a room left in the city, whole dang country is here to see Caruso. A man from Denver offered me a thousand dollars to find him two tickets. Two tickets. Must be an oil man. Never seen anything like it."

"I was hoping to get a ticket, even for just one night. I was also hoping to find a room somewhere, you know, like in a boardinghouse or something. I'm a seamstress and I'm planning to be a clothing designer. I came to see all the dresses and gowns at the opera tomorrow night."

Kaitlin noticed that most of the men making their way through the marbled entranceway were gazing in her direction.

"Name is Tavish. Andrew Tavish."

"Kaitlin. Kaitlin Staley. I really came to see Enrico Caruso. You think it's possible to find one ticket somewhere?"

"Not sure, let me look around," he hesitated. "Let me suggest you don't tell people you're a seamstress if sewin' is what you mean. In San Francisco, that's a nickname for a parlor girl. A fallen woman."

They were distracted by the horses in the carriage entrance whinnying and stamping. One bolted forward, crashing into another carriage, sending a gray-suited passenger toppling to the pavement, spilling the contents of his valise. Several bellmen rushed to his aid.

"I'll be glad when the automobiles replace these darn horses," Andrew said. "They've been demented for weeks. And the smell."

He took a few steps ahead of Kaitlin.

"Come. Let me show you the Palace."

—••◦∞◦••—

Chapter 23

TELEGRAPH HILL

APRIL 16, 1906. 1:50 P.M.

By mid-afternoon that Monday, I had finished setting up Hunter's rudimentary laboratory amidst the wine casks and cobwebs of the Fallon cellar.

I moved to a rough wooden table and slid a blank sheet of paper into his outdated typewriter—the letters on the old Remington #7 struck the page at the bottom of the carriage roll so you could not see them until they emerged several paragraphs later—and began my column.

Despite my lingering grief and worry, the words came easily.

THE HOUR OF CELEBRATION

One would be hard-pressed to find two more timely operas for the San Francisco audience than *Carmen* and *La Bohème*, which represent the secular and romantic school revolutionizing every contemporary art form.

When *Carmen* premiered at Paris' *Opéra Comique*, French aristocracy was scandalized as their teenage daughters, attending the spring *débutante*, were treated to the shocking sight of an amoral gypsy girl seducing the virtuous young army corporal, Don José, into abandoning both his fiancée and military duty. French society, it is rumored, has yet to recover.

La Bohème, a Giacomo Puccini masterpiece of *verismo*, affords an impassioned look at the bohemian revolution currently sweeping the Western world, a broad embracement of art and the human spirit in an increasingly mechanized and impersonal society.

Does not Carmen's saucy dance recall our own Libertine spirits, Loie Fuller and Isadora Duncan, and befit the suffragist movement sweeping through San Francisco and the rest of the country? Does not the noble but impoverished life of the Latin Quarter's young artists in *La Bohème* reverberate among our Latin Quarter, the lofts and studios of North Beach and Telegraph Hill? Is the unwavering voice of *Bohème*'s ardent young poet Rodolfo not heard distinctly in the uncompromising words of our Frank Norris and Jack London?

That God has sent his own voice, Enrico Caruso, to deliver His message of impassioned humanity is not to be lost among the glitter and hyperbole. By curtain call the night of April 18, we will have witnessed events that herald a new America, a new world, and a new San Francisco. The voice of God will have spoken to us.

How well will we listen?

As I reviewed my handiwork, I tensed at the sound of footsteps on the hardwood floor above, easing when I recognized Hunter's jaunty stride.

The smell of the morgue still clung to him, as did his anguish. "You saw your father?"

"I had to do the coroner's job for him."

Hunter moved past me to his rough-hewn bench. He put a slide into his microscope and leaned forward to the eyepiece.

"You performed an autopsy on your own father?"

"No cutting. Just blood and tissue samples, fingerprints, photographs." Hunter pulled the bare Edison bulb near the slide microscope. "This is the black substance I found on the steel cage by the boiler," he said, replacing it quickly with a slide he removed from his leather bag.

"And this sample came from beneath my father's fingernails." He examined it for a moment. "They look identical."

"What is it?"

"Too soft and spongy for rubber. Some kind of animal skin."

"There was an animal below?"

"Someone wearing an animal skin of some kind."

I sat at the Remington, inserted a fresh piece of paper, and typed as we talked. "Do you think someone hid below deck in the engine room?"

"Yes. Whoever was down there fell against the boiler cage when they hit rough seas. He left this black substance on the sharp edges, and then staggered around, leaving a zigzag trail of blood drops. Then he grabbed the door handle and stumbled when the boat heaved. That's how that bloody handprint got on the bottom of the door."

"Then he went up on deck to kill your father."

"My father grabbed him, that's how the same black substance got under his fingernails. He hit my father with something, a blackjack probably, there's a purple bruise at the base of his neck, oblong shaped, about six inches long. Then he cut the rope and shoved him overboard. From up in the pilot's roost, in that bad weather, Anthony saw none of it."

"But what happened to the killer?" I asked, typing frantically.

"There are a few possibilities. He drowned, or he rode the tide to one of the islands, or a boat picked him up before the cold did him in. Maybe he even jumped off near the dock and slipped away before I got there."

"You learned all this studying Sherlock Holmes?"

"Yes, I studied Scotland Yard's techniques. Most progressive police department in the world. I read every story I could find about them. It came in handy when I was helping the San Mateo Coroner. We had a minister once, claimed his wife committed suicide. She was on the bed, a revolver in her right hand an inch from her head. The cops were patting the good reverend on the back, offering him brandy and condolences. Only problem is, when someone shoots themself, especially with a .44 Colt, the recoil tears the gun from their hand. Not to mention his wife was left-handed. I compared the handwriting on the suicide note to the guest book from Sunday services. It matched the signature of the church bookkeeper. I went to her apartment and asked for her fingerprints, told her I was going to compare them to the suicide note and that I had already matched her handwriting. She started crying and confessed. She and the reverend were going to move to Scotland and live happily ever after on money the dead wife inherited. They were also pilfering from the collection plate. The cops weren't even going to investigate. That was when I decided once and for all to become a detective. That's all Sherlock Holmes did. Logic and simple observation."

I pointed to a box on the table filled with eerie photographs, all of people's faces. The faces were contorted, eyes cast in all directions, their lips pursed or protruding. "I'm not sure what you wanted me to do with those."

"That was an experiment for anthropology class. I'll explain later. Right now, do you think you can stomach another ride with me?"

Chapter 24

———◆◇◆———

APRIL 16, 1906. 2:25 P.M.

"What the hell are you trying to tell me, Kelly?" Adam Rolf shouted. "After weeks of planning this thing you don't have my papers?"

"They ain't found the bloody papers," Kelly replied casually. "How else would you like me to give it to ya'?"

Rolf leaned forward, placing his hands carefully on Shanghai Kelly's cluttered desk. It was the first visit he had paid to Kelly's seedy abode in years, and the cackling voices and buffoonish laughter in the bar outside Kelly's office added to Rolf's annoyance. "A lot of good it does me to have Byron Fallon in his grave, with those papers floating around."

"With good fortune, floatin' their incriminatin' little way to the bottom of the bloody bay."

"Luck is the province of fools and idiots, Shanghai. Right now, my Judas is still sipping my champagne and smiling at me."

Kelly turned his head to keep an eye on Tommy, dressed in his gray chauffeur's uniform and staring intently back at him. "I got my best men out looking for the papers right now," Kelly said. "Might help if I could offer up a little incentive to 'em."

"You tell those hoodlums to bring the papers directly to me and I will pay another ten thousand. They have twenty-four hours. Twenty-four hours. You bunco me and just remember I've buried better men for less."

Rolf turned on his heels and was halfway through the door when Kelly called after him. Rolf stopped without looking back.

"Better make that reward twenty-five thousand, Adam. Plus that supervisor's job you been wavin' in my face. Supervisor John Kelly. Got my dress suit picked out and everthin'. I'll throw your Judas in for good measure, head on a platter, just like last time. And Adam. Bloody Christ. Don't be making threats when you come 'round a man's office. You start a war with me, we'll see who's the first to mess his satin skivvies."

Rolf jammed his bowler hat in place and stormed through the dark, filthy Boar's Head saloon.

Tommy lingered behind to stare at Kelly. Tommy had worries of his own. If Byron Fallon had mentioned him in the missing documents, there would be no containing Rolf's fury.

"You sure you ain't workin' the old man, Kelly?" Tommy asked, examining Kelly's face for a sign he was aware of Tommy's betrayal. "You sure you ain't hidin' those papers somewheres?"

"Now why would I do a thing like that?" he responded.

Tommy fought the urge to kill him on the spot, knowing full well it would not guarantee recovery of the papers.

Rolf was seated in the Phaeton when Tommy exited the Boar's Head and climbed into the driver's seat next to him.

"Kelly probably has the papers in his safe," Rolf said as they started off. "He can't read them, and he sure as hell wouldn't trust anyone to read them for him. He's afraid they would sell the information behind his back. He wants to twist the knife, up the ante."

"Somebody needs to put a shank in the dirty Mick."

"Once I have the papers and the man who betrayed me, dispose of him by any means you find enjoyable."

While Rolf and Tommy drove toward Rolf's mansion on Nob Hill, Antoine Dugay entered Kelly's office.

"Mr. Kelly. I see *Monsieur* Rolf is just leave, 'e is not look so 'appy. I 'ave somesing maybe is make him smile very much."

"What might that be, Antoine?"

"A girl. Most beautiful girl Antoine ever sees. She is come by za train. Maybe Mr. Rolf is like zis girl very much."

"Where is the little twist now?"

"One of my spies, who is work at za Palace, tells me she is just leave there. She promise to contact heem laters. She is so much beautiful zis girl, blue eyes, big teats."

"You find her, Antoine. I'll make a gift of her to Mr. Rolf. Peace offerin'. I'll forget what you owe me in gambling debts."

Meanwhile, at a second-floor office at the Potrero Tannery near the

Hunter's Point ship building piers, the establishment's owner used a magnifying glass to examine the black substance Hunter had found beneath his father's nails.

"Seal skin," he said to Hunter and me. "Don't make a whole lot of it. A coupla coats for some of those society dames. Only skin we got that's black like that."

Gunter Erickson, a bearded Dane with one dead eye and skin more pickled than anything that left his tannery, handed the tiny sample back to Hunter, who handed it to me.

I turned it over several times, feigning the same ignorance Hunter displayed.

"This one has a coating on it, Mr. Erickson, slick, like some kind of waterproofing," Hunter said.

"Seems strange, waterproofing a seal," I added.

Erickson flashed the chipped ruins of tobacco-stained teeth floating in a sea of ebony gums and laughed, "It's only waterproof when the seal is wearin' it. Once you cure it, the oil in the skin dries up."

Hunter already knew that. Despite Byron's efforts to guide his son to other pursuits, he had schooled him since childhood in the subtleties of the detective trade, including the art of making a subject feel smarter than his inquisitor.

"What is this then?" I asked.

"Cold water suits. Somebody got the bright idea you could survive in the bloody bay if you wore a suit like this. Hell if I know if it works. Just what is your interest in this, you don't mind me asking?"

I gazed through the office window to the work floor below. In the strained sunlight streaming through the grimy windows, two dozen bearded, filthy men covered with sores and carbuncles used long wooden sticks to fish hides from enormous vats, dragging them to hanging racks.

"Mr. Erickson," Hunter said, "You employ a lot of Scandinavians. Danes, Norwegians, Swedes. Seafaring men, mostly?"

"Steady work's a shade better than a life at sea."

"Real popular with the shanghaiers," Hunter replied. "You ever lose anyone?"

Erickson hesitated, examining us carefully. "In the last two years I had three men up and disappear. Two of 'em family men. Ain't never heard from them again. You think this seal man had something to do with it?"

Once he let the "seal man" comment slip, Hunter gently closed in. "I think he killed a good man last night. A police officer."

"That detective they found floatin' near Angel Island?"

"That detective was my father."

The Dane let out a low, soft hiss. Hunter waited for him to bite.

"I'm sorry, son, I don't need no trouble around here. I pay them regular to leave my place alone. Buildin' inspectors, health inspectors, tax man, those thieves from City Hall like to bleed me dry. I don't want no trouble."

"You already have trouble, it sounds to me. My father was trying to put an end to it when they murdered him."

Erickson hesitated a long minute, staring nervously at the floor. "Guy with a long scar on his face come in about a week ago, askin' about the seal suits. We make 'em up special." He paused again, shaking off an obvious wave of fear. "Shanghai Kelly's man. One of my skinners seen him at Kelly's place on the Coast."

"And you made a seal suit for him?"

"A mate of his. This scarfaced guy, he give me the other man's measurements. Brought him in two days ago to make sure it fit proper."

"What did he look like, the other man?"

"Meanest lookin' bastard I ever seen, give me the shivers. Tattoos everywhere, like a bulldog he was built. They was up to somethin'. Never give me no names, nothin'. That's all I can tell you."

"Thank you, Mr. Erickson."

A few minutes later, I was enduring another hair-raising ride along the waterfront.

We arrived at Meigg's Wharf and walked to a dock where the Fallons kept a twenty-two foot Whitehall skiff.

We shoved the boat clear of the dock and jumped aboard. While I sculled the tiller, he untied the sail from the boom and hoisted it skyward.

"You ever sail one of these, Annalisa?"

"I started fishing with my father as soon as I could stand. He believed whatever a man could do, a woman could, too."

A fresh puff filled the sail and heeled us to starboard, the boat surging through the blue waters of the bay.

"How did you ever get Rolf to trust you, working for Fremont Older?" Hunter yelled over the stiff wind.

"Rolf tested me at first," I shouted back, "he'd tell me things, maneuvers he was getting ready to make. See if the information wound up in the *Bulletin's* editorials. After about six months, I managed to convince him I hated Mr. Older's crusade. I made sure Rolf's cronies and their wives got plugs in the society column. That made me very popular. I heard things no one else did. Not even your father or Mr. Older."

"You dance with rattlesnakes, Annalisa, you eventually get bitten."

"Not doing anything was more dangerous."

After struggling against a flood tide for nearly half an hour, we passed before the open mouth of the Golden Gate and stared out into the dark blue Pacific.

"It won't be that long before they build a bridge," Hunter said. "Then a sane man won't have to risk his life every time he needs to get to Sausalito."

"I don't know. The current is so strong, the water's so deep, how would they ever do that?"

"Thomas Edison believes that some time in this century, engineers will put a man on the moon and scientists will cure cancer. Building a bridge across this little mile of open water is just the beginning, believe me."

"Great. We can put all the ferry boats out to dry dock and fill the place up with the stink of all those God-awful automobiles," I argued. "Did you see the trough outside the tannery, dumping all that poison in the water? And the workmen, with skin you wouldn't wish on a leper? What good is all this progress if it kills us?"

The wind funneling through the Golden Gate suddenly stiffened. I jumped to the boom and reefed the sail.

"I tell you what's bothering me about your father's death. If someone was hiding below deck, in a custom-made seal suit, they had it planned for days, even weeks."

"That's what I've been thinking" Hunter said. He paused a long moment, looking a bit sheepish. "I had a chance to kill Scarface last night and I botched it."

"My God, before they murdered your father?"

"No. After. I should have killed him like Christian wanted."

"Then he couldn't lead us to the men who put him up to it. Your father believed in the law, not the cycle of murder and revenge. Without justice we're just barbarians trading places on the chopping block."

"I'd still like to know how they knew."

A flock of seagulls suddenly exploded from their roosts on Angel Island, squawking and swirling frantically.

"That's twice I've seen that," Hunter said. "Something is sure spooking them."

A half hour later, we scrambled off the boat at Angel Island, near the spot where the Spaniards first anchored in San Francisco Bay.

"We found my father's body near this cove. Let's keep a sharp lookout for your papers."

We hiked through thickets along the water's edge, an exchange of wistful looks between us managing, ever slightly, to ease the grim task.

I was staring into the brambles when I fell over something lying in the path.

It was a man's outstretched legs.

"Hunter!"

He ran over and pulled me to my feet, then leaned over to examine a thick body in a black seal suit. A pool of blood had formed on the man's chest, the result of two gaping holes. Near the right shoulder were two spent brass cartridges.

Hunter used a twig to lift one, inhaling the smell of fresh gunpowder. Then he examined the man's stiffened arms. On the right wrist of the seal suit were four small gouges. On the left arm a tear in the suit revealed a cut from the man's elbow to the wrist.

"Those gouges on his right arm are where my father grabbed him, that's how the seal skin got under his nails. The tear in the left sleeve is where seal man fell against the boiler cage and bled all over."

Hunter pulled a camera from his bag and clicked several photographs of the body.

We each grabbed an icy cold ankle and dragged him to the middle of the path. With a pocket knife, Hunter slit the suit up both sides and laid it open like a sandwich. I watched with a grisly fascination.

"What's that tattoo on his forearm?"

"A prisoner's identification number. You see the USMC tattoo above it? This guy was a Marine. A military prisoner. What do you bet his fingerprints and palm print match those on my father's launch?"

I spotted something near where the body had lain, partially obscured by thickets. I stepped into the weedy marsh, my ankles disappearing into the muck, and emerged with a leather portfolio, its exterior ashen gray from the salty water.

The clasp had been ripped from its mount. It was empty. I handed it to Hunter, who examined it, trying to soften his concern.

"Well, Hunter," I said. "Whoever killed the seal man has the photographs of Rolf's ledger. And my signed affidavits." It was not the cold wind that made me shiver. "What are we going to do with the body?"

"Drag him back in the bushes and try not to let anyone know we're onto them. There was a Chinese general named Sun Tzu, who said 'through subtlety and secrecy, the enemy is mine.' With my father dead, they think there's no one left to stand up to them."

I followed Hunter back to the boat, still a little jumpy. We shoved off in silence and caught a fresh breeze.

In barely half an hour, we were tying up at the landing on Alcatraz.

"Halt! Military Police! Who goes there?" At the top of the long wooden steps, a guard in blue uniform appeared, cradling a rifle.

"Hunter Fallon. San Francisco Police." Hunter steadied the boat and held up his badge.

"Since when did the department stoop to hirin' college boys?"

"Who is that?" Hunter called.

A young man with mutton-chop sideburns slid back his cap and offered a broad grin.

"Jesus, Ernie, last I heard, the Navy shipped you off to Panama."

"Hell, the Navy shipped me all over Creation. Said if I'd be a prison guard, they'd send me back to San Francisco. Been here almost a year, freezin' my ass off."

We tied the boat to a dock piling and trudged up the stone steps.

Hunter extended his hand. "Ernie, this is Annalisa Passarelli. Annalisa, Ernie Trombetta."

"Pleased to meet you, Miss Passarelli. Christ, Hunter. It's a God-awful thing I read. Your dad falling off his launch like that. My mother is just sick over it."

"Thanks. Tell me something. You got a Marine prisoner, number G368433 bunking here?"

Ernie searched Hunter's face for a clue and then walked back to the guard shack. He pulled the logbook from inside and started thumbing through it.

"Oh, yeah. Felix Gamboa. Meanest son-of-a-bitch on Alcatraz, even the guards stay out of his way."

"Not any more they won't. I found him over on Angel Island with two bullet holes in his chest. I was wondering how the hell he got there."

Ernie thumbed through the ledger to the back of the book. He ran his finger down several lines that looked like fresh entries. "I can't tell you how he got to Angel Island, but I can tell you how he got out of here. The assistant warden signed him out three days ago."

"Does it give a reason?"

"No, but I remember hearing a Lieutenant say Gamboa was testifying in a trial somewheres. That's a hoot. Only thing Gamboa knows about is shivin' people when their back's turned. Been on the Rock four years, most of it in solitary for tryin' to escape. Dumb bastard tried to swim the bay once, covered his self in grease from the boiler room." Ernie flipped to another page and found a notation. "The assistant warden turned him over to the police chief, it looks like."

"He turned Gamboa over to Jessie Donen?"

"Awful queer, ain't it? Police chief comin' out to Alcatraz just to escort a snake like Gamboa? Don't hardly make no sense."

"Thanks, Ernie."

"They havin' a service for your father?"

"Mission Dolores, tomorrow morning."

"He was a real good man, your dad."

"Ernie, you want to do me a favor? Don't tell anyone I was here. Don't say anything about Gamboa to anyone. Nothing."

Ernie nodded.

Hunter and I returned to the Whitehall and started across the bay.

"This is getting uglier by the minute, Hunter. Donen helping to murder his Chief Detective? How can this go on in the Twentieth Century?"

Hunter remained silent. We trimmed the sail as the sun sank in the Pacific, firing the sky in a rainbow of scarlet and gold.

"I want you to leave, Annalisa. I have a cousin down in Santa Cruz, a deputy sheriff. You can be safe down there."

"Your father risked his life every day. Christian and The Brotherhood do it. Now you're doing it. I'm not hiding from anyone."

"That's different."

"Because you're men?"

"Because it's a dirty, dangerous job that professionals should do and yes, that's a man's work."

"When Adam Rolf took control of City Hall," I said, "my parents had just opened a bakery on Fillmore Street. A Health Inspector came by demanding two hundred dollars for an oven permit. Then came a garbage permit for garbage they rarely collected, assessments for utilities that never appeared, levies for new sewers they never built. They suggested if we didn't want to pay we should join the Merchant's League and hire an attorney. One named Adam Rolf."

"Honest graft," Hunter said. "As long as Rolf can claim it's a fee for legal services, he can say it's not a bribe. Same old game dressed up in a fancy suit."

"My father refused to pay," I said. "They broke our windows and vandalized our store. Then our insurance was mysteriously canceled and the place burned down. My parents left Italy to avoid men like that. My mother sold her wedding ring to buy the tickets back to Rome. I was fifteen. I had just won a scholarship to attend Berkeley. They begged me to go with them. I was four when we came over; this was the only home I really knew. They're buried outside of Rome, along with a few thousand other influenza victims. They'd probably still be alive if it weren't for Adam Rolf. That makes it my fight."

Hunter had watched me attentively throughout the day, searching my face, appearing to record every gesture and movement.

"May I ask why do you look at me that way when I'm talking? One minute I think you're taking an interest in me, the next minute I think you're suspicious of something."

"Charles Darwin. *Emotion in Man and Animals*. You remember those photos in the cellar, with people's faces all skewed up? I took those for a research project. Darwin believes we can tell what people are thinking by reading their faces. Words lie. Expressions don't."

"You believe you can detect lies by reading people's faces?" I said, trying not to scoff.

"We do it every day. You ask a question, someone looks away, hemming and hawing. Stuttering. You ask something serious; they make a nervous joke of it. It worked so well I just got in the habit."

"You used it on me to determine whether I had anything to do with your father's death. If I tipped off Rolf or Kelly."

"It was nothing personal, Annalisa. Somebody betrayed my father; I just wanted to know who."

"I hope I passed the test."

"You did nothing wrong, Annalisa, nothing you're aware of."

"What else did you notice while reading my face?"

He hesitated and looked away.

"I guess that would be one of those evasive responses, no?"

He looked back, embarrassed. "Despite all the turmoil, you are becoming somewhat—enamored of me."

I was still too irritated to be embarrassed. "I guess the good news is I'm not a murderer."

"My father was murdered. I meant no offense, Annalisa."

"I would be obliged if you cease trying to read me in the future."

I pulled out my opera glasses, struggled with the adjusting screw and looked toward the illuminated clock above the Union Ferry Building. "We better hurry. The last thing I want is to be late and make Rolf suspicious. Assuming he doesn't already know me as Little Miss Judas."

Chapter 25

———••❦••———

LAKE TAHOE, NEVADA

APRIL 16, 1906. 5:10 P.M.

In Enrico Caruso's private Pullman car, Lincoln Staley finished a snifter of Louis XIII cognac, a gift from the Mayor of Carson City, Nevada, where Caruso had made a brief stop. The dapper tenor thanked the Mayor by launching into a few bars of *Pagliacci* from the rear platform of the train, sending the small crowd into delirium.

"'Ow you are like the cognac, Sheriff?" Caruso inquired.

"Fine, Mr. Caruso. Thank you. I'm not much of a drinking man."

"No, no 'Mr. Caruso.' Enrico, *per favore*. I am a simple persons from Napoli. I no like peoples who make, 'ow you say, *hairs*?"

Lincoln smiled. "Putting on airs, like *arias*. Enrico."

Caruso twirled his finger in the air and laughed. He swallowed his drink, rose, and tucked his thumb in the front of his pants, easing the pressure of the earlier dinner. "*Mi scusi, per favore*. I must go make the rehearsal."

Once alone, Alfred Hertz of the Metropolitan Opera turned his hawk-eyes on Lincoln. "Have you considered my proposal, Sheriff?"

Earlier that day, Hertz had told him about Caruso's tribulations in New York. A man had approached the tenor with a photograph of Caruso's family, demanding a ten thousand dollar tribute for the local boss of *Il Mano Nero*, the Black Hand. A phalanx of opera-loving Irish and Italian cops had rescued Caruso, shadowing him constantly, but the experience left the jovial tenor fearful and apprehensive.

"We would pay you handsomely for your efforts and provide you accommodations at the Palace, adjacent to Enrico's room," Hertz said. "It would certainly calm Enrico's uneasiness over all the wild stories he has read about San Francisco."

"I would love to help you, Alfred, but I must spend every minute looking for my daughter. The sooner I find her and drag her back to Kansas, the happier I am going to be."

The sound of the orchestra drifted from the car ahead, a dozen violins, softening the rumble and clacking of the wheels.

Hertz nodded for Lincoln to follow him.

They entered the rehearsal car as the tenor launched into song. Lincoln instantly recognized "*Il Lamento di Federico*," from *L'Arlesiana*, one of the arias Kaitlin played incessantly on her Gramophone.

"*È la solita storia del pastore/Il povero ragazzo voleva raccontarla/e s'addormir/C'è nel sonno l'oblio/Come l'invidio . . .*"

Instantly, the plaintive lilt, the aching emotion of the astonishing voice coursed through Lincoln and eased the vise around his heart. *This is an old story of a country boy/the poor boy wanted to tell it/but fell asleep/There in the oblivion of slumber/How I envy him*, he whispered. He had translated the song several times for Kaitlin, but it was the first time he recognized the tale as his own. The wistful country shepherd, imprisoned in loneliness on a barren prairie, lost in the sweet oblivion of his dreams.

Lincoln turned his face away, lest Hertz or Caruso see the pain in his eyes.

"*Anch'io vorrei dormir così/nel sonno almen l'oblio trovar.*"

And I would like to sleep like that/at least to find the sweet oblivion of slumber.

Hertz leaned close. "The gift of Caruso. He tells us our own stories, as though we are the only one to whom he sings."

Lincoln looked at Caruso, a beatific smile on the tenor's face as he soared gracefully, powerfully between the notes. In that moment, Lincoln understood what Kaitlin sought, why she would forsake her family.

The sweet oblivion of dreams.

Lincoln looked back at Hertz and nodded. He would stay close to Caruso. If he could not find his fearless and resourceful daughter in the crowded city, she would find her way to Caruso. Lincoln would be waiting.

In San Francisco, Kaitlin's dream was beginning to sour. She had left her exhilarating tour of the Palace Hotel hours earlier to ride the California Street cable car, marveling at the mansions of Nob Hill.

She had pressed her face to the window of the Ocean Beach trolley as it wended past the majestic cypress trees of the Sunset District to the Cliff House and Sutro Baths. Indulging in a two-dollar Hansom ride through Golden Gate Park, she stopped at the Japanese Gardens, at the giant lilies and the exotic Palace of Flowers. People stared at the unescorted girl, but she ignored them.

After taking the Sutter Street trolley back to Union Square, the warning of young bellhop Andrew Tavish began to haunt her. There was nary a hotel room anywhere. The few that did have a vacancy would not rent to a single woman.

And darkness was quickly setting in.

Using a directory she had bought at a tobacco shop, she called at the cheap boardinghouses south of Market Street. Her fashionable attire, with the jaunty broad-brimmed hat and wasp-waisted jacket, was out of place in the gritty neighborhood.

Young men on the stoops of tenements whistled and called suggestively as she passed. She clutched her drawstring purse and carpetbag and walked forcefully toward the waterfront, each street growing a little darker.

"I'm sorry ma'am, but we have nothing."

"Ain't had a room for rent in weeks."

"Been booked ever since the papers said Caruso was coming."

"We ain't lookin' for no trouble rentin' to a girl all by herself."

She worked her way down Howard and Folsom, then to Harrison and Bryant, past warehouses and foundries to the Southern Pacific Railroad Depot on Townsend. She slumped on the limestone steps of a nearby plumbing warehouse. Her feet ached inside her misshapen boots and everything was stiff from the four days she had spent sleeping upright on the train. She thought of telephoning Jeremy Darling, but knew the assistant professor of geology lived in a guest residence restricted to the University's male personnel.

From the corner of her eye she noticed a flickering light in the doorway of O'Connor's Cartage. A bearded man held a match to a companion's cigarette. Both were staring in her direction.

She raised her bag and shouldered her purse and headed up Townsend Street, away from the bustling train station.

At Fifth, she turned north and began walking briskly back toward Market. She looked over her shoulder and shuddered at the sight of the two men, bearded and sallow-faced, following through the eerie glow of the street lamps. The shorter one dragged his right leg behind him.

She quickened her pace and crossed to the other side of Fifth. They crossed the street behind her.

A knot tightened in her stomach. Kaitlin hitched her dress and ducked around the corner at Bryant, stealing a look over her shoulder as she trotted nervously across the street.

Her pursuers followed.

Her apprehension turned to fear. She thought to drop the carpetbag, but it contained everything she owned.

"Ma'am," one of the men yelled, closing within twenty feet of her. "Slow down, ma'am. You new in town, ain't ya?"

She turned to face them.

The shorter man, the one with the limp, wore a half-fallen face and dangling arm, as though the entire left side of his body had failed him. The side of his face that worked was leering and ominous.

The tall man bore a pockmarked face and a mouth devoid of teeth.

Kaitlin swallowed and stood her ground, raising her head in defiance.

"You lookin' for a place?" the tall man asked. "We seen you comin' out a boardin' house. We got us a place where you kin stay. Real nice place." A rollicking laugh rattled him, disintegrating into a soggy hack. Spittle and flecks of tobacco landed on his beard as he moved to Kaitlin's right.

His partner circled to her left.

"Whatsa matter, young lady?" the tall man asked. "Cat got your tongue?"

Kaitlin clutched her carpetbag and purse as her heart pounded wildly.

"Whatsa matter, you deef?" the tall one cackled. "We seen your bag, the nice duds you'se wearin'. You must have just come in from somewheres."

"Thanks for the offer. I'd really hate to barge in on you fellas and impose like that. You two look real happy together."

They looked at each other, confused by the inference.

"My father's a sheriff. I'm going to meet him here."

"That so? Too bad he ain't around now." The tall man leaned close, reeking of booze and moldy sweat. "Purty girl like you needs a daddy lookin' after her."

Kaitlin dropped the carpetbag and a groan escaped her lips as they jerked her backward into the shadows of an alley.

The gimp-legged man ripped her purse away while his tall, toothless partner pawed her blouse with filthy hands.

"I like me some nice big teats," said the gimpy one.

She jammed both hands into the chest of the taller man, driving him backward.

"Is this what you want?" she said, running her hand over her breasts. "Huh? Is this what you're after?"

The tall man and his partner looked at each other, tantalized by Kaitlin's response.

"Why be nasty about it, gents? Why not just have us some fun?"

"Now you're bein' sensible-like. We all have us a good time, ain't nobody gets hurt."

The sight of Kaitlin's pale skin and swelling bosom inflamed them. The tall man reached between his legs and rubbed vigorously.

Kaitlin inched back and popped the top button of her blouse, then quickly the second and the third, exposing a lacy camisole. "You boys ain't never seen any nicer than this."

The tall man lurched forward as Kaitlin eased her hand inside her blouse, her lilac-scented hair arousing him further.

She reached her left hand behind his head and pulled him closer. With his head six inches from her surging breast, she seized his hair and jammed a derringer between his eyes.

"How'd you like me to blow your little pea brain clean out of your skull?"

The sound of scuffling boots echoed softly as the gimp dragged himself down Bryant Street.

She thumbed the trigger back.

"Now, I asked a question, you rummy piece of filth. You wanna run or die?"

She tightened her grip on his hair, moving the derringer to his temple so as not to shoot her hand if she decided to pull the trigger.

He raised his hands. "No. Please. We was just funnin'."

"Funnin'? Maybe I should go easy then and just blow your balls off."

"No. No. Don't shoot. Please!"

She slid her fingers free and stepped back, gripping the derringer with both hands. The man cringed, half-closing his eyes.

"Run, you miserable snake. You hear me? You run and don't stop runnin' til you find the hole you crawled out of."

The tall man eased back, head down, hands still raised.

"RUN YOU BASTARD!"

He turned and sprinted away, stumbling several times. In seconds he had crossed Bryant Street, narrowly avoiding a collision with an over-loaded dray from Hotaling's Whiskey.

Kaitlin caught her breath and reached down for her purse. She froze, realizing the gimpy man had it. She searched frantically in the shadows, praying aloud.

Resigned that it was gone, Kaitlin lifted the carpetbag and broke into a trot she did not abandon until she made it back to the lights of busy Market Street.

She collapsed on a trolley bench, too angry to cry.

Chapter 26

UNION SQUARE

APRIL 16, 1906. 7:00 P.M.

Hunter stopped the Waltham in front of the City of Paris on Geary Street, where I climbed off and discreetly attempted to rub the painful tingling sensation from my legs.

The streets were overflowing with people streaming to the Nickelodeon a block away or to dinner at the crowded restaurants and cafés scattered near Union Square. Caruso's imminent arrival had invigorated the City.

"This is crazy, Annalisa, you can't show up at the Opera House. If they were onto my father, they could easily be onto you."

"If I don't show, Rolf will suspect me for sure. If he does have those papers, I'll see it in his face."

"Look, I'm sorry, Annalisa, I didn't mean to insinuate earlier . . ."

"I would give my life to bring your father back. Don't ever question me again."

His head dropped a notch or two. I took his hand and stared at him until he raised his chin and looked back at me. The feelings I had for him rose through the fear. I resisted the urge to kiss him.

"We'll finish this for your father. It will be a different city when Caruso leaves, Hunter."

"Then take a Hansom after the opera and meet me at the Conservatory of Flowers, Annalisa. I'll follow and make sure no one is tailing you. We need to be certain no one is onto you yet."

I abandoned my constraint, kissed his cheek, and ran toward the City of Paris.

I took the elevator to the women's department on the third floor. Donatella, a petite woman from Valle d'Aosta, a region in northeastern Italy where they speak both French and Italian, greeted me with her usual smile.

"Mr. Rolf, he is want me to choose something very special for you tonight, Annalisa."

"How nice. I'll have something special for him very shortly."

Several blocks away, Fire Chief Dennis Sullivan and his wife Maggie left Hoffman's Grill and crossed Market onto Bush Street. It was rare that they would eat out on a weeknight, but the heat in their small apartment on the third floor of the fire station made the thought of cooking unappealing.

"You've been distant all night, Dennis."

"It's this horrible situation with Byron Fallon. I feel like the heart has been cut right out of me. How long can this continue?"

She squeezed his arm for comfort as they walked.

"Mr. Spreckels invited us to his box to see *Carmen* tomorrow night," he said.

"Dennis. We have an invitation to hear Enrico Caruso sing and you're just now telling me?"

Maggie Sullivan knew better than press the issue. Opera and Caruso and fancy dress occasions meant little to him.

They crossed Dupont Street, the gateway to Chinatown, and were about to enter the firehouse when the roar of a motorcycle approached.

"Go on upstairs, Maggie. I'll be up in a few minutes."

Sullivan walked to the curb and waited for Hunter to kill the engine.

"I need your help, Chief Sullivan. My father was murdered and I can prove it."

Sullivan seemed none too surprised. "Why don't you come upstairs, Hunter? There are some things you should know."

Chapter 27

CHINATOWN

APRIL 16, 1906. 7:10 P.M.

Tommy guided the Rolls Royce through the Broadway tunnel and turned right on Dupont, scattering Chinatown pedestrians in front of him. In the back seat, Adam Rolf and Eugene Schmitz had barely spoken since they left the mayor's house.

"You sure you want to do this now, Adam?" Schmitz asked. "With all the newspapers in an uproar, perhaps a low profile would be in order."

"You miss the point, Eugene. Who has the power to challenge us with the meddling Lieutenant gone? Feeney? Fallon's hot-headed son Christian and those idiot crusaders in The Brotherhood?"

"And you still maintain you had nothing to do with it?"

"You know I despise redundancy."

Tommy jerked the Rolls to a stop in front of the Jade Dragon, Madame Ah Toy's restaurant.

A Hop Sing Tong enforcer in skull cap, black silk blouse, and braided queue opened the gilded door and led Rolf, Schmitz, and Tommy into the busy restaurant. They passed through the crowded kitchen and up the back stairs, crossing a rickety bridge above an outdoor courtyard to the loft of a faded brick warehouse.

On the warehouse floor below, Ting Leo stood among the four dozen girls, all still weak and bandy-legged from the ordeal at sea.

One by one, each was forced to disrobe while a Chinese doctor checked their teeth for rot, their hair for lice, and their skin for lesions. He ordered a trembling girl of perhaps ten to sit in a tall wooden chair while two of Ah Toy's houseboys spread her ankles apart. By the light of a flickering candle the doctor determined her maiden was intact. Several of the girls sobbed as they moved down the line in the doctor's direction.

Ting Leo gazed at the loft above where two men in black coats and a burly man in a gray cap stared down at them. She caught the cold gaze of the shortest man, the one with the thick mustache and watery eyes. She glowered and made a spitting gesture in his direction.

Rolf smiled as Ah Toy arrived at his side. Ting Leo, a half a head taller and more developed than the other girls, was ordered to disrobe. Rolf watched intently as she pulled her sack dress over her head and threw it on the floor defiantly.

"She is beautiful girl, yes?" Ah Toy asked, her dark eyes impassive in the rice-powdered face. She turned her gaze to Schmitz, who looked away uncomfortably.

Rolf watched intently as the doctor pulled Ting Leo's mouth open, exposing rows of perfect teeth, then checked her arms and legs for deformities.

She had been spared the barbaric practice of the "lily foot," unlike several of the other girls, their feet bound in infancy so that the bones fused together, the toes jammed between the metatarsals, the toenails curled like ram's horns and imbedded in the purplish lumps.

Ting Leo's strong shoulders and wide, calloused feet showed that her father had chosen instead to use her in the fields.

When she was placed on the chair and her ankles jerked apart, Schmitz turned on his heels and stalked away, much to Rolf's amusement.

"You are right, Madame Ah Toy," Rolf said. "She is splendid."

"I send her you first, Mister Rolf, as gesture of our friendship and good business together."

"I will return her in excellent health."

The houseboys released Ting Leo's ankles, and she climbed down from the chair.

Rolf handed Ah Toy a bulging portfolio.

"Here are forty-five work permits, two hundred dollars each."

"Two time what I pay last shipment."

"It's an expensive city, Ah Toy. This lot will fetch you a handsome price at auction."

Ah Toy nodded for Quong Lee, her burly foreman and principal enforcer, who handed a leather pouch to his mistress. She removed several packets of one-hundred-dollar bills and handed them to Rolf.

"Nine thousand dollar, Mr. Rolf."

"I hear you're attending the opera," Rolf replied, tucking the money inside his jacket. "I hope you'll stop by my home afterward for a reception I am having for Caruso. I believe in promoting harmonious relationships between our different cultures."

"Thank you, Mr. Rolf. I am delighted."

"Frankly, I was unaware the Oriental ear is so finely tuned to the subtleties of Italian opera."

"Is shortcoming of ours. I think all this time *Carmen* is in French."

Rolf fumed at being corrected. He bowed almost imperceptibly, and then followed Tommy back the way they came.

When the doctor finished with the last of the auction girls, a houseboy led him to a small storeroom where the two girls who had been recreation for the *Falmouth* crew were kept.

The doctor examined the whimpering girls while Ting Leo watched from the corner of the hallway. When the old man finished, he shook his head and walked away, reducing the girls to tearful shrieks.

The houseboy yelled for the girls to be quiet, then led them down a dirt passageway to a smaller storeroom, where he opened a heavy padlock and ordered them inside. They wailed and pleaded, sagging to their knees. He shoved them inside and ordered them to lie on the small wooden bunks that lined one wall, explaining the doctor would return to treat them. He set a small rusty bucket full of water inside and lit a candle in a holder on the floor, creating eerie strips of light between the slats of the bunks. He closed the door and locked the padlock.

Ting Leo slipped away, certain she would never see the girls again.

On Dupont Street, Schmitz was waiting near the curb when Rolf and Tommy emerged.

"Eugene! Such an interesting range of emotions this week. Now you look positively penitent."

"They're children, Adam. They're Chinese, but they're still children for God's sake."

"It never bothered you as long as they were out of sight in these dirty little *barracoons*. As long as you got your share."

"Very clever. Now that you rubbed my nose in it, I've gone from accessory to accomplice. It makes me wonder what you might have achieved if this cleverness had been used in service to humanity."

"And now you're having Father Yorke compose your speeches. You really do need a vacation, Eugene, you're bordering on irrational."

Chapter 28

The orchestra was already playing when I hurried up the marble stairway toward Adam Rolf's box, wondering if my name would soon be moving from the opera page to the obituaries, a fear I had downplayed with Hunter lest I add to his concerns.

From the moment I had gotten the job reviewing for the *Bulletin*, I had been wary of Rolf's attention, though his patronage as President of the Opera Association was essential to my work. The previous night, I inflamed his attentions with my gift of the silver watch chain, and now he might have discovered I was his betrayer.

And I was late.

"Annalisa!"

Rolf jumped to his feet. He looked me up and down, ostensibly examining the black lace French gown and emerald choker.

I smiled as best I could, reading his face for any sign he might be onto my ruse. His subtle leer neither confirmed nor eased my fears.

On stage, Sulamith warbled to her father, the High Priest, about her love for Assad. The elaborate stage costumes paled before the gowns and jewels arrayed in Rolf's double box, where everyone whispered softly, ignoring the dreary performance wafting from below.

"My God, Annalisa! Come, sit."

I placed a gloved hand atop Rolf's palm, lightly, in case I needed to retreat quickly, and followed him to my seat next to his.

"Eugene!" he called. "Doesn't she look stunning tonight, our Annalisa?"

"You are indeed a vision, Annalisa," the Mayor droned mechanically.

"I have to thank Mr. Rolf for that."

"I thought you were going to call me Adam from now on."

"Adam. Thank you, this is really a bit much. The gown is one thing, but this necklace. The other critics will be talking."

"You let me worry about the other critics. If they had half your charm and talent, they would be enjoying the same benefits."

"You're too kind, Adam."

"Eugene! Champagne for Annalisa," he called, his tone more dismissive and superior than usual.

Schmitz turned to Tommy, standing in the shadows nearby.

"Tommy, why don't you fetch some more champagne from the cold box in the other room?" Schmitz ordered.

Tommy bristled and moved off slowly.

"Tell me, Annalisa. How long have we been friends now?" Rolf asked.

"Almost two years."

"Two years. And what wonderful times we've had, have we not?"

"We have."

"And I trust that if you knew of someone taking advantage of my generous nature you would inform me."

I raised my eyebrows in surprise, hoping the sound of my heartbeat would not betray me.

"You see, someone here has been false to me."

"After all you've done for this city?" I shifted uneasily, crinkling my face in faux concern as the tepid soprano portraying Sulamith trilled on about handsome Assad.

"Whoever it was, Annalisa, Pierre was his accomplice. Tommy found Pierre hanging in his room two hours ago. I haven't even told the Mayor. The little fop had a thousand dollars and several rather indelicate photographs in his pocket. Whoever the swine was who did this, he . . ."

Tommy handed a fluted glass full of champagne to Rolf, who held it out to me.

I clutched it with both hands and sipped, trying in vain to find some comfort in the fact that Rolf appeared to consider his adversary a "he."

Chapter 29

———❦———

APRIL 16, 1906. 9:15 P.M.

Kaitlin sagged onto a bench in the teeming square, hesitant to cross the street to the Hall of Justice and ask for help. She worried that her father might have discovered she had gone to San Francisco—not New York, as the note she left had claimed—and that he had telegraphed the police with her description. Her head dropped into her hands and she teetered near collapse.

"Excuse me, ma'am. May I be of some assistance?"

"Go away," she said without looking up. "I don't have anything. I've already been robbed once tonight."

When finally she did look up, the sight startled her.

He was tall and appeared even taller, thanks to the towering headpiece of a Prussian officer, topped by an ostrich plume a foot and a half high. His square-shouldered military jacket bore gold epaulets and a row of gold buttons, minus one a third from the top. It was belted at the waist, clasped with a tarnished brass buckle. The trousers bore formerly white stripes down each side, disappearing inside a pair of faded beaver-skin boots.

Kaitlin was uncertain whether to laugh or run.

"Joshua Milton, Emperor of North America and Protector of Mexico, at your service, ma'am. If you'll accompany me, I'll see that proper restitution is made for your loss."

He offered the crook of his arm in a gesture of chivalry.

Kaitlin stared into the beatific blue eyes and reassuring face, framed by a regal salt-and-pepper beard.

"I'm sorry, sir. What did you say your name was?"

"I am the Emperor Joshua Charles Milton. At your service, ma'am."

"You're the Emperor of America?"

"Emperor of North America and Protector of Mexico. Everyone you see about you are my subjects, including, I'm ashamed to say, the scalawags who robbed you. They will answer for their callous deed."

He looked like a *Harper's* cartoon character come to life, and his gentle nature disarmed her fear considerably.

"Kaitlin Staley. I'm from Lawrence, Kansas. My father is sheriff of Douglas County."

"Lawrence? Oh, my. It was terrible what happened in Lawrence during the war, all those innocent people massacred."

"My grandfather was one of them. One of them that was killed, I mean. He was the sheriff before my father. Now everyone tries to make heroes out of the killers."

"Well, Kaitlin, making heroes of reprobates is not new to San Francisco either. I apologize that you have not encountered the kind of hospitality that we pride ourselves upon."

"That doesn't help much right now, I'm afraid."

"You have no money left? Nowhere to rest your head?"

"No," Kaitlin answered, a heartsick look on her face.

"Then come with me, please."

She rose cautiously and accepted a gently outstretched arm.

They sauntered across the park toward Telegraph Hill, Emperor Milton pointing to the spot in Portsmouth Square where California seceded from Mexico, and where the Tongs fought a hatchet war over the infamous slave girl, Lily Foot Fong.

"A Chinese gangster version of Romeo and Juliet," he said.

Kaitlin was delighted.

They stopped at the mouth of Pacific Avenue. Milton indicated the Bella Union, "a seedy rough house," explaining it was there that Eddie Foy and Lotta Crabtree began their climb to vaudeville stardom.

They crossed into North Beach, passing coffee roasters and cigar makers, overstuffed Italian delicatessens and colorful pastry shops, Kaitlin enraptured by Milton's tales of smoking cigars with Mark Twain and sipping brandy with Ambrose Bierce.

When they reached Washington Square, Kaitlin's distress had eased. The Emperor led her down Union Street and rapped on a leaded glass door.

"What is this place?"

"Someplace where you'll be safe." The door opened and Emperor Milton bid her enter.

From the top of a long stairway, a short Italian woman with gray hair smiled at them. "*Buona sera*, Joshua. What I a' do for you?"

"Good evening, Francesca. This young lady has encountered some misfortune. I was wondering if you might have temporary residence?"

"*Buona fortuna*, my *pensionero* is just a move out today."

Kaitlin's discomfort returned. "I, I, I . . ."

"They stole her money, is what she's trying to say."

He produced a small pile of over-sized banana-colored currency, counting out several bills into Kaitlin's hand. In the center of each bill was a line drawing of himself, complete with Prussian hat and ostrich plume. A hundred dollars in Milton money.

Kaitlin looked at him, astonished, and then stared up at Francesca.

"The room is a' five dollars a' week, *incluso* breakfast and supper," Francesca said. "Is good for everybodies, Joshua money."

Kaitlin climbed the steps, dazed and disbelieving, and handed over a five-dollar bill as Milton doffed his hat, bowed from the waist and slid quickly out the door.

"You are hungry, Kaitlin? I make some nice *zuppa*, *pasta fagiole* just today."

Chapter 30

GRAND OPERA HOUSE

APRIL 16, 1906. 10:50 P.M.

I excused myself before final curtain, having repeatedly declined Adam Rolf's invitations to a late supper at the Palace Hotel.

I hurried down the marble stairway as a smattering of polite applause succumbed to the jangle of hoots and catcalls over the execrable *Queen of Sheba.*

Once outside, I hailed a cab. "The Conservatory of Flowers."

"Lady, you sure? Ain't nothin' in Golden Gate Park this hour 'cept perverts and jack-rollers."

"Funny, I thought I just left them. Now let's go."

The horse clopped down Mission to Van Ness, and then up Fell Street toward Golden Gate Park. As we passed through the Panhandle, I looked back over my shoulder. Through the row of streetlights a motorcycle trailed behind me, a reassuring sight.

All night, I had tried to gauge Rolf's disposition. The lascivious attention he normally paid his female guests was missing, while he examined the faces of their husbands with a focused scrutiny.

Tommy, standing sentry a few feet from his boss, seemed more alert than usual, self-satisfied almost to the point of smugness. It made me wonder again if Pierre's death was indeed suicide or more of Tommy's handiwork.

Rolf knew he had been betrayed, he had made that quite clear. But he made no mention of the scope of it, offered no specifics. I was treated as almost a confidante. It was a relief, though marginal at best. I knew it could change at any moment.

I headed toward my rendezvous with Hunter Fallon, reasonably certain that wherever my affidavits were, they were not yet in the hands of Adam Rolf. I finally convinced myself that Pierre had committed suicide, the only way he could not have betrayed me before his death.

I settled back for an invigorating jaunt through the park, a welcome tonic. My thoughts turned to Hunter and I felt my poor heart, weary from all the turmoil, skip a beat.

The Hansom stopped before the glass-paneled Conservatory of Flowers, bathed in a lemonish light from the triple-headed gothic lampposts.

I paid the fifty-cent fare, and following a brief struggle with his edgy horse, the driver headed back toward the city. I pulled my wrap around my shoulders and waited excitedly for Hunter to arrive.

He started to lean the motorcycle against a lamppost, stopping in mid-motion to stare at me.

"My God, Annalisa. I don't think I've ever seen a woman more beautiful than you."

"It's the dress and jewels."

"I'm sure that's all it is."

"Officer Fallon. Are you flirting with me?"

"How nice of you to notice."

I put my gloved hand on his arm. We walked along the side of the Conservatory of Flowers, the spring air soft and perfumed.

"Does Rolf suspect you?"

"I don't think so. It makes me wonder if he really does have the papers. When his blood is up, he has difficulty masking his anger. Maybe the papers did spill out when the seal man was in the water."

"No," Hunter said. "The clasp was lying in the seal man's blood. The top was clean but the bottom was soaked in blood. That indicates they tore it off and threw it on the ground after they shot him. If Rolf doesn't have the papers, my guess is Kelly or one of his goons does."

He frowned, regretting that he may have alarmed me.

"Forewarned, forearmed, Hunter. I didn't make it this far deluding myself." I looked up at the moon, low above the firs and cedars.

"My God, you are beautiful, Annalisa."

"You said that earlier."

"I might say it a few more times."

"Sometimes that's all men see in women."

"This would not be one of those times."

Hunter looked away, the first time I noticed a touch of shyness. He was not sure what to do and neither was I.

"We better get you a change of clothes and go back to my father's place so I can keep an eye on you. I still have work to do."

I reached for his hand. "Are you sure you want me there?"

He held my gloved hand between both of his, rubbing it slowly. "I am quite sure."

I took his arm as we returned to the Waltham. Gathering my dress was a more formidable effort this time, but I managed to collect it well enough that it was not a potential danger.

I climbed on behind him, squeezing a little tighter this time.

In seconds, the park was flying by in a blur. We sped through the Western Addition and across Market Street, me in gown and jewels, he in goggles and leather, a sight even by San Francisco's standards.

In minutes, I was coughing up soot outside my building at Fifth and Folsom Streets.

"You'll have to wait outside," I told Hunter. "No men in the building with a single woman, not even the lobby, after six."

"Even a cop?"

"Especially a cop."

I stared at him for a long moment, nervous and excited about spending the night in the same house. Then I wheeled and headed quickly for the entrance.

I pushed through the creaking door and walked past the front desk, where my landlady Loretta sat reading the *Police Gazette*, her eyes bulging and her lips moving with each lascivious detail.

I skipped carefully up three flights of narrow steps to the dimly lit hallway, where I slid my brass key into the plate beneath the doorknob.

I crossed the cramped room, the only illumination the moonlight streaming through the single window. I pulled open the sticky sash and stuck my head outside.

"Officer Fallon! Excuse me, Officer Fallon!"

I took a flower from the vase on the windowsill, inhaled its waning fragrance and dangled it outside the window, calling down, "I would like to offer this rose in appreciation of your chivalry."

"*Il fior che avevi a me tu dato!*"

"Well, now. It's not often one meets a policeman who quotes Bizet. It's so downright—operatic of you."

Hunter circled clown-like beneath the falling flower, caught it, and pulled it through a buttonhole in his leather jacket.

I turned back inside, produced a stick match from an alabaster holder, and struck it. The slight flame illuminated the face of a man towering above me, bearded, cadaverous, a long scar down the right jaw. A glint shone off the keen edge of a very long knife raised above his head.

I gasped and dove away.

"Hunter!"

The knife just missed my ear, shearing the puffy shoulder of my gown. As I fell, the tip caught the edge of my dress, a foot from the hem, pinning it to my desk.

"Hunter, Hunter!"

As the man struggled to free the knife, I kicked him in the shin with all my strength. He recoiled and staggered backward.

Hunter had already bolted through the front door and was two strides from the stairwell when Loretta spotted him.

"Hey, hey, you can't come in here!"

He ignored her and charged up the steps.

I struggled to stand, my feet entangled in my clumsy gown. I ripped the dress free of the knife seconds before the intruder dislodged it. I crawled backward, kicking furiously as he advanced. He raised the blade again, his gaunt, scarred face ghastly in the moonlight. I realized who he was.

"HUNTER! HUNTER!"

My hand touched a wooden footstool as Scarface limped toward me, raising the knife. I gripped the stool with both hands and smashed his knee.

He screamed and toppled toward me like a fallen tree. I rolled away and struggled to my feet near the window.

"HUNTER!"

Hunter made the third floor and ran toward the sound of my cries. He smashed through the door, head over heels, landing on his knees to point the long barrel of the Colt at Scarface.

"Show me your hands or I'll kill you."

Scarface, his back to Hunter, turned slowly, his left hand above his head, his right hand hidden.

"Both of 'em!"

Scarface eased his body toward Hunter. In his right hand was a small revolver, the muzzle pointed at my chest. The sound of the hammer cocking froze us.

"Well, Junior," Scarface growled. "Looks like we got ourselves a Mexican stand-off."

Hunter eased to his left for a better look.

"I wouldn't be janglin' around too much, sonny. My thumb slides off'n this trigger, your sweetheart misses out on her next birthday."

Hunter stopped in his tracks.

"There's two more cops waiting for you downstairs. Drop that thing real slow."

"Funny, I only heard one motorcycle, seen two people gettin' off. Now, I'm gonna back out slow. My gun on her, yours on me. Real civil like. I hit that door, I'm gone. Be smart, everybody walks."

He backed away, one eye on Hunter, his gun steady on me.

Hunter moved aside slowly, his father's Colt no more than five feet from his adversary.

"Don't move, Annalisa."

"That's right, pretty lady, don't get fancy on me."

Hunter, arm extended and shoulders sideways, pivoted as the tall man stepped backward through the splintered door and into the shadowy hallway.

"I see your cherry face in the hall, sonny, I'll blow it clean off. Then I'll finish your lady friend real nice like. Understand?"

"You go ahead, run. We'll meet again soon. I promise."

Scarface offered a chipped grin and bolted down the hallway.

Hunter sprang to the doorway after him, crouched low, and leaned his head out. A slug splintered the wall two feet above his head. He ducked back inside as boot heels thundered away.

"You hurt, Annalisa?"

"I'm furious."

Hunter grabbed a kitchen towel and carefully wrapped Scarface's abandoned knife.

"Grab some things, Annalisa, and let's move before he returns with reinforcements."

Within minutes, we passed through a gauntlet of cackling neighbors inquiring into the ruckus.

We emerged on Folsom and climbed back on the motorcycle, this time with me clutching a cloth sack full of clothes and balancing my Gramophone, its brass horn as large as my torso.

I remember little of the ride other than clinging tightly to Hunter.

A few minutes later, we were in his wine cellar, leaning over his make-shift crime laboratory. Hunter produced a straight razor and started shaving a graphite pencil. He blew the powder gently onto the handle of Scarface's knife.

"Greasy hands make better fingerprints," he said.

He sliced inch-wide slips of white stationery paper and rolled each one onto the prints, then examined them with a magnifying glass. He compared them with the bloody impressions from the boiler room of Byron's launch.

"This really works?"

"The Persians and Chinese have been using fingerprints for centuries. An Englishman named Galton, Charles Darwin's cousin, developed this system ten years ago. Last month, the Army started fingerprinting soldiers to identify them if they're killed in battle. That's how backward we are in San Francisco."

He abruptly put the magnifying glass down.

"I got 'em. Scarface was in the boiler room; he probably helped Gamboa with the seal suit and then left. Someone was trailing in another boat, they picked Gamboa up after he killed my father, took him to Angel Island, and killed him to cover their tracks."

"How do you know there was another boat and he didn't just swim to Angel Island with that seal suit on?"

"The inside of my father's portfolio was dry. If Gamboa had swum any distance, it would have been soaked and the papers ruined. Rolf wanted those papers; he'd never risk a man having to swim San Francisco Bay. No. Gamboa hid below, and then he came up top and hit my father with a blackjack and cut his lifeline. He probably used an Eveready to signal a chase boat, swam a few strokes with the portfolio overhead to keep it dry. He would have killed Anthony as well, but Anthony never saw Gamboa anyway. This was Adam Rolf's doing. Shanghai Kelly could never concoct a plan like this on his own."

"What about the blood samples you took from your father and the boat?"

"Every part of us is unique: hair, teeth, fingerprints. One thing you find at crime scenes is blood. I just took it for future reference, in case we make a breakthrough and I can use it for evidence. What we have to worry about now is who knows your identity."

"Scarface and Kelly obviously do, but I still don't think Rolf does. Your father told me Kelly kept a man locked in his basement for two weeks once, a clerk who was supposed to testify against Rolf for extorting money on some big sewer contract. Kelly kept raising the price. When Rolf agreed, Kelly cut the man's head off as a present. That's why Scarface brought that big knife."

"We need to catch Kelly passing those papers to Rolf if we're going to pin the murder on them," Hunter said.

"Preferably with my head intact." I don't know why, but I smiled. If I had any doubts about my feelings toward Hunter, they had vanished.

I walked over and kissed him.

Chapter 31

TELEGRAPH HILL

APRIL 17, 1906. 6:30 A.M.

I passed the night in Hunter's old room, across the hall from where he slept in his father's bed. It was a restless night for both of us. Barking dogs and agitated horses had kept up a frenetic chorus that lasted until sunrise.

We were not the only ones who spent a troubled night. At his flat on Union Street, Christian had endured his most torturous dream yet, with the entire city engulfed in flames. When he tried to help firemen battle the blaze, he saw his own uniform on fire.

We ate a solemn breakfast, after which Hunter dressed quietly for his father's funeral, the pain seeping into his stoic face.

I kissed him good-bye and left, heartsick at being unable to attend the service lest I reveal my allegiance to the Fallons.

Outside, the sweet morning air failed to lift my spirits. I descended Kearny Street to Broadway, turned east to the Embarcadero and headed toward the Ferry Building.

A short while later, on the upper deck of the paddle-wheeled Alameda–San Francisco Ferry, Lincoln Staley leaned on the railing, sandwiched between dapper Enrico Caruso and scholarly Alfred Hertz.

"Is beautiful, yes? I hear many peoples say is beautiful city," Caruso said as they prepared to dock.

"Yes. I guess it is." Lincoln had other things on his mind.

The ferry bumped against the wooden pilings, and Hertz led Caruso down the gangway and into the Ferry Building.

Near the portal leading to Market Street, a dozen men dressed in splendid morning coats hurried in their direction.

"*Signor* Caruso! *Signor* Caruso," a beaming man cried, extending his hand. "I am Adam Rolf, President of the Opera Association. I am the man who made the arrangements to bring you to our beautiful city."

"Ah! So you are the one I must blame. If I travel two more hours I think maybe I am back in Italy again."

"I understand your reticence, *Signor* Caruso, but you will find my San Francisco as beautiful a city as any in America. And our hospitality second to none."

I stepped forward and extended a gloved hand.

"*Buon giorno, Signor Caruso. Benvenuto a San Francisco. Io sono qui per assistenza. Scrivo per un periodico, chiamato 'Il Bulletin.'*"

"*Bella città. Bella donna.*"

The group laughed. I recognized the man behind him as Metropolitan Opera conductor Alfred Hertz, conversing quietly with a tall man in duster and Stetson who resembled a Ned Buntline cover drawing of a Western sheriff.

Once outside, Caruso stared about the Ferry Plaza as hundreds of fans exploded in shouts and cheers, waving signs offering greetings in English and Italian. Placards bearing his likeness hung from poles and wires.

On a makeshift stage, Eugene Schmitz launched the San Francisco Orchestra into "March of the Toreadors" from *Carmen.*

The great tenor walked gingerly up the ramp, the horn section playing with such vigor it made his mustache quiver.

Schmitz waved his baton dramatically and stopped the band in midflight.

The crowd cheered wildly, tossing hats in the air and screaming, "*Bravissimo Enrico! Bravissimo!*"

Schmitz offered his hand to Caruso, addressing both him and the crowd. "This is a glorious day. The most glorious day in the most glorious city in all America. *Signor* Caruso, as Mayor of San Francisco, let me offer our warmest welcome to you and the Metropolitan Opera."

"Thank you, *Signor* Mayor. Thees San Francisco I think must be a great city, yes, if they are a' have as mayors a *maestro.*"

The crowd cheered.

Caruso walked to the edge of the platform and bellowed from his baritone depths. "I hear many times thees San Francisco is a wild place full of wild persons, but tonight, we make great music for thees wild place, no?"

Caruso removed his bowler hat and waved it at the crowd. The response was deafening.

"*Signor* Caruso," someone shouted. "*Signor* Caruso. What do you think of the eruption of Mount Vesuvius a few days ago?"

"I am very *paura*, 'ow you say, afraid for my peoples in *Napoli* who lives at the *piedi*, the . . . foots of thees volcano. I am believe God has sent me to beautiful San Francisco so I am safe from thees terrible thing." The crowd roared again.

Caruso waited for them to settle. "I am hope I can make some *concerto* to make monies to help my peoples in Napoli before I am leave." The applause, led by Italian compatriots who constituted more than half the crowd, shook the platform on which he stood.

"*Signor* Caruso," a reporter called. "Do you think that a volcano is more frightening than an earthquake?"

"I am never before see a' thees earthquake, but I no think thees is so much terrible as volcanoes. Now," he bellowed, "if you can please to tell me where in this San Francisco I am to find the best *piatto* of roast beef and macaroni?"

It sent the onlookers into frenzy. Schmitz launched the orchestra back into "March of the Toreadors."

Caruso descended the platform, tugged his mustache, and extended his arm to me.

I grasped the crook of his elbow and smiled.

"You are my *traduttrice*, *sì*, Annalisa?"

"It does not appear to me that you need a translator, *Signor* Caruso. Your English is most impressive."

"*Grazie, grazie.* Is some time difficult for me. Also sometimes I prefer to say somethings, in private. *Tutte delle personne non sono di fiducere.*"

I nodded. Caruso was not alone in finding some of those around him suspect. I noticed the man in the Stetson hat—I would not learn his name was Lincoln Staley until almost two days later—following behind and scouring the crowd intently.

Rolf climbed behind the wheel of his Phaeton while Schmitz held the back door for Caruso and me, as Tommy guided Lincoln and Hertz into the Rolls Royce behind us.

Rolf slipped the car into gear and the procession started down Market Street, weaving through cheering pedestrians, honking drays, and clanging trolley cars. Caruso leaned his head back and the tall buildings swam past in dizzying montage.

"*Io ho sentito molte volte che questa città e pericolosa. È, come si dice? The Wild West.*"

"It is the last of the Wild West," I replied, "but the parts that are most perilous are *sotto terra*. Below the surface."

Caruso leaned over, the throb of the Rolls Royce's engine masking his words. In Italian, he said, "I visit many places, and I have never seen a politician who is not full of . . ."

He trailed off, not wanting to offend, but I understood full well. I nodded toward Rolf and Schmitz. In Italian I told him, "These two here will not disappoint you."

He smiled and patted my hand. "I think I am like this San Francisco, Annalisa. I will be safe here."

A minute later, he caught sight of the Palace Hotel. He stood, hands on the back of Rolf's seat, mouth agape. Rolf wheeled down New Montgomery and through the two-story arched entryway into the circular Grand Court, cleared of traffic for our arrival.

Caruso stared upward at the seven tiers of balconies that surrounded the Grand Court. Hundreds of bronze torches, lit especially for him, adorned the marble columns, reflecting off the massive stained-glass dome a hundred feet above us like a thousand kaleidoscopes.

He was so enraptured of the dazzling sight his foot missed the running board and he stumbled forward. Two porters caught him beneath the arms.

"Be careful there, sir. You might hurt yourself," Andrew Tavish said. Schmitz and Rolf hustled to assist, but Caruso raised his hand to signal that he was fine.

"*Signor* Caruso, I regret that we must leave to attend an important civic function," Rolf said, turning his eyes to me. "The services for Lieutenant Fallon."

"A terrible tragedy," I said, leaving off *you murdering bastard.*

"We're planning a small celebration for you at my home on Nob Hill after the performance tonight, *Maestro*," Rolf said. "Some of our famous Dungeness crab, a little champagne. I'd be honored if you and Mr. Hertz would join us."

"*Grazie.*"

I spotted Alexander Sharon, the suave and charming manager of the Palace, walking swiftly toward us. I took Caruso by the arm and led him toward Sharon, away from the group.

Alfred Hertz turned to Rolf and Schmitz. "Thank you for your thoughtfulness. It has already eased Enrico's apprehensions. May I ask a small favor? This is Sheriff Lincoln Staley. Sheriff Staley joined us in Kansas City and agreed to help us with security for Mr. Caruso."

"I'm sure you won't find that necessary," Rolf said, sizing up the rough-hewn Lincoln. "We don't see a lot of shoot-outs here in San Francisco, despite the rumors."

"Sheriff Staley's daughter is missing, presumably a runaway. She's only fifteen. If there is anything we could do to help locate her?"

Schmitz beamed broadly. "Sheriff Staley, have you a photograph?"

Lincoln handed over the sepia-toned school photo he had shown to the ticket clerk in Kansas. "Her name is Kaitlin, with a K."

Schmitz examined the photo and handed it to Rolf, who perused it with quiet interest.

"A beautiful young lady," Rolf said. "You must be very proud. If you can spare this photo, I'll have Police Chief Donen post it on the Missing Persons board."

"It's my only one. Perhaps I might introduce myself to Chief Donen."

"I'll telephone and tell him to expect you," Rolf offered. He returned the photo and climbed into the Rolls with Schmitz.

Near the front desk, Alexander Sharon was pumping Caruso's hand. "This is such an honor to have you as a Palace guest, *Signor* Caruso. Such an honor indeed."

"Pleased to meet you, *Signor* Sharon, thees is my new friend, *Signorina* Annalisa Passarelli."

"I know Miss Passarelli well," Sharon replied. "She's our finest opera critic and a regular guest at Palace suppers."

He led Caruso and me through the marble entrance and into the tropical garden with its Roman fountains and statuary.

"Our architect, Mr. John Gaynor, studied all the great palaces of Paris and Vienna before he made a single sketch for the Palace Hotel. The property covers two and one-half acres and took more than a thousand craftsmen five years to build. Every piece of furniture was custom made in our own factory nearby."

In the Palace Grill, Caruso stopped to examine the mahogany bar and gilded mirror that stretched a city block. Exotic plants and hand-carved mahogany tables dotted a floor of polished marble.

"It takes thirty men to tend bar here," Sharon stated. "Our pantry holds twelve thousand specially made Haviland place settings, twelve pieces each, plus silverware. We have one hundred solid gold settings for special guests. Fred Mergenthaler, our *chef de cuisine*, has cooked for European royalty. I think you will find the food quite palatable."

"I am singing in many fine places; Buenos Aires, St. Petersburg, London, but I am never see something like thees."

"The original owner, Mr. Ralston, one of the Mother Lode's most prosperous silver barons, had a single objective in mind. To build the largest and finest hotel in the world. Every recent President has stayed here, including Theodore Roosevelt. There is more official business conducted in the Palace Garden Room than in the State Capitol building in Sacramento."

"*Signor* Sharon, peoples ask many times about earthquakes in San Francisco. Is happen very often?"

"The Palace was built to be the safest building in San Francisco, virtually immune to earthquake and fire. The foundation is sixteen feet thick. We have thermostatic fire detectors in every room, a one-hundred fifty-thousand gallon water reserve, and more steam-driven water pumps than any building in the world. There is a saying, *Signor* Caruso, 'If the Palace goes, so goes San Francisco.' You could not be safer in your mother's arms." Sharon's enthusiasm was infectious.

Caruso's apprehension had all but disappeared by the time we took the brass and mahogany elevator en route to suite 622.

Caruso entered the room and perused the redwood-paneled walls and heavy brown drapes.

"William Tecumseh Sherman, one of the great Civil War generals, stayed in this room after the war ended," Sharon said.

"Is too dark. Is look too much, 'ow you say? A place where they are make bodies for funeral?"

"Let's try another then," Sharon said, his ever-present smile in full bloom.

In short order, Sharon displayed suite 580. "Another of our war heroes, General Grant, who later became President, stayed in this one."

"Maybe after sleep in tent so many years, thees generals is happy to sleep in some bed."

"You're a man of candor, Mr. Caruso. We don't get that often."

Caruso strolled through the double parlors, examining the canopied bed, sandstone-colored carpeting, maroon satin curtains and sashes. Cut-glass chandeliers hung in every room and each parlor sported its own marble fireplace. "I am like very much," he stated.

Over the next two hours, Caruso's valet, Martino, directed the hotel bellhops in unpacking thirty-eight steamer trunks. Their contents included one hundred tailor-made shirts, fifty silk dressing gowns, a trunkful of hand-tooled boots, four trunkfuls of dress suits, forty topcoats, and six racks of Borsalino hats. They hung more than fifty self-portraits Caruso had sketched on his journey through America: Caruso greeting the Mayor of New York, Caruso visiting the animals at the Central Park Zoo, Caruso practicing his quick-draw from the Pullman car.

Above his bed, Caruso fixed a photograph taken with President Theodore Roosevelt on opening night at the National Opera in Washington, D.C. "He is my friend, President Roosevelt. Is very much love the opera."

Throughout the activity in suite 580, I occupied a peach satin arm-chair, pondering the somber event in progress in the Mission District.

Yet, whenever my thoughts drifted to Hunter, my spirits lifted. I was becoming so smitten with him that it was overcoming my fear.

Chapter 32

MISSION DOLORES

APRIL 17, 1906. 9:00 A.M.

Several miles from the Palace Hotel, at the entrance to Mission Dolores—the squat, adobe "Mission of Our Lady of Sorrows"—Hunter and Christian Fallon were greeting mourners. A half-hour earlier, with only The Brotherhood present, Hunter had explained his findings. Christian had listened impassively, his head hung in shame, the pain so palpable that Hunter was unable to chastise him. An unspoken peace between the Fallon brothers had begun to settle in.

Tommy jerked Rolf's Phaeton to a halt at the curb. Hunter and Christian watched, tense and angry, as Rolf and Schmitz strode up the steps with Tommy close behind.

Schmitz extended his hand. Christian and Hunter ignored it.

"We are very sorry about the passing of your father," Schmitz professed, lowering his hand self-consciously.

"I'll bet you are," replied Christian.

Rolf fought a grin and looked inside, where the small crowd of Byron Fallon supporters on the left side included The Brotherhood and perhaps a dozen other police officers.

On the right side, the rows were crowded with a sea of brass stars and heavy blue uniforms.

"We'll be over on the right side if you boys need us," Rolf said.

Tommy traded glares with Christian as he passed.

"Someday soon, you and me," Christian whispered to him.

"Chrissake, your Mayorship," Donen said as the party arrived at a center pew, "don't look so glum. You look like somebody died."

Donen's smugness dimmed as he looked across the church, where Charlie McBride and the Chinatown Squad took seats near The Brotherhood.

"Relax, Jessie," Rolf offered. "They're making it easy to flush out the troublemakers."

A stir swept through the church. All heads swiveled toward the entrance as Rudolph Spreckels, Prosecutor Charles Feeney, former Mayor James D. Phelan, Fire Chief Dennis Sullivan, and Fremont Older strode in. They were followed by Brigadier General Frederick Funston. Funston stopped, pulled himself up to his full five-foot-two-inch height, and sent a withering gaze toward Donen, Rolf, and Schmitz. Fearless Freddie let his stare drift to the supervisors, judges, and police officers spread out around them, until one by one they looked away.

A bead of sweat trickled from Schmitz' fan-shaped cowlick to his salt-and-pepper goatee. "If everything is just fine, Adam, then what the hell are Feeney and Fremont Older and General Funston doing here?"

Hunter and Christian closed the heavy doors and took their seats with Elizabeth, little Byron, and Katie. Elizabeth clutched Christian's arm and wept.

The rest of The Brotherhood sat directly behind them. Francis Fagen squirmed in his seat between his wife Eleanor and his brother Patrick. Next to them, the mother of the Rinaldi brothers, Cecilia Rinaldi, dabbed tears as Max and Carlo wrapped their arms around her, all the while fuming at the officers across the aisle.

The organ music ceased and a hush fell over mourners and antagonists alike.

Father Peter Yorke ascended the pulpit and gazed down at the open coffin of Byron Fallon. He bristled at the sight of his lifelong friend.

"We have come to bury another good man," his voice echoed off the adobe walls and through the nave. "As fine a man as ever walked a city street. A man who gave his life to protect the most innocent among us. A man who earned nothing but scorn and deceit from those who should have stood beside him. His blood is on the hands of those who turned their backs, those who violated the covenant of duty and Divine Word to line their filthy pockets."

He looked at The Brotherhood, his warriors, and then cast a mournful eye upon the other side. He cleared his straining voice. "Words will not honor him. Honor is a gift a man bestows upon himself. It is for his cowardly opponents we should pray. If Christ were here to walk among us, he would be seated on the side of Byron Fallon. If we do not end the wickedness that recognizes no value to human life, God's wrath will rain. If we do not drive out this evil that preys on helpless children and honest working men, God himself will intervene and the fire that descends from Heaven will be most swift and terrible."

As the assembly joined Father Yorke in a hymn, Rolf and Schmitz walked to the back of the church, preparing to traverse the center aisle to the pulpit.

Christian jumped from his seat and rushed along the opposite aisle to intercept them.

"What are you gentlemen doing?" Christian asked.

"As Mayor, I was preparing to say a few words in tribute to your father."

"I don't think that's such a good idea," Christian said as Hunter arrived.

Chief Donen joined them. "What seems to be the problem here, lads?"

"Officer Fallon here is challenging the Mayor's right to perform his civic duties," Rolf replied.

"Really? And why is that now?" Donen asked.

"I'm probably going to Hell as it is," Christian answered. "Stomping the Mayor in front of a churchful of people would just about clinch it."

Schmitz sulked off like a wounded adolescent.

"What a shame a man of your pluck earns what, twenty-eight dollars a week?" Rolf said, enjoying the confrontation. "Especially given the hazards inherent to the job."

"Tell me something, Mr. Rolf," Christian asked, leaning close, "how many more nine-year-old girls will it take before you feel like a man?"

Donen inserted himself between Rolf and Christian, straining to manage his long-simmering hatred. "A man who gets his dander up so easy can be a real danger on the street, Officer Fallon. Your next shift you and the rest of your lads report to me for jail duty. I'll see you get your minds right."

The chief stormed off behind Rolf.

"Felix Gamboa says 'hello,'" Hunter called out. "I saw him out on Angel Island."

Donen spun around, his face turning crimson.

"He looked surprised," Hunter added, "like he couldn't figure why everybody double-crossed him."

Donen's bluster cracked. His lip quivered and a fury spread across his face. He tried to answer but failed. Rolf seized the Chief's arm and pulled him to the street.

"Nice work," Christian said. "Now they have to try something really dumb and desperate."

"I just wanted to see their faces. Donen and Rolf were both in on it, sure as we're standing here. Now it's man to man, Christian. Just the way you like it."

"Then we better get dad in the ground before the lead starts flying," Christian said. The brothers clapped each other on the back, a look of determination in their eyes.

An hour later, a procession of a dozen horse-drawn carriages clopped over the cobblestone pathways of Laurel Hill Cemetery, on the edge of Golden Gate Park.

In the lead carriage behind their father's hearse, Hunter's eyes drifted to the downtown skyscrapers, imposing against a crystal blue sky. His memories came in staccato bursts: squeezing his mother's hand as they rode the elevator to the tenth floor of the *Chronicle* building, the first skyscraper in the West; running home to report his sighting of the City's first automobile; straddling Byron's and Isabella's shoulders as Mayor Phelan threw the switch that fired the City's first electric lights the length of Market Street.

At the cemetery, Hunter stood numbly over his father's grave as tears flowed from nearly all fifty of the mourners.

"*Gloria Patri et Filio et Spiritui Sancto,*" Father Yorke recited over the grave as Max, Carlo, Francis, and Patrick lowered the coffin.

Hunter raised a handful of dirt and let it dribble from his fist; it rumbled off the coffin's surface. He then turned and stumbled toward the carriages.

When almost all of the attendees had left, save for The Brotherhood and a handful of stragglers, Hunter raised his eyes to find Chief Sullivan standing before him. "I'm so sorry, Hunter. We're all so very sorry."

Christian arrived and shook hands with Sullivan as two somber men joined them.

"Hunter, Christian," Sullivan said, "this is Fremont Older, editor of the *Bulletin*. He's the man who started this graft hunt, who got the backing of the President. And this is Mr. Charles Feeney, the Special Federal Prosecutor sent by President Roosevelt himself to put Rolf and Schmitz and their cronies behind bars."

"I'm sorry to have to ask these things at a time like this," Feeney stated quietly, "but time is not an ally right now." He looked at Hunter. "Chief Sullivan says you believe your father's death was not an accident."

"A military convict named Felix Gamboa did the killing. His bloody finger and palm prints are all over the launch. Kelly's lieutenant, Scarface, brought him to the boat and helped Gamboa get ready. His fingerprints are there as well."

"Felix Gamboa?" Feeney asked. "His name came up in a case about a month after I got here. He's in Alcatraz."

"Chief Donen signed him out three days ago. His body is lying in the bushes over on Angel Island. Whoever put the bullets in Gamboa stole the evidence he took from my father."

"My Lord, the Chief of Police, conspiring to kill his Chief Detective," Older replied. "Father Yorke is right. God will intervene if we don't fix this, and quick."

Francis, Patrick, Max, and Carlo joined the group, fanning out around Hunter and Christian.

"Gamboa and Scarface are Shanghai Kelly's men," Christian offered, his voice thick and pained. "Kelly would never kill my father unless Rolf ordered it."

"Which presents us a real problem," Feeney sighed. "Fingerprints are not enough to convict any of them, even if we get them admitted into evidence. We need to catch Kelly passing the papers to Rolf, exchanging money. I better cable for Secret Service officers to assist us. President Roosevelt is fighting a war against graft, and he won't sit still for the murder of a police officer, I promise you."

"There's no time for that," Francis interrupted. "If Kelly has those papers, he's going to milk Rolf for all he can get. Rolf is in no place to bargain. He'll pay and get on with it before this gets out of hand."

"This is delicate work," Feeney said. "No offense to any of you. I have never seen braver men, but we need a seasoned detective, like your father."

"There's no time," Hunter blurted. "It will be over before your reinforcements get on the train. Last night, Scarface would have killed my father's informant if I hadn't stopped him. You want evidence, I'll get you evidence. I know I'm the low man here. But I have an idea on how to get them all."

"I'm sorry, Hunter," Fremont Older intoned, "but I gave my word to the President that this investigation would be handled by experienced men. I know you're a brilliant engineering student, but this is out of your realm."

"He can do it," Christian added. "If it wasn't for him, we wouldn't even know my father was murdered."

"My brother Francis here," Patrick added, "he turned down promotion to the detective bureau twice. He can run this as well as any man. We'll finish this for the Lieutenant if it kills every one of us."

"And you all support Hunter in this?" Older asked. "You believe his methods will work?"

"We do, sir," Francis responded. "Right now there is no one else."

"I should be chastised for even thinking this," Feeney said. "All right. Be smart and move fast. I'll sign the warrants the minute you bring me something. We were planning to arrest them all on Wednesday, the eighteenth. That may be all the time we have. Prosecuting them won't be easy. We could use a witness, someone who heard Rolf and Kelly arrange the murder, and we need those papers so we can connect them both to the crime."

"Christian," Sullivan added. "You sure you and the others are all behind Hunter on this? If there is any reservation or dissension, let's hear it now. Let's not compound sorrow with failure."

"He figured it out while the rest of us were napping, sir. He can do it." One by one the rest of The Brotherhood, even Max, nodded their consent.

"All right, Francis, you'll be the lead officer. I have the authority to appoint you special investigator," Feeney said. "Hunter will lead the evidence gathering. This isn't just a corruption probe anymore. This is murder of a police officer. They'll be digging in with a fury, so Godspeed to all of you."

Sullivan, Feeney, and Older walked away solemnly, leaving The Brotherhood on the windy hilltop overlooking Byron Fallon's grave.

"All right," Francis said, "the Lieutenant is watching over us. We close ranks, do this right. What happened is over. Understood?"

The group nodded.

"Good. Then let's get on with it."

The funeral party left Laurel Hill.

In the lead carriage, the weight of his father's death bore down on Hunter. Byron's lifelong dream had disintegrated into terror and desperation, with neither of his disobedient sons to help him. Hunter's tears fell, spotting his black trousers as the carriage wobbled down Fulton Street.

Across from Hunter, a grim Christian tried to comfort his weeping wife and children.

The carriage had just passed Fillmore Street when a patrolman spotted them and motioned frantically. Christian yelled for the driver to stop and jumped from the carriage, Hunter on his heels.

"What is it, Franz?" Christian demanded.

"Shanghai Kelly. Just got word on the call box he's throwing a party down on the Barbary Coast. Standing drinks for everyone."

"What's the occasion?" Christian asked.

"He's celebrating your father's death."

"Is he? Hunter, tell the driver to move the families to one carriage, you and me will ride with The Brotherhood. A party like that is worth attendin'."

Chapter 33

BARBARY COAST

APRIL 17, 1906. 11:00 A.M.

In the cluttered office behind his saloon, Shanghai Kelly yelled into the telephone, trying to be heard over the din of revelers outside. "What do you want me to tell ya'? I ain' got 'em. I got my best men looking but I ain't heard nothin' yet."

"Well, the dogs are nipping at our heels," Rolf shouted on the other end. "Fallon's sons found Gamboa's body out on Angel Island and con-nected him to Chief Donen. I want those papers, Kelly. And I better not find out you're working me again." He slammed the receiver into the cradle.

Kelly's bartender, Charlie Katevas, a hulking Greek with a face like a broken dinner plate, stuck his head inside the office. "You got little problem, Boss."

"And what might that be?"

"Christian Fallon is outside, he is scream your name."

"Then let's not keep the young man waitin'."

Kelly shoved his way through the crowded bar and swaggered out into the sunlight.

A phalanx of five hundred whores, thugs, and gamblers lined Battery Street, swaying from Kelly's rot-gut bourbon. They cheered wildly when he raised his arms. Kelly laughed. His bartenders would later slip laudanum into the booze and deliver enough bodies to fill every ship left crewless by the crackdown of The Brotherhood.

Kelly sauntered to the middle of the crowded street, where Christian stood with Hunter and The Brotherhood, all still dressed in mourning suits.

"Ahh, the bloody gang's all here." Kelly yelled. "Now, what seems to be the problem, Officer Fallon?"

"I hear you're celebrating my father's death," Christian shouted.

"S'matter of fact, we are. We're imbibin' a little Pisco Punch and some good cheap somethin' that might be bourbon, then again, it might not. We was figurin' on taking the trolley out to dance on his dirty grave a little later. Don't recall any city ordinance against it."

Hunter looked uneasily at Max. "What the Hell is he doing? We have more important business than this."

"Let 'em get away with this so no cop is safe down here?" Max said. "Just keep smiling, Hunter. They see a trickle of sweat and you're a dead man. Keep your hand on your revolver and your eyes wide open and you might learn something."

Christian took a step closer to Kelly and stretched his arms out to the side, playing to the crowd.

"Ah, but there is an ordinance against it, Shanghai."

"And which one might that be, sonny?"

"The one I'm about to tattoo across the face of the biggest motherless whore on the Barbary Coast."

The crowd convulsed with howls and laughter. Kelly's mustache inched upward into a defiant smirk. He pulled out a hundred-dollar bill, raised it above his head and gave it a crisp snap.

"You a sportin' man, Officer Fallon?"

"I'm a sportin' man, Miss Kelly."

In an instant, gamblers began to circulate through the crowd, soliciting bets.

Christian walked to The Brotherhood, peeled off his jacket and vest, and handed them to his brother. "If you were smart, Hunter, you'd get a bet down. Judging by the fact Kelly's got thirty pounds on me, you should get three to two for your money."

"This is crazy, Christian. We have other needs besides making a circus down here."

"What we need is to restore the natural order of things," Christian replied.

"Who you doing this for, dad or yourself?"

For the first time since Byron's disappearance, Christian managed to look Hunter in the eye. "I'm sorry for what I did. I'll go to my grave sorry."

"Then let me fight him. I'm his size, you're not."

Christian clapped his brother gently on the head. "You gotta stop trying to save everybody, Hunter. This is my way, not yours. One in the family is enough."

Christian peeled off his shirt and laid it atop his jacket. He flexed his knuckles, thick from years pounding the weighted bag. His rock-hard torso offered a road map of close calls; a scar on his bicep where a bullet had passed, a jagged scar where an ice pick had nicked a kidney, another on his clavicle from an encounter with an anchor chain.

Hunter looked over at Shanghai Kelly, also now stripped to the waist, baring the chest and shoulders of a blacksmith and a stomach like a stack of cordwood.

"What a fine day this is," Kelly bellowed. "Byron Fallon sleeps with the worms and me, a simple son of Belfast, has the honor to put a lacin' on his bastard son."

Christian smiled and stretched his arms overhead. "Keep talking, Kelly. The more you talk, the worse the beating I'm going to give you."

"Do we have a bet here, Officer Fallon? Shall we say a hundred? Maybe two?"

"Let's make it five."

"A lot of money for a flatfoot cop. Will you be payin' when it's over?"

"I'll be paying my condolences to your next of kin."

The crowd roared, circling the combatants in a forty-foot human ring.

Christian started to raise his fists, changed his mind, and lowered them slowly. He leaned forward, pointing to his chin, offering Kelly the first blow.

Kelly raised his ham hock fists and shuffled forward.

Christian stood still, inching his chin closer.

Kelly launched a vicious right at Christian's jaw, missing by a foot. The force spun him around, whereupon Christian kicked him squarely in the seat of his pants. The crowd gagged on its laughter.

Kelly gritted his teeth, his face flushed, and squared up. Christian leaned his chin forward and another Kelly right found nothing but air. The crowd howled.

"You come to fight like a man or dance like a damn sissy?" Kelly bellowed.

Christian got up on his toes and danced a little jig, swinging his hips from side to side, rousing Kelly to fury. Then he launched an overhand right that caught Kelly flush on the mouth and sent him to the cobble-stones.

"I'll kill you, you little bastard, I'll kill you!"

"This is no good," Hunter muttered to Francis.

"Have some faith in your brother," Francis replied.

Kelly scrambled to his feet and charged.

Christian slowed him with a left jab and straightened him with a right uppercut, and then danced away.

"I'll kill you and dump you in the box with your old man."

"The more you talk, the worse the beating you get, remember?"

Kelly circled deliberately, backing Christian toward the crowd. Kelly swung a roundhouse left and an overhand right, which Christian ducked. Kelly moved in again. He faked a roundhouse, then lowered his head and charged.

As Christian stepped backward to avoid the charge, he stumbled.

Shanghai Kelly hit him like a bloodied bull avenging itself. He lifted Christian off his feet and slammed him to the ground with a sicken-ing thud, kneeling quickly on his chest. Kelly landed a vicious right to Christian's jaw that bounced the back of his head against the cobblestones.

Max pinned one of Hunter's arms to his side while Carlo grabbed the other.

"You stay out of this," Max growled softly, "Christian started it and Christian finishes it."

Kelly landed another right to Christian's face, then another. Kelly's fist came up again, red with blood from Christian's nose and mouth.

Hunter tried to break free but Max and Carlo tightened their grip.

As Kelly's fist came down again, Christian freed an arm, lunged to grab Kelly's hair, and jerked him forward. Kelly's fist thudded against the curb.

Christian landed a short hook to Kelly's face, threw him clear, and sprung to his feet. He wiped the blood from his mouth, waiting for Kelly to rise. The instant Kelly's feet were beneath him, Christian moved in, landing a right hook to Kelly's ribs.

"Come on, Christian," Hunter yelled, "kill him!"

Kelly charged, throwing punches from every angle.

Christian backpedaled, using his quickness to counter Kelly's attack.

Kelly caught Christian flush with a left hook that staggered him, and then moved in.

Christian sidestepped, fighting back furiously, jabbing to Kelly's face and hooking to his body. The crowd grew quiet, holding its breath.

Kelly pounded away at Christian's ribs.

Christian fired back with combinations; three, four, five punches at a time, tearing at Kelly's fleshy face. Blood poured from Kelly's mouth and nose, covering Christian's fists in a sticky mess.

Still Kelly came, banging away furiously at Christian's midsection. Christian countered, peppering his opponent's face. When Kelly's hands came up, Christian attacked his ribs with short, vicious punches.

Kelly lunged forward and caught Christian with an uppercut, staggering him. His torso red with blood streaming from his nose and mouth, Kelly pushed his advantage.

Christian recovered, planted his feet, and landed an overhand right that sent Kelly flying into two prostitutes.

The crowd lifted Kelly and threw him back into the middle. He spat a mass of blood and raised his scarlet fists.

"Kill him, Shanghai," the rabble yelled.

Christian spat a mouthful of blood.

Kelly, chest heaving and eyes bulging in fury, charged at Christian, firing a lethal right.

Christian turned his head in time to deflect the blow. He sprang to his toes, dodging every wild blow that Kelly offered; leaning clear of a jab, ducking below a hook, leaning away from Kelly's uppercuts.

When Kelly waned and gasped for air, Christian counterattacked. A jab to the mouth, a right cross to the ear, a left to the jaw. He pummeled Kelly's ribs and stomach, the blows taking their toll.

Kelly lunged, caught Christian in a bear hug, and tried to squeeze the life from him. Slick with blood and sweat, Christian slipped his arms free, grabbed Kelly's head, and butted the bridge of his nose, the crack echoing down Battery Street.

Kelly dropped him, half-blind and bellowing in rage.

The crowd winced as Christian stepped in and pressed his assault. A right cross to the jaw, a left hook to the ribs, an uppercut to the solar plexus that lifted Kelly to his tiptoes. When Kelly sagged to his right, Christian straightened him with a left.

A straight right hand knocked Kelly out cold on his feet. Christian hoisted him on his shoulder, staggered thirty yards, and heaved him into San Francisco Bay. The water parted and settled back, turning red.

The Brotherhood sprinted to Christian's side. Hunter used his shirt tail to wipe his brother's bloody face.

"Don't you try to save him," Christian told his brother. "He drowns, it'll just save me havin' to shoot him."

Christian clapped Hunter on the shoulder, forced a smile, then turned and bellowed to the crowd. "This bar is closed! I catch any man, anywhere on the Barbary Coast with anything to say about my father, he'll get worse than Kelly!"

Hunter put Christian's jacket around him, examining the cowed and impassive faces of the onlookers.

Order had been restored.

Chapter 34

———— ·◆◇◆· ————

HALL OF JUSTICE

APRIL 17, 1906. 11:20 A.M.

Six blocks from the bare-knuckle bout outside Shanghai Kelly's saloon, a carriage from the Palace Hotel stopped at the Hall of Justice.

"Much obliged," Lincoln said to the driver.

"You're welcome, Sheriff."

Lincoln paused to marvel at the collection of humanity across the street; garish whores and pigtailed Chinese, scarred sailors and jaunty Negroes, savvy pimps and sweet-faced school kids teeming through Portsmouth Square in jerky syncopation to the honking horns and tinkling saloon music.

He pushed into the Hall of Justice, walking purposefully to the scarred desk where the duty sergeant sat riffling papers.

"I'm looking for Chief Donen."

"He's a bit irked at the moment," the desk sergeant said. "We just buried the Chief of Detectives and the scribblers been on him like flies, but try your luck. Fifth floor."

Lincoln made his way to the elevator, past a squad room where half a dozen patrolmen played poker on a wobbly table.

Arriving on the fifth floor, he spotted the burly chief inside a glass-lined office.

"Chief Donen?"

Donen was busy digging through Byron's desk. He slammed a drawer shut without looking up. "Who the hell are you?"

"Lincoln Staley, Sheriff of Douglas County, Kansas."

Donen found a letter opener and went to work on a drawer lock, barely registering Lincoln's presence.

"I'm looking for my daughter."

"Somebody snatch her?"

"Runaway. Caught the train a couple of days ago."

"Wanted all that stuff she couldn't get in Kansas, right?"

Lincoln remained silent.

"How old is she?"

"Fifteen. Probably passing for older. Big girl. Tall for her age."

Staley handed over the photograph of Kaitlin.

Donen stopped and whistled softly. "She's a beauty. Look, we got four hundred and fifty thousand people in this city, Sheriff. A thousand new vagabonds show up every week. Kids by the boxcar, bloody runaway capital of the world. As if I ain't got enough headaches already." He looked at Lincoln. "You packin' a sidearm?"

Lincoln slid back his duster.

"You any good with that thing?"

"We already buried them that ain't."

"Try to keep the thing holstered while you're here. There's a board downstairs, you can post her photograph. No promises."

Lincoln returned to the first floor and entered the squad room. Beneath a handmade sign that read "MISSING PERSONS," he found an entire wall covered with school pictures, wedding photos, candid snapshots, pencil drawings, and watercolors, tacked on top of each other an inch thick. Some of the missing looked no older than eight or nine.

He put Kaitlin's photo in the inside pocket of his duster and walked out, his disgust for big cities and big city cops growing by the second.

Six blocks east, Kaitlin crossed Market Street and made her way to the Palace Hotel. There she entered the Garden Room, filled with the syrupy smell of violets, as a string quartet played *"Danza Pastorale"* from Vivaldi's *I Quatro Stagioni*.

"Hello, Kaitlin."

She turned to find a smiling Andrew Tavish.

"My, you look different. Did you find a place to stay?"

"A little boardinghouse on Union Street, right on Washington Square with a nice Italian lady."

"I know the place. You're very lucky."

Kaitlin looked toward the lounge, where Assistant Professor of Geology Jeremy Darling rose from his armchair and started toward her. "Andrew," she said. "If anyone should come around asking, not that they would, I don't want anyone to know where I'm really staying. I sort of let on I was staying here. Please. That's why I'm meeting my friend here."

"Is that your beau?"

"I met him on the train; he's offered to escort me for the day."

"A gal's gotta be careful in San Francisco."

Excusing herself, she walked to Jeremy, extending a gloved hand.

The sight of her sent Jeremy's heart careening. "Kaitlin, my gosh, you look so different! What did you do?"

"I had my hair cut and dyed. Henna, actually. Some man named Emperor Milton gave me this strange money last night, with his picture on it. They accept it everywhere in San Francisco. Do you like my hair?"

"It's quite different."

"So, where are you taking me?"

"On a picnic."

Kaitlin's jaw dropped as she gazed toward the elevators. Jeremy followed her stare.

Enrico Caruso, dressed in a pencil-striped gray suit and a coal black Borsalino hat, walked directly toward them. As he passed, the great tenor gazed up at Kaitlin and smiled, the corners of his mustache rising with the olive cheeks.

Kaitlin appeared ready to faint. She was so engrossed in the sight of Caruso that she did not recognize me walking just behind him.

"So," I said, slowing to address her. "You managed to survive your first day in San Francisco."

"My gosh. Annalisa. The reporter. Are you accompanying Mr. Caruso?"

"I'm his translator, not that he really needs one. We're on our way to rehearsals. Enjoy your stay."

I hurried to catch Caruso, who smiled back at Kaitlin, bowing slightly.

She held a gloved hand to her mouth. "My God, I don't believe it. No one back home would believe this! This is heaven."

"My aunt lent us a carriage," Jeremy resumed. "She packed us a lunch." He tried gamely not to stare at her, but it was useless.

She took his arm and walked to the carriage entrance. Kaitlin was a half-head taller, and Jeremy self-consciously tried to avoid the stares of all they passed. He helped Kaitlin into the carriage, handed a nickel to the livery man, and climbed in next to her. They headed out through the archway and onto the cobblestone street, turning south.

"What are those boxes and tripod for? Are you a photographer as well?"

"I have to take some photographs and measurements near the lake where we're going. I thought you might find it interesting. I've been monitoring a fault line."

"A what?"

"I told you on the train, remember? Where one big earthen plate pushes against another, that's called a fault line. The biggest one we know of runs down the middle of the San Francisco Peninsula. When they move abruptly, that's when you have an earthquake."

"As I said before, I'm not planning on having any earthquakes while I'm here. And I plan on being here for a very long time."

Kaitlin watched the scenery swim by as they swung along El Camino Real, skirting the shimmering blue bay. She loosened the buttons of her burgundy waistcoat and breathed the salt air, leaning her head back to feel the warm April sun on her face.

"My God. Is there anything about San Francisco that isn't wonderful?" she asked, her memory of the previous night's travails quickly fading.

An hour later, Jeremy turned off the main highway and spurred the horse up a narrow dirt road, where wild coastal sage and purple bush lupine perfumed the crisp breeze. Atop a ridge overlooking a crystal blue lake, he stopped the carriage.

He ran quickly to Kaitlin's side and helped her down. "Welcome to San Andreas Lake. Are you hungry? Or shall I take my measurements first?"

"I had a biscuit and coffee in this darling little café in North Beach. In Kansas, most places won't even serve a woman by herself. Let's walk and build up an appetite."

She smiled her big, gleaming smile. He stared back like a lovesick adolescent.

At the south end of the lake, Jeremy adjusted the legs of the tripod and screwed a brass instrument atop it as a fascinated Kaitlin looked on.

"What is that thing?"

"A transom. It's for surveying. Road construction and building layouts, mostly. I use it to determine soil and rock movement."

He focused the transom and stared through it, swinging it in a small arc several times. He pulled away from the eyepiece with a look of concern, checked his settings, and sighted again.

"My God. It's moving."

"What's moving?"

"The fault line. You see those stakes over there, along each side of San Andreas Creek, where it feeds into the lake?"

Kaitlin squinted and pulled the enormous brim of her hat lower to shade her eyes.

"Here," he said. "You can see better through this."

She tipped her hat back and put her eye up to the transom.

"Do you see how those stakes are not in line with each other?"

"Yes."

"When I left for New York they were perfectly in line. It looks like the fault line has moved several inches in just the last few months."

"I don't understand."

"If the plates move without causing a tremor, I believe the pressure is building somewhere. North of here would be my guess."

"You're frightening me, Jeremy. What's going on?"

"People at the university think I'm daft, that's why I'm still an assistant professor." He rubbed his hands together nervously. "Yesterday," he continued, "I stopped at a dairy farm in Berkeley. Three heifers dropped their calves prematurely in the past two weeks. The county dogcatcher has dozens of reports of cats and dogs running away and every horse within miles has been on edge."

"You've lost me. What do heifers and lost cats have to do with earthquakes?"

"Everything." He looked at Kaitlin glumly. "If you don't mind, I'd like to take a few more measurements before we eat."

"Fine with me. I'm starting to lose my appetite."

Chapter 35

NOB HILL

APRIL 17, 1906. 1:50 P.M.

On a telephone pole across from Adam Rolf's mansion on Mason Street, a repairman donned climbing spikes and quickly ascended to the top. The workmen hustling in and out of the Fairmont, attending to details for the next day's opening, scarcely noticed.

Hunter Fallon, an oversized black beret hiding his face, reached the top of the pole and began to unbolt a junction box when a Rolls Royce, with Tommy at the wheel and Rolf beside him, lurched onto Mason Street just below.

Hunter pressed his face against the pole until the Rolls turned into the circular livery entrance and disappeared behind the mansion. Sweat trickled down Hunter's face as he quickly spliced into Rolf's telephone line.

When he finished, he shimmied to the ground and hurried inside the Fairmont, blending with the army of workers scurrying through the lobby.

Inside his mansion, Rolf entered the expansive kitchen where Pierre's former *sous* chef oversaw a half-dozen helpers preparing the evening's banquet. "Malcolm! Have I received any phone calls?"

"A Mr. Clyde Ebbens telephoned from the Senator's office in Sacramento," Malcolm replied. "He said he would be phoning you back sometime this afternoon."

"How about Mr. Kelly?"

"Nothing from a Mr. Kelly."

Rolf reached into a brass tub piled high with ice and extricated a crab. "How many do we have?"

"Six dozen, sir."

"Telephone Alioto's at the wharf and get another six dozen. And make sure they're fresh. I don't want Mr. Caruso or the Senator getting the runs like people at the last party."

Rolf left the kitchen and strode into his study, where he locked the door behind him. He threw his bowler hat onto the desk and went to his safe, deftly spinning the numbers. He pulled open the massive steel door and extracted ten bundles of hundred-dollar bills, one hundred thousand dollars, and placed the money into a portfolio. He took the accounting ledger from the top shelf of the safe and set it atop the blotter on his desk.

He opened the red leather cover and froze. The ledger was upside down. He replayed his movements, checking that he hadn't turned it inadvertently. He looked back at the safe, wondering if he could have returned it improperly when he last replaced it. It was not a mistake he had made before.

He walked to his office door and opened it. "Tommy," he called out, "fetch the Rolls and let's get to the Opera House."

At the rear of the Fairmont, Carlo steadied a dump cart while Max set blocks before each wheel.

"What the hell is this contraption?" Max asked Hunter above the blanket-covered cargo. "We like to bust a gut moving the damn thing."

"I'll explain upstairs. We have to hurry, Rolf is home."

They rolled the machine through the chaotic lobby, into the elevator, barely making it through the doorway into room 434.

"All right, damn it," Max demanded as Hunter removed the cover, "What the hell is this thing?"

"A Victor recording machine, same kind Caruso uses in New York. Only one like it in San Francisco. Feeney said we need someone who overheard Rolf and Kelly discussing the murder of my father. I'm going to fix it so he and the jury can hear for themselves."

"You're one of those modernist clowns," Max growled. "Got a dentist livin' two doors down, last month he puts a toilet in the closet next to his bedroom. Too lazy to use his outhouse, so he shits in the house. Every time I see one of those cars stinkin' up the streets, scarin' the horses, I'd like to put a round up his ass."

"Get used to it, Max," Hunter replied. "Someday everybody will be shitting in the house."

While Max, Carlo, and a battered Christian watched in bewilderment, Hunter wired the earpiece of the telephone to the horn of my Gramophone. He then set it six inches from the square brass horn on the recording machine.

"I learned this trick from Thomas Edison when I visited his plant in New Jersey last summer. The electrical impulse running through a wire can feed more than one telephone. Whenever Rolf talks to someone, their voices will travel through this auxiliary telephone. The sound is amplified by the horn attached to the earpiece, then passes through the recording horn onto the revolving disk."

"Y-y-you think R-R-Rolf is go-going to discuss kill-killing the-the-the Lieu-Lieutenant?" Carlo asked.

"I doubt Rolf wants to be in the same room with Shanghai Kelly, except to exchange the money and the documents. Rolf has a private line, not a party line. He would never dream that someone is tapping into his conversations. If we get lucky, Adam Rolf will be the first man ever to hang himself with his own telephone line."

"Max is right," Christian said. "This is way over my head."

"Wave of the future, gentleman. Climb on board or step aside," Hunter said.

"I can see every cop in the country rolling one of these things around to listen in on somebody's telephone," Max said. "Nothin's better than a good old-fashioned beating."

"I think that's the optimum phrase," Hunter replied. "Old-fashioned."

Chapter 36

———•⟨∞⟩•———

GRAND OPERA HOUSE

APRIL 17, 1906. 2:00 P.M.

A mile below Nob Hill, at the Grand Opera House, Enrico Caruso was engaged in a battle of his own.

"They're buffoons," Olive Fremstad bellowed. "Look at them. Tripping over each other's feet! They couldn't afford a professional chorus because *you* got all the money."

Fremstad, the two-hundred-pound Teutonic soprano who thought opera died with Wagner, had little use for the Verdi- and Puccini-loving Caruso.

Hertz set his baton aside. "Be reasonable, Olive. We're tired. We have all come a long way."

"Reasonable? I'll show you reasonable! I quit! I will not work under these circumstances," she yelled.

Caruso pulled himself up and leaned close to Fremstad. "You know what is happen in thees place last night? The audience is hate *Queen of Sheba*, they are almost make a riot. Now you are quit on Caruso? I tell you somethings, you stuffed cow. You are sing best Carmen in your fat life tonight. Or I make sure you are never sing in any Opera House where Caruso sings."

Fremstad turned purple and stormed off, the floor squeaking under her furious gait.

"Enrico, Enrico, please," Hertz implored as sixty fully dressed gypsies and Spanish dragoons watched their dream disintegrate. "You know Olive is temperamental."

"I am tell you in New York that I do not wish to be in same city with thees woman. Or come to thees crazy place."

"Enrico, please. We need her. After the performance last night we must show these people the greatness of Caruso. We cannot do that without our Carmen."

Caruso took a deep breath and stretched the collar of his shirt, allowing the color in his face to drift toward normal. He stared at the *chorines* who had all been staring at him. "You tell Olive that I no insult her but she no insult Caruso. You tell her she is sing tonight or she is *finita*."

"I will, Enrico." Hertz signaled for the understudy, a petite Dutch woman, to take Fremstad's place.

She moved close to Enrico, barely able to look at him. The cigarette girls returned to the mock factory and prepared to enter the mock plaza with their substitute Carmen.

I sat in the wings, scribbling quickly. I looked up into the auditorium and saw a door open in the box of Adam Rolf. The silhouettes of two men passed through the rectangle of light and the door closed behind them. I slid my chair behind the stage curtain, safely out of sight, and fished my opera glasses from my bag, cursing as I struggled to adjust the worn-out focus knob.

In his box, Adam Rolf removed his bowler and held his hand out to his guest. It took me a few moments to recognize the pointed goatee, slicked-back hair, and long, aquiline nose of William H. Herrin, whose appearance earned him constant lampooning as the Devil. He was chief counsel of the Southern Pacific Railroad, a political fixer and power broker for one of the nation's most powerful trusts, a man bereft of principles and flush with bribery funds.

After several minutes of what appeared to be a heated discussion, Rolf and Herrin smiled and shook hands again. Rolf clapped Herrin on the shoulder. Then Herrin left.

I stowed my notes and walked swiftly toward the stage door.

I bolted to the California Street cable car six blocks away and hopped aboard. As the cable car hit the steep grade above Kearny, I stared up at the onion-domed Stanford Mansion, the towering Hopkins Art Institute, and the sandstone Fairmont.

I jumped off below the Nob Hill summit and ran inside the Fairmont, barely slowing until I reached room 434.

Hunter answered my knock and pulled me inside, where I spotted my disassembled Gramophone, its horn mounted to a telephone and face-to-face with an even larger horn.

"I hope you can put that back together," I said sternly.

"I've done it many times."

I stared at the enormous machine, trying to identify it.

"We're going to record Adam Rolf's phone conversations on a disk."

"You can do that?"

"Haven't tried yet, but it should work."

I looked to the opposite corner and caught a glimpse of Christian's battered face.

"I heard you and Shanghai Kelly had a slight altercation," I said.

"Don't tell me you were dad's secret witness," Christian said.

I looked at Hunter for approval, then smiled and nodded. The pain on Christian's face seemed little to do with his injuries.

I turned to Hunter. "I think I know what Rolf is up to, why he's bribing the Senator. Can you leave here for an hour?"

"Christian. When the telephone rings, just throw the switch. When the disk runs out, flip it over. When that's finished, replace it as fast as you can. Write down the time they called and who is talking if you can."

"They can't hear me?"

"I only wired the ear piece, not the mouth piece. You can scream and cuss at them all you like."

Moments later, we were roaring down California Street on the Waltham, past the Southern Pacific Station on Townsend. We followed the Bay Shore Highway, gaining speed until we reached El Camino Real.

South of San Carlos, I tapped Hunter's shoulder. He swung onto a narrow dirt road, which he followed for several miles. The air grew saltier and cooler as we approached the bay.

He killed the engine and hid the motorcycle in a thicket, careful not to let anything touch the engine or exhaust pipe.

We followed a path through the high thistles and up a sandy hill until we reached the crest. Below lay a wide marsh that disappeared into the crystal blue water of the bay. Wagons dotted the flats as white bosses and Chinese laborers ran about. A steam engine powered a massive pump sucking water from the marsh. Behind it, a rusted paddy shovel threw dirt and garbage atop the muck. Two giant steamrollers followed and compressed the reclaimed land into a flat surface.

"I came down here with Rolf for a luncheon at the Ralston mansion in Belmont a few weeks ago, hoping I might find something of interest for your father."

I produced my opera glasses and handed them to Hunter.

He fiddled with the adjusting screw and examined the site below. "Must be a hundred men down there. Let's walk a little further."

Careful to stay out of view, we traveled along the ridge, well past the workers. After walking a mile or so, we spotted piles of heavy wooden timbers near freshly laid railroad tracks that stretched into the horizon.

"Surprise me, Annalisa. Tell me Adam Rolf owns all this land."

"Who else would buy up useless swampland in San Mateo County? Rolf asked me how a railroad line would look running through here. I thought he was making a joke."

"I'm still not sure what this has to do with bribing the Senator."

"About an hour ago I saw Rolf shaking hands with William Herrin, chief counsel of the Southern Pacific Railroad. He and Rolf have been at odds since Rolf got Schmitz elected Mayor over Herrin's lackey in the Republican Party."

"They fight every time there's an election," Hunter said, "then they kiss and make up whenever there's money that needs stealing." He was temporarily drowned out by squawking gulls overhead. "Rolf controls San Francisco, but Herrin and his boss, E. H. Harriman, control everything else in this country."

"Rolf just made some kind of deal with them," I said.

Hunter clasped his hands behind his head and walked anxiously in a circle.

"My God," he muttered, "I don't believe this."

He stopped and pointed across the bay. "You see that finger of land jutting into the water? Dumbarton Point. Shortest distance across San Francisco Bay is from here to Dumbarton. Right now, the transcontinental railroad terminus is in Oakland, not San Francisco. If the government authorized a Dumbarton Bridge, the railroad could bypass Oakland, cross the bay, and run all the way to the San Francisco waterfront. You marry shipping and railroad together, you couldn't move a crate of lettuce, a ton of steel, or a bolt of silk from Tokyo to New York without Rolf and Herrin taking a cut. They could buy anyone. The White House, the whole damn country would be theirs."

"That's what the hundred-thousand-dollar bribe to Senator Payton is for," I said. "Rolf's going to get the federal government to pay for it, just like Stanford and Crocker did when they built the railroad. Even this swamp would be worth millions. One endless row of little bedrooms from San Francisco to San José. That hundred-thousand-dollar bribe is just a down payment."

"It's tonight," Hunter said, grim and emotional. "Tonight was going to be my father's triumph. Now it's Rolf's. All he had to do was eliminate my father, the one man with the fortitude to bring him down. This is it. Tonight we get them all."

He raised my opera glasses and stared along the marsh.

"What is it, Hunter?"

"You see that section? Where the tracks are meandering, like a long, slow S?"

He handed me the opera glasses. I watched as several apprehensive-looking men walked along the twisted section taking measurements and shaking their heads in bewilderment.

"When we were doing the water survey for Chief Sullivan, we helped a geologist from Berkeley map a lake about twenty miles from here. That big earthquake fault they discovered runs right through the middle of it."

"The San Andreas."

"Professor Darling believes earthquakes give off warning signs and nobody listens to them," Hunter said. "This is bad. Filled land is the worst. That bend in the tracks means the fault is moving."

---◦◦∞◦◦---

Chapter 37

PALACE HOTEL

APRIL 17, 1906. 3:30 P.M.

Jeremy Darling stopped the carriage on Market Street, near the corner of New Montgomery. "You sure you want me to let you out here, Kaitlin? I thought you'd like pulling into the Grand Court."

"This is fine." She extended her hand. "It was a wonderful afternoon, Jeremy. I can't thank you enough."

"Kaitlin?"

She was suddenly distracted, staring toward Montgomery Street.

"Kaitlin? I know I'm not one of those wealthy San Francisco nabobs. I'm not even a full professor yet, but I hope to be soon."

Kaitlin did not hear a word. She was frozen in her tracks, staring with a look of horror.

Jeremy failed to notice. "I was hoping I might call on you in a more formal manner. I feel it imperative to be honest about my feelings."

Kaitlin was oblivious to Jeremy's overtures. She saw the telltale Stetson bobbing above the crowd, then the tan duster. Her mouth fell open as her father stepped off the curb and started across Market Street in her direction. She skirted behind the carriage.

"Kaitlin, what's wrong? Why are you hiding like that?"

"Quiet, Jeremy! Don't say my name."

Kaitlin trembled as Lincoln crossed twenty feet in front of Jeremy's carriage and disappeared behind the corner of the Palace. When her father was out of sight, she dashed across Market Street without a word. Jeremy stared, confounded, as Kaitlin ran up Kearny and disappeared from view.

She ran through the Financial District, her panicked look attracting as much attention as her beauty. She passed Portsmouth Square and the Hall of Justice, finally slowing beneath the unfinished, triangular-shaped skeleton of the Rolf Building. She moved on through teeming North Beach until finally tromping up the stairway of her boardinghouse.

Safely inside, she sagged against the wall in her tiny room and wondered how Lincoln had tracked her so quickly. Then she noticed her carpetbag and sketchbook were missing from the chair where she had left them. She jerked open the faded bureau where she had carefully arranged her clothes. Empty. She heard footsteps in the hallway and wheeled to find Francesca drying her hands on a stained apron.

"Where are my things? What did you do with all my clothes and my drawings?"

"You are lie to me, Kaitlin. Thees is why you cut off hairs and make different colors, so you can a' hide."

"What?"

"Your pimp, 'e is come thees morning and look for you."

"My what?"

"Some French mans with leetle mustache and *brutti* teeth. He ees tell me you are in troubles with police. He is take your things."

"Why did you let him do that?"

"He says you stole much monies from him. He have a policeman downstairs who tells me thees is true." Francesca pulled a slip of paper from her apron pocket. "'Ere is address where he is take your things. He is say if you bring back his monies, he gives back your things."

Kaitlin's hand shook as she tried to read the scrawl on the paper.

"Ees on Jackson Street, on Barbary Coast where all thees other whores is working. Now, you go from a' my 'ouse."

Kaitlin ran down the stairs and into Washington Square, collapsing on a park bench. She stared through teary eyes at the children and lovers basking in the warm sunlight. After a few moments she fought back the tears, and walked stiffly to Montgomery Street.

After six blocks, she stopped and stared down Jackson Street to the Barbary Coast, rife with the noise of honky-tonk pianos and an unsettling odor. Barkers called to passersby, trying to entice them into sampling the house's wares.

She braced herself and started forward, forcing each foot in front of the other. Several wary-eyed whores stared from balconies above.

Two blocks later, she stopped and looked up in disbelief, checking the slip of paper for confirmation. The building stood in stark contrast to the neighborhood. The green four-story Victorian sported a wide, pillared porch, double leaded-glass entrance doors, and windows shaded by lace curtains.

A burly Negro doorman dressed in a butler's suit stood at the front door and examined her sternly. "May ah he'p you, Miss?"

"I was given this number by someone."

"Well, excuse me, ma'am, but that don't tell me a whole lot now, do it?"

"A man with a French accent," Kaitlin said haltingly. "He was on the train. His name was Anton."

"Yo' means Antoine? Got his self a little thin mustache."

"He took my things and told the lady where I was staying a bunch of lies about me."

"Thass Antoine. Lass time he tol' the truth the devil was in sho't pants."

He turned the large brass handle of the door, letting it drift open slowly.

"I ain't going in there till I see Antoine and get my things back."

"Miss Tessie, she takes care all the bidness here. Yo' wants sumpin', yo' talks to Miss Tessie."

Kaitlin stepped hesitantly toward the porch.

"Ain't nobodies gonna hurt you, ma'am, ain't that kind of place. Now, you wants to speak to Miss Tessie . . ."

Kaitlin gathered herself and stepped through the open door. It clicked softly shut behind her.

"Do you have an appointment?" a voice with a soft French lilt inquired.

Kaitlin turned to find a doe-eyed woman in a maid's outfit.

"I'm here to get my things back. The colored man outside told me to see someone named Tessie."

"I'm Tessie," a voice called.

Kaitlin stepped through the wide parlor entrance onto the Turkish carpet, the full expanse of the room coming into view. Even in her frightened state, the room seized her attention. Chintz curtains, ornate Chippendale loveseats, and a gold-edged fireplace highlighted a room larger than her house in Kansas.

Tessie Wall stepped forward, dressed in flowery brocades of satin. The body matched the voice: thick, brassy, and domineering. "You must be Kaitlin. Antoine told me you and he had a nice journey together on the train."

"That filthy little worm stared at me the entire time. Now he steals my things and tells my landlady I'm a whore. I came to get my clothes and drawings back."

"Nicolette, would you get her belongings and bring them here?"

"Yes, ma'am."

"Have you eaten? I have a chef here, quite a good one."

"No, thank you. I just want to get my things and leave."

"Leave for where? Home?"

Kaitlin trembled. "This is a whorehouse, isn't it?"

Tessie smiled. "My girls are courtesans. Those girls you passed on the street, those are whores. My girls are rewarded for beauty and intelligence. They provide companionship and conversation, they are treated like princesses."

"They're whores who dress better."

"My girls have married some of San Francisco's most prominent men. Tonight you'll find them in their opera boxes, explaining the intricacies of *Carmen* to their husbands."

"Must be hard to do with her head in his lap," Kaitlin said, recalling the sight of Antoine's "cousin" delivering a "Parisian Kiss" on the train.

Tessie laughed aloud.

Nicolette arrived with Kaitlin's carpetbag and sketchbook.

"You'll find all your things are intact," Tessie said. "I'll reprimand Antoine when I see him. You're welcome to take them and leave."

Kaitlin stared down at her faded bag, unsure of what to do.

"Why don't you sit a spell?"

"Why?"

"I'm not an evil woman. I have never forced a girl to do anything against her will. You look like you've had a spell of bad luck. I'll call the Palace and get a room for you as my guest. How would you like to see Caruso tonight?"

Kaitlin's head swam from fatigue and fear. She stared at Tessie.

"And what do I have to do for all this?"

"You have to be nice to someone. Someone very important."

"How nice?"

"Just be nice. Nothing more."

"Who is it?"

"Adam Rolf, the most powerful man in San Francisco. President of the

Opera Association. City Attorney. He can open more doors for you than anyone in San Francisco."

"And just where do those doors lead?"

"Why don't you think about it? I'll have Joseph call a cab. By the time you get to the Palace, your room will be waiting for you."

Kaitlin fought back tears. "What do I have to do for this room?"

"An unhappy girl is of no use to me, Kaitlin. What my girls do, they do of their own free will. They have lives and opportunities they never dreamed of."

"And this Adam Rolf?"

"He likes the company of attractive and sophisticated young ladies. You'll be amongst dozens of people, it would be impossible for anyone to do anything unacceptable. And you'll be seeing Caruso."

"I'll have to use a different name," Kaitlin said, "if I'm to stay at the Palace."

"The room is under my name," Tessie said. "It's a marvelous place. You think about it. I'll telephone after you get settled."

Kaitlin gave Tessie a last uncertain look as Nicolette took her carpetbag and headed toward the door.

On the front porch, Joseph raised a whistle and gave a long shrill blast. A horse-drawn Brougham appeared almost instantly. Joseph helped Kaitlin into the carriage.

Tessie watched through the window as they drove away. She walked to the rear of the house, into a small dining area.

Antoine was seated at the table, smiling his hare-lipped grin. "She is beautiful zees girl, yes?"

"You didn't tell me she was a redhead."

"She was no red head when I am see her on za train. Is even better now, yes? Wiss red head?"

"I'll tell Mr. Kelly you came through with your part of the bargain and delivered the girl. Come back tomorrow. If Mr. Rolf wants her, you'll get your bonus. Depending on what condition she is in when I get her back."

Antoine rose and bowed. "Is good when everyone makes mow-nees."

Chapter 38

---∙⟨∞⟩∙---

APRIL 17, 1906. 4:50 P.M.

Hunter stopped the Waltham in front of the City of Paris on Union Square, amidst a crowd dramatically larger and more animated than the usual dinner and theater throngs.

"Where are all these people going?" he asked me. "They can't all fit into the Opera House."

"They just want to breathe the air Caruso breathes," I answered, my legs cramped from the jarring trip.

"Annalisa. You can't go to the opera. If Scarface knows who you are, then Shanghai Kelly knows, and if he hasn't told Rolf yet, he will."

"Rolf would not dare try anything there. If he knows, I'll see it in his face. Just be at the Fairmont afterward so I can signal you from the party. A few more hours and we'll be done with all this craziness."

I threw my arms around his neck, kissed his face, and hurried away.

While I pushed through the heavy doors of the City of Paris for what I hoped would be the last of Adam Rolf's largesse, Hunter charged up Nob Hill. At the Fairmont, he stowed the motorcycle, went in the service entrance, and charged up four flights to the room.

"Anything happen, Christian?"

Christian pointed to a pile of black disks. "Let's see. The new chef ordered six dozen crabs, four more cases of champagne, and twelve boxes of cigars. Then Rolf called the City of Paris to have a dress delivered to the Palace. They're going to have to start making longer disks. I used up half of them on groceries."

Christian held up a disk and smiled. "But not this one."

Hunter grabbed it from his brother's hand. He disconnected the amplifying horn from the earpiece, re-attached it to the gramophone, and cranked the handle several times. The voices that came through were clear and strong.

"Mr. Rolf?"

"This is Mr. Rolf."

"This is Clyde Ebbens, the Senator's personal aide. We're up here in Sacramento, meeting with the Governor and some key state legislators. The Senator asked me to telephone to see if all the arrangements we discussed have been completed."

"I have the donation here in my office. We'll finish our arrangement at the party after the opera."

"Excellent. The Senator will be happy to hear that."

"How long will it take the Senator to introduce the bill on the railroad project?"

"The wheels are in motion. You can provide the services we discussed earlier?"

"I'm acquiring the Union Iron Works to manufacture the steel girders for the bridge. A crew is already laying tracks."

"Isn't that a little premature, Mr. Rolf?"

"Ambition breeds success, Mr. Ebbens. Please tell the Senator we're looking forward to seeing him this evening."

Two distinct clicks ended the recording.

"It works," Hunter cried.

He examined the face of his brother. Christian's upper lip and cheek were swollen and purple, but his left eye, nearly closed earlier, had shrunk considerably. Hunter noticed two small puncture marks on Christian's eyelid.

"Slimy little thing sucked so much blood he keeled over and died," Christian said, grimacing.

Hunter looked at the trashcan. A swollen leech lay in the bottom. "You might want to dump that thing out before some tourist from Missouri checks in and faints," he laughed.

Christian started to laugh and stopped himself, raising his left hand to the side of his face. He stared at his brother for a long moment. "I haven't had a drink in two days. It might be a while before I have another one."

"I think that would be a good thing."

Hunter watched a single tear slip from Christian's right eye and run down his cheek. Another followed and then another. Christian turned and held his head down.

"Gamboa might have killed you both, Christian. He probably would have killed Anthony, but he didn't have to. The weather was so bad Anthony never saw him."

Christian was about to answer when his jaw dropped and a stunned look spread across his face.

"What is it?"

Without replying, Christian bolted from the room, slamming the door so hard the molding creaked. He sprinted down the fire exit and onto California Street.

Hunter was left to worry what havoc his headstrong brother might cause next.

At the bottom of Nob Hill, Christian turned onto Powell and ran through Union Square. He dodged the trolley cars and automobiles and crossed to South of Market.

At the corner of Brannan and Fourth, Christian charged through the door of a dingy tenement. He bounded quickly to the third floor and knocked on a thin, tired door.

"Christian? What are you doing here?" Gertrude Fallon, Byron's widowed sister-in-law—a gray-haired woman with thick glasses and a perennially worried demeanor—stared uneasily at the panting Christian.

"Is Anthony here, Aunt Gertrude?"

"He just got home from Agnews a couple of hours ago. I'm sorry we didn't make the funeral, Christian, but he was in bad shape."

"I need to talk to him. Alone. Police business. Maybe you could take a walk to the store or something so we could talk?" Christian put his arm around her shoulders and gently moved her from her own apartment, closing the door behind him.

She listened at the door for a minute, fearful of her hot-tempered nephew, and then descended the creaking stairway.

Christian moved through the cramped kitchen into the tiny living room. The shades were drawn, the room so dark it took Christian's eyes a minute to adjust. Anthony sat in the corner on a threadbare couch, rocking back and forth and mumbling to himself.

Christian peeked into a bedroom, where Anthony's older brother Jessie, still pale as a corpse, snored beneath a faded comforter.

Christian returned to the living room and threw back the curtains, flooding the room with light. Anthony squinted and leaned forward, his chin almost in his lap.

"Anthony. It's me, Christian."

"Don't hurt me, Christian." His voice was barely audible. "There was just me and him. Me and him," he gasped. "I tied him to the rail, there was water everywhere. I couldn't see nothin'. It was so dark. I swear to God I don't know what happened."

Christian moved to Anthony's side. He leaned close and took a whiff of Anthony's ratty sweater, then stuck his hand in Anthony's pocket and found a vial. He twisted the cork loose and inspected the sticky black substance in the bottom. Opium.

Anthony continued to sway and mumble. "I didn't kill him. I swear I didn't kill him."

"Anthony. I want you to listen to me."

"I didn't kill him," he sobbed. "I swear to God. It was just the two of us. It was so dark. So dark. Water everywhere."

"Anthony. Who did you tell that dad was gonna be on that boat? Who knew?"

"I didn't kill him. I swear to God. I swear to God I didn't kill him."

"Anthony. Are you listening to me?"

Anthony buried his head in his arms, still swaying.

Christian knelt and pressed his forehead against his cousin's, pulling Anthony's hands away from his face. "You know I always find out what I want, don't you? You're my flesh and blood, Anthony. Don't make me beat it out of you."

"Don't hit me Christian, please." Anthony gasped and sobbed, his body shaking.

"That was my father, Anthony. Tell me everything or I will beat you bloody right here in your mother's living room. You want her to find you like that? You want her to know what you did?"

"I didn't know they were going to hurt him, Christian. I swear to God!"

"Anthony."

"He just wanted to know where Uncle Byron was going."

"Was it Chief Donen?"

He sobbed and shivered, nodding his head several times. "They caught me taking opium from a Chinese peddler. They were going to fire me, they said I would lose my job and no one would give me another one. How's my mom going to eat without me? Huh, tell me that, Christian? Elliot and Jessie was gone, it was just me and her. Chief Donen wanted to know what Uncle Byron was up to so they could protect him."

Christian rose, fighting his rage. "Don't tell anyone what you told me Anthony, not even your mother. Understand? You say a word to Chief Donen or anyone, I promise I'll come back and kill you. Understand? I'll kill you."

He left Anthony wailing like an infant.

In room 434 of the Fairmont, Hunter was about to leave when he was startled by the sound of the telephone ringing. He threw the switch to activate the recording machine.

"This is Adam Rolf."

"How you doin', Adam? Gettin' ready for the big shindig?"

Hunter's heart leapt. He grabbed the notebook and fountain pen and scribbled as quickly as he could.

"I hear you got a little visit from Christian Fallon this morning, Shanghai."

"The next visit the little bastard is going to make is Laurel Hill to join his daddy. No extra charge."

"You owe me that much after the way you botched this thing with his father."

"Next time you want a cop in the ground, do it your bloody self, Adam. Fallon is in his stinkin' grave like I promised. The guys that did the job got a little sloppy with the papers they found is all."

"Tell me you got the papers."

"I got the papers."

"Who was it that double-crossed me?"

"Ain't had a look yet."

"That's right. How are you going to be a city supervisor if you can't read, Kelly?"

"I can't read but I can count real good. You'll be telling me how to vote anyway."

"One more delay, Kelly, one more of your little games and things get ugly, understand me?"

"One more thing, Adam. They raised the price on me. Fifty grand is what my boys are askin'. A bloody pittance considering we saved your arse. Have the money ready, I'll deliver the goods tonight when the party is windin' down. Just an old business acquaintance droppin' by for a taste 'a that good whiskey you're pourin'."

Rolf slammed the phone so hard it hurt Hunter's ear, though it did nothing to temper his jubilation.

"I got you, I got you, you murderin' swine!" He grabbed the disk from the recording machine and sprinted from the room.

Inside his mansion, Rolf stormed through his office and screamed for Tommy, who appeared from the front parlor.

"Kelly's bringing the documents tonight. I want you to take care of him and the two-faced bitch who betrayed me as well."

"You're pullin' my leg, boss. It was a skirt put the shiv in your back?"

"Let's just say I got a hunch. I will know tonight for sure."

Chapter 39

PALACE HOTEL

APRIL 17, 1906. 6:00 P.M.

In an elaborate suite on the third floor of the Palace Hotel, Kaitlin scribbled unsteadily in her diary. She had plenty to record. In less than thirty-six hours she had encountered Enrico Caruso, learned from an infatuated geologist that the world was about to end, survived an attack by thugs, befriended the Emperor of North America, been robbed by a French pimp and solicited by a wealthy madam, and somehow wound up at the world's most luxurious hotel, free of charge. Kansas, she wrote, seemed like a lifetime away.

Now she had gained an invitation to the heart of San Francisco society to see the great Caruso. But at what price? She ended the entry with "Who is this Adam Rolf?"

She put the diary down and rubbed her aching temples, then walked to the window and stared over bustling Market Street. Once enlivening, the constant clang and clamor, the rumbling, honking, and shouting had melded into an annoying discord. She thought to flee but again was unsure where to go. Save for eighty dollars in Emperor Milton money, she was penniless. The dream of San Francisco had somehow become a gilded nightmare.

A knock at the door startled her. Kaitlin froze, her heart pounding. Another knock. She moved to the door, fighting to compose herself. A third knock had her reaching for the door handle.

Andrew Tavish grinned at her over a large white box tied with a green lace ribbon and bow. "Kaitlin! What a surprise!"

She opened the door wider and Andrew stepped inside. He placed the box on a low table in front of a gray satin divan. A snow-white envelope was tucked under the box's ribbon.

"What's this, Andrew?"

"Don't know. They told me at the desk to bring it up."

She tilted her head to read the gold printing on the end of the foot-deep box. "City of Paris. That's the most expensive store in San Francisco."

"I swear. For someone who has never been here, you know the city better than me."

Kaitlin stared at him. The warm, accommodating smile she had encountered the day before now seemed patronizing and shallow. It wilted slightly under her gaze.

"I just realized something," she said.

"What's that?"

"I guess I am more naive than I thought." She hesitated. "A man came to the place I was staying and told the landlady I was a prostitute. He took all my things and got me thrown out."

"That's awful."

"Except that you're the only person I told where I was staying. Who paid you? Antoine or Tessie?"

His smile faded and his eyes slipped downward. "I, uh, I didn't say anything to anyone."

"We're not sophisticated where I grew up, but we can sure identify the smell of horse manure when it's right in front of us."

"I gotta be going. They need me at the desk."

"Does your boss know you work for pimps and thieves?"

"Have fun. With the opera dress, I mean."

"Dress? My, they work fast here in San Francisco. I thought you said you didn't know what it was. You try to hurt me again, Andrew, and I'll make a gelding out of you. Understand?"

He stalked from the room and slammed the door behind him.

Kaitlin raised the white box and felt its heft. Inside the envelope she found a card with gold lettering: "Mr. Adam T. Rolf." She turned it over.

"Dear Kaitlin," she read aloud from the handwritten note, "Please accept this welcome gift. My driver will call at seven-thirty. I hope you enjoy the music of Enrico Caruso. At the post-opera party, you will have an opportunity to meet him in person. Warmly, Adam Rolf."

She set the card aside and fumbled to untie the ribbon. She pulled out a black lace embroidered dress with a gathered waist and flared skirt. She held it up. A perfect fit.

Miss Tessie obviously knows her girls.

In the bottom of the box she found a pair of long black fingerless gloves, an ivory choker, black silk stockings, garters, and a pair of dark gray short-heeled pumps. She looked at the card and read the words again, searching for a clue to Rolf's intentions. She tried to convince herself that perhaps all Adam Rolf wanted was her company.

She entered the spacious tiled bathroom and twisted the ornate silver handles on the claw-foot tub. She inhaled the steam rising from the torrent of hot water and laughed nervously. She had never had a bath without first heating the water in buckets on a wood-burning stove.

Chapter 40

APRIL 17, 1906. 6:40 P.M.

Three floors below where an uneasy Kaitlin primped, Enrico Caruso and Alfred Hertz climbed into the chauffeured Rolls Royce that Adam Rolf had provided. Caruso was weary from his journey and the tumultuous rehearsal. The prospects of a ruinous opening night complicated his melancholy.

"*Signorina* Fremstad is maybe correct," Caruso said. "Thees chorus are *imbecilli*! They no know where to stand, where to sing, *niente*."

"Enrico, everyone will come to hear the great Caruso. Look around you. Look at the banners and the poster cards. This is the most exciting thing that has ever happened here. If the chorus failed to show up for the performance, no one would even notice. Tonight, you will make history."

Caruso let Hertz' words sink in. "You are right, Alfred. They are pay to see Caruso. Tonight, I am give best Caruso ever."

Out in Pacific Heights, in the bedroom of his Italianate Victorian on Fillmore Street, Eugene Schmitz paced like a condemned man. The crushing suspicion that Adam Rolf, despite vociferous denials, was behind the death of Byron Fallon had deeply unsettled him. The visit to Ah Toy's house of horrors had been the final straw.

He walked through the French doors to his rooftop terrace and leaned against the rail, staring through the Golden Gate where the silver canopy of evening hung above the dark water. He scanned the bay to Angel Island where Byron's body had been found.

"Eugene. Eugene!" his wife called impatiently. "You haven't bathed or shaved yet. You know how upset he gets when you're late."

"Telephone Mr. Rolf and tell him we're not going."

"What do you mean, we're not going?"

"We're not going, Julia, and I'm not in any mood to argue. Just tell him we're not going. Tell him I'll explain later."

At the Central Fire Station on Bush Street, Dennis Sullivan rose from his desk on the third floor and rubbed his tired eyes. He stared at the roll of blueprints that covered the desk and hung over both sides. His last chance to overcome the greed of Rolf and Schmitz and get the resources he needed would come at nine o'clock the next morning when he would present the plans to Judge Morrow.

Maggie was in the bedroom at the end of the hall, putting on her earrings when he entered.

"I thought maybe I'd take you to the Palace Grill and have a quick glass of champagne before the opera," he said.

"You did, did you? Then you better hurry."

He smiled and kissed her warmly.

"Dennis. You haven't kissed me like that in so long I can't remember."

"Then shame on me." He stepped to his dressing closet and pulled out the black tuxedo. "I really do hate these things," he muttered.

"How many times in our lives will we get to see Enrico Caruso? Let's look sharp and enjoy ourselves."

Sullivan stripped off his coveralls and unbuttoned his wool shirt. He had one leg into his tuxedo pants when the fire bell went off. In the iron cage hanging in the corner of the room the other Sullivan, a blue-green cockatiel, started squawking, "Fire! Fire! Fire!"

"Oh, Lord," cried Maggie, "not now."

Sullivan stepped out of his trousers and hurried to the small brass horn on the wall next to his bedroom door. "What is it?"

Assistant Chief Dougherty shouted through the hollow tube from three stories below. "Spotter at North Point Station called it in. Looks like the California Cannery on Bay Street. It's a doer."

"Let's send every pumper and Hayes truck from North Beach, the Financial District, two companies South of the Slot. I'm on my way down."

A glum Maggie stared at him and started removing her earrings.

"Why don't you go by yourself, Maggie? You'll be sitting with Mr. Spreckels and his guests."

"And worry myself sick about you the whole time? I don't know why you can't let Mr. Dougherty handle it."

"The man's sixty-eight, Maggie. I can't take the chance."

"And as long as these thieves in City Hall keep stealing all the money, you'll have to keep rushing off every time a kitchen stove flares up." She threw her earrings onto the dresser.

Dennis Sullivan recognized the futility of another response. He pulled on his britches and hurried to a hallway closet, sliding down the slick brass pole to the firehouse below.

On Dolores Street near Seventeenth Avenue, in the working-class Mission District, Angela Feeney, a plain woman with streaks of graying hair, answered the door to find a handsome young man in a blue suit and tie.

"I'm Hunter Fallon. I'm here to see Mr. Feeney."

She smiled politely and ushered him inside. She led him past a parlor filled with stodgy furniture and down a narrow hallway to a miniscule study.

Charles Feeney was busy typewriting a report. He looked over the top of his spectacles. "Hello, Hunter. What do you have for me?"

Hunter produced two black disks and handed them to Feeney, who raised his eyebrows.

"The first one is a recording of Adam Rolf discussing his bribe with the Senator's aide. They're planning to reroute the railroad from Oakland into San Francisco. The second is Kelly demanding fifty grand from Rolf for killing my father and delivering the papers he was carrying."

Feeney removed his spectacles and stood, staring at Hunter. "You recorded these conversations? How in God's name?"

"It was work, but we did it, sir. It's their voices, talking over the telephone, incriminating themselves as sure as we're standing here."

"Fingerprints, voice recordings from a telephone line," Feeney said. "It's a bit farfetched but maybe we'll get lucky. My biggest concern is for Miss Passarelli's safety."

"Kelly is withholding her name from Rolf so he can raise the price. I'll be watching her."

Feeney handed over a manila folder. "Arrest warrants for Mayor Schmitz, Police Chief Donen, and Adam Rolf for bribery, extortion, corruption, and slave trading. There are others for Donen, Rolf, Kelly, and

Scarface—his real name is Willis Polk—for murder of a police officer. A guaranteed trip to the gallows if we can make it stick. This should send a wave of fear through every dirty politician from here to Boston."

"Right now, all I'm thinking about is justice for my father and making sure Annalisa lives to tell her story."

Feeney looked at the recordings in his hand. "You know, if these things hold up in court, it will change police work. It will give us tools we never dreamed of."

"It's the Twentieth Century, Mr. Feeney. It's about time."

Chapter 41

GRAND OPERA HOUSE

APRIL 17, 1906. 7:30 P.M.

In his dressing room backstage, Enrico Caruso slipped into the trousers of the Spanish corporal Don José. His valet, Martino, knelt and pulled the white stockings over the tenor's thick calves. A knock came at the door.

Martino answered and admitted Lincoln Staley. Caruso brightened immediately.

"Ah, Lincoln. Now you are come I am feel better. You know, last night, they are almost to make a riot here."

"No one who hears you sing, Enrico, will think of rioting."

Caruso smiled. "Lincoln, you are sitting on side of stage for me. Okay? In case someone is go *pazzo*."

"I'll be in the wings."

Lincoln's forlorn look answered Caruso's next question before he asked it.

"We are find her, Lincoln. You tell me she is come to San Francisco for Caruso? Then tonight she comes. I know thees in my hearts."

When he finished dressing, Caruso walked the dimly lit hallway to the wings, with Lincoln and Martino trailing close behind. He trod across the stage and peeked out through the curtains, just as the audience broke into applause.

The applause was not for him. All eyes were on Emperor Milton in full-dress regalia of towering beaver fur hat and blue Prussian military coat with polished brass buttons and gold epaulets. He walked slowly down the center aisle, waving to his subjects. Milton bowed politely, and then settled in the middle seat of the front row.

"They are all crazy in thees crazy place," Caruso muttered.

At the railing of Rolf's box, Senator Payton sipped champagne and stared at the scene below.

"Emperor Milton," Rolf explained. "A financial wizard. Downtown businessmen would not buy a spittoon without consulting him. Went off the deep end when his efforts to corner the rice market went belly up. He has front row seats to all the opening nights."

"I heard things are a little different here, Mr. Rolf," the Senator said.

"We lock up half our lunatics and make celebrities of the other half. A distinctly San Francisco tradition."

Backstage, Caruso found Martino and pulled him aside, out of Lincoln's earshot. The pair conversed in Italian.

"Do you have my pistol?" Caruso asked.

"It's in the dressing room, *Maestro*."

"You go bring it to me, please."

Martino hesitated, but knew better than to challenge Caruso's orders.

In the dressing room, Martino reached into a chest of drawers and removed the pistol from beneath a pile of shirts. He flipped open the cylinder and removed all six cartridges, stowing them in his pocket.

Caruso was pacing anxiously in the wing when Martino returned. He took the pistol and stuffed it in his cummerbund. "These people are crazy in San Francisco," Caruso explained. "They make riots at the opera, they put crazy people in the front row. I am no take any chances."

My Hansom arrived and I joined the last arrivals in their anxious charge toward the entrance.

Once inside the Opera House, I rushed up the circular stairway. I was dressed in a borrowed gray silk taffeta gown, black suede pumps, long black gloves, and an ivory choker. Whatever happened, I was certain it would be the last time I had to endure Adam Rolf.

"Annalisa. Annalisa!"

I turned and spotted Hunter at the bottom of the steps, dressed in a dark blue suit. He was beaming broadly. I hurried back down and ducked under the stairway, pulling him out of sight of prying eyes.

"Hunter. What are you doing here?"

"I had Mr. Feeney telephone Mr. Spreckels and ask if I could join him in his box so I could keep an eye on you. I'm worried."

"Don't worry, I made it this far." The sight of him—the blue eyes and chiseled face—made my heart race faster than it already was.

Hunter reached inside his coat and produced a pair of opera glasses with mother-of-pearl inlay and polished brass eyepiece. He slipped the silver chain around my neck and stared into my eyes.

"My mother brought these from Italy. She had two dreams before she died: to vote and to see Caruso. I guess you will have to do both for her."

"What she really wanted, Hunter, was to see her son become as good a man as his father. I imagine she's a happy woman right now."

I examined the opera glasses. "I can't possibly keep these."

"She gave them to me the day before she died. We loved going to the opera together. She said someday my wife should have them."

I clutched my gloved hand to my face and forced the tears back.

"I'm sorry I don't have a ring, but I'm asking you to marry me." He then asked me again, in Italian.

I hesitated, fighting the flood of emotion.

Hunter went on. "I was thinking about tomorrow. It's my birthday, April eighteenth. Then I'll have two reasons to celebrate every year."

"I think tomorrow is going to be a very good day." I threw my arms around his neck and kissed him. It would be a very good day, provided we survived the night ahead of us.

"Go, Annalisa. Be careful. And remember, I'm watching out for you."

I kissed him again and struggled up the stairs.

I hesitated at the door to Rolf's box, switching to a practiced, guiltless face. I entered without knocking.

"Annalisa!" Rolf hesitated before breaking into a grin that looked strained and unconvincing. "Annalisa. One runs out of superlatives."

"Good evening, Adam. Where is Mayor Schmitz?"

"He's not coming."

"Is he ill?"

"I don't believe so." His tone was unsettling. "Annalisa. Allow me to introduce you to our honorable Senator George Payton and his wife. Senator, this is Miss Annalisa Passarelli, one of our brilliant opera and theater critics. She has been assisting Mr. Caruso."

"Senator. Mrs. Payton. It's a great honor."

On the opposite side of the Opera House, Hunter slipped into the private box of Rudolph Spreckels, who greeted him with Fremont Older in tow.

"How goes it?" Spreckels inquired.

"I have all the warrants. The informant will signal us when Rolf has handed the money to the Senator and again when Shanghai Kelly has delivered the papers taken from my father. We don't expect any of that to happen until the party."

"Splendid," said Older. "When it is finished I will cable President Roosevelt. Teddy is a man who values results."

Chapter 42

APRIL 17, 1906. 7:40 P.M.

At their tiny cottage on Webster Street, Francis Fagen's wife, Eleanor, went to the back porch where her brother-in-law Patrick rested on a cot, reading his Bible.

"Patrick," Eleanor said. "You better come eat."

Patrick stretched his long legs and walked to the small kitchen table where Eleanor set down plates of rabbit stew and potatoes. The three of them joined hands in prayer.

A half block away, near the corner of Webster and Golden Gate, Carlo Rinaldi sat at the kitchen table cleaning his revolver.

His mother Cecilia entered and removed a macaroni casserole from the wood-burning oven. "Carlo, *per favore, porta via la pistola dalla cucina. Chiama il fratello a' pranzare.*"

Obediently, Carlo stowed his weapon and walked to the stable. Max lay on a crude wooden bench, huffing as he pressed a rusty barbell up and down.

"Max. M-m-mom wants you to c-c-come eat."

Max lowered the barbell, sat up, and caught his breath.

"Y-y-you b-better sa-save som-some strength for tonight."

"Worry about the other guys when I get my hands on them," Max replied, wiping his sweaty brow on his shirt.

The brothers joined their mother at the kitchen table and bowed their heads as she prayed for their safety. They were distracted by horses kicking at their stalls.

"*I cavalli sono pazzi*," Cecilia said. "Morning, noon, nights, crazy all the times the horses."

When they finished eating, Max and Carlo kissed their mother. They donned their pistol belts and stuffed their pockets with extra cartridges. They pulled on long black dusters and slid sawed-off shotguns into long narrow pockets inside, then distributed extra manacles in the pockets of their coats.

Max and Carlo joined Francis and Patrick for the walk to the United Railway trolley line, several blocks away on Geary Street.

In the dummy car at the rear, empty save for the four of them, Patrick produced a biblical passage he had hand-copied and read aloud.

"*But it is good to be zealously affected, always in a good thing and not only when I am present with you. Tell me ye that desire to be under the law, do ye not hear the law? Now we, brethren as Isaac was, are the children of promise. Stand fast therefore in the liberty wherewith Christ hath made us free and be not entangled again with the yoke of bondage.*"

The four earnest young officers muttered, "Amen."

It would be the last such moment they shared.

Chapter 43

APRIL 17, 1906. 8:05 P.M.

Tommy stopped the Rolls Phaeton in front of the Opera House for the second time that night.

"Do you think he'll be angry that I'm late?" Kaitlin asked.

"You sit here yakking, you're gonna be even later. Why don't you climb down and get on in there?"

Tommy's brusqueness did nothing to ease Kaitlin's nerves. She gathered her strength and her gown and slid out of the Rolls.

Tommy screeched off, leaving her alone with her mounting fear. *Nothing's going to happen. It's the opera. It's Enrico Caruso. This is why you came here.* She took a step forward and then another, gaining momentum as the sound of the orchestra wafted through the open doors.

She barely made it into the lobby when the sight of it stopped her in her tracks. It was brimming with massive arrangements of orchids, narcissus, and roses. Elegant women in peacock displays of lace and satin, dappled with glittering diamonds and precious jewels of every color, hurried for their seats. She inhaled the fragrant air, her attention suddenly drawn to a massive three-tiered crystal chandelier that cast kaleidoscopic dots about the lobby.

"It's the largest cut-glass chandelier in the world."

She wheeled to find a smiling, cherub-faced usher in a black coat and striped trousers.

"Fifty-five feet in diameter. Weighs two tons. It was a gift from the Opera Society President, Mr. Rolf. May I help you find your seat?"

"Yes, uhh, Mr. Rolf is expecting me."

"He has a double box, C and D. Top of the stairs, third door to the left. Knock at C and someone will let you in."

"Is he a nice man?"

The usher hesitated. "I'm sure he is, ma'am. Enjoy the performance."

Kaitlin nodded politely and ascended the stairs, her knees wobbly beneath her. She knocked timidly on the door, waited an uncertain moment, and rapped a little harder. The door lurched open and a butler's face appeared.

"I'm sorry I'm late. I'm Kaitlin Staley. I believe . . ."

The flood of light brought a wave of well-coiffed heads turning in her direction. A short man with a bushy mustache rose from his seat and walked to greet her.

"You must be Kaitlin," Rolf said.

"Yes, sir."

She offered a gloved hand. Rolf clasped it firmly, staring up into fathomless blue eyes. Behind his smile was a cold, hungry look Kaitlin had seen in the carpetbaggers still working Douglas County.

"I'm Adam Rolf. I am glad you could join us."

She nodded and swallowed hard. Rolf took Kaitlin's arm and led her forward.

From the railing where I had been chatting with Alma de Bretteville, I spotted a beautiful young woman slipping into the seat next to Rolf—the one most often reserved for me. My spirits sank when I recognized her: Kaitlin spotted me and waved, relieved at the sight of a familiar face.

In the orchestra pit, a cymbal crashed, launching a torrent of strings and brass into *Carmen*'s frenetic prelude. The melody swirled through the audience and sent heads bobbing, fingers fluttering, engulfing all in buoyant abandon. San Francisco faded and sensuous Seville exploded into the Opera House.

The prelude yielded to a jaunty "March of the Toreadors," heralding the arrival of Don José's rival, the dashing bullfighter Escamillo. The joyous motif crested, and then spiraled into an ominous phrase, finally dissolving to a plaintive oboe that prophesied the fate of tempestuous Carmen and troubled Don José.

I raised my beautiful opera glasses, panning across the exuberant faces in the expensive seats until I found the box belonging to Rudolph Spreckels. Spreckels and his very pregnant wife Eleanor sat next to Fremont and Cora Older. Behind them, in the shadows, Hunter gently mimed the conductor, his cheeks puffed slightly as he hummed the melody.

Hunter raised my battered old opera glasses and scanned the boxes, until he stared at me staring at him. He subtly mouthed, "I love you."

I lowered my binoculars and stole a glance behind me as Rolf slid his arm onto the back of Kaitlin's seat.

"The dress fits you perfectly," he whispered to her.

"Yes, sir. It fits just fine. Thank you, sir."

"We're an informal lot in San Francisco, Kaitlin. Call me Adam. All my friends call me Adam."

She nodded, tight-lipped, fighting the urge to lunge for the door.

"Have you been to many operas?"

"This is my first, sir."

"Call me Adam."

"Adam. I had a Victor back home. I bought it with my sewing money. I listened to Caruso so much I wore out the recordings."

"And where's home?"

"Lawrence, Kansas. Where William Quantrill and Frank James gunned down all those people during the war. My Grandpa was one of them. One of them who was killed, I mean." Kaitlin turned her head to avoid Rolf's carnivorous grin and stared intently at the stage.

To the sound of fifes and bugles, the chorus of street boys heralded the arrival of the Spanish relief guard. Kaitlin leaned forward, distancing herself from Rolf's advancing arm, losing herself in the spectacle.

"Kaitlin," Rolf said, his mood darkening. "Your father? He's a farmer? Or a rancher?"

"He's the sheriff in Douglas County."

The door opened and a man moved through the shadows, leaning over Rolf's shoulder. Rolf smiled and patted the man's hand.

"Kaitlin," Rolf said, "say hello to Mr. John Barrymore."

Kaitlin's head swiveled and her mouth dropped. She had fallen asleep many nights beneath photos of Caruso and Barrymore tacked on the rough-hewn wall of her room. He grinned broadly, the profile unmistakable, his white teeth gleaming, his breath bathed in gin.

Rolf excused himself and walked to Tommy, who had just arrived to take his usual station near the door. "We have a little problem, Thomas. The girl Tessie Wall sent? Her father's that hick sheriff, the one playing bodyguard for Caruso."

Tommy looked over Rolf's shoulder to where Barrymore now sat in his boss's seat, jabbering softly to a transfixed Kaitlin. "She's somethin' all right, boss. Could get downright nasty if daddy shows up at the party just as you're about to break the little filly in."

"Deviousness is your true talent, Thomas. Quietly make this disappear."

A ripple shot through the audience as Enrico Caruso, bedecked as Spanish Corporal Don José, entered the stage with his fellow soldiers. Caruso stopped near the cigarette factory as young women poured into the plaza for their lunch break, twirling their hips and shamelessly teasing the young men.

Don José watched with disdain as the seductive gypsy Carmen appeared, playing her castanets and singing her saucy *Habañera*, the lilting aria punctuated with stirring bursts from the chorus.

"*L'amour est un oiseau rebelle.*"

Love is a rebellious bird, I scribbled as lumpy Olive Fremstad, in Carmen's ruffled skirt, fumbled through a graceless entry. Enticed by the sight of handsome Don José, she sauntered over, her ardor further piqued by his aloofness. She produced a flower from her ebony hair and handed it to him, declaring him the only man for her. As Don José inhaled its intoxicating fragrance, Carmen ambled away, casting an alluring look over her shoulder.

In Spreckels' box, Hunter reached into his jacket, produced the flower I had dropped to him from my tenement, and inhaled its waning fragrance. I vowed him a kinder fate than Carmen would offer Don José.

Caruso began to sing, rejecting Carmen and swearing his allegiance to his fiancée, Micaela, the audience riveted by the astonishing voice that filled every corner of the house.

While Enrico Caruso kept us enraptured at the Grand Opera House, Francis Fagen spread a hand-drawn map of Nob Hill on the floor of room 434 of the Fairmont Hotel. Patrick, Max, and Carlo looked on.

"This can go easy," Francis said, "if everybody keeps their wits about them. Last thing we need is a gun fight inside Rolf's mansion." They all jumped as Christian burst through the door, his face a mass of purple bruises.

"Speakin' of the Devil," said Max.

Christian slipped next to Patrick and said nothing.

"All right," Francis resumed, "Rolf's guests will be entering through the front gate on California. We need to watch the entire house so the informant can signal from anywhere inside."

"That would be Annalisa Passarelli," Christian added.

"Whoa," Max said. "That knock-kneed girl who used to live at the bottom of Filbert Street? The Society reporter? You tellin' me all this time the Lieutenant's informant is a damn woman?"

"That's what I'm saying," Christian answered.

"Now," Francis resumed, "the construction crews are going to be at it all night getting the Fairmont ready for opening tomorrow. Carlo, you and Max will linger in the lobby. I know the foreman, it's already arranged. Keep a sharp eye on the east side of the house, especially Rolf's office—the three bay windows in the middle of the first floor."

Francis hesitated, the gravity and fatigue causing a moment's hesitation. "The Crockers across California Street hate Rolf. Patrick and I will take up station behind their wall and watch the front."

"Hunter wants me to stay up here and man this recording contraption in case another incriminating telephone call comes in," Christian said somberly. "Him and me can watch the second floor and livery out back."

"Tommy and Shanghai Kelly will die before they let us drag them out in handcuffs," Max said. "Especially if they think there's a noose waitin'."

"We can accommodate that," Christian said. "Remember what they did to my father when I wasn't there to watch over him."

It was the closest Christian had come to admitting wrong. His subdued and chastised nature took them all aback.

The howling of the neighborhood dogs, sporadic all night, reached an unnerving crescendo.

"M-m-m-maybe th-th-they j-just hate opera." Carlo's joke did little to ease the tension.

Chapter 44

———◦◦◦———

GRAND OPERA HOUSE

APRIL 17, 1906. 9:50 P.M.

The Grand Opera House filled with the mournful sound of a clarinet, wafting over the audience like a gull gliding on the ocean breeze. A staccato violin deepened the tender entreaty to a phrase of resignation and foreboding.

The audience straightened, necks straining as though the extra few inches might bring them closer to the magic unfolding before them.

Caruso stepped to center stage to intercept Carmen, now his fugitive love. From inside his tattered shirt he pulled the faded flower Carmen had given him on first meeting. *"La fleur que tu m'avais jetée,"* Caruso sang. *The flower that you gave me.* He ignored Olive Fremstad, digging into an emotional well.

"I felt but one desire," I whispered, "one desire, one hope."

"Te revoir, O Carmen, oui, te revoir."

"To see you again, Carmen," Hunter recited in perfect unity as I watched him through my opera glasses. "To see you again."

Caruso soared from baritone depths to heavenly notes seemingly beyond the range of the male voice. He told Carmen how the scent of the flower, her scent, had sustained him during his lonely, desperate hours in the brig after abandoning his post for her. He begged Carmen to return to his arms.

All around the Opera House, people held their breath.

I caught a quick glimpse of Kaitlin, a tear streaking her face.

"Carmen, O ma Carmen." Caruso's plaintive cry dissolved into the melancholy notes of a French horn.

I dropped my notebook and leapt to my feet with the audience, all cheering madly.

Caruso, breathless and stunned by the response, waited for his Carmen to respond.

The music and drama heightened the aching in Lincoln's heart. He squirmed in his chair backstage as Fremstad's Carmen stepped forward to challenge the distraught Don José.

Lincoln jumped when a hand touched his shoulder.

Tommy nodded for Lincoln to follow him. The two men squeezed through the props and pulleys until they found a quieter spot near the dressing rooms.

"Mr. Rolf sent me down. He just got word," Tommy said. "The cops may have spotted your daughter at Tessie Wall's place on the Barbary Coast."

Lincoln tensed. "And just what kind of place is Tessie Wall's?"

"Ain't the kind of place a man wants to find his daughter. Neighborhood's rough, don't cotton much to strangers. Once the show's over . . ."

"Let's go now," Lincoln demanded.

Lincoln followed Tommy through the stage door onto Mission Street, where the Rolls sat at the curb.

He climbed into the passenger seat as Tommy gave the crank a whirl and jumped behind the wheel. They thundered down Fifth Street, crossing Market with bone-rattling jolts as they bumped over the four sets of trolley tracks.

Tommy wheeled onto Jackson Street, working the bellows of the brass horn to clear unsteady prowlers from his path. He slammed the Rolls to a halt in front of an ornate Victorian and honked again.

A Negro doorman peeked through the leaded glass door, and then signaled to someone inside. Moments later, a heavy-set woman wobbled down the steps.

"Evening, Miss Tessie," Tommy called. "Adam got a message you might have seen a young girl we been lookin' for."

Tessie eyed Lincoln as two women in corsets, black stockings, and garters appeared at the front door.

She can't be in a place like this, Lincoln thought. Then he remembered Kaitlin exposing her breasts to Rusty for a dollar. He passed Kaitlin's photo to Tessie.

"She looks different now," Tessie mused. "Redhead, cut real short. I sent her away. I've seen too many runaway schoolgirls in my time. I run a clean business."

"Where's she now?" Tommy demanded.

"One of the other girls sent her to a saloon where they ain't so particular. The Boar's Head down on Battery. Poor kid looked awful desperate."

Tommy eased the brake and the Rolls lurched forward. The throbbing of the engine echoed off the buildings as Tommy worked the horn. The closer they got to the waterfront, where a sea of masts bobbed at anchor, the darker and dirtier the streets became. Lincoln had seen dangerous streets in St. Louis and Kansas City where he hunted rustlers and bush-whackers, but nothing as unnerving as the malevolence infecting the Barbary Coast.

Tommy wheeled onto Battery Street and jerked to a stop before a bar with a half-fallen sign that read THE BOAR'S HEAD.

A wary Lincoln stepped onto the wooden sidewalk in front of the faded exterior, which appeared ready to collapse into the garbage-strewn street at any moment. He watched Tommy push through the creaky swinging doors. Lincoln hesitated a moment, then followed.

The stench of bad cigars, cheap whiskey, and syrupy perfume assailed Lincoln's nostrils. Men as scarred and mangy as alley cats pawed garishly painted women who had been reduced to lumpy residues of femininity. A singer screeched and someone pounded what may have been a piano. A dozen men lining the glass-topped bar stared at him as though examining their next good meal.

Lincoln inched closer to the bar. Beneath the filthy glass top was a display of black, decaying human noses that had obviously been gnawed free of their original owners. Each was denoted by a small brass plaque with names and dates of acquisition, all under the heading "the Whale's Scrapbook."

Tommy shouldered through the crowd, shoving aside clawing whores. After questioning several of the saloon's wobbly denizens, he moved to the end of the bar and had a whispered conversation with the bartender. The man pointed toward a curtain.

Tommy nodded for Lincoln to follow him.

They pushed through the shredded curtain, stopping abreast of an enormous, tattooed bouncer. The dimly lit hallway had a dozen stalls, each covered by a filthy curtain. A chorus of grunts and squeals filled the air. In one stall, Lincoln could see a soldier, green wool breeches down around his campaign boots, rooting atop a woman whose stocking-clad legs were wrapped about his naked rump.

"You got a new girl, come down from Tessie's place?" Tommy asked the bouncer. "Tall redhead, Kansas farm girl, sweet lookin'."

"She busy. You wait one minutes," he answered in a Polish accent, arms crossed in front of his chest. "Nice beeg teats I like. You wait."

Lincoln grabbed Tommy's beefy bicep. "My daughter would never set foot in a place like this."

"Young girls, they come to town, no family, no money. Ain't nobody starts out like this, Sheriff. More of 'em winds up here than the opera."

Lincoln stared about, trying to catch a glimpse inside the stalls.

"Up to you, Sheriff. We can stay or we can go," Tommy offered.

Lincoln nodded. Tommy handed a gold coin to the bouncer, who bit it and nodded his consent. Tommy started down the hallway, followed close by Lincoln, whose hand enveloped the butt of his Colt.

Lincoln watched as the soldier groaned and arched his back. The whore's plump legs shuddered convulsively and a short-heeled shoe thumped to the floor, revealing a silver dollar-sized hole in her black stocking. His head swooned at the thought of Kaitlin doing the same, a wave of fear dulling his senses.

He never saw the heavy oak dowel that hit him.

Halfway to the floor, he caught the bouncer's second blow behind the right ear, an inch from where the first had landed, the sickening crack echoing down the hallway. Lincoln collapsed on the dirty floor as the grunting from the stalls continued unabated.

Tommy knelt over him, and in the dim red light saw the blood trickling from the side of Lincoln's head. "Don't kill him, you dumb bastard. He's worth ninety dollars alive."

"He live okay." The bouncer removed Lincoln's gun belt and the gold coins from his pocket, then shouldered him like a side of beef. He carried him to the end of the hallway, kicked open a door, then threw the limp body down a chute.

At the bottom, someone dragged Lincoln across the dirt floor, leaning him against the wall with four other unconscious men.

Chapter 45

GRAND OPERA HOUSE

APRIL 17, 1906. 11:55 P.M.

On stage, Carmen was approaching the bullring where her new lover, Escamillo, was doing battle.

A wild-eyed Don José burst from the shadows.

"I was told to fear for my life," Carmen sang. "But I am brave and have no intention of running away."

Don José replied, "I'm imploring you, beseeching. Yes, together we can begin another life, under new skies."

Kaitlin gripped the arms of her chair, oblivious to Rolf—and to the drunken Barrymore snoring softly on the other side of her.

She slipped from her seat and inched along the wall to stand behind me at the railing.

Caruso sang every note as though it was his last. His hands trembled, his eyes misted, his voice soared gently as he pleaded for Carmen's love.

Carmen responded defiantly, "*Libre elle est née et libre elle mourra.*"

"Free I was born and free I will die," I said, steeling myself.

A distraught Don José pulled a knife from his cummerbund as shouts poured from the bullring and Carmen mocked him, defiant and unrepentant.

The audience braced.

Don José lunged, his knife came down, and Carmen fell.

The audience gasped in unison, sobs and tears streaming from people in every corner of the hall.

"*Ah! Carmen! Ma Carmen adorée.*"

Weeping, Caruso threw himself on the body of Carmen. Had the audience been closer, they might have heard Olive Fremstad grunt and order Caruso to get off her.

Hertz brought the music to an abrupt and stirring end. In unison, three thousand sprang to their feet, the roar of exultation shaking the chandelier above us.

Something truly extraordinary transpired here tonight, I scribbled. *This was not an opera, this was a revelation. Those of us who witnessed Caruso's Don José will be united forever by the simple fact that we were there. Nothing like it may pass our way again.*

While the audience called Caruso back to the stage again and again, each time more zealously, Hunter slipped out of Spreckels' box. He bounded through the lobby to Mission Street, and dashed between the long lines of polished cars and gleaming carriages. He was soon roaring off toward Nob Hill.

As the applause continued unabated, reaching a thunderous crescendo, I looked at my watch.

One minute after midnight. Wednesday morning. April 18, 1906. The beginning of a glorious day. Caruso's triumph. The arrest of Rolf and Schmitz. My marriage to Hunter Fallon.

A glorious day, indeed. Or so I thought.

Chapter 46

NOB HILL

APRIL 18, 1906. 12:20 A.M.

At the Fairmont Hotel, Hunter clanged up the rear iron stairwell to the fourth floor, and burst through the door so quickly that Christian pulled his revolver.

"You're still trying to shoot me, aren't you?" Hunter asked.

Christian tried to smile. He set the revolver on the table, more forlorn than Hunter had ever seen him.

"Anything happen while I was gone?"

"Not unless you're a champagne salesman or a crab. They must be planning to feed half the city over there."

"Did you bring me a change of clothes?"

Christian motioned toward a valise in a corner. Hunter began ripping off his tie as his brother rubbed the smooth stock of the double-barreled Remington.

"I wanted to ask you something, Christian. How long has it been since you shot somebody? Before the other night, I mean?"

"A year maybe. That was the first I ever killed three in one night. Would have been four of a kind if I had found Scarface."

"How many does that make? All together."

"Eight."

"Eight? How could you kill eight men?"

"I didn't shoot that well at first. I mostly winged a bunch of 'em."

"Eight. Jesus. That's more than dad and grandpa put together."

"I ain't as forgiving as they were." Christian paused. "Not that I really give a damn, but how was it?"

"Life's too short not to love opera. Too bad dad isn't here." Hunter hesitated, fearful the comment would seem like a further attack on his brother. "Anyway, they'll be talking about this night for a long time."

"I ain't been to the opera since we were kids. I threw a fit at *Rigoletto* once and mom promised she'd never take me again."

"Tonight is *La Bohème*," Hunter said. "My favorite. Though it's going to be hard to beat *Carmen*." Hunter whistled "March of the Toreadors," grinning broadly.

"You can't be that giddy over an opera. You get some tail somewhere?"

"Better than that."

"She brought her sister?"

"I'm getting married tomorrow. Today, actually. April 18, 1906. It's my birthday, remember? Twenty-three."

"I must have something stuck in my ears. Who did you say is getting married?"

"Annalisa is going to marry me. The minute this is over."

"So much for a long courtship."

"How long did it take dad to propose? He met mom at noon at a church social for the Orphan's Asylum. He asked her to marry him when? Four o'clock?"

"I ain't never seen a man who could ask and answer his own questions as fast as you, Hunter."

Christian walked to the window and stared at the mansion across the street, where a trickle of automobiles discharged their tony guests. "This is never going to be over," he said.

"What?"

"I said this is never going to be over."

"It's your sunny disposition I was always envious of."

"You put the pinch on Rolf and Schmitz, two more take their place. It's never over," Christian said.

"Well, at least we'll always have a job."

Christian laughed half-heartedly. "If mom could see you packin' a revolver and a badge, she'd have a conniption. She really thought you were going to build that bridge or find a cure for somethin'."

"I'm just sorry she won't be here to see me marry Annalisa. Do you want to be my best man?"

"You sure you want me?"

"There's only the two of us left."

Christian closed his eyes and rubbed his weary face. Abruptly, the clanging of the cable car outside became the clanging of fire bells. A mountain of flame swirled upward into a plume of smoke that separated into the Devil's grin. His body jerked. He opened his eyes and stared at Hunter, whose face grew smaller as though he was falling backward down a well.

"Christian? Are you all right? Christian!"

"I think I need a drink."

"Not until this is over."

"I've been having nightmares. A big earthquake, the city on fire. Now I'm having them when I'm awake."

"When a man stops drinking, it does strange things to him. A little gunfight, a good night's sleep, you'll be fine. Maybe you'll get to put a round in Rolf or Kelly, then you'll really feel better."

Hunter moved behind Christian and gazed over his shoulder as the Phaeton arrived at the curb in front of Rolf's mansion. Rolf quickly emerged with an uneasy Kaitlin, followed by Senator Payton and his wife.

"This Rolf is something," Christian said, "Probably told the Senator that girl is his niece. Guy's got more nieces than a Chinese pimp. I'm going to enjoy thumpin' him."

Christian raised a small brass telescope, checking the position of Francis and Patrick behind the gate of the Crocker mansion across California Street. Then he checked the heavy brass clock on the corner of California and Mason.

Twelve forty-seven A.M. And the dogs were still howling.

A half-hour later, Enrico Caruso leaned back in the rear seat of the Phaeton as Tommy drove us up California Street, the stars swimming above in a sparkling blur.

"When I am sing tonight, Annalisa, I am think of my peoples in Napoli and thees terrible Vesuvio. They are my Carmen. They are my, 'ow you say, *amore perso*."

"Lost love."

"My lost love, *sì*. When I sing tonight, I close my eyes—also so I no see that fat cow who is play Carmen—and I see my beautiful Napoli. Thees night I am sing *più meraviglioso* a' my life."

"It is a good thing the other tenors did not hear you. They might have to retire the part of Don José."

Tommy brought the Phaeton to his usual lurching stop in front of Rolf's mansion.

I climbed down and entered through the brass gate, clutching Caruso's arm, clandestinely stealing a look at the window on the fourth floor of the Fairmont. The shade jiggled, helping still my anxiousness.

We entered the massive front door into Rolf's festive double parlors. The stuffy crowd burst into applause as Caruso, in a gray suit and black porkpie hat with maroon satin band, strode beneath the enormous cut-glass chandelier.

I used the opportunity to maneuver toward Kaitlin. "Not bad for your first opera," I said. "Assuming it was your first."

"My God," she gushed, snatching a fluted glass of champagne from a passing waiter and guzzling half of it. "My heart is still pounding."

Kaitlin swallowed the other half of the champagne, trading the empty glass for a full one. She had passed less than an hour at the party and her eyes were already swimming.

"You'd better go easy on that stuff," I cautioned. "You might want to keep your wits about you tonight."

"Introduce me to Caruso. Please, Annalisa, oh please," she said.

I took her hand and pulled her through the crowd to where Caruso received well-wishers like an incumbent politician.

"Enrico, this is my friend, Kaitlin. She just arrived in town. We passed her in the Palace yesterday."

"Pleased to meet you, Mr. Caruso. This is so wonderful. I came all this way on the train just to see you."

"I am very much pleased to meet you, Kaitlin."

Caruso's eyes widened as he marveled at Kaitlin's shimmering blue eyes and flawless skin.

"My God. I'm shaking hands with Enrico Caruso."

"You are come a long ways to see Caruso, Kaitlin?" he asked.

"All the way from Lawrence, Kansas. I doubt you ever heard of it."

"Kansas? I am meet a man from Kansas." Then it hit him. The hair was shorter, the look more sophisticated. But the slim nose, the full lips, the strong jawline were identical to the photo Lincoln carried.

"I am meet a man who is look for his *figlia*. His daughter. A sheriff, *chiamato* Lincoln Staley."

Kaitlin turned pale and the champagne struck home, making her light-headed and unsteady. I grabbed her arm.

"'E is your father, Lincoln, no? I am meet him on train and he becomes, 'ow you say . . . my *guardia del corpo?*"

"Bodyguard," I offered.

"He's here? My father? In this house?"

"'E was at opera, then I no see him no more. 'E is leave with Mr. Rolf's chauffeur. Big man. *Muscoloso.*"

I shuddered at the revelation, instantly fearing for Lincoln.

"Why don't we sit down, Kaitlin?" I urged. I led her away, carefully avoiding Adam Rolf as he chatted with Senator Payton.

Kaitlin slumped onto a divan. "My father. I saw him going into the Palace this afternoon. God. He's staying with Mr. Caruso."

"You're a runaway? How old are you?"

"Fifteen. They all think I'm eighteen."

I looked at Rolf, who walked to the foyer where Ah Toy entered clad in her trademark green silk. Behind her trailed Ting Leo in ivory pajamas, her angelic face framed by long black hair. Ah Toy nudged Ting Leo and spoke to her in Cantonese.

Slowly, Ting Leo offered her hand to Rolf. Rolf delicately pinched her smooth cheek, drawing a scowl.

I signaled a waiter, who recognized Kaitlin's condition and brought a glass of water for her.

"Drink this, Kaitlin. All of it," I told her.

I turned back to watch Ting Leo, dots of spectral light from the chandelier dancing across her face as she struggled to comprehend it all. I wanted to scream for Hunter and Christian to burst in and bludgeon Rolf and arrest them all.

Clyde Ebbens, the Senator's aide, walked over and touched Rolf's arm. Rolf excused himself, smiling down at Ting Leo.

Ebbens then nodded for the Senator, who left his wife to join them in the march toward the host's office. The jangle of forced laughter and tinkling glass swelled into a vortex.

I turned my attention to Kaitlin to avoid trading looks with Rolf as he passed.

Inside Rolf's office, Tommy locked the office door as his boss led Senator Payton to the safe.

"This is quite a home you have here, Adam," Senator Payton observed. "You must have collected things from all over the world."

"I hate to travel, actually. My San Francisco is everything to me. I buy from collectors. May I offer you a Havana cigar or a decent cognac?"

"Thank you. We have to be back in the capital to meet with the Governor first thing tomorrow. Mrs. Payton refuses to ride with me if I smell of cigars or have too much to drink. Much to my regret."

Rolf removed the leather portfolio and plopped it onto the middle of his desk. Ebbens and Payton stepped forward as Rolf opened the catches, spinning the case around to reveal the stacks of money.

"I usually prefer not to be involved in these sorts of transactions myself," the Senator said, a little wide-eyed.

Rolf laughed. "Quite the contrary, Senator. I don't let anyone handle these transactions for me. It is my personal philosophy that if a man trusts no one, he cannot be betrayed."

"So the rumors of your pending legal problems are just that? Rumors? You have not been betrayed?"

"If you're not the subject of gossip, you are not working hard enough," Rolf replied.

Rolf shoved the portfolio closer to the edge of the desk. Ebbens thumbed through a stack of hundred-dollar bills.

"You are a man of vision, Mr. Rolf," Payton declared. "Consolidation is our destiny. Commerce and transport, rail and shipping. The consolidation of San Francisco's stature as the seat of power, the land of empire-builders. It's the only way to choke off this vile Labor movement, these Socialist rabble-rousers and so-called 'Progressives,' to keep power in the hands of men bred to use it."

In the main parlor, a rejuvenated John Barrymore burst through the door and staggered toward Caruso. "Enrico, my God, what a performance!" he bellowed. Barrymore tripped over the carpet, spilling into Caruso's arms and kissing the tenor on both cheeks.

Barrymore beamed even more brightly when he spotted Kaitlin. "Kaitlin! My Kaitlin, you left me all alone!"

Kaitlin regained her equilibrium and rose to greet him. Barrymore tripped over the carpet again and nearly brought Kaitlin down with him, wrapping his arms around her.

"Kate," he said, his eyes swimming. "Why don't you come away with me? I have a bottle of some marvelous champagne back at the Palace. In fact, I have almost anything marvelous you might want."

I nudged Kaitlin and nodded, knowing she could escape a besotted Barrymore easier than Rolf.

"Go. Please," I said to her.

Kaitlin seized his arm and pulled him across the room and out the door.

Through the window in the parlor, I could see workmen hustling in and out of the Fairmont. Bulging drays made their way to the front entrance in an endless parade, where workmen stripped their cargo and sent them for another load.

From the fourth floor of the Fairmont, Hunter and Christian watched as Barrymore stumbled down the front steps toward a Hansom. He chivalrously tried to take Kaitlin's arm and help her in, but she thought it better the other way around. When he stalled half-way, she put her hand on his rump and shoved.

"That must be a record even for Barrymore," Hunter said. "How long was he in there? Thirty seconds?"

He looked over at Christian, who was pacing anxiously, working his knuckles and fondling his revolver.

Inside the mansion, the door to Rolf's office opened and Senator Payton emerged. He was followed closely by Ebbens, who now carried a heavy valise.

I gathered my gown and headed for the front door, forcing myself to slow as a butler opened the door for me.

On the expansive walkway between the porch and the brass fence, I dug in my shoulder bag and produced a machine-rolled cigarette, then fumbled to strike a match. The wind blew it out. I tried another, and again the wind blew it out.

From the window of room 434, Hunter spotted me. "Christian! Christian! I see her."

Christian bolted to the window, where they watched as I cupped my hands, turning my back to buffer the wind. I lit the cigarette and a puff of smoke escaped my mouth. I coughed.

"All right," Hunter said, "the Senator has the money. We should have Max or Carlo arrest him as he boards the ferry."

"No. We'll have Patrick arrest him when he gets *off* and turn him over to the Oakland police. That way San Francisco cops can't tip off Rolf."

"I guess that's better," Hunter replied.

While the Fallon brothers decided his fate, Senator Payton, his wife, and Ebbens exited the Rolf mansion and walked toward me.

"Good evening, Senator, Mrs. Payton. I hope you enjoyed yourselves this evening."

"It was most enjoyable, Miss Passarelli," Payton said. "We will look forward to reading your column. I'll hope you'll give us a kind mention."

"Thank you, sir. I think you'll find it very interesting."

The trio headed toward a Rolls Royce idling at the curb. I puffed nervously as the automobile chattered away down California Street.

"Annalisa. What are you doing out here?"

I wheeled as the sound of Rolf's voice startled me.

"Is that a cigarette I see you smoking? I have never seen you smoke before. Not very ladylike, I must say."

"It's one of those secret little vices," I whispered, trying to stifle a cough that threatened to unmask the lie.

"One you may wish to discontinue. Why don't you come back in before you catch yourself a death?"

I resisted the urge to flee. I raised the hem of my dress and started up the steps, distracted momentarily by the frantic whinnying of horses at the Fairmont.

"I'll be glad when these miserable nags are gone," Rolf said as he took my arm. "You, smoking: I'm afraid you are just full of surprises."

Hunter eased back from the window, reaching for his revolver. "Maybe we should go in now, Christian."

"And charge him with what? Making a campaign donation? You lose your nerve, your ass follows in this game. Sit tight. He's not going to hurt Annalisa in front of all those people. Last thing we want is Rolf and those clowns walking the streets again."

Inside the mansion, Rolf looked about, his expression souring. "Where's Kaitlin, Annalisa?"

"I thought I saw her leaving with Mr. Barrymore. I'm not sure where they were headed."

Rolf examined my face with a look that stoked my uneasiness. "Another one of my guests who lack the most common courtesies. It amazes me, Annalisa, how some people mistake my kindness for weakness."

He stared at me for a few seconds, then spotted Ah Toy and Ting Leo in the adjacent parlor. "Enjoy yourself," he said. "The night is just begin-ning." He walked away.

"Annalisa," Caruso said, approaching from behind. "These are won-derful peoples here. I never expect that they are love so much the opera. I think before they are *barbari* but now I am not so sure."

"They're barbarians, just better dressed." I leaned close and spoke softly. "Enrico, I have a secret I would like to share with you."

"Enrico is do two things very well, Annalisa. 'E is sing and 'e is keep *i segreti*."

"I am getting married today. He asked me at the Opera House, just before you sang. You are the only one I am telling."

"You are no tell your *genitori*?"

"My parents are both dead. So are his."

"Then I come and sing just for you."

He leaned forward to kiss my cheek and I threw my arms around his neck. From the corner of a misty eye, I caught Tommy glaring at me.

The clock was ticking loudly on the mantle.

Chapter 47

—··◆◇◆··—

APRIL 18, 1906. 5:00 A.M.

Two tense hours later, I stood before the window of the lady's second-floor powder room, trying to signal discreetly to Hunter that I was still safe. I could see his weariness and fear, even at that distance in the shadows of room 434.

In the streets below, the last of Adam Rolf's guests sauntered to their cars and carriages, all glimmering beneath the streetlights.

A few blocks east, at Central Fire Station, Dennis Sullivan examined the blueprints on his desk. His breathing was fitful, his eyes red and swollen from the fire he had battled past midnight.

He leaned back in the creaky chair, forcing his weary eyes to focus on the calendar. April 18, 1906. He retrieved his pencil and scribbled on the corner of the blueprints: *Thirteen years and thirteen days as Fire Chief.* A superstitious Maggie would have considered it a bad omen.

Outside the third-floor window, the sun peeked above Mount Diablo, painting a small patch of clouds with pale gold, a radiant splash of light amidst the darkness; an entire city in *chiaroscuro*. People who believed that sunrise was a perfect ending to the day traded places with those who thought it a better beginning, tuxedos and topcoats passing carpenters' coveralls and butchers' aprons. Hooves clopped and engines rattled up and down cobblestoned Bush Street.

The Chief returned to his blueprints, circling the long-dormant cisterns beneath the city's streets. His head drifted forward slowly, his sandy eyes closing. By the time his forehead touched the desk, he was asleep.

Across Bush Street, Fremont Older pecked at his editorial for a special edition.

THE DAWNING OF A NEW SAN FRANCISCO

The open-minded spirit that has graced San Francisco since the discovery of gold in the American River does not extend to tolerance of thieves, thugs, kidnappers, and child peddlers, no matter how well-heeled or well-connected they may be. The arrests of Adam Rolf, Eugene Schmitz, and all their glue-handed puppets on the Board of Supervisors will send a signal that resounds clear to Washington. The days of wholesale corruption, the days of municipal government by grafters and predators, have been dealt a serious blow this day, April 18, 1906. By the time Caruso takes center stage tonight to follow his astonishing *Carmen* with an equally anticipated *Bohème,* San Francisco will be a different place. By nightfall, the Paris of the West will glow as never before.

Older scrawled his signature, tucked the sheaf of paper into his coat pocket, and donned his faded bowler.

Once outside, he inhaled the sweet morning air and headed toward the Palace Hotel, where Cora slept in the suite that served as home.

A mile away, where Washington Street crests between the cramped squalor of Chinatown and the splendor of Van Ness Avenue, Frederick Funston was awakened by muffled gunshots. He had been asleep an hour, having spent the night working on the war games he was to lead that month with all of the Army troops on the West Coast. He slid into his britches, tucking a revolver into his waistband, and hustled outside.

The crisp air invigorated him. Another gunshot told him the culprits were more than a dozen blocks away, in the midst of the Barbary Coast, and finding them would be impossible. He lingered, staring up Jones Street to Nob Hill where a lone painter tried to capture the morning sky.

All around the bay, brigantines and clippers, paddle-wheel ferries and graceful Whitehalls carved their foamy wakes.

At the Palace, Enrico Caruso had just fallen asleep. An hour earlier, after promising for the fourth time to sing at my wedding, he had arrived at the Palace in Rolf's Phaeton. At the hotel's entrance, he saw a threadbare old man huddling against the chill. Caruso removed his overcoat, stuffed a handful of bills and coins into the pockets, and handed it to the old man.

The triumphant tenor now snored contentedly, surrounded by his sketches and the photograph of himself with Theodore Roosevelt.

At the Fairmont, Hunter Fallon stared from the window, past the Golden Gate to the amber light that spread across Mount Tamalpais.

"*La luce splendida*," he muttered.

"What?" Christian asked.

"The splendid light. I decided to keep up the tradition."

Their attention swiftly turned to Rolf's mansion as Ah Toy shuffled to her covered carriage, where a Tong bodyguard opened the door.

Christian raised his brass telescope in time to catch Patrick jumping off the California Street cable car. The younger Fagen ducked behind the wall of the Crocker mansion to rejoin brother Francis.

Patrick looked toward the Fairmont, shrugged his shoulders, and raised his arms out in defeat.

"Damn it to Hell," Christian spat. "Something happened. The Senator got away."

"It won't matter. When Rolf is facing the hangman, they'll all trip over their tongues implicating each other," Hunter said.

"Bad start. Bad omen, Hunter. This ain't the way to do it."

The steeple bell on St. Mary's Church in Chinatown chimed five times as a battered carriage bearing Shanghai Kelly and Scarface stopped at the rear of Rolf's mansion.

"This is it," Christian said excitedly.

He and Hunter grabbed their weapons and pulled on long black dusters.

"Do me a favor, little brother. If either of these sons of bitches even looks at you wrong, blow a hole in him the size of the Broadway Tunnel."

"If they draw on us, I'll kill them. Otherwise, no. Feeney wants them on trial and so do I."

"Write that in their obituaries if it makes you happy."

They bolted from the room, taking the steps two at a time.

"I was startin' to think that stinkin' Kelly was never gonna show," Max snapped when they arrived in the lobby. "I oughta kill him just for messing with my sleep."

"Carlo," Christian said, "when Annalisa signals, you go in the back door with Francis and Patrick. Hunter, you'll go in the front door with me and Max. Let's keep our eyes peeled. Rolf likes to fight his wars in a courtroom. Those other guys ain't that fussy."

I was sprawled in an armchair in Rolf's front parlor, exhausted and on edge. Ting Leo dozed fitfully across from me, on the divan, her small frame curled into a ball.

"Annalisa!" Rolf's voice suddenly commanded.

I sat up quickly as he stepped into view. "Adam! You frightened me."

The lines in his face were deeper than I had seen them. The light from the chandeliers, gay and invigorating earlier, created ghoulish shadows in his icy stare. "Annalisa. There's someone here to see you."

I tensed. "It's awfully late. I had better take Ting Leo back to Chinatown."

Rolf extended his hand and motioned toward his office.

Tommy appeared and lifted Ting Leo from the couch.

I glanced behind me and shuddered to see Scarface in the front entrance. I forced myself to rise, looking about for an escape route, my legs a pair of rubbery bands.

Shanghai Kelly waited inside Rolf's office, his face a mass of bruises. Tommy set Ting Leo down. She cringed at the sight of Kelly.

"Annalisa, you remember Mr. Kelly?"

"Of course. He sat in your opera box and built an alibi while his men killed Lieutenant Fallon. One of his men tried to kill me. Kelly's had your precious papers all this time," I said, trying to stall for time.

"So, Kelly," Rolf said. "You did have the papers, just as I suspected. This is what, twice you've pulled this on me?"

"Ain't like it'll break you, now," Kelly scoffed. "All the dirty work I done for you."

I inched slowly toward the window as they argued.

Tommy took a step to head me off. He raised a finger to his lips to silence me, his hand on the revolver beneath his coat. He appeared ready to kill me before I could blurt out that he too had betrayed Adam Rolf.

Rolf turned his attention back to me. "When I found my ledger upside down in the safe, I knew Pierre had let someone in but the little poof killed himself before I could squeeze it out of him. If I hadn't been playing with the silver chain you gave me, I might never have suspected. Is there something in the papers that gives you away?"

Ting Leo moved across the room and leaned her head against my arm.

"I was plannin' on bringing her head over on a platter," Kelly said, handing Rolf the papers. "A little gesture like I promised."

"You might still get the chance," Rolf replied. He thumbed through the papers, growing angrier by the second.

My gaze drifted to the window facing Mason Street.

"How thorough you were, Annalisa. You must have spent every second trying to put a dagger in my back."

"It was a pleasure, Adam. Really it was. A predator who rapes children and profits from their misery, a pathetic little man who wouldn't have a friend in the world if he didn't buy them. Did you really think you could murder Byron Fallon and get away with it?"

"Let's see. I own the Police Chief, the Mayor, half the judges in town. I would say the odds are favorable."

He walked toward us, eliciting a whimper from Ting Leo.

"You know, Annalisa," Rolf said, leaning close. "I rather fancied you. But your little friend will provide me more pleasure than you ever could."

He stepped back. "Kelly, help yourself to Miss Passarelli. When you finish, sell her to the filthiest crib on Pacific Avenue. Now, if you all will excuse me."

Tommy grabbed my wrist as Rolf seized Ting Leo. The moment they pried her from my grip, I wheeled and kneed Tommy in the groin with all the strength my tired frame could muster.

He groaned and buckled as I sprinted to the window and ripped the shade from its mount.

"Hunter! Hunter!!"

Tommy recovered and tackled me from the rear.

Ting Leo grabbed a pearl-handled letter opener and plunged it into Rolf's thigh. Rolf screamed and staggered to his knees.

Across the street, The Brotherhood pulled their weapons and charged across California Street. Hunter and Christian shoved through the brass front gate as beefy Max trailed behind.

The corner clock hit five-thirteen.

The horses outside the Fairmont reared as the ground began to tremble. The shaking grew in intensity until the six men in long black dusters began to stumble.

Rolf pulled the letter opener from his leg as the floor bucked, glass tinkled and books began to fall.

Tommy looked at the chandelier dancing wildly above his head, affording me the chance to escape his grip again.

I rolled away and covered Ting Leo with my body.

Then it hit.

PART THREE

THE RIP

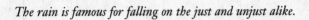

The rain is famous for falling on the just and unjust alike.

— MARK TWAIN

Chapter 48

NORTHERN CALIFORNIA COAST

APRIL 18, 1906. 5:13 A.M.

I lay on the floor of Adam Rolf's mansion, trying to shield Ting Leo, while the end of the world advanced toward us with astonishing speed.

As Professor Jeremy Darling had long speculated, somewhere on the ocean floor west of the Golden Gate the jagged edges of the opposing Pacific and North American plates crumbled, like teeth breaking on two enormous sets of gears.

The San Andreas Fault slipped by twenty feet.

A rip in the ocean floor opened and shut with such force it spit a plume of water toward the surface more than two miles above. The watery blast slammed the hull of the wooden fishing yawl *Old Manassas*, lifting it clear out of the water. Four thousand pounds of salmon and a sleeping crew of five floated in air, and then crashed to the sodden deck. They bobbed frantically as the sea parted and a mountain of water rained down on them, threatening to sink the helpless boat.

The fissure sped across the ocean floor, shooting a serpentine tail arcing above the dark blue surface. A mile off California's northern coast, the watery tail struck the steamship *Argonaut* with such force the rivets exploded from its steel hull as though they were fired from a Gatling gun.

One hundred fifty miles north of San Francisco, the fissure burst ashore, cleaving Alder Creek in two, and rumbled into the fishing village at Point Arena. It cracked the Point Arena Lighthouse like a bull whip and tossed the sleeping light keeper into the opposite wall, inches below the window.

The rip tore across Humboldt County like an invisible plowman, leveling mile after mile of ancient forest, swallowing cabins and farmhouses, tossing livestock and laborers, catapulting a deliveryman through the window of a grocery store where he was buried beneath tins of beans and pork. It lifted the mountain above Mill Creek, dropping a million tons of dirt and shale, fir and redwood on the lumber mill below, burying fifteen lumberjacks, mule tenders, trimmers, and pond monkeys. Ripping south, it moved a farmhouse twenty feet, dropping it intact before a barn where its owner was trying unsuccessfully to milk his frightened Jerseys.

In Sonoma County, it pulverized the old Russian church at Fort Ross and splintered thousands of virgin oak and redwood trees, the deafening staccato echoing for miles through the surrounding canyons.

The rip dove back toward the sea, shattering miles of Sonoma County cliffs, burying pristine beaches under tons of shale and granite, shoving long-submerged shoals above the waterline.

It re-emerged near the promontory of Bodega Head, flattening the Bodega Bay Hotel and a dozen sleeping occupants like a phantom steamroller. At Marshall, it lifted the town's waterfront hotel and dropped it into the bay, submerging the lobby in water, leaving the sleeping tenants on the floor above unharmed. It split Tomales Bay down the middle, moving the western shoreline eighteen feet north.

Engineer Andy McNab, shoveling coal into the boiler of his locomotive at Point Reyes Station, heard a grinding sound and turned to see the ridges above him rolling like waves at sea. Paper Mill Creek before him narrowed by six feet, its wooden bridge bent like a giant toothpick. The wave bucked McNab and his train's four cars into an adjacent poppy field.

At the tiny village of Bolinas, the rip cleaved the cliffs in two and tossed heavy redwood docks into the sea. A barren field became a lagoon, its cloverleaf indentation swelling with water from the Pacific.

The rip rolled on through southern Marin County, a giant serpent beneath an earthen blanket. It raced past Alcatraz, leaving the island untouched, the prisoners still snoring in their bunks.

The trembling beneath San Francisco grew as thirty-five thousand structures began a violent hula dance. Along the Barbary Coast, chandeliers bucked, tables overturned, and gamblers were hurled from their seats. The Red Rooster and The Olde Whore Shoppe collapsed, burying their drunken patrons.

In Chinatown a few blocks away, terrified occupants clung to their airborne beds as the flimsy tenements burst at their mortared seams, pitching everything and everyone to the streets. In the dank basements, floors collapsed on opium smokers, fan-tan players, and prostitutes.

Along the waterfront, a thousand boats slammed against the docks, spilling cargo into the sea, pitching crews overboard. San Francisco Bay rose two feet, the water sloshing back and forth for a hundred miles.

The Palace Hotel, with twelve hundred sleeping guests and staff, swayed in an enormous circle, grinding and wrenching against its steel bracing, the upper floors leaning out over the sidewalks of Market Street and New Montgomery. Enrico Caruso awoke to the sound of tinkling chandeliers and the sensation of his bed hopping about the room, his carefully hung self-portraits raining down on top of him.

Along regal Van Ness Avenue, the cobblestones resembled popping corn and the hills undulated like blankets being shaken out by unseen hands. A young man was bucked into the air and landed on ground that was several feet below where he had stood.

On Mission Street, six *vaqueros* and sixty steers tumbled and rolled. The animals sprang to their feet, stampeding and trampling fallen passersby.

Inside the mansion on Nob Hill, I prayed aloud and waited for the building to collapse on top of us. I saw Rolf's massive safe spring to life and dance about the room. Ivory tusks took flight, heavy vases shattered, bookshelves ripped loose and crashed on the hard oak floors.

Just outside the front gate, the six members of The Brotherhood were pinned to the ground, unable even to crawl. California Street became a giant roller coaster, the cable car tracks twisting and snaking, fire hydrants blasted skyward.

The rip tore south along the Peninsula, smashed through the mansions of Hillsborough and Belmont, and leveled building after building at Stanford University, including the stable Hunter Fallon had called home. It shattered the booming downtown area of San José.

Finally, it dove back into the Pacific at Monterey, sending shock waves south to Los Angeles, and rattled windows in the small beach town of Santa Monica.

Then it stopped. It had lasted less than a minute.

At the crest of Nob Hill, Hunter and Christian struggled to their knees as the city fell silent for a moment, save for the maniacal clanging of a hundred church bells.

Carlo scrambled over the buckled street shrieking, "Max! Max!" His brother lay crushed beneath an iron lamppost. Carlo's cries were soon drowned by the mounting thunder of hundreds of buildings spilling into the streets. Billowing clouds of dust poured skyward, blocking the eerie sunrise.

Inside Rolf's mansion, I struggled to free myself from beneath a mound of books and shattered porcelain. In the dim light ten feet away, Adam Rolf stirred, a bloodstain welling on his trousers where Ting Leo had stabbed him. I realized she had crawled out from beneath me and was lying several feet away, breathing in staccato bursts, her eyes full of terror.

Everything seemed detached, slow, as if we existed in some netherworld. I looked up to find Tommy standing over me, blood streaming from a gash above his eyebrow. He jerked my head back and slid the blade of a large knife against my throat. I tried to move but my limbs seemed soft as dough.

To my left, a muffled shotgun blast tore the door open and Hunter and Christian burst in. Hunter ran toward me, his revolver pointed at Tommy's head. Tommy dropped his knife and stepped away.

Across the room, Christian pointed the double-barreled Remington at Scarface and Kelly.

Adam Rolf struggled to a sitting position and reached for the papers scattered on the floor. The next I knew, my foot was atop his fingers. He cursed, though the words were distant and unclear.

Francis rushed in, clutching his revolver. "Max is gone," he shouted. "We'll need a crane to pull that thing off of him."

Shanghai Kelly smirked and muttered, "Good riddance."

Christian smashed Scarface across the face with the butt of his shotgun, dropping him to his knees. He then shoved the barrel beneath Kelly's chin.

"You got something to say, Kelly?" Christian demanded.

"Let's get the bracelets on these guys," Francis ordered.

They quickly manacled Scarface, Kelly, Tommy, and Rolf and forced them facedown onto the floor.

Christian, Hunter, and Francis convened in a corner of the room, out of earshot of their prisoners. I walked unsteadily toward them and handed Francis the photographs and affidavits.

Hunter asked if I was all right, and I must have nodded. I was distracted by the sight of Patrick pulling a distraught Carlo away from Max's mangled body.

Francis cleared his dusty throat and spoke quietly. "All right. Hunter, you and I will take these birds to jail. Christian, check on Elizabeth and your kids, then take all the papers to your father's house for safekeeping. Patrick and Carlo can check on our families and talk to Max's mother. We'll arrange a proper burial later. We'll meet up in North Beach in an hour."

"Take my motorcycle," Hunter said to Christian. "It will be a lot faster."

"Let's move," Francis urged, "I got a hunch this is going to be a long day."

—◦◦◦◦◦—

Chapter 49

BUSH STREET

APRIL 18, 1906. 5:18 A.M.

"Dennis! Dennis! Oh, God, please help me. Dennis!"

Choking and blinded by the dust from his shattered firehouse, Dennis Sullivan crawled across the jagged oak floor toward Maggie's screams.

"Dennis. Oh, God. Dennis!"

Sullivan had heard heart-wrenching pleas all his life, but nothing tore at him like Maggie's barely human screams. He pulled himself forward, disoriented by the rising steam and the hiss of the boiler three stories below. He felt his way over a pile of bricks that had composed the spire of the California Hotel next door.

"Maggie," he uttered hoarsely, "Maggie!" He got to his feet and staggered forward, Maggie's cries getting closer.

Then Sullivan stepped into an abyss, falling headfirst, suspended for a moment in the billowing dust and steam.

"Dennis!"

Maggie's voice lingered in his ears, as if her lips were pressed against him. Sullivan's head struck the flue of the boiler, his wife's pleas fading as his body pitched over in the scalding spray.

On the fifth floor of the Palace Hotel, Alfred Hertz shoved his way against the tide of half-naked people. He knocked at the door of Enrico Caruso's suite but the shouting of guests and groaning of the still-swaying building drowned him out. A small jolt sent Hertz sprawling to the floor amidst a sea of writhing bodies, all of them shrieking in terror. He propped himself against the doorframe, praying for the circular motion to stop lest the hotel crash to the streets below. When it finally ceased and the stampede resumed, he heard wailing through a small crack where the latest shock had sprung the door ajar.

He shoved into Caruso's anteroom and stopped cold, stunned at the disarray. Caruso's drawings lay amidst mountains of clothes tossed from the dresser drawers. A bonnet-top chest had skipped the width of the room and crashed atop an armchair, reducing it to kindling. At Hertz's feet lay a Turkish carpet, neatly rolled, as if the temblor had prepared it for removal. Shards of mirror strewn about gave the unnerving scene a funhouse look.

Caruso staggered in from his bedroom, clad in satin nightshirt. Impossibly heroic on stage just five hours before, he appeared as dazed as an orphaned child. Hertz ran to keep him from walking barefoot across a pile of broken glass.

The singer clutched his throat. "Alfred," he whispered hoarsely, "I am lose my voice. *La voce è morta*. Is died, my voice." The building swayed again, casting the distressed tenor to his knees, a pose as comic and tragic as his beloved clown in *Pagliacci*.

In her room two floors below, Kaitlin picked her way around the fallen chandelier and overturned furniture to find John Barrymore in an armchair, snoring contentedly. In one hand he clutched a half-empty bottle of champagne; the front of his shirt bore the other half.

"Mr. Barrymore, Mr. Barrymore!"

She shook him several times. A chorus of lurching, guttural hacks was all the effort earned her. She stumbled across the room and slipped into the hallway, where she was pinned against the wall by the rush of people shoving to escape as the hotel continued to waver.

Atop Washington Street, Frederick Funston emerged from his house for the second time that morning. He stared toward the waterfront, tracing the sea of destruction. Clouds of dust obscured portions of North Beach, the Barbary Coast, and the Financial District as the unending collapse of buildings rumbled through the morning air.

The General marveled at the throngs of people rushing about him, dazed but silent, their paths jagged and footsteps wobbly. He had seen the same phenomenon in Cuba and the Philippines, when hardened soldiers returned from battle, unable to perform tasks as simple as opening a canteen.

What he saw next sent a shudder through him: seven distinct plumes of smoke stretching from the waterfront to the Financial District, their dark tails rising through the clouds of dust. He ran into the house and dressed in his uniform.

At his house on Fillmore Street, Eugene Schmitz fumbled with the buttons on his suit, his house intact save for a handful of broken knick-knacks. The impact of the tremor had seemed so mild at the Schmitz residence that the Mayor had considered returning to bed.

A honking horn drew him outside, where Chief Donen's red Model N Ford idled at the curb.

"Just how bad is it?" the Mayor asked.

"Half the buildings downtown look like somebody took a paddy shovel to 'em. All the telephone and telegraph lines are down, everything's busted."

Schmitz shivered. They motored down the cracked cobblestones of Fillmore Street as shopkeepers picked gingerly among the broken windows and fallen shelves.

Donen wheeled east onto Bush Street, the damage worsening by the block. Houses leaned against each other at comic angles, telephone and electric lines lay entangled in piles of bricks and mortar. Scores wobbled from their houses naked or in nightclothes, silent and rudderless. Schmitz gripped the dashboard and mumbled a prayer.

Donen whipped onto broad Van Ness Avenue, its mansions virtually undamaged. The Ford's rubber tires began to slip as a torrent of water poured over the shattered street.

"That water is from one of the three main Spring Valley lines," Schmitz said. "It runs right below Van Ness. This is worse than bad."

In the eerie light ahead of them loomed a sight so alien that Schmitz' foggy mind dismissed it as an illusion. A colossal steel skeleton, like a giant birdcage, towered over Market Street where City Hall should have been. The Mayor searched for other landmarks to confirm he had misjudged the site's location.

Donen stopped the Ford in the middle of Larkin Street, directly across from City Hall.

"Sweet Mary, Mother of God," Schmitz uttered. Not a square of marble or a slab of granite still covered the steel skeleton. The enormous support columns were shattered to their bases. To their left, the massive dome of the Hall of Records had collapsed upon itself, taking the interior of the building with it. Piles of expensive waste surrounded the ruins of the entire three-block structure, with floating papers and clouds of dust hanging so heavily above it that the sunlight was divided into shafts.

Schmitz stepped over the twisted noodles that had once been trolley lines. At the rear entrance of City Hall, he stared down into the hollow core of the shattered pillars. Mounds of compressed newspapers, which corrupt contractors had used for filler, stared back, several of their headlines still legible.

A young reporter from the *Bulletin* stepped up next to him. "I wouldn't fret, Mr. Mayor. Concrete is expensive. It scarcely leaves enough money for bribes."

Schmitz stared at the reporter for a moment, and then turned to Donen. "We still have a Hall of Justice, do we?"

"It ain't pretty, but it's standing."

Schmitz looked past Donen to the new Central Emergency Hospital a block away. Each of the six floors had collapsed onto the one below. Doctors and hospital staff tore at the wreckage with bare hands, trying desperately to reach patients and nurses who had fallen into the first-floor operating room. Schmitz at last realized the piercing sounds he heard were cries for help.

To their left, across the wide plaza from the damaged hospital, the enormous Mechanics' Pavilion seemed intact. "That's the biggest open floor in the city," Schmitz said to Donen. "Let's set up a makeshift hospital over there."

On Bush Street, the men of Central Fire Station fought desperately to reach Dennis Sullivan. Steam pouring from the station house boiler hindered their efforts to pull a mountain of bricks off their beloved Chief. An aftershock sent more debris raining down on them. The sweating, choking men finally pulled Sullivan free and slid him onto a stretcher as blood seeped from the right side of his skull. They cut through his clothes to find several broken ribs, at least one of which had punctured a lung. Steam had scalded half his body.

They lifted his stretcher as two firemen carried a bleeding Mrs. Sullivan down the shattered stairway.

"Where's my husband? Where's Dennis?"

"He's here with us, ma'am," one of them answered. "We need to get him to Southern Pacific Hospital as fast as we can."

She stepped forward, and her eyes focused on her husband's burns and the blood streaming from his head. Mrs. Sullivan shrieked, collapsing into the arms of her rescuers.

Sullivan's men hoisted his stretcher onto their shoulders and ran toward the hospital at Fourteenth and Mission Street, twenty blocks away.

On Market Street, shock had given way to mounting alarm as Donen and Schmitz bumped their way through a carnival of the bizarre. A woman ran across their path, naked beneath her fur coat, carrying a broken lantern. Sleepy-eyed children dragged their mattresses and favorite toys down the filthy street. A businessman clad in striped undershorts and tuxedo tails stumbled about, holding an empty birdcage. A man on crutches struggled over the jagged cobblestones, a candelabrum dangling from a long black scarf draped around his neck.

A psalm-chanting young woman ran pell-mell, holding a naked baby by its ankles like a boiled chicken. Scores of trunk rollers and trunk draggers struggled to move their belongings over lumpy streets and sidewalks. To complete the carnival, masked and costumed roller skaters from the previous night's *Mardi Gras* at the Mechanics' Pavilion glided in and out of the wreckage.

At the corner of Fifth and Market, Schmitz caught sight of something that frightened him more than any thing yet. Above the tenements South of the Slot rose four plumes of smoke. Another two stretched behind the Emporium near Fourth Street. Before Schmitz and Donen turned left on Kearny, they noticed another black tail arching skyward just beyond the Palace Hotel.

They bounced through the Financial District, dodging businessmen shoving roll-top desks and claw-foot chairs stacked with files. Schmitz gripped the door of the Ford, fighting a wave of dizziness.

Donen stopped the car before the Hall of Justice, cracked in a jigsaw pattern up its entire six-story façade. Across the street, Portsmouth Square was filling with shouting people who had escaped the devastation in Chinatown. Two dozen police officers had set up a cordon in front of the Hall and struggled to control a crowd that had already reached two hundred. A young patrolman ran to Donen. Shouts and calls from the crowd made it difficult for Donen and Schmitz to hear.

"Chief. We got reports of looting breakin' out all over the bloody place. These people here got family trapped in the rubble. They're demandin' we help 'em."

Schmitz inserted himself in front of Donen. "Listen, officer. I want you to take Chief Donen's car and go to every precinct in the city and see that every officer reports for duty. I want a full damage report on every station house, firehouse, and hospital as fast as you can get them, understand?"

"Yes, sir."

"Chief Donen, I want you to round up every clerk in this building and have them meet us in the basement." Schmitz hesitated, watching a dozen plumes of smoke growing in the distance. Then he shoved through the cracked front door and skipped down the steps.

Several employees, left over from the night shift, were straightening cabinets and shoveling debris from the floor. "All right," bellowed Schmitz. "Listen to me. I need everyone's cooperation. Is there a printing press anywhere that is still functioning?"

"Yes, sir," replied a bearded secretary. "There's one just up on Sacramento Street, near the Bank of Italy. I was picking up some forms when it hit."

Schmitz found a writing tablet amid the debris and scribbled a note with his fountain pen. "If that press isn't working, find another one. Have this proclamation printed as fast as they can get it out. If they refuse, I'll have them arrested. Understand?"

"Yes, sir."

"I want every bar and liquor store in the city closed down. Anyone who dispenses alcohol will have their stock destroyed immediately. I smelled gas when we were driving in. People are not to use their gas or electricity until further orders. No fires, no indoor cooking is to be done until we get a handle on this thing."

Schmitz handed the order to the trembling young man, who saluted him half-heartedly and ran out. The sound of desperate cries carried from somewhere above them.

"What's that screaming?" the Mayor demanded.

"The prisoners, Mr. Mayor," someone responded. "The jail cells are leaning and the roof looks like it might give in."

"Close the doors and ignore them until we can find a place to transfer them. Now, I want situation boards set up on everything, the hospitals, the fire department, the police department, the telephone and telegraph lines. Casualties, relief efforts, damage reports, everything. Does anybody have any idea how we can send a message?"

"Yes, sir," called a lanky clerk. "A man come by, said the Army office over in the Phelan Building has got a line."

"Get a message to the Governor in Sacramento, the Mayors of Oakland and Berkeley. Tell them we need pumps, fire hoses, and all the men they can spare. And we're going to need drinking water. Send a telegram to the Navy at Mare Island and see what they can do." It dawned on Schmitz that there might not be a Berkeley or an Oakland. "Get those telegrams off," he said, "and find out their conditions. Where is Fire Chief Sullivan? Has anyone seen Sullivan?"

"He's on his way to Southern Pacific Hospital," a gravelly voice called from behind him. Schmitz turned to face Assistant Fire Chief Dougherty, a slumped and white-cheeked man. "He's unconscious. His head is busted; the steam from a boiler burned him something awful."

The news almost knocked Schmitz off his feet. He wanted to close his eyes and pretend that none of this had happened, that the one man he desperately needed had not been lost.

"He was the first casualty recorded," Dougherty added solemnly. "First name to make it onto the sheet."

Schmitz stared into the cloudy blue eyes of the sixty-eight-year-old Assistant Chief, whose engineering expertise had kept him in the department long after his days as a firefighter had ended.

"Mr. Dougherty, that leaves the burden of the department on your shoulders."

"Yes, sir," he said. "I'm a bit long in the tooth, but I will do my best."

"What is the condition of the department?" Schmitz asked Dougherty.

"Every fire station I passed is damaged. All the wet cell batteries in the central alarm office over in Chinatown are busted, which means the whole alarm system is down. There's fires burnin' everywhere, and the main feed lines from the Spring Valley are split wide open and spittin' water up through the cobblestones."

"We need a map of the city," Schmitz bellowed. "Somebody find us a map!"

Three blocks east, Hunter and Francis turned from California onto Kearny, shepherding Tommy, Scarface, Adam Rolf, and Shanghai Kelly in front of them. Ting Leo squeezed my hand tightly as we trailed behind.

"How long have you been on the police force?" Rolf demanded of Hunter.

"I'm a veteran," Hunter said. "Today makes four days."

"Four days. Four days and you think you're going to arrest me and get away with it?"

"There are a lot of surprises coming, Mr. Rolf," Francis interjected. "Especially how fast you hit the end of the noose when the trapdoor drops."

I tapped Hunter's arm and pointed to a furniture store two doors down on Sacramento. Three ragged men threw a trash can through the window and began pulling out expensive lamps.

"Hey, you!" Hunter yelled. "Police! Stop!"

Two of the men started to run. The third hesitated and extended a raised middle finger in Hunter's direction, then bolted and dropped the lamp, which shattered on the sidewalk.

Shanghai Kelly scowled. "Don't you bloody Fallons ever mind your own business?"

We approached the growing mob scene on Kearny. Behind the crowd, four columns of soldiers, rifles on their shoulders, turned the corner and headed toward the Hall of Justice. At the head of the pack strode Frederick Funston, his face lost beneath the brim of his campaign hat.

"I'm not sure I like the looks of that," Hunter said as we squeezed past the crowd.

In the basement, Schmitz barked orders to two dozen men working feverishly around him. "I want someone to make a list of the city's business leaders. I don't care which party they belong to. I want them down here as fast as we can find them."

He was interrupted by the arrival of a limping Adam Rolf, still in his evening attire, his hands manacled behind him. Following him marched Tommy, Scarface, and Kelly.

"Adam," Schmitz called, "what the hell is going on here?"

Francis stepped from behind them and lowered his shotgun. "These men are under arrest, Mayor Schmitz."

"On what charges?"

"Three of them for the murder of Lieutenant Fallon, Mr. Rolf's body-guard for the attempted murder of Miss Passarelli."

Jessie Donen stormed over. "What the hell is this?"

Francis looked his chief in the eye. "We have proof that Mr. Rolf and Mr. Kelly here conspired to kill Lieutenant Fallon. Scarface and Felix Gamboa did the dirty work, but I guess you already know that since you sprang Gamboa from Alcatraz."

Donen turned livid, growling through clenched teeth. "Talk like that can you get you and your dippy cousin here in a lot of trouble, Officer

Fagen. Who the hell gave you the authority to march the City Attorney through town with a shotgun in his back?"

"Prosecutor Feeney."

Donen started unlocking Rolf's manacles. "And where would you have us keep 'em? You hear that yellin' and bangin' upstairs? Them that's locked up now like to bust their way out."

"This is a murder charge," Hunter said angrily. "These men murdered my father and we have enough evidence to hang every one of them."

"This earthquake must have made you boys as loony as the rest of them," Donen answered, his fury growing.

"What I'd like to know, Annalisa," Schmitz inquired, "is what you have to do with all this."

"I collected evidence against Mr. Rolf that helped lead to the indictments."

Before Schmitz could reply, Brigadier General Funston stormed into the room.

"What can I do for you, General?" the Mayor asked.

"It's what I can do for you, Mayor Schmitz. On my way from the Presidio, I chased off a half-dozen looters and counted a dozen fires. In a couple of hours, the whole South of Market is going to be on fire. This city is going to require order. Military order. I've got two thousand men at arms, ready to follow my every command and protect this city."

"You can't do that, Mayor Schmitz," Hunter argued angrily. "You cannot declare martial law without the authorization of President Roosevelt!"

"And who are you?" glowered the impatient general.

A frightened, baby-faced police officer ran into the room and pushed his way to Chief Donen. "Chief, Mr. Mayor. We got a situation outside. There's rumors runnin' wild a gang of two hundred men are gatherin' down to the train station and fixin' to rob the Mint."

"There's millions in gold bullion in the Mint. General Funston," Schmitz barked, "I want a detachment of your men to surround the building. And I want you to coordinate all the other activities of your troops with me. Is that clear?"

Funston motioned his duty officer over. "Send twenty riflemen to guard the Mint, tell them to double-time over there."

The officer saluted and ran off. Funston returned his attention to Schmitz. "And what about looters?" Funston demanded.

"Shoot them" Schmitz ordered. "Anyone caught looting is to be shot on sight."

I struggled to control myself. "Mayor Schmitz," I blurted. "You're going to let privates and corporals shoot people like they're hunting rabbits?"

"Who is this woman?" Funston demanded.

"I'm a reporter for the *Bulletin*."

"Ma'am," Funston responded, "if you say another word or try to interfere with the military authority, I'll arrest you and have you carted off to the brig at the Presidio. Now stand back."

Donen finished removing the manacles from Kelly and Tommy.

"Sir," Hunter implored Schmitz, "These men killed the best police officer in the city and we have proof. If you can't keep them in custody, we'll take them to jail in Oakland."

"Listen, son," Schmitz said, "Mr. Rolf isn't going anywhere. If anyone was involved in the death of your father, I will see they answer for it. But right now, I have much bigger problems to contend with."

"No," Francis argued, stepping back, and gripping his shotgun. "You can't do this. These men killed the Lieutenant, sure as we're standing here."

"I'm going to give both of you boys one last chance," Donen warned. "Stand down or I'll have you disarmed and arrested."

Hunter and Francis glowered at the smug Adam Rolf, and then stormed from the room. Ting Leo and I scurried after them.

Rolf moved close to Schmitz. "This would be a very bad time to develop a backbone, Eugene."

"No, Adam, this is precisely the time. If I find evidence you or anyone murdered Byron Fallon, God help you."

Rolf limped away, his jubilant goons trailing behind him.

Dougherty huffed back to Schmitz' side and spread a tourist map on the table. Funston stepped in next to them as Dougherty pointed.

"The most important buildings south of Market are the Mint on Fifth and the Southern Pacific Depot on Townsend," the old man said nervously. "We're going to have to make a firebreak somewhere. Right now the wind is blowing south, toward the train depot. If we make the break along Brannan, we can save the station. As for the Mint, they have an artesian well and the building is made of granite. They can fend for themselves unless the wind changes."

"And how do we make a firebreak along Brannan if we have no water, Chief?" Schmitz asked.

"Dynamite," Funston interjected.

Schmitz stared at the map, his spirits sinking by the second. "And what do we dynamite? Boardinghouses, hotels? There's a hundred thousand people in that neighborhood. Except for Chinatown, it's the densest area in the whole damn city."

"We have no choice," Funston argued. "It's either water or dynamite, and right now we have no water."

Schmitz tried to steady himself. "We never trained anyone to use dynamite. That and a supplemental saltwater system were part of Chief Sullivan's proposal."

"My men will carry out the assignment," Funston countered. "They have experience with ordnance."

"Ordnance, yes," Dougherty replied, "but cannon and dynamite are not the same, General. The improper use of explosives can be disastrous."

"Do you have a better plan, Mr. Dougherty?" Funston inquired. Dougherty's silence shook the anxious men around them.

Outside the Hall of Justice, the smoke wafting skyward from South of Market grew by the minute.

"I guess God figured our efforts were too little, too late," I said. "And now, we set cop killers free and turn the Army loose to start shooting people!"

"I'm worried about what Christian will do when he finds out they let dad's killers go," Hunter answered.

"You leave Christian to me," Francis countered. "The only one who can straighten this out is Prosecutor Feeney. Right now there are people all over the place desperate for help. Let's go find Christian and get to it."

I grabbed Ting Leo's hand and the four of us hurried up Montgomery, past the battered Barbary Coast. Garbled music and raucous laughter poured from buildings that appeared to stand by nothing but force of habit.

Near Broadway, we heard the Waltham approaching, followed by the sight of Christian bouncing over the twisted trolley tracks and broken bricks. He skidded to a stop in front of the Montgomery Museum, where the formaldehyde-filled jar that bore the head of Joaquín Murietta had fallen through the window and shattered on the sidewalk. The frantic people running by scarcely noticed the pickled skull staring up at them.

"My place survived okay," Christian said. "I packed Elizabeth and the kids onto old man Hazifotis' fishing boat. He's taking them up the Delta to his brother's place near Sacramento. Dad's place is a mess but it's still standing. I hid the evidence in the wine cellar, behind the panel. Where's Rolf and Kelly?"

Our glum looks stopped Christian. "Don't tell me. They turned them loose? I'll kill every one of them."

"Right now, we got other things need doin'," Francis argued. "The fire department is lookin' at a nightmare, especially South of Market."

Shouts and screams resounded from Dupont Street a block away. In seconds, dozens of Chinese came pouring from the alleys, fleeing some unseen terror.

Hunter turned to Francis. "We'll meet you South of Market. Sixth Street looks like it got the worst of it. We'll see what's going on in Chinatown and meet you there."

Ting Leo, Hunter, Christian, and I ran toward Chinatown.

What awaited us on Dupont Street looked like a moving sketch of Dante's *Inferno*. The flimsy façades, designed to conceal opium dens, brothels, and gambling joints, had tumbled into the streets, leaving their occupants exposed as if on some pornographic stage. Bodies jutted from mounds of debris, bloodied prostitutes dug among the ruins for their silk robes, dazed customers struggled to find their britches. A few opium habitués clung to the wooden slats of their bunks, trying to relight their pipes, waving nonchalantly to passersby.

A flood of terrified Chinese ran down the middle of Dupont. Through the sea of frantic bodies we spotted the cause: a bull with massive horns, goring and trampling the poor souls in its path. A dozen young men ran alongside it, yelling and striking the enraged animal with bricks and stones.

The bull charged into a shop whose frantic occupants jumped through the shattered window to escape. Three prostitutes ran from the adjacent building, stumbling on their rocker shoes, shrieking in terror.

"The Chinese believe the world is held up by four giant bulls," Hunter explained. "They must think the earthquake was caused by this one leaving his post."

The bull charged back out through the broken window, shards of glass slicing its belly.

I noticed Christian walking calmly down the middle of Dupont, waving his arms, throwing chunks of cobblestone and screaming, "Hey! Hey!" The furious animal pawed the ground, snorting, and then charged from fifty yards away. Christian removed the Colt from his belt and walked forward. At thirty yards, he aimed and cocked the trigger. At twenty yards, he fired, and fired again, three times in all, the bullets slamming into its skull. The bull bellowed and stumbled, its momentum carrying it forward until Christian danced aside, barely avoiding the horns. He emptied his revolver into its flank.

People surrounded the animal, weeping and screaming. They dipped their fingers in its blood and held their hands to the heavens. Several old women ran into the street and fell to their knees, clasping their hands and praying.

"My Cantonese is weak," Hunter said, "I know a few hundred words. One of them is 'death.'"

"Peepers dies," Ting Leo said.

Hunter and I looked at her in astonishment.

"Aw peepers dies," she said, waving her hand to show the old ladies were talking about the whole city. Ting Leo struggled with the words she had memorized from the *Falmouth*'s crew. "Peepers dies." She waved her hand again. "Aw peepers dies."

"We better drop her off with Miss Cameron at the Chinese orphanage," Hunter said, "if the building is still standing. I have a bad feeling these old Chinese ladies may be right."

Chapter 50

APRIL 18, 1906. 7:15 A.M.

On the rooftop of his mansion, Adam Rolf handed Citizen's Police badges to Tommy, Shanghai Kelly, and Scarface.

"Where the hell did you get these?" Kelly asked.

"I'm the City Attorney," Rolf explained. "Chief Donen and I can appoint special Civilian Officers in an emergency. I think this qualifies."

A butler appeared, bearing a silver tray with a bottle of cognac and several monogrammed snifters. He poured each of them a healthy drink. "Tell me something, Kelly," Rolf asked, "what do you see out there?"

Kelly stared South of Market, where the scattered fires had begun to merge and grow. "A lot a' whores and pimps out of work."

"That's why you're still knocking rummies over the head for a living. You know what I see? Unlimited economic opportunity. A chance to rid ourselves of a few enemies."

"That ought to be worth what, Adam? Five grand a head?"

"After you shook me down for fifty grand with that sham story about not having those papers? Right now, I'm inclined to hire someone less likely to get himself stomped by Christian Fallon."

Kelly's face contorted into a rainbow-colored scowl: bloodshot eyes, purple jaw, a solitary gold tooth swimming in a sea of its brown-chipped cousins. He gazed over at Tommy, who stood with his hands over his midsection, where he carried his pistol. "You find better muscle, Adam," Kelly replied. "You let me know."

Rolf pondered a moment. "I'm going to give you one last chance, Kelly. One. I want everything they have. Evidence, affidavits, maybe a head or two for posterity."

"Five grand a head for The Brotherhood, ten a piece for Feeney, Spreckels, Older. A bargain to my way of thinkin'."

"Evidence first, bodies second this time, understand me?" Rolf swallowed his cognac. "Tell me something, Kelly, what is it with the Fallon brothers? One of 'em is a drunk; the other's a college boy. You sure you're up to it?"

Kelly raised his glass in a toast. "To some very expensive cadavers." He guzzled and wiped his mouth on a dirty sleeve.

Rolf watched Kelly and Scarface depart, and then turned to Tommy. "Find my broker and tell him to buy up every lumber mill, cement factory, and plumbing supplier from Santa Cruz to Santa Rosa. And hurry back. After they dispose of the Fallon brothers and the rest of that lot, I want you to eliminate Kelly and Scarface. Whatever they would have collected for their efforts is yours."

"Be my pleasure, Mr. Rolf."

"And, Thomas. Stay away from the hop-head dens until this is over, understand?"

On Sixth Street, four blocks south of the Palace Hotel, Captain Charles Cullen and nine firefighters of Engine Company No. 6 had an immediate problem. The rear of the firehouse had sunk three feet into the muck of old Mission Swamp, filled in with the debris of the earthquake of '68. The sinking had split the long, narrow building in two and shattered the front doors.

Christian arrived outside the firehouse. A blaze across the street at Prost's Bakery was threatening the entire block. Christian ran to Cullen and his men, who were desperately trying to drag their heavy Clapp and Jones steam pumper over a pile of rubble.

"Charlie," Christian yelled, "where's your horses?"

"They went plumb loco, like to tear themselves to pieces squeezing out the busted door." Cullen tried to catch his breath, staring at Prost's as the flames climbed higher. "It's bad down here, Christian. Real bad."

Cullen's lieutenant, a bearded man of thirty, ran back to the station. "Captain," he yelled. "There ain't a drop in the hydrants. You can see the water pouring up through the streets."

"Then drop a hose in the sewer," Cullen ordered.

A disheveled man, waving his arms as if he were trying to fly, rounded the corner of Howard and ran straight toward them. "You gotta come!" he yelled. "There's people trapped. Hundreds of 'em! Hundreds of 'em and the fire is coming!" The man grabbed Christian's upper arm so hard his fingers dug into the flesh. "Oh God! You gotta see it! It's awful. It's somethin' awful!"

"Stay here and help pull this engine," Christian ordered the man as he sprinted toward Howard Street.

Minutes after we left Ting Leo in the care of Dolly Cameron on Sacramento Street, Hunter and I reached Market near the Palace Hotel. We drove through a mounting stream of refugees pushing wheelbarrows bulging with personal possessions, balancing suitcases atop bicycle seats, or towing armoires with wheels nailed to the legs. Smoke had darkened the sky and flames cast an orange glow on warped buildings and anxious faces.

We got to Mission Street as a building exploded a block ahead, shattering windows and sending a mountain of flaming wreckage skyward. Hunter jumped the motorcycle over the curb and skidded into the alcove of a brick warehouse as flaming shingles and ceiling joists crashed around us.

A half block away, twenty soldiers milled around a horse-drawn caisson.

Hunter drove back into the street. When the officer in charge of the demolition squad spotted us approaching, he raised his revolver and yelled, "Halt!" his voice almost lost in the roar of the fire.

Hunter produced his star. "Officer Hunter Fallon, SFPD!"

"I have orders to clear this area," he shouted at Hunter.

"And I'm a police officer whose authority supersedes the military in civilian affairs," Hunter yelled.

"Not today it doesn't. I am ordering you to clear this area, Officer Fallon."

"What's your name, Sergeant?"

"Levert Stillman."

"Who gave you orders to blow up these buildings?"

"General Funston ordered a firebreak to keep this thing from spreading to the train station on Townsend. Now, run along and mind your own damn business." Stillman turned away as a soldier ran from the warehouse of a lamp wholesaler, screaming "Fire in the hole!"

The building exploded with such force the concussion nearly knocked us over. Our ears pounding, we stared skyward as bricks and cases filled with flaming paper crashed down over the entire block.

"Sergeant," Hunter yelled, "that smells like black powder! You're not stopping the fire, you're spreading it!"

"If you don't get out of here," Stillman replied, "I'm going to have you hauled off in irons."

Stillman stepped back and raised his revolver across his chest. "The last thing I want to do is draw down on a police officer," he said, "but if you don't move and stop interfering with my orders, I will."

"Let's go, Hunter," I pleaded. "Nothing is going to stop these men."

Hunter turned around and pointed us toward a large plume of smoke billowing above Sixth and Howard.

At Sixth Street, my eyes refused to believe what lay before us. The Nevada House, a cheap three-story hotel in the middle of the block, had fallen against the Lormor Hotel next door. The Lormor had crashed into the Ohio House, which in turn rammed the massive Brunswick House on the corner with such force that the latter now sprawled across Howard Street, the bodies of pedestrians and horse-drawn wagons tangled in the debris. A chorus of agonized screams pierced the mounting roar of the inferno.

"My God," I said, "those hotels are nothing but tiny rooms filled with immigrants and transients. There could be a thousand people in just those four buildings." Less than twenty yards away, I spotted the lifeless foot of a child protruding from the wreckage of the Lormor.

Hunter pointed to the Brunswick Hotel, whose fourth-story roof was now but ten feet off the ground. There we could see Christian, Francis, Patrick, and Carlo struggling to lift a beam from the legs of a young woman who writhed convulsively.

"Annalisa, stay here," Hunter yelled, and ran to them.

An aftershock hit and the wreckage shifted, drawing a chorus of screams from the entrapped. Patrick, Hunter, and Christian put their backs to the beam and managed to raise it a few inches, the woman screaming as Francis pulled her clear, her legs crushed beyond recognition. She pointed frantically to a gaping hole in the wreckage, unable to speak in anything but animal grunts.

Patrick dropped to his knees and peered into the opening, where he spotted the motionless bodies of two small boys. He turned back to the mother as the last gasp of air escaped her lungs.

"The Lord has her now," he said. He took the St. Christopher medal from his neck and wrapped it in the woman's hand.

I watched in a daze, clasping at the St. Christopher beneath my dress, the first I realized I was still wearing my opera clothes. Francis climbed through the opening and after a few minutes passed a weeping girl up to Christian and Hunter.

Carlo and Patrick tied a rope to her waist and lowered her toward the ground, where she collapsed, gasping and sobbing in my arms.

Francis next lifted out a boy of about ten, then a girl who might have been the boy's twin sister. Christian put his arm up to shield his face from the flames eating across the rooftop as Hunter pulled a naked, mumbling woman through the hole.

"Francis, you gotta come out. Now!" Christian screamed.

Francis looked at the pleading face of a man trapped in the wreckage of a brick fireplace.

"Now, Francis. Now!" Christian and Hunter yelled from above.

Francis jumped for Hunter and Christian's outstretched hands. They pulled him clear and ran for the edge of the building, jumping to the ground as the roof exploded in flame.

A voice, high-pitched and barely human, pierced the roar of the fire. "Kill me! For God's sake, someone please shoot me!"

Through a skewed window frame, we spotted the trapped man and the fire eating across the beams that pinned his legs. "Kill me!" he screamed.

Francis raised his revolver and aimed. "I can't do it," he said. "God would not forgive me."

Christian pushed Francis' arm down and then raised his own pistol. The shot echoed down the street, freezing the bevy of soiled onlookers.

"Shoot me, someone shoot me, don't let me burn for God's sake!" another voice cried, too fractured for anyone to tell if it was male or female.

Christian moved a dozen steps to his left and fired again.

Another building exploded behind us, sending a shower of burning debris skyward. When it landed, another dozen buildings were set ablaze.

"We have to find a way to stop this," Hunter yelled in my ear. I looked at the flaming refuse and realized that one of the buildings just blown to bits was my rooming house: the flames were now consuming my clothes, photographs of my parents, mementos of my childhood.

Chapter 51

———••◦◦◦◦◦••———

MARKET STREET

APRIL 18, 1906. 8:00 A.M.

Enrico Caruso, a topcoat covering his silk pajamas, entered the Palace Grill to a sight that belied the horror a few blocks away. The post-temblor frenzy of the hotel's guests had vanished. Scores of people lounged amidst the clinking of bone china and the patter of small talk, eating and drinking as though nothing unusual had transpired.

Caruso approached the headwaiter, who tried not to stare at the tenor's attire. "Hotel ees safe?" Caruso asked.

"Yes, sir, Mr. Caruso. Mr. Sharon has assured us the building survived intact. He has activated the pumps and has men waiting if the fire turns in our direction. You know the saying, 'if the Palace goes . . .'"

"I know. San Francisco is go *boom*."

Kaitlin appeared in the entranceway, timid and uncertain. Relieved to spot Caruso, she traversed the room in long, jerking strides. "Mr. Caruso. I can't find my father. I've looked all over the hotel. Have you seen him?"

"I no see him since he is at Opera House."

"Oh, God. He came here because of me and now no one knows where he is."

"I am sure is okay. 'E is strong, your fathers."

Tired and ashen, Kaitlin slumped into a silk-covered chair.

"Why you are leave the party last night, Kaitlin? You are look for your father?"

"I was afraid of that horrible Mr. Rolf," she said. "I came back here with Mr. Barrymore. He got drunk and fell asleep. He snored through the whole earthquake."

Caruso raised an eyebrow.

"Don't worry," Kaitlin assured him. "I think he likes champagne more than women. I know one thing. I won't be forgetting this any time soon."

Six stories above them, on the Palace roof, a fearful Alexander Sharon watched as his men hastily stretched fire hoses across the rooftop. The myriad of small fires that had flared between the hotel and the waterfront had merged into three distinct walls of flame that had begun to block the view east of the hotel, obscuring the bay and the Berkeley Hills. He looked at the flagpole above, where the Stars and Stripes flapped steadily toward the southeast. He was relieved that the wind continued to push the flames away from his beloved hotel.

His relief turned to horror. The flag luffed, flapping about the pole in limp circles as black soot drifted down around him.

Chapter 52

—••⟨∞⟩••—

NORTH BEACH

APRIL 18, 1906. 9:20 A.M.

In the basement of the Hall of Justice, Eugene Schmitz struggled to comprehend the escalating stream of reports and rumors. A written plea for help had just arrived from the Mayor of Santa Rosa, fifty miles north. The entire town now lay in rubble and the ruins were engulfed in flames. Stanford University reported that a majority of campus buildings had been leveled, and the famed botanical gardens destroyed.

San José reported scores dead and hundreds injured. Nearby Agnews Asylum had split in two, killing patients and staff. The Sheriff reported surviving mental patients were running about naked, attacking anyone they encountered. Deputies had captured several and were forced to tie them to trees, where they lay shrieking in the Santa Clara Valley sun.

Schmitz looked over at Donen, who was at a chalkboard recording rumors of unfathomable calamities. Chicago and New York had been leveled. A chasm drained the Great Lakes into the Mississippi River, now flooding the Midwestern Plains. Denver had been reduced to flat land. Los Angeles had been swallowed whole and San Bernardino was a waterfront.

"Mr. Mayor!" a messenger shouted, thrusting a paper into Schmitz' hand.

Donen watched as Schmitz studied the most recent missive. For a man whose most difficult decision until that day had been what to wear to the opera, the Mayor seemed remarkably forceful.

Schmitz beckoned to Donen. "I have a report here that says a number of General Funston's troops are engaged in looting. Mostly liquor stores. You know anything about this?"

Before the Police Chief could reply, another messenger burst into the room. "I just came from the British Consul's Office," he exclaimed. "He saw soldiers take six men into an alley behind his office and execute them."

Schmitz looked calmly at the messenger. "The Army has orders to shoot looters on sight."

"Yes, sir," the messenger replied, "but he says the men they shot took axes and blankets from a store to help with the rescue effort."

Schmitz turned back to Donen. "Find General Funston! Get him in here as fast as you can. I don't care where he is. Find him! And I want any soldier involved in looting disarmed and arrested."

"You want me to arrest soldiers?"

"I don't care who it is. Go find General Funston."

Schmitz spotted his secretary, Bertrand, who sported unmatched shoes and a case of apoplexy greater than his norm. "We sent a message to the Navy at Mare Island two hours ago requesting drinking water. Where the hell is it? And send a telegram to the Governor. I want every man who wears a uniform in the State of California as fast as they can get here. National Guardsmen, cadets from the military academies, every one of them."

"Sir," Bertrand offered. "Perhaps we should post warnings about looting. Maybe give people a warning before we gun them down."

Chapter 53

BUSH STREET

APRIL 18, 1906. 10:15 A.M.

Hunter and I reached Central Fire Station after a journey made difficult by the growing stream of refugees. Through the shattered doors of the firehouse we could see that a spire of the California Hotel chimney had cut the place in half.

"That's Chief Sullivan's office on the third floor," Hunter replied. "It looks like the front part of it is still standing."

"What exactly are you looking for?"

"He was working on a disaster plan for his meeting with Judge Morrow. It's up there somewhere."

We were ten feet from the door when another aftershock sent us to our knees. A shower of bricks fell from the hotel onto the rear of the fire station, smashing a portion of what it had missed in the previous assault. Hunter struggled to pull me to my feet, fatigue making our every movement an effort.

"Stay here, Annalisa, it's too dangerous."

"What? And let you have all the fun? This is my story, remember?"

"How silly of me," he replied. He took his pocket knife and cut the hem loose from my tattered opera dress, freeing my legs. We stumbled forward, stepping over bricks and timbers from the hotel's spires and entered the station.

Another small jolt sent bricks from the upper floors crashing to the concrete floor three stories below, setting loose a swirling mass of dust that stung our eyes and nostrils. We pressed against the wall for several agonizing minutes as debris spilled through the abyss.

"The whole building is unstable," Hunter said. "Stay here. Please."

I shook my head. Finally, the dust subsided and we scampered up the cluttered steps to the second floor landing. Through the broken windows overlooking Bush Street, we could see the towers of smoke drifting in our direction. We steadied ourselves and tiptoed across the uneven floor to the stairway leading to Sullivan's office.

"I'll go first," Hunter cautioned. "If something happens, get the plans to Assistant Chief Dougherty as fast as you can." He kissed me and started up the creaking steps as another pile of bricks crashed off the lifeless fire engine below. Hugging the brick wall, Hunter inched his way to the third floor. I took a deep breath and followed, stepping delicately.

When I neared the top step, I saw there was a two-foot gap between it and the landing. I reached for Hunter's hand and jumped. The stairway collapsed beneath me.

Hunter seized my wrist with both hands and jerked me forward, carrying me onto the landing atop him. We lay there as the stairs crashed to the floor below.

"We have to keep moving," he said.

We forced ourselves to stand and moved cautiously into Sullivan's ruined office. On the other side of the room a birdcage lay crushed beneath a ceiling joist, tufts of blue feathers scattered about. A set of blueprints on Sullivan's desk was partially buried by bricks and plaster. A chasm of twenty feet lay between us and the desk.

"Here's where I need a bridge," Hunter said. "Something simple, maybe two towers and a nice handrail."

Hunter found a two-by-ten ceiling joist in the hallway outside. He dragged it in, set one end on the floor, and let the other end swing through the air toward Sullivan's desk. It came down a foot short, flipping end over end until it crashed three stories below.

"I think that one was a little short," I observed, laughing ridiculously and battling a wave of nausea.

Hunter looked around and spotted another ceiling joist. He grabbed hold and pulled, grimacing as splinters tore his hands.

"Some wedding day," he gasped.

"At least we won't have any trouble remembering the date."

Frustrated and desperate, Hunter shoved the beam across the breach. One end landed in the center of Sullivan's desk, the other end at Hunter's feet.

"We better hurry, Hunter!"

We piled bricks and timbers under our end of the joist until it was fairly level. Hunter climbed on and walked gingerly over the chasm, peeking at the still-steaming boiler three stories below. "I just thought of something," he yelled. "What if those aren't the right blueprints?" He took a breath and danced over the final stretch.

At Sullivan's desk, he lifted the beam with one arm and slid the blueprints from underneath. "This is it!" he called. "'Emergency Plans For Disruption of the Spring Valley Water System.'"

Through a hole in the brick exterior, Hunter could see the waterfront, where a Navy fireboat fed water to firefighters, whose pumpers sent towering streams onto a block-long wall of fire.

Hunter turned and spotted something behind me. "Annalisa. Work your way to the door left of the stairs."

I climbed over a mound of debris and jerked at the knob several times before the door sprung open. "It's a fire pole!" I called. "I can't see what's down there. It's too dark."

"We'll just have to take a chance," he called back.

Hunter tucked the blueprints inside his shirt and walked swiftly across the beam. He slid down the fire pole, landing on the sign from the California Hotel. I quickly followed.

"The wind has definitely shifted," Hunter said as we hit the street. "If those fires merge and jump Market Street, there may be no stopping it."

A block from Mission Dolores, at his home on Seventeenth, Charles Feeney packed his books and legal papers as his wife loaded keepsakes into a steamer trunk.

"Angela. Just take the things that absolutely cannot be replaced. Photographs, marriage license. Put the most important stuff in one small bag so we can keep it with us."

A resounding knock came from the front door. Feeney headed down the narrow hallway, yanked the warped door open, and stared upward at a man with a large scar on the right side of his face.

The man flashed a seven-pointed star in a hand the size of a dinner plate. "You folks are gonna have to pull out of here," he said.

"Who are you?" Feeney demanded. "The fire isn't anywhere near here yet."

"Special police, deputized by the city. We got orders to move everyone out of this neighborhood."

Feeney gazed passed Scarface at three thugs, all sporting pistols in their belts.

"I'm Federal Prosecutor Charles Feeney. You have no authority here."

Scarface rested his hand on the revolver in his belt. "I don't give a damn if you're President Roosevelt. You don't clear out, we're gonna have to clear you out. Get movin'."

"Charles, what is it? Charles, what's wrong?" Angela fretted, pushing next to her husband. The sight of Scarface sent a chill through her.

"I'll grab my papers," Feeney replied.

Scarface slid the revolver from his belt, his thumb on the hammer. "You ain't leavin' with nothin'. Now get movin'." He stepped aside and motioned for the Feeneys to leave.

Angela took her husband's arm and pushed him forward, onto the broken sidewalk, where Feeney stopped to stare back at Scarface. "Charles. Please. Don't start a confrontation. Please."

The pair moved slowly up the hill. At the crest of Mission Dolores Park, three blocks away, they stopped to look at the city below. A curtain of flame stretched all the way from the waterfront to Van Ness Avenue. Angela put her hands to her face and sobbed.

Feeney turned his attention to his Mission District neighborhood, scarcely recognizing it. The walls of the foundries and bakeries had collapsed. In the open fields near the stockyards and livery stables, cattle and horses stampeded. He looked for the Valencia Street Hotel, the most prominent structure on its block.

It took a moment before he recognized it. The building had pancaked, the fourth floor resting where the first once stood. Rescuers chopped frantically at the roof as shrill cries drifted from the wreckage. Adjacent houses leaned against one another like barroom inebriates, their windows and doors twisted into cocky grins.

"There's no reason to evacuate our house! The fire is still two miles away," he shouted. "Wait here, Angela."

"Charles, what are you going to do? Don't go back there, please."

He was already running down the hill.

A half block from his house, he spotted Scarface loading his papers into a horse-drawn wagon.

"Hey! You! Stop that!"

Scarface turned and smiled as Feeney hurried toward him. He threw the last of Feeney's legal papers into the wooden bed, climbed into the wagon with his men, and pulled away.

Feeney arrived at the short walkway to his house, struggled to regain his breath, and headed inside.

He was just inside the front door when the house exploded.

Angela was less than a block away when the concussion knocked her to the ground.

Chapter 54

———⟨∞⟩———

APRIL 18, 1906. 11:30 A.M.

Frank Leach stepped off the Oakland ferry with the enthusiasm of a man who had taken a wrong turn into Hell. A crush of frightened humanity surged onto the ferry, almost knocking him backward.

He made his way across the Ferry Plaza, fighting the human tide. On Market Street, he dodged the abandoned remnants of their hasty exodus, temporarily heartened that the city's main thoroughfare had not yet been touched by the flames.

He turned south at Fifth Street, picking up his pace until he reached the U.S. Mint. The iron shutters, imposing columns, and granite façade showed barely a crack, while across the street, Lincoln School had fallen halfway across Fifth Street.

A Sergeant appeared from behind a column at the Mint and pointed a rifle at him. On the rooftop, a dozen more soldiers hoisted their rifles to ready arms.

Leach raised his hands slowly. "I'm the Superintendent," he sputtered, the fire's clamor nearly drowning out his words.

The Sergeant stepped from behind the column and approached.

"I'm Frank Leach, Superintendent of the Mint. I must get inside!"

"I got orders not to let anyone past the front door."

"Sergeant, listen to me, please. If the place catches fire and you shoot the one man who can save it, how's that going to look?"

"You got proof?"

Leach reached carefully into his pocket, producing a letter from the previous mayor, James Phelan, that appointed him Director of the Mint.

Before the Sergeant could peruse the paper, another soldier approached.

"I'm Lieutenant Armstrong, the officer in charge of this detachment."

The calm, handsome young officer was a welcome sight. The Sergeant handed him Leach's paper.

"Mr. Leach," Armstrong said. "My job is to protect this Mint at all costs."

"Then you better come with me, Lieutenant. And Sergeant, if any of my employees show, I would appreciate if you would let them in to assist us."

Leach sprinted up the granite steps of the Mint with Armstrong next to him.

Once inside, the two men pushed themselves up four flights to the roof, where a half dozen soldiers loitered, watching the flames.

"Gentlemen," Leach called, "unless you're willing to burn up with us, I suggest you rejoin your fellow soldiers down below."

A corporal saluted and led the other men from the roof.

Leach and Armstrong hurried to the southwest corner and stared out over the burning warehouses and tenements as the pace of explosions quickened. The wind swirled and the temperature soared as heat and smoke from the inferno raging between Harrison and Folsom three blocks away began drifting in their direction.

"This roof is tar," Armstrong said, "it will burn like hell if sparks hit it. We better strip it down and start soaking it best we can."

"There's a pump and artesian well below," Leach replied.

He ran to the front of the roof and looked below, where soldiers argued with a handful of his employees. From Mission Street, a fire captain in uniform ran to the group, pointing at the chest of the Sergeant, then at the building. The Sergeant stepped aside and the men charged up the steps.

Leach rushed down to meet them, noticing for the first time the mass of debris that filled every office in the building.

"I'm Captain Jack Brady," the new arrival announced anxiously. "The wind is shifting on us. I know there's a pump in the courtyard, how much hose do you have?"

"About three hundred feet."

"That's all the hose you have? For a building this size?"

"Thank Schmitz and his cronies. They'd rather risk the whole damn Mint than spend a hundred dollars for a second hose."

Chapter 55

HALL OF JUSTICE

APRIL 18, 1906. 12:11 P.M.

A soot-covered messenger stormed into the basement of the Hall of Justice, shoving through a dozen men. "Mr. Mayor! Mr. Mayor!"

The urgency in his voice seized Schmitz' attention.

"Mr. Mayor. The wind is shifting." The words silenced everyone within earshot. "The wind is shifting, sir," he said. "The whole mornin' it's been blowing the fire toward the train station and the waterfront. Now it's bearin' down on Market Street."

A collective gasp went up. The messenger gathered himself, embarrassed as if the news were his fault. "That's not all, sir. A fire department spotter saw smoke rising from the Hayes Valley."

"What? We got a report an hour ago that Dougherty's men had a handle on everything west of Van Ness!" the Mayor exclaimed.

"Yes, sir, they did. There's one hydrant still working out there. As soon as they left, a woman on Hayes Street was making breakfast in a cracked fireplace and set her attic on fire. Now the wind is whipping it up so fast it's heading toward City Hall."

"Damn it!" Schmitz bellowed. "Five thousand houses, all the city's records in danger because somebody had to have ham and eggs for breakfast?"

"I think that's about what happened, yes, sir," the messenger said.

Schmitz looked around at the men who had come to save the city: former Mayor Phelan, *Chronicle* publisher Michael de Young, several bankers, and Schmitz' adversary, Rudolph Spreckels. They had survived wars, currency crises, lawlessness, and crippling strikes, as well as their political animosities. Nothing had prepared them for the horrors raging about them.

The door banged open and General Funston strode in. He walked across the room, imperious and annoyed, stopping abruptly before Schmitz.

"You wanted to see me?" Funston asked. The General was not happy.

"Yes," Schmitz answered, shuffling a stack of papers. "I'm not sure where I should start. I have reports of your men looting stores, your men drinking on duty, and your dynamite squads blowing up buildings without consulting me!"

"Maybe you should step outside and see for yourself," the fuming General urged, his jaw clenching, his face reddening. "Half the city is about to catch fire and a couple of hundred thousand people are on the short road to hysteria. Now, you call me in for a bunch of ridiculous rumors!"

Assistant Chief Dougherty returned and pushed his way to Funston and Schmitz.

"Chief Dougherty," Schmitz called, "we just received a report that the wind has shifted and Market Street is now in the path of the fire."

"It's worse than that," Dougherty replied. "I was on the roof. The South of Market fire is spreading in two directions. The western tail jumped Tenth Street and is headed toward the Mission District. If it merges with the new fire in the Hayes Valley, it could surpass everything we've faced so far. And the wind has not only shifted but strengthened. The main wall is now bearing down on the Mint and the Palace Hotel. If it leaps Market, the entire Financial District is in its path."

"Half of the City," Schmitz replied, voice trembling.

Funston jabbed his finger at the map. "We have to extend the firebreak. Take out all the buildings on the east side of Van Ness. That will protect Pacific Heights and the Western Addition. And we have to dynamite Mission Street and the south side of Market. That's the only way to protect the Financial District, North Beach, Chinatown, every bloody thing all the way to the waterfront."

The implication left everyone stunned. Rudolph Spreckels cleared his throat and stepped forward. "General, you're asking us to sacrifice the Grand Hotel, the Palace, the *Chronicle* Building. Two, three hundred million dollars worth of real estate. Maybe more."

They were all too preoccupied to notice Hunter and me pushing toward them.

"Every building on the south side of Market Street," Schmitz repeated. "Their records, their assets, everything."

"You don't have to do any of that," Hunter interrupted. As the two dirtiest people in the building, it took little effort to clear a path.

Hunter unfolded Dennis Sullivan's plans atop Schmitz' map. "I was the lead surveyor on the Stanford team that did the water study for Chief Sullivan. This is his map."

Bertrand offered me a glass of water. I guzzled half and then passed it to Hunter, who gulped the other half.

Hunter pointed to the plans. "Dennis Sullivan is a genius. Here's a schematic of the entire Spring Valley Water System. That thick dark line running through it is the San Andreas Fault, mapped by a geologist from Berkeley. The breaks in the thirty-inch conduits are directly above the fault, in filled land, just like Chief Sullivan predicted. Now, look at this."

Hunter wiped his forehead on the back of a dirty hand before turning the next page. "A list of every iron works and pipeline supplier in San Francisco. It's pretty obvious. Chief Sullivan is telling us to splice into the Spring Valley system at the breaks and run pipe above ground. Has anyone even tried splicing into the ruptured lines?"

A dull silence was his answer. He flipped to the next page. "Here's a list of every Navy vessel on the West Coast with firefighting capacity. We don't need the Army. We need the Navy! If we can splice into the Spring Valley system we can hold back the fire until the Navy gets here. We can keep it from jumping Market and Van Ness and devouring the whole city if we move fast enough."

"Dynamite is the only way to stop it," Funston argued, banging the table, "and the more we stand here talking, the less likely it is to work."

"It's not working," Hunter argued. "Ten percent of the city is in flames and the other ninety percent will be if this continues. All your men are doing is spreading the fire. If they dynamite Market Street, we won't need the fire to jump to the other side. All that burning debris will do it for us. Dennis Sullivan said that unchecked, it would take a week for this city to burn. With the Army in charge, it will be gone in two days. We don't need dynamite, dammit, we need water! Instead of starting fires, maybe General Funston's men could start running pipes and hoses!"

Funston shook, barely able to contain his anger. "What it comes down to is whether the administration is going to trust a Brigadier General in the United States Army or a smart-mouth college kid!"

Hunter glared at Schmitz. "The question, Mr. Mayor, is whether you're going to let General Funston blast the city to smithereens or listen to Dennis Sullivan, the best firefighter in the country."

"All right. All right," Schmitz said. "Here's what we're going to do. Is the telegraph still operating at the Postal Office?"

"Yes, sir," Bertrand replied, "but if the fire leaps Market Street, we will be completely cut off."

"All right. Send a telegram to the Navy. We want every fireboat, every foot of hose, every sailor on the West Coast as fast as they can get here. General Funston, I want a specific plan for the expansion of the dynamiting in ten minutes."

"It won't work," Hunter countered. "The more we dynamite, the faster the fire is going to spread and the harder it's going to be for the Navy to stop it. I saw one of General Funston's teams blasting away with black powder, setting everything around it on fire. You can't use black powder and you can't blast firebreaks if you don't have water. You have to soak those buildings first, soak the buildings around them and be prepared to douse any fires they set. That's just common sense. If we use every resource we have, we can slow it down until help arrives."

"You've made your point," Schmitz replied, "but we can't sit by and do nothing. That will be all, Officer Fallon. They need you on the rescue operations."

Hunter started to roll up Sullivan's plans.

"You better leave those with me," Schmitz said. "When the Navy does arrive, we may need them."

"It will be too late," Hunter said. He stuffed the plans into Schmitz' arms and stalked away.

I lingered behind, staring at Schmitz and Funston. "If Chief Sullivan were here to speak for himself," I said, "he wouldn't stand for any of this. Not the military taking over, not people who know nothing about explosives blowing the place to Kingdom Come. The world is watching. When there's nothing left of us, there will be Hell to pay for ignoring what Chief Sullivan is saying to you."

I stormed off as a soot-encrusted fireman burst through the door, almost knocking me over in his rush toward Schmitz. I stopped to listen.

"Mr. Mayor," he gulped, "the Hayes Valley fire just hit City Hall. It's spreading toward the Mechanics' Pavilion. Every hospital in town has been sending their wounded over there. Must be a thousand people laid out on the floor."

Schmitz looked ready to sag to his knees. He scratched his head as if trying to raise an idea. "We better evacuate the injured."

"We can't take them to the train station," Dougherty said, "if the fire jumps Tenth Street, they'll be cut off. One entire escape route would be gone."

"Good God, man," Funston said. "Listen up. I want every automobile and wagon in the city commandeered and the wounded moved to Army General Hospital at the Presidio." He pulled a notepad from his pocket. "Have a messenger run this note to the duty officer. I want a tent city set up on the Presidio grounds and every blanket and spare ration on the West Coast sent here immediately. Now, gentlemen, if you'll excuse me, there's a fire that requires my attention."

Funston shoved past me as he exited. Dennis Sullivan had been denied again, this time by a man he thought an ally.

I trudged up the steps to teeming Kearny Street, trying to stave off the fear. To my left, a fiery mountain towered behind Market Street's tallest buildings. The fire had taken on a frightening sound, a tick tick ticking like a million cicadas. I grew light-headed in the heated air as people scuttled about with strange, jerky motions, a marionette show bathed in unearthly crimson light.

I spotted Hunter pacing in Portsmouth Square, waving his arms and muttering, head and shoulders above a sea of displaced Chinese. A halo of red and yellow, the fire's reflection, danced about his head and soiled face.

A burst of laughter escaped me, which abruptly turned to joyous tears. Hunter had become a man before my eyes, simply because a man was needed. He found his best, as his father did, when things were at their worst. An emotional shiver swept through me, a welling that brought a momentary calm.

"Those idiots," Hunter said when I reached his side, his tone more pity than rancor. "How do pathetic little men like that come to power? What is this obsession the world has with grinning imbeciles with the backbone of a pimp?"

He swung me gently in his arms as tears streamed down our dirty faces. I wanted to tell him how proud his parents would be, how much I loved him, but I was unable to speak.

I stared at the fire and my melancholy turned to horror. The inferno was growing by the second.

Chapter 56

---•⟨∞⟩•---

APRIL 18, 1906. 12:18 P.M.

In the dining room of the St. Francis Hotel, where he had gone to escape the pandemonium at the Palace, Enrico Caruso used the last wedge of toast to wipe the last smear of egg from the corners of his plate, washing it down with his third glass of orange juice. A stifled belch signaled the finale of an enormous breakfast.

The other guests had switched from discreetly watching Caruso to staring at him in disbelief. Even Kaitlin, whose three brothers would devour a horse if given the liberty, sat transfixed.

Caruso patted his stomach, slid back his chair, and wobbled across the dining room. He shoved his way through the kitchen's swinging doors and promptly found the headwaiter, who was quietly relating Caruso's gastronomic feat to the chef. "Is wonderful *prima colazione*. I am thanking you very much," the smiling tenor declared, handing over a five-dollar bill.

They stared at the biggest gratuity they had ever received and nodded politely to the tenor, who wore a smear of jam across his mustache. Caruso bowed politely and exited.

He was halfway across the dining room when an aftershock sent him to his knees. Cups and dishes crashed and moans echoed across the cavernous room. When it stopped, Kaitlin ran to the tenor's side and helped him to his feet.

"'Ell of a place," Caruso said hoarsely as Kaitlin helped him to his feet. "I never sing here again."

They stepped outside the St. Francis, where the sight of the fire arching above Market Street added to their malaise. Caruso took Kaitlin's hand and pulled her through the crowd gathering around Union Square.

They crossed Market; the faces of those in flight toward the waterfront grew more anguished each minute. A mother, father, and two young boys struggled to shove a piano over the tracks and cobblestones, the motionless body of an elderly woman sprawled atop. A legless man on a wheeled board clung to a rope trailing from a manure truck now loaded with antiques.

They entered the Palace lobby, where Alexander Sharon made a beeline to Caruso.

"*Signor* Caruso, Mr. Hertz is in your room having your belongings packed. We are evacuating the hotel as a precaution. The fire has shifted directions. I am so sorry."

"What is thees, *escavazione*?"

"Evacuation, Mr. Caruso. They want us to leave," Kaitlin replied.

"The Grand Opera House has just surrendered to the flames," Sharon added apologetically. "Everything was lost. Your costumes, instruments. Everything."

On the Palace roof, a mismatched crew of security guards, bellmen, and waiters braced as the fire reached Mission Street a block away. A janitor beckoned them to the edge of the building, where they watched soldiers moving the crowd away from the unfinished Monadnock Building next door. A sapper ran out from the steel girders as his comrades scattered. Seconds later, a dynamite charge exploded and sent the Palace shaking from foundation to roof.

The men on the hotel roof staggered away, holding their ears as a storm of sparks and cinders showered down on them. Scores of tiny fires sprung up on the expansive, black pitch roof. A burly waiter turned a brass wheel and three hoses bulged with water, the streams so powerful the force almost ripped the nozzles from the men's hands. They quickly extinguished the flames.

On the west side of the hotel below, crews on each floor ran the hallways, kicking in doors where the explosion had shattered windows and set curtains and carpeting ablaze. They doused the flames, cursing Funston and the Army.

In his suite at the opposite end of the Palace, Caruso finished dressing in a blue striped suit and entered the parlor where Kaitlin and Hertz awaited him. The calm that ushered him through breakfast had disappeared. He clutched his most prized belonging, the photograph with President Roosevelt.

"My voice," he croaked, "my voice ees died."

"Enrico," Kaitlin soothed, "your voice is fine. Have you tried to sing?" She looked at Hertz, busy directing bellboys struggling with Caruso's trunks.

"Yes," Hertz called, "why don't you try? Sing something, Enrico."

Caruso's eyes darted fitfully between Hertz and Kaitlin.

"Please, Enrico," Kaitlin said with a touch of her alluring smile. "For me."

He handed her the Roosevelt photo and walked to the window. Hertz ripped back the curtains and shoved open the broken sash, offering Caruso a smile.

"See, Enrico, there is no fire here," Hertz declared. The statement was a hollow one. The light of the fire behind the Palace danced eerily off the buildings before them. It sent Caruso's spirits plummeting.

"You are the greatest voice in the world," Kaitlin said, "sing something."

"What are you like me to sing, Kaitlin?"

"The one about Mimi and Rodolfo, the poor seamstress and the poet who falls in love with her. From *La Bohème*. I love it because I'm a seamstress who loves poetry."

Caruso stared at Kaitlin's earnest face and his spirits revived. "*Che gelida manina*. Is 'ow you say?" patting his head to dislodge the words. "*Froze little hand*. Is Rodolfo sing to his poor Mimi while 'e is a' try to warm hand. Is aria I was sing tonight."

Kaitlin nodded, choking back tears. She wanted to tell him how many times she had fallen asleep, her ear pressed against the horn on her Gramophone, dreaming of Rodolfo. Caruso squeezed her hand and the gesture steadied them.

He cleared his throat and faced the window, Kaitlin on one side, Hertz on the other.

"*Che gelida manina/se la lasci riscaldar/cercar che giova?/Al buio non si trova/ma per fortuna è una notte di luna/e qui la luna l'abbiamo vicina.*"

Kaitlin mouthed "How cold your tiny hand is/let me warm it/what's the use of looking/we won't find it in the dark/but with good fortune it is a moonlit night/and here we have the moon so close." They were the words that Lincoln had translated and she had written in her diary. A tear ran down Kaitlin's face. The stoic Hertz succumbed as well.

On Market Street below, Hunter and I rode through the torrent of refugees struggling toward the waterfront. Fearful and exhausted by their efforts, many left sewing machines and bassinets, hope chests and hand baskets, rocking chairs and coat racks, family portraits, bicycles, a sidewalk bazaar of personal memoirs.

Hunter swerved between piles of the debris. He slowed as we stared up at the Palace Hotel, crowned by the flame and smoke a block behind it. Streams of water played across the fiery backdrop as desperate men fought to keep the jewel of the city from the encroaching holocaust. All around us, people were stopping to gaze upward.

I tapped Hunter's shoulder and pointed to the fifth floor.

Through a shattered window frame, Caruso appeared, his miraculous tenor drifting down, piercing the thunder and the fear. "*Chi son/Chi son/ Sono un poeta/Che cosa faccio?/Scrivo!/ E come vivo?/Vivo!*"

"Who am I? Who am I? I am a poet. What do I do? I write," I whispered in Hunter's ear, hugging him from behind, "And how do I live? I live!"

Caruso's voice soared, reaching ever deeper into his storied baritone, soaring to lyrical heights that once again seemed impossible. The horror faded and an eerie feeling of peace swept through the crowd.

"*In povertà mia lieta/Scialo da gran signore/Rime ed inni d'amore/Per sogni e per chimere/E per castelli in aria.*"

"In my carefree poverty/I indulge like a rich man/in rhymes and poems of love/by dream and fantasy/by castles in the air," Hunter called back to me.

I noticed streams of people pouring from the Palace. "Hunter, they're abandoning the hotel. We can't leave Caruso on his own."

"He has a manager, a valet . . ."

"Who don't know anything about the city. They can't get to the railroad station and the Ferry Building must be overwhelmed. That's Enrico Caruso, we can't leave him here like this."

"All right," Hunter said. "Take him to my house and get some rest before you collapse. Telegraph Hill is the safest place in the city right now. I'll come back for you. Go, I have work to do."

I climbed from the Waltham and quickly kissed Hunter's dirty face, momentarily struck by the fear that I might not see him again.

"*Ma il furto non m'accora/poiché v'ha preso stanza/la speranza!*" Caruso soared to the airiest heights on "*speranza*" and held it effortlessly as a shiver went through the crowd.

"But the loss does not bother me/because its place has been taken/by hope," I said softly as Hunter powered up Market Street, Caruso's voice fading behind him.

On the fifth floor, Kaitlin wiped her tears. "You see, Enrico," she said, "your voice is fine."

I sprinted across Market and up the littered stairwells of the Palace as the last of Caruso's trunks were being removed. Exhausted by the effort, I burst into his room, almost butting heads with him.

"Enrico" I called, "You must come with me. Please."

"Annalisa! Where must we go?"

"My fiancé has a house on top of Telegraph Hill where you should be safe. It is too difficult to leave the city now."

Caruso looked at Hertz and Kaitlin. "They are come with me?" he pleaded.

"No," Hertz replied, "I must look after the others. Go, Enrico. Take Kaitlin. I will be relieved to know that you are safe."

"If you see my father," Kaitlin said to Hertz, "please tell him where I am."

"Telegraph Hill. I will tell him. Now go, all of you."

Halfway down the hall, we passed a soot-covered Alexander Sharon as he hurried from the roof.

"Mr. Sharon," Kaitlin called. "Have you seen Mr. Barrymore? He was still in my room when I left."

"Oh, God," he said. Sharon banged through the fire door. After running frantically down three flights of stairs, he burst into Kaitlin's room. Barrymore had just begun to stir.

"Ahh, Mr. Sharon," Barrymore inquired through his fog, "is it me, or is it warm in here?"

A mile west, in the cavernous interior of the Mechanics' Pavilion, Christian and Carlo used a blanket to carry an old woman, her broken arm still unset, toward the street.

"Save me, dear God. Somebody please save me," she begged, her cries lost in the nightmarish dirge of moans and shrieks from a thousand other victims. In the rafters overhead, *papier mâché* masks, remnants of the previous night's *Mardi Gras*, twisted in the sinister red glow streaming through the windows, adding a Luciferian quality to the already grisly scene.

Christian stared at Carlo, who had been mumbling periodically since Max was killed. They struggled toward the exit, stepping over bodies, bumping into desperate rescuers.

On the sidewalk outside, Francis and Patrick hog-tied a sandy-haired young man who had gone mad, trampling the wounded and flailing at anyone who got in his way.

Carlo and Christian spotted a bakery truck on Grove Street and out-ran the other rescuers to secure a place for the wounded woman. Within seconds, a dozen more injured were piled around her.

A few feet away, two soldiers carried the body of a teenage boy who had succumbed to head injuries. He was covered with red dust and par-ticles of brick, the obvious result of a wall falling on him. They placed him in the gutter. No sooner had they released him than several more bodies were piled atop like cordwood. The wagons were only for the living.

Christian seized Carlo's arm and pulled him through the jostling crowd to Francis and Patrick. A motorcycle roared toward them.

"Where you been, Hunter?" Francis asked. "We need all the hands we can get!"

"I took Chief Sullivan's disaster plan to Mayor Schmitz to try to stop the dynamiting." As if on cue, a volley of explosions thundered through the air. "Instead of looking for water," Hunter continued, "those idiots are going to let Funston blow up the whole damn city."

Hunter looked over Christian's shoulder and spotted a woman clutch-ing at rescuers, pleading for attention. "Mrs. Feeney," Hunter yelled, "Mrs. Feeney!"

Hunter pushed through the crowd and seized her arm. "Mrs. Feeney. It's me, Hunter Fallon. Inspector Fallon's son, remember?"

"They killed him, they killed him," she babbled repeatedly. "They blew up our house. They just blew it up. He went back for his papers and they blew it up with him inside." She sobbed and her knees buckled.

Hunter caught her as Christian, Francis, and Patrick ran to them.

"Who killed him?" Hunter pleaded. "Mrs. Feeney, listen, please. If someone killed him you have to tell us. Who killed Mr. Feeney?"

"I don't know," she gasped. "They had badges, but they weren't police-men. They were hoodlums."

"Mrs. Feeney," Francis implored. "You have to help us. What did they look like?"

"A scar on his face. Tall. Another man, bald, tattoos all over."

Francis spotted an automobile approaching the curb. He and Hunter grabbed Mrs. Feeney and carried her through the crowd.

"Mr. Howard, Mr. Howard!" Francis yelled to a passing car. Charles Howard, owner of the fledgling automobile dealership on Van Ness, slammed his Buick to a halt.

"Mr. Howard," Francis said as they lifted her onto the seat next to him. "This is Mrs. Feeney, the wife of the Federal Prosecutor. You must get her to the Presidio! Take her to the Duty Officer, tell him she is to stay in his protective custody, do you understand me?"

Soldiers and volunteers loaded more wounded into the Buick's back seat. "I'm going there anyway," Howard called over the fire's roar, "been ferrying people to Army General Hospital, only one still working!" He offered a half-hearted salute and drove off.

"We got a war on our hands," Francis said. "Scarface and Dumbrowski, the tattooed gorilla. We put him away for beating one of Kelly's whores to death. Bastard. Kelly promoted him to replace the Whale."

"They killed Feeney," Hunter added. "They're using this chaos to go after their enemies. They'll go after Spreckels, Older, every damn one of us."

Francis examined the victims being carried to the sidewalk. Above the carnage, he could see towering St. Ignatius where he had been baptized and married, now being devoured by flames. The embers drifted onto the roof of the Mechanics' Pavilion.

"We can't let them run around the city killing people," Francis said. "Hunter, you go get Annalisa, she's in danger. My guess is they'll go after Spreckels next, he's got all the documents stored in his mansion on Van Ness."

"Carlo, you have to snap out of it," Francis said. "Carlo, do you hear me? Are you with us?" Carlo put his head down and looked away.

"This is war," Christian said. "No prisoners this time. They get in our way, they're dead men."

A mile north, on flooded Van Ness, a soot-covered Ford zigzagged between columns of rifle-wielding troops and made a sharp turn onto Sacramento. It swerved into the driveway of the corner mansion and stopped near the stables. A frantic Rudolph Spreckels jumped out and ran inside, his face a mask of worry.

He bounded up the winding staircase to the second floor and slipped into the bedroom, where Mrs. Flaherty, the plump Irish housekeeper, attended to his wife. He sat on the edge of the bed and pressed Eleanor's hands as her breath came in quick, short gasps.

"I tried t' telephone the midwife, Mr. Spreckels, but none a' the bloody things was working. Ain't a doctor in the city not tendin' the wounded and dyin' somewheres."

"I know," Spreckels said, "it's just the three of us."

"It'll be the four of us in a few minutes here," Eleanor smiled, her face covered in sweat. "This baby is not waiting for anyone."

Spreckels placed his hand on her belly and felt the child move. Through the window he could see City Hall burning a mile away, the peak of the fire waving in his direction. He was jarred by pounding and shouts of "open up" coming from his front door.

"Stay with her, Mrs. Flaherty."

He ran down the wide stairway and jerked open the front door. A tall man with a scar on his face and a badge in his left hand stared down at him.

"We're clearing out these houses," Scarface said. "We got orders from the city."

"The fire is a mile from here," Spreckels argued. "It might not even make it this far."

Scarface stepped aside, revealing a bald, tattooed Dumbrowski and three other men, all sporting ominous scowls and the badges of the Citizens Police. "We got our orders," Scarface said threateningly. "Now git."

"I'm Rudolph Spreckels. You have no right to order me from my own home. You can tell Mayor Schmitz I said so."

"We'll be sure to let him know," Scarface replied, fingering the Colt in his waistband. Scarface looked over his shoulder and spotted a detachment of soldiers. They stopped in the middle of Van Ness, fifty feet away. Several of them stared back at him.

He turned and glared at Spreckels. "Let's get moving," he hissed.

"Look," Spreckels said, "my wife is about to deliver her child. I'm not moving her."

"If your missus is about to drop a foal, you better get her the hell out before things get burned up. Now get movin'. And don't plan on cartin' anything with you."

Spreckels slammed the door and hurried outside to the stables, where two Chilean grooms were trying desperately to calm the horses.

"We have to move Mrs. Spreckels," he yelled.

They followed Spreckels back into the house and dashed to the bedroom.

"Rudolph, what's happening?"

"We're going to move you, Eleanor."

"Oh, God. No."

"We have no choice. We're being ordered to evacuate."

"Can't they wait? Please!"

"We can't."

Spreckels nodded to Mrs. Flaherty and the two nervous grooms. They hoisted the corners of the bed sheets and struggled down the hallway.

"Rudolph. Rudolph! Put me down."

Near the back door, Spreckels saw the tattooed man and several others staring at his car and examining his stables. "Let's take her out the side door toward Clay Street," he said softly.

Halfway to the street Mrs. Spreckels gasped and her breathing quickened.

"She's not going to make another meter," Mrs. Flaherty warned him. They set her gently on the lawn. Mrs. Flaherty knelt and pulled the blanket up. "This little one's got a mind all its own," she said. "It ain't waitin' for no one."

Spreckels looked at the throng hustling down Van Ness toward the bay. "Let's raise one of the bed sheets and at least give her some privacy," he ordered.

"All right," Mrs. Flaherty said, "the head's comin' through, we need you to push, ma'am. Push!"

Spreckels looked toward the attic, where he often had met with Fremont Older, Byron Fallon, and Charles Feeney. Documents crucial to the investigation were stacked about the room. A figure scampered past the dormer window: moments later, flames raced up the curtains, through the dormer window, and began climbing up the bone-dry roof.

Spreckels looked toward the rear of his home, where the scar-faced man leapt from the back porch and hurried toward his surly companions near the stables.

The flames spread rapidly, fanned by the hot wind. By the time Mrs.

Flaherty tied the umbilical cord with a shoestring, the house was engulfed in flames.

Eleanor Spreckels clutched her daughter to her chest and squeezed her husband's hand.

"We'll call her Eleanor, after you," he said. "The bravest woman I know."

She looked into her husband's damp eyes and saw the reflection of the flames devouring her home.

Chapter 57

APRIL 18, 1906. 2:42 P.M.

On the second floor of the San Francisco Mint, Frank Leach, Army Lieutenant Armstrong, and Fire Captain Brady teetered near collapse. The smoke and heat made it painful to breathe, their hands were raw and blistered from touching the brass nozzle and fittings. Even worse, the lone fire hose was not enough to cover the dozen new fires that seemed to break out every minute.

They heard screaming from above.

On the roof of the Mint, a dozen men had been hoisting pails from the well five stories below, their shoulders aching, their faces baked and swollen. They had soaked curtains and slapped desperately as sparks from the fire at Lincoln School across the street rained onto the Mint's roof.

One of the men pointed to the *Call* Building two blocks north, which had caught fire at the top. Window after window, hundreds of them, exploded. Massive columns of flame rushed up the elevator shafts and along the granite exterior, turning the building into an eighteen-story Roman candle. A giant fireball exploded above the dome and arched high into the blackened sky. The concussion shook every building within blocks.

The men atop the Mint suddenly realized they were trapped against the wall overlooking the courtyard. In unison, they screamed for Leach until his face appeared in the window below.

They lowered a rope to which Leach tied the fire nozzle. They pulled it up and attacked the roof fires, several of the men stumbling to their knees, weeping with exhaustion. As they extinguished the flames, they pointed the nozzle skyward and tilted their heads back to let the cool water bathe their faces and swollen tongues.

On the roof of the Palace, Manager Sharon felt the wind shift again. It carried sparks and embers from the *Call* Building, igniting fires where his exhausted men had just doused them.

"Up," Sharon screamed. "Up, dammit!" Sharon turned the wheel on a rooftop water tank as his men staggered to their feet. The hoses spat and sputtered, then ran dry.

Sharon ran to the roof's edge. Down below, he saw that city firemen had attached their hoses to spouts on the hotel wall, draining his reservoirs. He cursed the firemen with what little voice he had and then followed his men through a whirlwind of cinders to the stairwells.

Kaitlin, Caruso, and I watched the terrifying spectacle from the porch of the Fallon house, where we had sat since the strenuous climb up the southern slope of Telegraph Hill.

I had changed from my opera clothes into bicycling bloomers and a cotton blouse while a weary Enrico Caruso sketched a portrait of himself singing from the hotel window. In the scant minutes since he had looked away from the Palace, the hotel's roof had caught fire.

"*Dio mio,*" he said to Kaitlin and me, "they are say to me Palace Hotel does not burn."

I had no answer. I stared at the rooftops of buildings scattered about the corners of the city, and noticed a strange and distressing sight. From Cow Hollow north and Russian Hill west and Rincon Hill to the east, all the flags that had so far survived were pointing toward the center of the fire on Market Street.

I held my arms out to test the wind. "Feel that," I said. "The fire is coming toward us, yet the wind is coming from behind us. The fire is creating its own draft, like a giant chimney sucking air from every direction."

"Is getting closer, the fire," Caruso said. "You are think maybe is come here?"

I turned my gaze from the Palace to the waterfront, where thousands of people pushed and shoved, trying desperately to board boats to ferry them to safety.

"I don't know, Enrico. I don't know if anything can stop it now."

Kaitlin stared westward, toward the Fairmont Hotel on Nob Hill, then along Russian Hill and Cow Hollow to North Beach below us, a colorful sea of picturesque Victorian houses and flats that had suffered significantly less earthquake damage than those South of the Slot. "You mean the fire could come this far? It could burn all those houses?"

I rubbed my soiled face, afraid to answer. I felt some relief to hear the growl of the Waltham approaching, moments before it emerged from the overgrown lot on Kearny. Hunter skidded to a stop a few feet in front of us.

"We have a problem," Hunter shouted.

"I can see that."

"Rolf's goons—" he choked, "those bastards killed Prosecutor Feeney."

"Oh, my God," I said, clasping my hands to my face in horror.

"They blew up his house. They're using this pandemonium as a cover to strike back. If they went after Feeney, they're going to come after all of us."

Hunter looked to Kaitlin and Caruso. "The two of you have to get to Golden Gate Park. It's past the fire line, you'll be safe. They're setting up tents and kitchens."

"That's Broadway," I said to Kaitlin, pointing to the bottom of Telegraph Hill. "Take it until it gets steep. Turn left, then go right on Fulton Street. Fulton leads to Golden Gate Park."

"I have a map," Kaitlin replied. "I can find it." Her stoic demeanor wavered. She reached in her bag. "Can I leave this in your house?" she asked, ready to cry. She handed me her diary. "I'm afraid I might lose it." I nodded. "Please find my father," she said.

I turned to Caruso. "You must go with Kaitlin, Enrico. Stay in Golden Gate Park as long as you can. We'll find you when this is over."

I hugged Caruso and ran into the house, placing Kaitlin's diary on the bench near Hunter's toppled instruments.

When I returned to the street, I climbed on the seat behind Hunter. We flew back down Kearny, my arms wrapped tightly around him, my head buried against his back so I could hear and feel his heart thumping. The temperature rose block by block as ash and soot swirled around us.

A few blocks from where we passed, Lincoln Staley was beginning to stir in the dank cellar below Shanghai Kelly's saloon.

His first conscious moment was terrifying. A blinding flash of light, followed by a jarring throb threatened to rend his skull in two. Liquid fire rose through his gullet, burning his mouth and tongue as he vomited bitter coffee and laudanum.

Praying he was still alive, he reached out to stop the room from spinning and forced himself to open his eyes. Through the darkness he saw a thin trickle of flickering red light. He reached into his duster for a container of stick matches. He fumbled the lid off, spilling them in the dirt. He felt around until he found one and then struck it on the lid. The match sizzled to life.

Several heavy beams lay at jagged angles ten feet away. At the end of one, two men lay crushed in a moon of blood-soaked dirt. Lincoln looked around for his Stetson hat but could find it nowhere.

Then it came to him. Following Tommy down the whorehouse hallway. The bald, tattooed man, the sharp crack and the blinding light. The match burned Lincoln's fingers. He struck another and crawled toward the flickering light outside, fighting nausea and vertigo.

Lincoln struggled to a kneeling position and rammed his shoulder upward, toward the light. He did it again and again until the wooden door popped open. He heaved his body through the opening and collapsed on the broken sidewalk, where he lay for a minute, listening to a horrendous roar, the air as hot as a boiler room.

Move. You have to move, Lincoln. You have to keep moving.

He pulled himself to his feet and rubbed his eyes. Every building on the street lay in some form of ruin. Shards of broken glass sparkled crimson on the wooden sidewalks, roofs and porticos lay sprawled across the cobblestone streets, several buildings appeared to be holding each other up. He tried to breathe through his mouth, his throat raw, the heated air so painful he felt he was swallowing glass. He realized the roar was not coming from inside his head but from behind him.

Lincoln reached the middle of the street and looked skyward, bewildered by a towering shroud of fire and smoke.

Earthquake. A damn earthquake. The whole city is on fire.

He looked up Battery Street, trying to recall the route he had taken with Tommy.

Lincoln navigated the wrecked neighborhood, straining to clear his thoughts and dodge the Barbary Coast's garish survivors. Garbled laughter drifted from a saloon, where dozens of people crowded around a barrelhouse piano. A whore with rouge-stained cheeks and matted hair limped through the swinging doors to stare at him, the fire's glow adding a ghastly tint to her cadaverous face.

The battered sheriff spotted the closest thing to salvation. He plunged his head into a half-empty horse trough, the water stinging his blistered mouth.

On Clay Street, Lincoln approached a familiar house. A Negro butler deposited a trunk into an automobile parked askew on the crooked sidewalk. Through the house's open door, Lincoln recognized a heavy-set woman.

He hurried up the steps as gamely as his legs allowed.

"Hey, you! Where you goin'?" the colored man yelled as Lincoln slammed the door, flipping the bolt behind him.

"What the hell do you want?" Tessie asked defiantly, then shouted. "Joseph! Joseph!"

Lincoln grabbed her by the throat and slammed her against the wall. By instinct, his other hand found the derringer in a small pocket inside his duster. He cocked the upper cylinder and rested it against her chin.

"My daughter," he said in a raspy voice.

"Your daughter. Who the hell is your daughter?"

Joseph banged at the door. "Miss Tessie! Miss Tessie! You all right? Miss Tessie!"

Lincoln shoved the barrel of the derringer deeper into Tessie's ample chin.

"Ah, yes. I remember. Rolf told me to help get rid of you. If it wasn't for this damn earthquake you'd be halfway to Shanghai."

"Where is she? If you lie, I'll kill you."

"That'd be the day Adam Rolf is worth dying for. Try his house on Nob Hill. Top of California Street. That's the last anybody saw her, at the shindig after the opera. Now, get the hell away from me."

Chapter 58

APRIL 18, 1906. 4:00 P.M.

Christian, Francis, Patrick, and Carlo arrived at the Spreckels mansion, the only building ablaze for a mile in any direction.

"Damn," said Christian, "they beat us here. I'll kill them, I swear to God."

An old man ran toward them, waving to attract their attention. "Are you friends of Spreckels?" he gasped.

"We're police officers," said Francis, "we came to help him."

"You're too late. Mrs. Spreckels had her baby on the sidewalk. He took them to the hospital at the Presidio." The old man caught his breath. "I'm James Stetson. I live on the next corner."

"Did you see who did this?" Christian asked.

"I saw some men running out. The kind of swine you see on the Barbary Coast. One was real tall, had a big scar, his pal looked like one of those circus strongmen, tattoos and a bald head. Mrs. Spreckels was still lying on the sidewalk with the baby, the whole damn place was on fire."

"Is anyone hurt in your house?" Francis asked.

"I live alone. I got my bathtub and all my pails filled with water and I'll fight if it comes knocking on my door."

"Feeney's dead, Spreckels is probably safe at Army General Hospital," Francis said to the others. "Ain't nothing down Van Ness in that direction except Christian's place. I got a hunch Kelly and his thugs are out to settle a score." He looked at Carlo, who stood staring at the ground, his breathing labored.

"Mr. Stetson," Christian said, "my brother is supposed to meet us here. Hunter is his name, he should be on a motorcycle. Tell him we're at my place on Union Street."

"You're Byron Fallon's boys. Cryin' shame what happened. I'll wait for your brother as long as I can."

"Thank you, sir." Christian turned to Francis. "I'm about ready to finish this."

A mile east, Hunter and I worked our way down Montgomery Street through the mounting debris and flood of refugees, the sound of dynamiting now as rapid as an artillery barrage. On California Street, Hunter spotted Amadeo Giannini and two clerks carrying sacks from his Bank of Italy office to two dump wagons loaded with vegetable crates.

"Mr. Giannini," Hunter cried, "are you alright?"

"Yes, Hunter," he replied, settling onto the wooden bench and seizing the reins. "I've got every dime of the bank's money in these sacks. I'm going to try to make it to my brother's house just down the Peninsula a few miles."

"Are you armed?"

"I have an old pistol. I'm not sure it works, don't think I've ever fired it."

"You best go up Broadway, cut across to the Great Highway and El Camino Real. It's the only way."

Giannini saluted. "Please share my condolences with Christian. Your father was a great man." His horses had barely moved when an explosion down the street panicked them.

While Giannini fought to steady his team, Hunter and I looked skyward as flaming debris spread over two blocks in each direction. A burning couch landed atop a three-story building a hundred yards away. In seconds, the wood shingle roof, bone dry from the heated wind, burst into flames.

A group of twenty soldiers stood in the center of California Street near a caisson full of black powder, admiring the results of their handiwork.

Hunter appeared ready to intervene when I tugged at his arm.

"It's useless, Hunter, they're following Funston's orders." We were about to leave when we heard the soldiers shouting "Halt! Hey, you! Halt!"

Half a block up California, a man ran from a butcher shop, a box of food in his arms. Two soldiers raised their rifles and aimed at his back.

"Hey, you! Halt!" a Sergeant yelled.

The man kept running. They fired. He pitched forward, spilling meat and sausages across the cluttered street. He rolled onto his back, motionless.

Hunter ran to the Sergeant in charge. "Are you crazy?" he yelled. "How could the poor bastard hear anything that far away?"

The Sergeant moved toward Hunter menacingly. Hunter produced his badge.

"I got my orders to shoot any looter on sight" the Sergeant answered.

"How do you know he didn't own that butcher shop? How do you know he wasn't taking food to his family in Golden Gate Park so they could eat tonight?"

"I got my orders. Now, you get the hell out of here before I take you in for interfering with the military." The Sergeant headed toward his troops.

"This is insanity," Hunter raged. "No one has the right to suspend the Constitution and order summary execution. Funston couldn't wait to make himself emperor."

A few doors from where the body lay, soldiers emerged from a liquor wholesaler, carrying wooden boxes filled with whiskey. Several empty bottles already littered the sidewalk where they set the cases down.

"Looters. They got soldiers shooting people for looting, then looting stores themselves," Hunter said.

"And he'll answer for it," I argued. "Come on. We can't stop the whole Army. There's nothing we can do except find Francis and Christian."

I seized Hunter's arm and pulled him away as another building exploded, showering flaming wreckage on top several stores, instantly setting them on fire.

"April eighteenth, nineteen-oh-six," he said. "The day the world went crazy."

We motored up Sacramento Street to avoid the soldiers. Block by block, we passed troops forcing people from their homes, the occupants pleading for the right to salvage their possessions or stay and fight the flames. Just below Nob Hill, we could see the Stanford, Crocker, and Rolf mansions still intact and imperious.

At Van Ness, we found James Stetson standing before the flaming Spreckels mansion.

"You Hunter Fallon?"

"Yes, sir. Did Mr. Spreckels and his family get out?"

"He took his wife over to the Presidio, she just had her baby. Your brother Christian was here. They went to his place. I think they're gunnin' for the scum that did this."

"Are you going to be alright?" Hunter asked.

"I'm old and rich and I lived a good life. I got nothing to complain about."

Hunter re-engaged the gear lever and powered down Van Ness, through streams of water as broken mains continued to gush.

It dawned on me that horses had become scarce, trolleys and cable cars non-existent. With the ruptured streets and fallen buildings and abandoned possessions piling up everywhere, Hunter's motorcycle and a handful of automobiles were the only vehicles moving.

We wheeled onto Union Street, raucous music and drunken laughter pouring from dozens of barely upright saloons.

Two short blocks from Christian's flat, Patrick jumped from the shadows and flagged us down. Hunter killed the Waltham's engine and coasted to the wooden sidewalk, where he leaned it against an iron lamppost.

"You don't want to go down there just yet," Patrick warned. We followed him through the splintered door of a boarded-up storefront and up narrow wooden steps to a loft on the second floor where Christian and the others waited.

"What the hell are you guys up to?" Hunter asked.

"Staking out a burglary," Christian replied.

"We're chasing burglars now?"

Hunter moved next to Christian. Beyond the rooftops of Union Street, the reflection of the billowing flames, a mile behind us, danced off the surface of the bay, adding a disturbing crimson hue to the dark water. Christian pointed toward his flat, where Shanghai Kelly stopped a heavy dump wagon near a pile of familiar furniture.

"They're robbing your flat!" Hunter said.

"Elizabeth's mother bought that furniture during the Civil War. Good riddance. Besides," Christian added smugly, "it's insured. Three grand. Way more than it's worth."

We watched as Shanghai Kelly pulled the hitching pin and led the horse to a water trough farther down the street. Scarface and Dumbrowski emerged from Christian's flat with a wooden file cabinet, hoisted it above their heads, and smashed it on the cobblestones. They laughed like jackals.

"How many are there?" Hunter asked.

"Kelly, Dumbrowski, Scarface," Christian answered. "Plus three more rummies from one of Kelly's crews." He noticed me for the first time. "Annalisa."

"Hello, Christian," I replied. He looked pained and worn, his face still bruised. He smiled, but it was a hollow effort.

"That was a brave thing you did," he said.

"Your father was worth it."

"I meant agreeing to marry my brother."

Everyone laughed, a scant respite from the tension and ominous task at hand.

"What say you, little brother?" Christian asked. "Time to settle the score?"

"I'm in," Hunter said.

"Are you going down there to arrest them, or pick a gunfight?" I asked.

"That's up to them," Patrick interjected, fondling his revolver, his pale blue eyes intense, unflinching.

"That's just what they want," I answered. "Draw you out in the open so they can kill you."

"We tried doin' it civil-like," Christian said. "The time for talk is over." He shouldered his shotgun and started for the door. Francis, Patrick, and Carlo followed, the latter without looking up from the floor.

I seized Hunter's arm. "You are the man who was going to change things, remember? The one who is going to do things differently?"

"I'm part of them now, Annalisa. If Kelly and his men raise their hands and throw down their weapons, we'll arrest them."

"And if they don't?"

"A gunfight makes for better copy."

The cavalier response dismayed me. "I thought you were taking after your father. Now you're starting to sound like Christian."

"We're family, Annalisa, you get a little bit of everything in every one of us." Hunter gazed anxiously toward the stairway. "Either way, Kelly and his lot have killed their last good man."

"I pray to God you're right, Hunter."

Hunter pulled his revolver and ran down the steps to join Christian, who was waiting in the doorway, gazing up Union Street.

"You think they've spotted us yet?" Hunter asked.

"No, but they will if we march down there like Pickett's Charge. That's what Kelly's hopin', that's why he's makin' a spectacle out of bustin' up my place like that."

Christian spotted an abandoned camelback trunk ten yards away with a mound of women's clothes spilling out. He crouched low and ran to the trunk, where he pulled out an antique blue gingham dress, holding it against his chest.

"This lady here ate real well," he said grinning. "There's enough fabric in this one for a small tent."

Outside Christian's flat, Kelly and Scarface were on alert, watching for trouble as their cohorts carried Christian's belongings to a wagon.

From the window, I could see Kelly fix his gaze on two women who approached from a block away, partially hidden by a trunk they pushed atop a child's wagon.

Kelly turned away and took a fire ax to a chest of drawers.

Christian and Hunter, crouching behind the trunk, maneuvered the wagon over the craggy surface of Union Street. Hunter tried to shove the floppy brim of his flowered bonnet back far enough so he could see, with little success.

"Elizabeth has a fit deciding what dress to wear," Christian said, "and look at you. Gussied pretty as an oil painting. Nice strand a' pearls and maybe Annalisa can get you in the society page."

"Too bad I couldn't find a purse to match the outfit," Hunter added, peeking over the trunk as they closed within half a block.

"It was Anthony," Christian blurted.

"What?"

"Anthony. I always thought he was just plain loopy, but it looks like opium cooked his brains. Donen found out, told Anthony if he didn't keep him apprised of dad's activities, he'd fire him."

"What did you do to him?"

"He's a foot away from a straightjacket, permanent. Killing him would be a favor. It was my job to protect dad and I couldn't even do that."

"Seasick as you get, Gamboa would have killed you both. Let's just get the guys who did it."

I paced frantically at the second-floor window, watching as Francis, Patrick, and Carlo slid from the doorway to a debris pile, fifty yards behind the dress-wearing Fallon brothers.

Somewhere, a tinny piano and a screeching woman's voice played "It'll Be a Hot Time in the Old Town Tonight."

Christian clutched his sawed-off shotgun against the back of the trunk and wiped the sweat trickling down his face. "Once the shootin' starts, don't stop until all of them are dead."

"We should give them a chance to surrender," Hunter said.

"You're not going to start that again, are you? Just keep your head down, keep squeezing, and cover each other while we reload."

They closed the gap, my fear mounting so that I had to force myself to watch.

Kelly studied the enormous trunk moving down the street in his direction. A gust of wind lifted the bonnet of the shorter one, revealing the battered face of Christian Fallon.

"Cops!" Kelly screamed, jerking the revolver from his belt.

Christian and Hunter ripped off the restrictive hats and dresses.

Kelly fired first, splintering a corner of the trunk.

Christian squeezed the trigger of his shotgun and ripped a hole in the dump wagon a foot from Kelly's head.

Hunter aimed at Scarface as the big man dove toward an overturned table. The slug missed, smashing into the cobblestones.

Francis, Carlo, and Patrick, outlined by the devilish red light, fired as they charged.

Hunter saw a man emerging from the flat, his revolver aimed at Christian. Hunter fired: the bullet exploded in the man's chest and dropped him in the doorway.

Kelly's shot bounced off the trunk and grazed Christian's shoulder.

A blast from Christian's shotgun smashed the oak table where Kelly had crouched and sent the Irishman scampering for better cover.

Carlo, howling like a madman, charged down the middle of the street firing repeatedly at Dumbrowski. A slug from Carlo's revolver shattered his lower leg and sent the giant sprawling.

Someone leaned out from a doorway and aimed at Carlo. Before the man could fire, Christian dropped him with a single shot.

"Carlo, get down!" Hunter screamed.

Scarface put a shot through Carlo's side; Dumbrowski put another through his shoulder. Still, Carlo charged.

"Take cover," Patrick yelled. Carlo never heard him.

Dumbrowski, trying desperately to crawl to cover, screamed as Carlo's next shot caught him in the groin. The next silenced the tattooed giant by taking off the top of his head.

Carlo's revolver clicked empty. He threw it down and pulled a hunting knife, closing on Scarface from twenty feet. Christian and Hunter fired furiously, trying to keep Kelly and Scarface pinned down as Carlo closed.

Scarface leaned around the edge of the oak table and pumped another shot into Carlo's side. Carlo stumbled, but still he charged.

Francis opened up on Scarface, desperately trying to keep him from firing at Carlo.

A bullet from Scarface's revolver entered Carlo's open mouth and exited the base of his skull. Carlo staggered and collapsed at the tall man's feet.

I sagged to my knees and sobbed, clinging to the window sill.

Christian put a round close enough to the oak table to take off most of Scarface's ear.

A red-bearded man poked a rifle from the window of Christian's flat. Francis and Patrick fired, peppering the man with lead. He fell headfirst onto the sidewalk, a bloody spray arching from his shattered skull.

Kelly poked his head from behind the dump wagon, firing at Christian and Hunter, bullets ricocheting inches from their legs.

Patrick and Francis moved forward, ducked into a doorway, and fired at Kelly, who pulled another revolver from his belt and fired back. Kelly's round shot off a doorframe and caught Patrick in the shoulder.

Patrick staggered onto the sidewalk, grimacing, blood oozing through his shirt. Francis stepped in front to shield him, firing at Kelly and Scarface until his revolver ran dry. He grabbed Patrick's revolver and fired one shot before it too expired.

Christian finished reloading and saw Francis and Patrick exposed. He leapt from behind the trunk and charged, firing his revolver, trying to keep Kelly and Scarface pinned down.

"Christian, get down," Hunter screamed, his hands trembling as he reloaded.

Hunter fired at Scarface, tearing a hole in the oak table as Christian dove toward the wagon where Kelly hid.

Francis pulled Patrick back into the doorway.

Christian crouched behind one end of the wagon, five feet from Kelly, who reached up and jerked the brake loose. The wagon rolled forward, leaving Christian's legs exposed.

Kelly leaned beneath the wagon's bed and put a bullet in Christian's knee. Christian stumbled and dropped his gun.

I held my hands to my mouth as Hunter jumped from behind the trunk and dashed forward to protect his brother. He fired a bullet through Kelly's shooting arm while Scarface hid behind the pock-marked table.

Christian writhed in pain and crawled toward his revolver.

Hunter shot Kelly in the leg and then his gun ran dry. He dove behind a chest of drawers and dumped the spent shells from his revolver while Francis stepped from cover to fire at Kelly.

Scarface grabbed Dumbrowski's revolver and sprinted toward the flat, firing at Francis as Hunter frantically reloaded.

Kelly raised his revolver and drew a bead on Christian's head.

Hunter finished reloading and fired first, the bullet slamming into Kelly's side. Two more shots from Hunter's pistol ripped through Kelly's chest and finished him.

Christian clutched his leg as Hunter moved to his side.

In the deep shadow of Christian's doorway, safe from Hunter's view and Francis' line of fire, Scarface turned and fired.

The shot ripped through Christian's heart.

Hunter wheeled and fired into the doorway as Scarface disappeared into the shadows. When his revolver ran dry again, Hunter turned to his brother.

"Christian, Christian!"

I was already racing down the sidewalk. I slowed and looked at Patrick, who was dazed and mumbling a prayer.

Francis stood guard as I dropped next to Christian and put my arm behind his neck, a pool of blood widening into a giant red crown beneath him.

I gazed over at Carlo's lifeless body, then back at Hunter, whose face was a mask of pain and resignation. He leaned forward and kissed his brother on the forehead.

"Tell mom and dad I love them," he whispered.

"I think Scarface is gone," Francis said. "He took the rear exit on Filbert. Let's hook Kelly's horse back up to the wagon. We have to get to the Presidio."

"How bad is Patrick?" I asked

"The bullet nicked his collarbone. He hasn't lost a lot of blood, he should be all right. We better move, ain't none of this over."

Chapter 59

KEARNY STREET

APRIL 18, 1906. 7:15 P.M.

At the Hall of Justice near the border of the Barbary Coast and Chinatown, aides frantically shuffled stacks of messages as Schmitz held a tense
conference with General Funston, Assistant Fire Chief Dougherty, and
Police Chief Donen.

"The effort has been too little and too late," Funston growled. "A two-
block firebreak is not enough. We need a much wider firebreak along this
route." Funston produced a filthy map from his back pocket, and traced a
crescent-shaped line from the residential area of the Mission District,
down Van Ness Avenue to the waterfront, reciting the names of the streets.

Schmitz was stunned. "Six blocks wide and four, five miles long? What
is that, five thousand buildings? There's not that much dynamite in the
whole state."

"We found a ton and a half of gun cotton at the Naval base on Mare
Island and another two boxcars of black powder at the Southern Pacific
Depot."

"General," Dougherty said, "what does it matter if we blow the city to
smithereens or let the fire have it? Admiral Goodrich is on his way. We
should position ourselves to help the Navy when they arrive."

"Where were they when they got the distress call?" Funston asked.

"San Diego," Schmitz replied.

"San Diego. Maybe they'll arrive in time for our funeral. I've already
given the orders. My men are expanding the dynamiting from California
Street to Jackson to keep the fire from spreading to Chinatown and

North Beach. We have teams positioned on Van Ness to take out every building on the east side and keep the fire from jumping to the western part of the city."

An explosion blew out the windows on the east side of the building, sending everyone to the floor in terror. Shaking off slivers of glass, their ears echoing with the concussion, Schmitz and the others climbed to their feet.

Bertrand stumbled across the room, covered in ash, a handkerchief pressed to his mouth and nose. "Mr. Mayor," he implored, "we must go now, sir. The fire is racing up Kearny, it's barely a block away."

Schmitz looked to Funston as the building creaked ominously. "General, if your men are blasting a firebreak to protect Chinatown and North Beach, what's the fire doing outside our door here?"

"You told me to keep you informed," Funston growled as he rolled up the map. "So, now I've informed you."

"Let's go, sir," Bertrand begged. "Nob Hill is still safe. The car is waiting to take us to the Fairmont."

Schmitz turned back to Funston, but he was already gone.

Donen seized the Mayor's arm and dragged him from the building.

Outside, a blast of heated air almost knocked Schmitz off his feet. He pulled his collar to his face and jumped into the Ford next to Donen.

With Bertrand and Dougherty in the back seat, they lurched up Washington Street, through Chinatown, Donen working the horn. Schmitz stared to his left, where half the Financial District was now ablaze, the flames so high it was impossible to see above them.

Help was closer than he realized.

The USS *Chicago*, flagship of the Navy's Pacific Squadron, plowed past Big Sur, just south of Monterey. Admiral Casper Goodrich, a lean, regal figure, lowered his binoculars and looked to the men fanned out behind him on the bridge.

"Jesus and Mary. Seventy-five miles from San Francisco and you can see the flames already. Ensign Arthur, tell the engine room to squeeze every ounce of speed we have. And pray there's something left to save when we get there."

Goodrich looked back over the stern at the *Marblehead*, *Boston*, and *Princeton* churning in formation behind him. Hundreds of sailors and Marines crowded the rail, transfixed by the flickering glow and mountain of smoke to the north.

"Keep trying the wireless," Goodrich ordered a young seaman. "Let the Mayor and Fire Chief know I want a situation report the minute we dock." Goodrich raised his binoculars. "If there's anyone there to give us one."

We had arrived at the Presidio after an arduous struggle with the horse and wagon that bore the bodies of Carlo and Christian. A tent city had sprung up, with row after row of torch-lit streets, complete with dining tables and makeshift kitchens where soldiers fed a growing stream of refugees. It was the first I realized that night had fallen. Tents with big red crosses painted on their sloping panels received the burned and wounded, where field medics and nurses treated those they could and sent the more serious cases on to the doctors at Army General Hospital. Compared to the chaos behind us, it was a model of calm and efficiency.

Through the tidy rows moved Eda Funston, the Brigadier General's wife, a dignified woman dressed in a long black dress. She stopped at every tent to offer comfort.

I was staring back toward the city, at the wall of flame that towered several hundred feet, my fatigued mind unable to estimate how far it had advanced.

A stoic Hunter returned from his meeting with the duty officer and tapped me on the shoulder. "We gave Christian and Carlo to the make-shift morgue. We'll bury them when this is over."

"What about Patrick?"

Francis was standing on my other side. "He's proof God loves the Irish," he said. "As long as he keeps still and doesn't use that shoulder, he'll be fine."

"Annalisa," Hunter said. "Francis and I are going after Rolf and Scarface before they find new recruits. I want you to wait somewhere safe for us."

I let slip a pained laugh, so alien it startled me. "Somewhere safe? Like where? Switzerland?"

Hunter wiped the tears washing lines down my ragamuffin face. "I'm going to stay with you," I said. "And I won't argue." I was afraid that if I let him go, I might never see him again.

"If we stand still too long, we'll never move," Francis said.

Eda Funston approached and offered us food and water. We gratefully accepted.

An hour or so after our arrival, we headed back toward the inferno. With the Waltham now out of fuel, and no drug stores from which to purchase gasoline, we walked. Francis, Hunter, and I trudged up Filbert Street, each of us carrying two canteens of water.

At the peak of Russian Hill, it appeared that the fire creeping from the Financial District into Chinatown was close enough to touch. We sagged onto fractured Taylor Street and tried to catch our breath. Through a vacant lot between two collapsed buildings, I was able to see once-stately Van Ness Avenue. Water from the broken Spring Valley line still gushed over the cobblestones, soaking discarded mattresses, family heirlooms, and suitcases. As I watched, light-headed, the cool, undulating stream turned into a watery tongue, seeping from the mouth of the fiery Demon behind it.

I was shaking from the delusion when, near the corner of Sacramento and Van Ness, three houses exploded, flaming remnants soaring into the air, crashing down on rooftops over a four-block radius.

"They expanded the dynamite line," Hunter raged somewhere behind me. "Those stupid fools!"

A tiny woman hurried toward us, her efforts made difficult by the cracked streets and piles of refuse. Struggling close behind her was Ting Leo. "Miss Cameron," I called hoarsely, drifting toward her. "Miss Cameron!"

"Annalisa! Dear Lord. We've just come from Chinatown. The girls who came over with Ting Leo are trapped in Ah Toy's place. The fire's only a few blocks away, they're going to burn alive."

"What about the girls at the Mission?" I asked.

"They're in North Beach, in Washington Square with the other poor souls. I'm not sure how long even that will be safe."

"You go to them," Hunter said. "If we can get the others out, we'll bring them to you."

Miss Cameron started off, but Ting Leo shook her head, refusing to go. She grabbed my hand and started pulling us in the direction of Ah Toy's.

"Go ahead, Miss Cameron," I called. "I'll tend to her. You see to the other girls."

We hurried toward Chinatown, grateful that the path was downhill.

When we arrived outside the Jade Dragon restaurant, Ting Leo found a crack at the base of the façade. She cupped her hands to her mouth and called out.

"Ting Leo," one of the girls shouted back. "Ting Leo!" The trapped girls screamed her name repeatedly.

Terrified, the girls had huddled all day amid debris and dust, weeping and crying for help. Through a small crack in one wall, they could see other girls in the room next to them, crushed and lifeless. Squealing rats crawled over the bodies, their red eyes illuminated by tiny shafts of flickering firelight.

Ting Leo shouted several times, and the girls shouted back.

"Dead? Many girls dead?" I asked. I closed my eyes and feigned death. Ting Leo did not understand.

"How many girls alive?" I asked, pointing to Ting Leo's fingers and then the screaming girls inside. "How many alive?"

Ting Leo shouted and the tearful voices replied. Ting Leo shouted again. She turned and flashed both hands and two fingers.

"Twelve," I said, repeating the gesture. "Twelve girls alive."

Ting Leo nodded frantically. "Twel' gills rive."

Hunter examined the building. The entrance on Jackson had collapsed into the basement, pitching the roof and brick façade halfway across the street.

Scores of Chinatown residents ran before the approaching wall of flame, ignoring the adolescent screams.

"We might be able to chop our way through the side of the building," Francis yelled.

"Too dangerous, it could bring the building down on top of them," Hunter called back. "We'll have to find a crawl space beneath the floor and basement wall to get them out of there."

Ting Leo watched intently, trying to decipher our words. I pantomimed an opening and pulling the girls through. She turned and exchanged shouts with the girls below. Then she sprinted to the back of the building.

Without a word, she wiggled through an opening beneath the floor.

In the dark space, barely a foot high, she crawled toward the source of the wailing. She shouted to the other girls and was shocked by the sound of her own voice. She cleared her throat of the dust and called again, to no avail. She felt her way over jagged pieces of concrete, splintered floorboards, and rusty nails, through the stench of rodent urine and droppings. She squeezed under a cracked beam and into a section illuminated by the glimmer of fire through a cracked wall to her left. The wailing grew closer.

Finally, she slid her hand between a heavy floor beam and the basement wall. The girls below clutched frantically at her. She shook them off and felt along the opening. It was too narrow for even the smallest to slide through. Tracing the floor beam above her with her hands, she crawled to the wall closest to us, yelling through the crack she had used earlier.

"Hunner, Hunner!"

"Hunter," I said. "She's calling your name."

Hunter was across the street, throwing a brick through the window of a hardware store while Francis kept watch, hoping no soldiers were close enough to shoot them. Hunter crawled through the shattered window and quickly emerged with a new Eveready and a fire ax. He ran toward us, shining the light through the small crack to illuminate Ting Leo's wide, desperate eyes.

"Twel' gills rive!" she yelled, pointing to the beam above her head and motioning upward.

"How does she know your name?"

In the light of the Eveready, Hunter recognized the angelic face. He smiled. "We met in the harbor."

Francis chopped at the adobe wall, delicately, widening the hole enough so that Hunter could slip the Eveready through. Ting Leo wiggled forward and accepted it uneasily, pointing the light along the wooden beam.

The gleaming red eyes of an enormous rat stared back. When Ting Leo jiggled the light, it fled.

"If we can raise this beam a foot," Hunter shouted, "she might be able to pull them out of there."

He and Francis sprinted to Dupont Street. Once they passed beyond the relative shield of the buildings, the heat from the rapidly approaching fire hit them like an open furnace. Half a block up Dupont, a middle-aged Chinese merchant ran from his shop with a large paper box and climbed into an overloaded two-horse wagon.

They ran to him, trying to explain, by Hunter's fractured Chinese and frantic gestures, the situation at Ah Toy's. The man shook his fists angrily and grabbed the reins. Francis stepped in front of him and seized the horses' tack, sending the man into a fury. He lashed out with a buggy whip, striking Francis' shoulder.

Hunter pulled his revolver and jumped into the wagon, jabbing it in the man's ribs, forcing him out.

I heard horse's hooves approaching, the sound almost drowned out by the roar of the fire moving steadily closer.

While Francis steadied the fractious animals, Hunter knotted a rope to the horse's yoke and threw it high over a lamppost. He tied the other end around the beam that ran under the restaurant and directly above Ting Leo's head.

Clutching the bulky Eveready to her chest, Ting Leo inched toward the screaming girls. Then she signaled to me by motioning upward with the beam of light.

Francis slapped at the horses' haunches with the knotted reins. The rope grew taut and chattered over the lamppost. Slowly the beam began to rise.

Lying on her belly in the dirt, Ting Leo watched the opening slowly widen.

"More. More," I yelled. They slapped and shoved the horses, the animals growing more unruly as the heat and the roar of the fire grew by the minute.

The beam groaned and dust rained down on Ting Leo. The girls fought frantically, shoving each other, ignoring Ting Leo's screams to push the smallest one up. Finally, she threatened to leave them unless they obeyed.

"Hurry!" I yelled to her as the rope stretched and the lamppost bowed under the weight. I could see the fire now surging above the rooftop of the restaurant, the sound ever more deafening. "Hurry!!!"

The smallest one was boosted up and Ting Leo pulled her through the opening, shoving her in my direction.

"Here, over here" I yelled. "Come, come, come," I shouted.

I realized the hole in the exterior was not big enough to crawl through. I raised the fire ax, so weak the back swing almost toppled me. I grunted as the pointed tip struck the wall, barely widening the hole. Three more times I managed to swing the ax until the adobe crumbled. I clawed at the hole until my fingers bled, fighting the urge to panic, and then I finally pulled free a tiny girl no older than seven.

Hunter and Francis struggled to keep the horses digging forward as the first girl collapsed, gasping, her eyes burning with dust, sobbing hysterically. I opened a canteen, splashing her eyes and mouth. She gulped the water, choking, rolling over to her knees to vomit. I grabbed her hair and pulled her head back, dousing her mouth and face until she spit up clods of dust.

Ting Leo, screaming orders, pulled the second girl through and then the third. The beam slipped, wedging the fourth girl and knocking the wind from her.

I yelled to Hunter, who put his back to the yoke while Francis flailed at the backsides of the straining animals. Slowly, they inched forward.

Ting Leo pulled the fourth girl free, then the fifth, each one coming through more quickly. I doused each of them with water, emptying both of my canteens as I counted aloud, "six, seven, eight," lest one be left behind.

The last two girls refused to help each other, jumping desperately for Ting Leo's hand. She screamed that she would leave them, ordering the tallest to boost the other. Finally, Ting Leo strained to pull her through.

The last girl was unable to reach Ting Leo's hand. She fell to her knees, paralyzed by fear as the collapse of a burning building several doors away shook the walls. Ting Leo dropped into the basement, seizing the girl by the back of her dress and shoving her upward, the girl kicking Ting Leo in the face as she squirmed.

Alone, Ting Leo shone the Eveready around the filthy room, searching for something on which to stand. Nothing. Then she shone it through the opening and waved it frantically.

I saw the light waving in the dark, just below the beam. I realized Ting Leo was trying to signal me, and that she herself was trapped.

"These horses cannot hold any longer!" screamed Hunter. "Get her out of there!"

I somehow squeezed through the exterior opening and pulled myself toward Ting Leo. The stench and my exhaustion made me retch. The building creaked and the beam slipped several inches, sending down a mountain of dust.

"Annalisa's going to be trapped," Hunter screamed. Francis grabbed a wooden cane from an abandoned wheelbarrow and flailed at the horses' flanks as Hunter strained against the yoke. Slowly, the horses inched forward and the beam creaked upward.

I grabbed Ting Leo's wrists. She wriggled desperately, her nails digging into my flesh. I tried not to scream or drop her. Digging in the dirt with my toes and knees, I inched backward until she popped through the opening.

We crawled toward the street, Ting Leo in front, unconsciously kicking dirt in my face as we scrambled forward.

"Hurry!" Hunter screamed as the lamppost started to buckle and pull loose from its mooring.

Ting Leo squirmed through the hole in the outside wall, then turned and pulled me clear as one horse stumbled, dragging the other one backward.

Hunter cut the rope and sent the building crashing into the basement, the horses stampeding down Jackson Street.

Hunter lifted me to my feet as the rooftop of the Jade Dragon burst into flames. We rushed the weeping girls down Jackson under the canopy of searing heat.

"Annalisa," Hunter said when we reached Montgomery, struggling to catch his breath. "Take these girls to Miss Cameron at Washington Square. Please."

I was about to argue when I realized the girls would be lost without a guide. "I will if you'll tell me where you're going," I said.

"We're going to do what we have to do. Meet us at Meigg's Wharf. Please."

"You're going to Rolf's house after him and Scarface."

"Scarface killed my father and then he killed my brother. On Rolf's orders."

"And what if they kill you?"

"If I had killed Scarface the first night, on the Barbary Coast, Christian might still be alive. He's not going to kill someone else."

I knew it was useless to argue. I gathered the weeping girls and steered them up the hill toward North Beach.

Before she crossed Broadway, Ting Leo turned to smile back at Hunter. She would later talk about seeing him in the harbor, about the light shining on her face, the light that came from his hands, and about the prophecy she had heard in her village about a man who would come to save them from the dreaded emperor. "Hunner," she said, gazing up at me with a dirty, beatific smile.

I hurried Ting Leo and the others along. Though we had won a small victory, it was not over yet.

In fact, it was about to get worse.

Chapter 60

NOB HILL

APRIL 19, 1906. 12:30 A.M.

Eugene Schmitz leaned on a banquet table in the ballroom of the Fairmont Hotel, examining his map, the air rife with the smell of burning buildings and the thunder of constant dynamiting. He gazed over at Police Chief Donen and Assistant Fire Chief Dougherty. "Any word from the Navy, anyone?"

"Nothing," Donen said. "The telegraph office burned down an hour ago. Unless they're still operating a line out at the Presidio, we're completely cut off from the world."

What Schmitz did have was a stack of disturbing reports. An elderly Italian immigrant, a witness claimed, had been bayoneted for refusing to help soldiers on the fire line, an order he could not understand. Two other reports claimed that soldiers had executed a dozen men in a vacant lot near the Townsend Street Train Station. The Reynolds & Company tobacco firm had been looted so many times by men in uniform, an employee reported, that their entire stock had disappeared.

Schmitz threw the reports into a trashcan, where, unbeknownst to him, an aide would shortly retrieve them.

"Does anyone have an update on the fire situation?" he demanded.

Dougherty finished conferring with a soot-covered firefighter and walked to the map table. Everyone squeezed in around him. He began to point out locations, his slumped shoulders sinking toward collapse. "The fireboats from Mare Island are still pumping enough salt water to keep the fire off the Ferry Building," the old man stated. "That's the only good news. If the front that hit Chinatown jumps Broadway into North Beach, it could burn all the way down Montgomery to the waterfront. It's like the bloody Devil himself is at the wheel. Every time we think we have him cornered, it outflanks us."

Dougherty pointed to Van Ness. "Nightmare number two. If we don't keep the fire from jumping Van Ness, we'll lose Pacific Heights, Golden Gate Park, the Sunset, the Richmond, maybe even the Presidio. The whole Western Addition, the damn thing could burn all the way to the ocean. Won't be a building in the city left standing."

"The whole bloody city," Schmitz croaked. "Thirty-five thousand buildings. Dear God."

A lanky fireman ran into the teeming ballroom, a pair of binoculars dangling from his neck. "Chief Dougherty, Chief Dougherty!"

Everyone turned to listen.

"I've been up on the roof, spottin'. It's a bloody miracle. Colonel Morris, he used so much dynamite on the east side of Van Ness he blew the fire out! Busted windows for a mile but damn if he didn't blow it out! Somehow a couple of Spring Valley water guys hooked up a hydrant a block or two from Van Ness and the boys doused all the sparks."

A cheer resounded throughout the room.

"That's not all, sir," the firemen said. "The wind shifted. Chinatown is gone, but the fire didn't jump Broadway. It's blowin' toward the Barbary Coast."

Schmitz checked the map. "My God. If we move all the firefighters from Van Ness to the Ferry Building, we can use water from the Navy's pumper boat to hold the fire back until it burns itself out on the Barbary Coast. Save the waterfront. We do that, it's over."

"Whoa, that's invitin' trouble," Dougherty argued. "It's too early to pull those men off Van Ness. If it flares up, won't be anyone to stop it."

"If we lose the waterfront, we lose the lifeblood of the city," Schmitz argued. He stared at the map. "Victory is at hand, gentlemen. Chief Dougherty, I want all your men moved from Van Ness to the Ferry Building, as quickly as they can get there."

"I don't like it," Dougherty argued. "My men haven't eaten or slept in twenty-four hours. You move all those men and equipment, it will be impossible to move them back."

"They'll do what needs to be done, Chief." A triumphant look spread across Schmitz' face. "Bertrand! Find General Funston and tell him to stop the dynamiting immediately. No more dynamite, understand? Then send someone to the Presidio and telegraph Washington. Tell President Roosevelt the city is out of danger."

"A bit premature, Eugene," Donen offered sternly. "Maybe you better look out the window."

"Thank you for your input, Chief Donen. You all have my orders."

Donen walked to the back of the Fairmont ballroom, staring at the mountain of flame advancing on the Barbary Coast. Three feet from the enormous window, he could feel the heat radiating through it.

Earlier that day, he had been as impressed with Schmitz' uncharacteristic decisiveness as had everyone else in the room. Now, Donen was convinced that the grinning buffoon had returned.

"Washington likes to hear good news," Schmitz announced to anyone in earshot. "President Roosevelt is not one for pessimism. He'll think twice about indicting me now."

Dougherty walked away in disgust.

"Mr. Mayor," Chief Donen called. Schmitz raised an eyebrow and moved to the window, apart from the others. Their faces reflected the glowing hues that seemed to dance on the window. "If the fire is winding down like you say," Donen offered, "we're going to have to make a report. The higher the body count, the harder it's going to be to rebuild the damn place. Who the hell is going to invest in a deathtrap?"

"How could we ever count the dead?" Schmitz countered. "You heard what Dougherty said earlier. The fire is well over two thousand degrees, exactly what it takes to cremate a body."

"Precisely. The papers will report any figure you give them. No way to ever count 'em up proper."

"Thank you, Jessie. Your civic-mindedness never ceases to impress me."

Donen looked across the massive ballroom at the city's business leaders. Many of them were Schmitz-haters a day earlier. Now all of them worked harmoniously, managing tables with handwritten placards denoting their assignments: Restoration of the Water Supply, Relief of the Hungry, Citizens Police, Restoration of Abattoirs. Nineteen committees in all. Schmitz had included all of the city's leaders except Rolf and the Supervisors, a calculated move to distance himself from the threatened *coup d'état*. In the midst of a horrific crisis, his instinct for self-preservation had survived intact.

"Your popularity seems to be on the rise, Mr. Mayor," Donen added with a pursed smile.

"Nothing like a little war to boost a man's public image," Schmitz replied.

He turned and addressed the others. "Gentlemen! Despite the difficulty, the city has drawn upon its great resources to steer us through this trying hour. This should harken a new era of cooperation and community that will last a lifetime!"

No one seemed overly moved by the homily, perhaps due to the conflagration, fifty stories high, that framed the grinning Schmitz.

From the roof of his mansion, Adam Rolf watched the stream of civic leaders that continued to arrive at the Fairmont. Above the GRAND OPEN-ING, APRIL 18 sign on the roof, the flames and smoke obscured the sky.

"Kind of ironic, isn't it?" he said to Tommy. "I own that charlatan Schmitz, and here I am at the front door, not even invited to the party."

"Makes you wonder what the world's coming to, boss, the lack of gratitude and all."

"I've been thinking about something, Thomas. That little faggot Pierre, timid as he was, where did he find the blarney stones to hang himself like that? No. Seems to me like Pierre might have been hung contrary to his own free will."

"I don't know who would do something like that," Tommy said, returning Rolf's stare. "Seems real lean on potential." Tommy stood there for a moment and considered strangling Rolf and throwing him off his own roof when they were interrupted.

A bloody, disheveled man appeared behind them.

"Ah, Mr. Scarface," Rolf called. "Since you're alone and missing an ear, shall we assume your encounter with The Brotherhood was only marginally successful?"

"Depends on your way a' thinkin', Mr. Rolf. We killed Feeney and Christian Fallon. And poor Mr. Spreckels. His place up and caught fire with all them valuable papers in it."

"Who does that leave us then?"

"The Fagen brothers and Fallon's youngest kid, the college boy."

"The Stanford graduate and Francis Fagen. Congratulations. You killed the dumb ones and let the two smartest cops in the city walk. The ones most likely to put us behind bars."

"It ain't over yet."

"And my elusive papers, the ones that provide the road map to our mutual gallows?"

"They probably burned up somewheres, most likely Feeney's house."

"Mostly likely," Rolf bristled. "And who put the bullet in Christian Fallon?"

"Yours truly."

Rolf looked back over the city, waving his arms as though conducting the symphony of explosions. "Look at that, will you? Frederick Funston, blowing the city to pieces so he can save it. A bloody genius at work. Every one of those little explosions rings my cash register. Remind me to put him on my Christmas list."

"I can raise a few men and go after the Fallon kid and his pals, Mr. Rolf," Scarface offered.

"Hunter Fallon saw you put the bullet in his brother?"

"Standing maybe ten feet away when I done it."

"And he thinks I put you up to it. That's the danger of educating a cop. They start thinking. No. I think we'll just sit tight and wait for him right here."

Rolf pulled a cigar from his vest pocket, clipped the end and handed it to Scarface, clipped one for Tommy, and a third for himself. "All told, it's been a pretty good day," Rolf said. He looked at Scarface's bloody cheek. "Give or take an ear."

Tommy, growing more wary of Rolf by the minute, watched as they puffed away.

It is doubtful any of them took notice of a solitary man below, dressed in a filthy duster and struggling up California Street.

Lincoln Staley, his features so obscured by dirt it's doubtful anyone would have recognized him, stopped under the vast portico of the Fairmont. He caught his breath as best he could and headed toward the hotel lobby.

A bellhop dipped a silver ladle into a brass tub and offered him a drink. Lincoln sipped slowly, the cool water stinging all the way to his spastic stomach. "Much obliged," he said, and accepted the offer for another. "I apologize for the appearance."

"Hell of a grand opening, isn't it, sir?"

Lincoln nodded politely, fingering the derringer in his pocket. He walked outside on quivering legs, fighting another wave of nausea. He leaned against a pillar, his eyes on the mansion across Mason Street.

Chapter 61

——··◇··——

GOLDEN GATE PARK

APRIL 19, 1906. 6:44 A.M.

Kaitlin Staley stirred next to the great tenor, against whom she had cuddled for warmth throughout the night. She forced herself to sit up, jabs of pain from sleeping on the cold, damp ground reawakening the ache of the previous day's treks.

Caruso teetered to a sitting position next to her, stretching for his toes.

They noticed it at the same time. Spread out on the trash-strewn lawn was a sea of human beings. Acres of them, each family huddled together and clinging to the things they prized most. Victors and Gramophones, stacks of musical recordings, tubas, bass fiddles, string guitars, sewing machines, fur coats, favorite suits, straw hats with flowers and bows, felt hats plumed with pheasant and egret feathers, oak chopping blocks, an enamel bathtub filled with a life's effluvia, brass cooking pots and iron sauté pans, prized carving knives, framed photographs of weddings and baptisms, crutches, roller skates, bicycles, scores of dogs and cats of every breed and disposition, leather baby carriages with sleeping pets and infants, wagons overflowing with boxes of precious documents.

"I never see so many sad peoples in my life, Kaitlin." Caruso stared skyward. There was no sun, no moon or stars, not a speck of blue, nothing but rolling patches of smoke above a pale gray haze, with shafts of amber light occasionally slipping through. He had no idea what day it was, if it was sunrise or sunset.

"We're safe here, Enrico," Kaitlin offered.

"They tell me thees every places we are go."

331

She clutched the arm of the once heroic figure, noticing how much smaller he seemed than on stage. The cool breeze, blowing steadily throughout the night from the Pacific Ocean just a few miles west, suddenly shifted.

The air warmed instantly, the faint roar of the fire two miles away became a mounting crescendo that woke many of those sleeping around them. The cries of frightened children melded into an unnerving symphony.

Kaitlin wrapped her arms about her knees, rocking softly, tortured by the horror her foolishness had caused her father. She muffled a sob and gazed out over the array of pitiful souls. It looked to her as if a giant wave had thundered ashore and left behind its human flotsam.

An old woman, who seemed to be wearing every stitch she owned, begged change for a dollar, as if there was something on which to spend it. She passed a young man clutching at something bundled in shelving paper as other people, possibly his friends or family, urged him to release it. He handed it over, and a child's hand flopped loose, dangling lifelessly.

Kaitlin let her head sag so Caruso would not see her tears. *If my father was here, he would know what to do.* And she sobbed some more.

Caruso spotted a teamster with a one-eyed mare pulling a dump wagon. He grabbed Kaitlin's hand, jerked her to her feet, and ran to flag him down.

"'Ow much to take my friend and me to boats?"

"Three hundred dollars."

"Three hundred dollars? This is, 'ow you say? Robbers?"

"I took a Hansom ride two days ago," Kaitlin argued, "and it cost two dollars for the whole afternoon."

The teamster reached for his buggy whip. "Price of poker goes up closer you get to Judgment Day."

"Wait," Caruso said as he stared at the flames and smoke billowing above him. "We are not wait for whole city to burn up, *poof.*" He counted out three hundred dollars in gold coins into the teamster's hand.

"A wise decision there, *paesano.* Climb on up."

Caruso took Kaitlin's hand and helped her on. He was halfway on himself when the wagon jerked and nearly spilled him over the back.

In seconds, the carriage was thundering down Fulton Street, taking corners on two wheels.

"I think you're right," Kaitlin said to Caruso. "Maybe San Francisco is a little crazy."

Chapter 62

NOB HILL

APRIL 19, 1906. 9:33 A.M.

In the ballroom of the Fairmont, a bone-weary Eugene Schmitz dozed in a silk upholstered chair, the first rest he had gotten in more than twenty-four hours.

Bertrand grabbed his shoulder and shook until the Mayor jerked awake. "Mayor Schmitz, sir. You better come up to the roof. Now, sir." Schmitz forced his eyes open, struggled to clear his head, and wobbled toward the stairwell with Bertrand, Donen, and a wheezing Dougherty trailing close behind.

On the roof, Schmitz stared at the fire eating its way toward them, up the eastern slope of Nob Hill.

"That pocket around Union Square was safe," Dougherty raged, "the fire went right around it!"

"A police officer saw some soldiers break into Delmonico's," Bertrand answered sheepishly. "They lit a fire in the kitchen stove to make coffee. They caught the place on fire."

Schmitz stared, disbelieving, as the fire moved up toward the most expensive real estate in the West. "Remind me to have Funston court-martialed and shot," he said to Donen.

Schmitz marched to the other side of the roof and looked above Rolf's mansion. His heart sank at the sight of a long, thin tail of smoke trickling skyward from Van Ness. Seconds later came the sound of three explosions.

"What the hell is that?" Schmitz asked.

"Looks like smoke, sir," Bertrand answered.

"I can see the smoke, Bertrand. I want to know what those noises are! I thought Funston was going to stop the dynamiting!"

"That's not dynamite," Donen responded. "It sounds like cannon fire."

A second plume of smoke began wafting skyward along Van Ness.

"It's flaring up again, dammit," Dougherty said. "Maybe telegraphin' Washington how great things were was a bit premature after all."

"Bertrand, send a messenger to the firefighters we pulled off Van Ness. Have them return to their former positions."

Dougherty fumed. "After they lugged all that heavy equipment down to the Ferry Building, you want them to haul it back up Van Ness?"

"That's what I said," Schmitz answered, his patience at breaking point. "Get the car, Bertrand. We're going to pay General Funston a visit."

"Sir, I can't do ten things at once," Bertrand pleaded.

"Then get nine people to help you! Grab all the maps and situation reports and evacuate the hotel! After I deal with the General, meet me at the Fort Mason Officers' Club. If the fire makes it that far, we can strip to our drawers and swim to Sausalito from there."

"Strip to our drawers and swim from there, yes, sir."

Schmitz charged outside and climbed into the passenger's side of the Ford. He looked anxiously over his shoulder at the flames advancing up Nob Hill toward the Stanford mansion.

Donen cranked the Ford and jumped behind the wheel as Dougherty settled into the back seat behind Schmitz.

They approached Van Ness as the explosions grew louder and more frequent. "Funston won't need a court-martial when I'm through," Schmitz stated angrily. "I'll just have him hung and call it civil defense."

Donen stopped the car at Van Ness near Clay as soldiers fired a cannon at an apartment building on the east side of the street. The iron ball ripped through a fourth-floor window and tore off half the roof. The shot from a second cannon shattered the wall and sent the building crashing into the street.

While the men reloaded, Donen slipped the Ford into gear and roared up next to them.

"General Funston?" Schmitz screamed. The soldiers pointed to their ears and shook their heads in bewilderment.

"Funston!" Donen screamed, running three fingers across his shoulder to indicate stripes. The soldiers gestured toward the bay.

Funston was reading a map atop a caisson full of dynamite when they arrived. He set the map aside and sauntered toward them as slowly as he could, his bloodshot eyes bulging from his grimy face. "What the hell is it this time?"

Schmitz was distracted, staring toward the bay. Through the Golden Gate streamed a small flotilla led by the flagship of Admiral Goodrich.

"What the hell do you want?" the General demanded. "I've got work to do."

Schmitz leaned his face closer to Funston's. "Yes, you do, General. Your first job is to stop. I told you hours ago to stop the dynamiting. I did not tell you to replace the dynamite with artillery fire! I want you to send runners to every dynamite team and artillery position and order them to stop at once. The Navy's here. I want you and your men to assist them and the fire department in any way they require, understood?"

"You forgot who is giving the orders here, Mayor Schmitz."

"That's right, General, I did. But it all came back to me. You have no authority in civilian affairs unless granted by President Roosevelt. If you disobey my orders, I will have Chief Donen haul you off to jail in Oakland where you can stay until your court-martial. Now, stop blowing us all to hell, and help us put this damn fire out while there's still something left! Is that clear, General?"

Funston wheeled about and started toward a nearby artillery team. He held his hand up just as they were about to fire.

On Nob Hill, from behind the wall of the Crocker estate, Hunter and Francis studied the Rolf mansion. They were convinced that only Rolf, Tommy, and Scarface were inside.

In his ruined office, Rolf pulled a folder full of papers from his safe and gave them to Scarface, then handed a box to Tommy. Rolf closed the heavy door and turned the dial.

"You two go ahead," Rolf said. He reached into his desk drawer, withdrew a revolver, and stuffed it into the pocket of his coat.

He was halfway to the door—Tommy and Scarface already in the front hallway, near the front entrance—when the door exploded inward.

Tommy and Scarface dug for their guns as Francis burst in with a smoking shotgun, Hunter right behind him.

Tommy fired, the bullet whizzing inches from Hunter's neck.

Scarface fired wildly, missing Francis, and bolted toward the library.

Francis' next blast caught Tommy flush in the chest, ripping him open like a ripe melon. He was dead when his hulking form hit the oak floor.

Scarface ran into the library across from Rolf's office, where he leapt over mounds of fallen books. He banged through the swinging door at the rear and entered the main dining room, his boot heels crunching through piles of broken crystal and shattered china.

Hunter made the dining room as the door to the kitchen was swinging back. He took several steps and launched himself a few inches above the ground, crashing headfirst through the door.

Scarface was waiting on the other side. When the door burst inward, he fired at where he thought Hunter would be, splintering the door chest high.

Hunter slid across the floor, firing wildly. One of the shots tore through his opponent's calf.

Scarface stumbled backward through the kitchen's rear door and into the hallway. He dragged himself down the hall, toward the servant's entrance in the rear, leaving behind a bloody trail.

Hunter sprang to his feet and followed cautiously. Peering into the hallway, he spotted the rear entrance ajar and Scarface limping down the steps. Hunter approached the rear porch. "Drop your weapon!" he screamed.

Scarface wheeled, raising his revolver.

Hunter squeezed his trigger: the cylinder would not move. He squeezed again, still the gun would not fire. He spotted a fragment of metal shell casing wedged in the cylinder. He dropped to a knee, popped open the cylinder, and dug at the hot sliver.

Scarface aimed, snarling, "Nice work, cop!"

Francis ran toward the rear entrance, saw Hunter crouching, Scarface towering just ahead of him, his gun pointed.

A shot rang out. Then another.

Scarface toppled over.

Hunter cleared his revolver and pointed his gun at Scarface just as the big man crashed to the ground.

A filthy man in a filthy duster stood in the circular driveway, his smoking derringer pointed at Scarface, who convulsed on the ground, blood foaming in his mouth. The man in the duster walked over and took Scarface's gun. He kept his gun trained on the prostrate man until the shaking stopped and a final breath escaped Scarface's lungs.

"You a cop?" he asked Hunter.

"We're both cops," Francis said as he emerged, his gun pointed at Scarface's body.

"I'm Sheriff Lincoln Staley. I'm looking for my daughter, Kaitlin."

"She's with Enrico Caruso," Hunter said. "We sent them to Golden Gate Park. She was fine last I saw her."

"Much obliged. You should always carry a backup weapon, young man. These little derringers come in real handy."

"We better move," Francis said to Hunter.

They heard footsteps behind them.

I had my hands up before they could raise their weapons. I breathed an enormous sigh when I saw that Hunter and Francis were unharmed.

"Rolf, is he dead?" I asked

"Not unless he died of fright," Francis said. "I got him manacled in the other room. Let's grab him and get the hell out of here."

After refusing our pleas to accompany us, Lincoln left for Golden Gate Park to look for Kaitlin.

Hunter, Francis, and I guided a scowling Adam Rolf up California Street, toward the waterfront. On Van Ness, we passed rows of weary soldiers as yet another fire sprang to life along the east side of the boulevard. A groan traveled up and down the ranks.

We arrived at the Hunter's boat. Francis loaded Rolf aboard and climbed in next to him.

The dozens of fires had merged into three major infernos. The only areas untouched by the conflagration were North Beach and Telegraph Hill.

I climbed aboard the boat and reached out for Hunter's hand. He hesitated and looked at me.

"You're a good sailor, Annalisa, you and Francis can handle the boat."

"This is getting to be a very old story, Hunter. Where are you going this time?"

"After the documents Christian hid at the house. Without them, my father might have died for nothing."

"You can't go back there, Hunter. It's crazy."

"The fire's not there yet and we need those papers."

It took all my strength to mount even the feeblest debate. "Don't do this, please. I'm begging you. The wind can change again, the fire can move."

Hunter stared at Telegraph Hill, silhouetted by the flames eating through the Barbary Coast behind it. I realized it was not the papers drawing him back.

"Hunter, it's a house, not a life," I pleaded, tottering from fatigue. "We can rebuild it, you and I. Please, Hunter."

He gently pressed my arms against my sides. "That house is all that's left of my family, Annalisa. It's safe now but if things change, I won't give up without a fight."

Hunter kissed me, an act that set my head spinning further. He dropped me into Francis' arms and shoved the boat clear of the wharf.

Before I could scream, we were twenty feet from shore and Hunter was running down the pier.

I sat down hard in the boat and looked toward the Ferry Building, to a sight that might have rallied my heart had it not been leaden with fatigue.

Preparing to dock were five ships of the Navy's Pacific Squadron, their decks crammed with young sailors and Marines, many of them with fire hoses coiled around their shoulders.

------•⟨∞⟩•------

Chapter 63

THE EMBARCADERO

APRIL 19, 1906. 1:10 P.M.

At the Spear Street pier near the Ferry Building, Eugene Schmitz paced fitfully as the *Chicago* was secured to the dock. The Mayor's face was drawn, his eyes bloodshot, his mouth unable to raise an ounce of spittle.

Hundreds of sailors and Marines lined the decks before him, ready to face the biggest inferno men had ever fought. The gangplanks fell and the young men charged ashore, not a trace of fear in any of them.

At the head of the column, a lean man in an officer's uniform approached. "You Mayor Schmitz?" he asked calmly.

"Yes." The Mayor's voice was barely audible.

The officer motioned to Ensign Arthur, who handed over a canteen. Schmitz guzzled and passed it to Dougherty.

"Admiral Goodrich, at your service, Mayor Schmitz."

"This is Police Chief Donen and Assistant Fire Chief Dougherty. The situation is ugly and getting uglier. Every time we have a grip on it, the wind shifts and the fire outflanks us. Our problem is lack of water."

Schmitz brushed soot from atop a bollard and unrolled Sullivan's map. "This street is the city's widest boulevard, Van Ness Avenue. Right now, the east side is in ruins."

Donen touched Schmitz' shoulder and pointed toward Russian Hill. The buildings on its eastern slope, facing Telegraph Hill, had begun to smoke and embers had begun to glow along the roofs. One by one, the houses burst into flame, the fire racing up the hill, rooftop to rooftop, gaining momentum until a fireball arched into the sky.

Schmitz clutched his chest, having taken almost all he could stand.

"We have to evacuate the city, Mayor Schmitz," Dougherty barked. "Washington Square is full of refugees. If the fire races down the hill and hits North Beach, you'll have thousands trapped."

"Chief Donen. Take the car and get every police officer and soldier to evacuate the city!"

"The only way out is the waterfront," Donen replied. "We're going to need boats, every damn boat we can find."

He ran to the Ford and sped away.

"Commander Badger," Goodrich yelled to a stocky man standing behind him. "Send out launches, commandeer every barge, fishing boat, pleasure craft, and ferry on the bay, I don't give a damn who they are or what their business is. At gunpoint if necessary. Establish an evacuation line the entire length of the waterfront."

"Aye, aye, sir."

"Alright, Admiral," Schmitz said, trying to shake the fatigue. "Van Ness. If the fire leaps to the west side, it will burn to the Pacific Ocean. A couple of thousand buildings, Golden Gate Park, the Presidio."

"Is there a place we can dock near there?"

"There's a pier at the foot of Van Ness. The second line is the obvious one," Schmitz gasped. "This waterfront is everything. If we can't hold the fire back, we'll never evacuate all these people. Without the docks and piers, we might never rebuild this city."

"How long is the fire line along the waterfront?" Goodrich shouted over the roar.

"At the rate it's going, the fire on top Russian Hill will spread down the eastern slope to North Beach, then follow Montgomery Street to the waterfront. We have a few hours maybe, depending on the wind. The fire on the east side of Van Ness—the western slope of Russian Hill—is already headed this way. That's maybe three miles between those two fires. If they link up, the fire line would be that long."

The scope of it gave Goodrich pause. "Three miles. And what about Van Ness?"

"We have to save the west side of it. At least a mile," Dougherty replied, "from the bay to California Street. That's four, four and a half miles of fire lines we need between the whole lot. Can you do it?"

"I have five ships, a thousand good men, and more than five miles of hose. We can pump a greater volume of water, faster, than anyone on earth. If there's any chance it can be stopped, we will stop it."

Goodrich motioned Ensign Arthur over. "Divide the men into two teams, Ensign. Signal one team to dock at the foot of Van Ness, that wide street on the edge of the fire line, and run hoses to the highest point of the hill. Have the other half of the crew run hoses along the waterfront and be prepared to save these buildings."

"Aye, sir."

Goodrich turned again to Schmitz and Dougherty. "We can run our hoses along the waterfront directly from the ships but we'll need your pumpers to attack Van Ness."

"They should be there by now," Schmitz replied, and turned to Dougherty.

The old man was already hurrying toward a passing buggy. He flashed his fireman's shield, shoved the driver off, and seized the reins. Before Schmitz could call to him, Dougherty was gone.

"I'll be setting up a new command post at Fort Mason," Schmitz told Goodrich. "Right at the foot of Van Ness there. These people are going to need everything we can muster when this is over."

"We'll take it from here, Mayor." Goodrich saluted and ran back aboard his ship.

Dougherty sped along the waterfront to Van Ness, whipping the unwilling horse up the cluttered street toward the jaws of Hell. Exhausted firemen lay next to their equipment, unable to lug their pumpers another foot. On the east side of the street, building after building was ablaze.

Dougherty charged among his men, screaming with all the fury his tired lungs could muster. "Get up, dammit, you lazy bastards! No man lies down until the job is done, understand me? Pull these engines and run those bloody hoses! Any man caught slacking on the job, he answers to me! Get up, dammit, and do your bloody jobs!"

Enraged by Dougherty's taunts, the filthy men rose, tears streaming down their swollen faces, and dragged their hoses and engines.

At the Ferry Building, spent firefighters and soldiers witnessed a miracle. Hundreds of sailors and Marines trotted toward them, rolling out hoses, coupling brass fittings, and organizing fire lines with mechanical precision. Some passed out canteens of water and rations, seizing hoses from exhausted men, who collapsed to their knees, weeping, unable to open their broiled fingers. A gravelly cheer sped along the fire line.

Hunter Fallon was unaware of any of it. After witnessing the fire billowing above Russian Hill, he had to struggle upstream against the crowd abandoning North Beach. He labored up the slope of Telegraph Hill, the temperature climbing with each weary step, his clothes little more than sweat and soot-caked rags.

He paused at the summit, a half-block from his house, sipping from a canteen and struggling to catch a breath that did not sting his lungs.

Hunter gained momentum the final hundred yards and stumbled into the house, his boots crunching over layers of broken glass.

He ran down the basement steps to the wine cellar. In the dim light, he discovered his laboratory in rubble. All four of the fifty-five-gallon wine barrels had rolled from their mounts, crushing his slides and test tubes like a steamroller, and yet the barrels had not yielded a drop.

He pried open a wall panel normally hidden by the wine barrels, and removed the telephone recordings, photos, and affidavits that Christian had hidden there the previous day. Stepping gingerly over the wreckage, he took a shovel and dug a deep hole in the dirt floor, the earth so cool he finished the hole with his bare hands.

He buried the evidence along with Kaitlin's diary, which he had found on the table. He ran to Byron's bedroom on the second floor, which was littered with smashed furniture and shards of broken mirrors.

In the bathroom, Hunter shoved a pail beneath the faucet, rejoicing when water streamed out. He filled his canteen and drank, wincing as the water hit his parched throat, and then splashed his burning face and neck. The faucet sputtered to a stop.

The kitchen faucet did the same. The sound of the inferno a half mile away on Russian Hill built into an endless, rolling thunderclap that shook Hunter's house, rattling the doors and shaking loose slivers of glass from the broken windows.

He covered his ears and put his head down. *Think, dammit, think*. He sipped from the canteen. Then it hit him.

He ran back to the basement, retrieved an ax, and chopped through the wall to the steep yard alongside the house. He found a block and tackle, squeezed through the hole, and tossed the pulley rope through an upstairs window.

In minutes, he was hoisting pails of Byron's wine to the second floor.

At the Powell Street pier, Kaitlin clung to Caruso as the frightened crowd surged around them. "Passengers only," a young seaman yelled in his high-pitched voice. "No luggage, no nothing. Bodies only."

Caruso noticed Dolly Cameron shouting orders to a group of terrified Chinese girls, not a word of which they understood. Caruso waved to a young sailor on board the ship and then pointed to the Chinese girls. The young man was about to turn away when he noticed the pleading in Caruso's face. He signaled for the girls to be handed up.

Caruso seized the smallest of the Chinese girls and tried to lift her to the ship but could not reach. Kaitlin climbed atop an abandoned steamer trunk, grabbed the girl, and thrust her into the sailor's arms. Caruso and Kaitlin boosted the girls aboard until their arms ached.

Dolly, Kaitlin, and Caruso were pulled aboard.

On deck, Kaitlin slumped against the cabin wall next to Caruso, leaning her head against his shoulder.

The sailors cast their lines, trying to ignore the pleas of the terrified people they left behind. The boat maneuvered out into San Francisco Bay, gingerly weaving through hundreds of bobbing vessels laden with refugees.

"'Ell of a place. I never sing here again," Caruso muttered.

On Van Ness Avenue, firefighters came alive as Marines and sailors spliced hoses to the barren pumpers.

A sailor at the crest of California Street waved his semaphores. A mile away, sailors aboard the *Slocum* turned the giant wheels. Water rushed uphill, puffing and straightening the feeder line. One by one, the hoses splaying from the fire engines jerked to life, their precious streams lashing at the mounting fire.

Soldiers seized the hoses and rallied the firemen. Neighbors, hopeless and defeated minutes earlier, charged from their homes to join the fight. On the side streets west of Van Ness, ladders appeared and people climbed on roofs to slap at the sparks and flames with wet towels and pillow slips.

At St. Mary's Cathedral on Van Ness, young Father Charles Ramm rose from prayer to fulfill a promise made hours earlier. He filled a knapsack full of wet towels and began to scale the outside of the church tower, digging his toes and fingers into gaps and cracks. Soldiers ran to his aid with a twenty-foot ladder. By the time they raised it, he was already out of reach.

The heat and effort caused Father Ramm to stall just below the spire; the worried crowd shouted for him to retreat. He wrapped a wet towel around his neck and climbed the final twenty feet to the steeple.

Near the top, he clung precariously with one hand, slapping at the flare-ups with a towel held in the other. When he extinguished those sparks, he moved horizontally around the steeple, battling others.

Atop Telegraph Hill, Hunter finished stripping the living room of things flammable, throwing the last of the furniture out of the windows. His efforts were met by a hail of sparks pouring in, stinging his face and arms.

The sparks danced across the oak floor like fireflies. Hunter grabbed a wine-soaked towel and slapped at them. When the towel ignited, he tossed it in a metal pail and seized another, lashing furiously as flames started climbing up the walls.

He recoiled as a shadowy figure appeared in the doorway.

"At least you didn't try to shoot me this time."

"Annalisa, what the hell are you doing here?"

"I jumped ship to a small schooner heading in to pick up refugees. I figured you needed me more than Francis did."

I cupped my hand and scooped liquid from the pail and had a sip. It burned like acid.

Hunter quickly uncorked a canteen and passed it to me. "Sorry, I thought you had noticed. That was my father's best Zinfandel in years."

I caught my breath. The wind shifted and the sparks subsided. I hugged him and gingerly kissed his tender, dirty face.

We gazed from the window, our eyes so dry and bloodshot it hurt to open them wide.

The side of Russian Hill that faced us had yet to catch fire. Unburned, as well, was the Montgomery Street corridor below and Telegraph Hill where we stood.

The venomous smell of blistering paint and varnish told us that was about to change. Soldiers ran from house to house and shop to shop, ordering everyone out.

People poured into the streets and alleyways, running north down Stockton and Powell and Montgomery toward the waterfront, the heated air began to pulsate, like giant hands clapping against everyone's ears. Small flames, like a thousand tiny candles, suddenly began to glow on the rooftops.

"Here it comes," Hunter said, pulling me down so that our eyes were barely above the sill.

A giant tongue of flame suddenly shot down Russian Hill. It danced across the rooftops, tumbled through the air in great swirling balls, ripping through the wooden corridors of Union and Filbert Streets, igniting everything it touched.

When the flame reached the bottom of the hill, a crosswind sent it rushing down Montgomery toward the waterfront, incinerating all before it like toy figures tossed into a blast furnace.

We watched in abject horror as the flame tore across Washington Square, igniting trees, bushes, and human beings.

The firestorm disappeared down Montgomery, leaving Russian Hill and Montgomery Street ablaze, the odor of flaming buildings and burning bodies drifting up Telegraph Hill.

The fire clap blocked the moans and screams from the poor souls below. We thought to run to their aid but knew the effort would be in vain.

"Telegraph is next," Hunter said. "We have to move."

He soaked a towel in the wine as sparks again poured through the window. "You hit the rooms," he shouted. "I'm going up to the roof. Remind me never to install wood shingles."

I ran to the small dining room and slapped at sparks. They pitted the floor wherever they landed, crackling like Chinese fireworks when the towel struck them. I tried to cool my face in a wine-soaked towel, crying out as the alcohol hit my skin.

Hunter shinnied up a porch column and pulled up several pails. He ran across the shingled roof, slapping at a shower of embers.

Along the waterfront, sailors and Marines, soldiers and firefighters stood with their backs to the piers as several fires rushed toward them. Fueled by a wind behind it, the inferno gained strength, growing taller and more ferocious as it advanced.

The *Chicago*, *Marblehead*, *Boston*, and *Princeton* opened their pumps. Along the three-mile stretch of waterfront, the air filled with towering plumes of water that vaporized before they reached their targets. Admiral Goodrich and Commander Badger ran along the lines, shouting through megaphones to spur their men forward.

Anxious evacuees lining the docks turned to watch as the young sailors advanced.

From the middle of the bay, Enrico Caruso watched the blaze reach crescendo, an undulating kaleidoscope of molten gold and pale rose with streaks of purple and splotches of darkest crimson. The fires' colorful reflections quivered on the water as the ceaseless roar echoed off Alcatraz and Angel Island.

"A thousand feet high, the flames," the young sailor told Caruso. "Navigator just measured it."

Kaitlin stirred. She and Caruso could see Telegraph Hill, like a stone mountain refusing to yield to the flames.

In the dining room of the Fallon house, flames trickled across the floor, backing me into a corner. I lashed out with a wine-soaked towel until it caught fire, then flung it into an empty pail and seized another. I was dismayed to find it was the last one. I fought back, sick with exhaustion, and still the flames advanced, so close they threatened to ignite my clothes.

My eyes closed against my will and I could feel myself teetering. The hiss and smell of burning wine forced my eyes open, to the sight of Hunter pouring pails of it across the floor, dousing the flames surrounding me.

His face was suddenly next to mine, hands clapping at my blouse to extinguish tiny sparks, his voice so hoarse that every word sounded like a whisper.

"We've got to get to the roof. Can you make it? Annalisa! I need you on the roof! Annalisa!"

I nodded and stumbled forward, the boiled wine scalding my bleeding knees. The pain jolted me awake. I screamed. Hunter jerked me to my feet.

"Stand up! Stand up, Annalisa, or we'll die."

He pressed a towel to my swollen face, hoping the pain inflicted by the alcohol would revive me. I groaned and pushed him away, the shock helping to steady my woozy head.

"I need you on the roof. Can you do it?"

I nodded and followed him outside, where Hunter pushed me onto the roof. Using a wooden door as a shield, its varnished surface smoking and blistering, we climbed to the peak of the gable roof.

"Annalisa! Annalisa, I need you to soak the towels and drop them to me."

We were in the eye of a maelstrom. Below us to the east, fire advanced on the central waterfront. To the west, flames raged along Russian Hill and North Beach; to the south the Barbary Coast burned unchallenged. If we could hold off the sparks and firebrands, we had a chance.

Hunter soaked a towel and handed it to me, motioning over the side. I nodded, my eyes swollen so that I had to tilt my head back to see through narrow slits. The closest fire was still a quarter-mile away, advancing from Washington Square to begin its ascent up Telegraph Hill.

I crawled down the roof to the edge, where Hunter propped the door up, one end in the gutter, the other against a broken rake handle. He took the rope on the block and tackle and tied it around his waist. With a wine-soaked towel over his head and neck, he lowered himself down the side, swinging in a giant arch while slapping at the flames.

After a dozen awkward swipes, the towel dried up and blistered paint stuck to it, burning his hands. He threw it back to the roof and tried to scream, but the fire clap drowned him out. I crawled from behind the makeshift shield and doused the burning towel in a pail, trying to avoid looking at the forty-foot drop.

I chucked the towel back over the edge and he barely caught it in his outstretched hand. A rainbow of sparks fell on the roof behind me. I crawled up the hot shingles, grunting as I walloped away.

Along the waterfront sailors and Marines tore strips from their shirts, wrapping their hands to protect them from the heat of brass nozzles and couplings. Flaming debris drifted over their heads and onto the deck of the *Princeton*. Teams of sailors trained their hoses on the ship. Up and down the line, men fainted while others advanced to take their places, pulling the fallen ones to safety. The hissing of steam grew incessantly as the blaze fought back, hungry to jump the wide Embarcadero and devour the hundreds of wooden docks and warehouses.

But the young men refused to yield.

On Van Ness, Dougherty's men saw their maniacal leader everywhere as the battle line of fire and firefighters wavered back and forth. Giant clouds of steam and vapor billowed along the inferno's edge, the product of massive streams of salt water.

The fire leapt the west side of the boulevard and surged two blocks. The Assistant Chief roused an army of soldiers and volunteers to counter-attack, beating at the flames with their shirts, tearing at bits of burning wood with bloody hands.

At the Fallon house, the situation had shifted. The fire in North Beach and Russian Hill had slackened, victim of its own avarice, moving toward the northern waterfront. The main fires had passed us by. All that remained a threat were the flames climbing steadily up Telegraph Hill, devouring the houses several blocks below us.

Something mechanical inhabited us, a practiced response that kept us moving. I climbed back down from the roof and filled pail after pail with wine and attached them to the pulley line for Hunter to hoist.

I battled the sparks and flames inside the house while he did the same above. We soaked rags in what little water we had left, wrapping them around our faces and necks, leaving only our eyes exposed.

I watched everything, even my own movements, as though I was outside of my own body, an apparition watching someone who barely resembled me engaged in an absurd task. The pain kept me rooted: my skin crawled, my shoulders ached, and my lungs cried for relief.

Then a miracle arrived. Mercifully, the wind shifted, blowing the fire back on itself before it reached us.

The fire began to die.

I sagged to my knees and sobbed, though not a tear was left in me. I could not tell how much time had passed, what day it was, if the sun had risen or set or if any of those things still occurred. Perhaps I was already dead and this was Hell and the whole thing was about to begin anew.

Hunter scrambled back along the roof as the last halo of sparks drifted down on him. He stamped them out and retreated behind the peak of the roof. He rolled to his side and for an instant, drifted to a dark, dizzy place where he could hear his mother's voice.

I limped out on the porch, barely able to see, and drained the last drop of water from my canteen, the warm liquid burning all the way to my stomach.

Hunter jolted awake and crawled, sick and spent, back to the peak of the roof, where he stared toward Montgomery. The fire was almost gone: several houses, including ours, had been spared.

He lowered himself to the ground and entered the house, returning with a canteen he had hidden in the basement to keep cool. He doused my face and forced me to drink. I gagged and placed my hand over my swollen lips, forcing the water down again.

We collapsed beside each other on the porch. In seconds, we were asleep. The nightmares came instantly, more hideous than any I could ever imagine: crushed children and burning women, rats with gleaming eyes, and devils laughing at people being tortured. I saw my parents racked by plague, Byron drowning, Christian bleeding in the street, and Hunter being burned alive.

Only exhaustion kept me from awakening.

Chapter 64

———◦◦◦———

TELEGRAPH HILL

APRIL 21, 1906. SUNRISE

When Hunter and I awoke hours later it was from the sting of fresh water on our faces. I coughed and rose up halfway, afraid to touch my face. I heard Hunter gag and cough. I tried to open my eyes but my eyelids would not budge.

"Hold still," a soothing voice said. "Open slowly."

I felt cool water running over my face again, seeping into my eyes and freeing my eyelids. I could hear Hunter cough again as water was poured over his face and neck.

Hunter struggled to a sitting position, gasping for breath and reaching out for something to help anchor the spinning in his head. Somehow, my fingers wrapped themselves in his. It helped steady and comfort me.

"Hunter. It's Doctor Genovese, Hunter. Do you understand me? Hunter!"

The best Hunter could do was grunt.

A cup was placed against my lips and, despite the burning, I forced a swallow.

"Take it easy, both of you. Real easy." It was a male voice that I did not recognize at first.

Flashes of light shot through my head and a wave of pain wracked my body as I was pulled to my feet. My skin was on fire, every bone and muscle ached, every movement stabbed with bolts of electricity.

"Annalisa, it's me, Francis. Take another sip."

He pressed the cup to my lips again. I gagged, coughing soot through my nose and mouth into the cup.

"I'm Dr. Genovese, a neighbor of the Fallons," the other man said as he dabbed an ointment on my face.

Hunter managed to look at me, scarcely recognizing the puffy face and soot-encrusted hair of the woman he had asked to marry him. I looked back in shock. Blisters and soot covered his cracked face. His eyes were almost shut, his lips and tongue so swollen he could barely mumble.

My mind began to steady and my vision cleared. The wind had freshened and the sun carved long shafts through the gray, swirling dust. The smell of ruin was everywhere.

I recognized Francis' face—though ragged and sweat-stained, he appeared unharmed. After the Navy had commandeered the boat he was using to take Adam Rolf to authorities in Oakland—Rolf had been freed yet again—Francis attempted to come to our aid, only to be driven back by flames. He had gone to the Mission District and joined three thousand residents who used a single working fire hydrant to save their neighborhood.

There were other, no less astonishing tales I would learn.

At Rincon Post Office, employees had used mail sacks to beat out flames in a struggle that lasted twenty-four hours. The Mint was saved by its superintendent, Frank Leach, Army Lieutenant Armstrong, Fire Captain Brady, and a few dozen courageous men.

The fire line along the western side of Van Ness Avenue had wavered numerous times, but held. Young sailors and Marines had made the difference; with residents and firefighters, they had refused to yield the Western Addition.

Hunter and I fought to gain our bearings. Francis and Dr. Genovese spooned some sort of canned vegetables into our mouths, the first food we had consumed in days.

"I want to show you something, Hunter," Francis said. "Can you walk?"

We could barely hear, the fire still pounding in our ears. Francis and Dr. Genovese took us by the arms and got us moving forward.

We descended the porch of the Fallon house and walked across the cobblestones, still hot beneath our feet. Our clothes were so crusted with wine, sweat, and soot that we crackled with each step.

We stumbled to the edge of Telegraph Hill and forced our eyes to open wide enough to gaze at the waterfront below. The entire stretch of the Embarcadero was covered with a blanket of murky soot and ash. As the wind stiffened and the air continued to clear, we could see the soot shift and undulate as something stirred beneath its surface.

Slowly, shapes began to form. First heads, then torsos, then arms, and knees, all black with soot. Soon entire figures emerged, as though the dead were rising from their graves. We strained to keep our eyes open, stunned and disbelieving, as hundreds of civilians, firefighters, sailors, and Marines rose from the places where they had collapsed from exhaustion. Many had their hands still tied by rags to their fire hoses. Some crossed themselves; some crawled onto their knees and prayed.

Behind them, the Ferry Building was still standing. Along the waterfront, every pier and warehouse was soiled but intact. Not a single one had been lost.

Epilogue

—◦◦∞◦◦—

TELEGRAPH HILL

MAY 30, 1906. 8:00 A.M.

When you first dream of becoming a writer, you never know when the chance might come, or whether you have the gifts the task requires. You wonder if you will ever craft the indelible line, record a treasured character, expose some festered evil, offer up some moving insight. You never dream the opportunity might come as mine has, a jolt in the night, a call when least prepared, an event so momentous that no matter how inventive the effort, how deft or impassioned the juggling and re-arranging of your thoughts, the words still seem trifling.

I have done what I could. I mixed first person observations with third person reportage, as did my hero Nellie Bly, stirring together observation with hear-say, conjecture with fact. Light and shadow, terror and mirth, heartbreak and romance, all blended as well as I am able.

I used the diaries of Kaitlin Staley and the expansive letters she has sent—the post office has never stopped working—nearly a dozen letters, all crafted in a marvelous, flowing hand. In her most recent, Kaitlin, now sixteen, vows to return and create "elegant but inexpensive fashions" to replace those lost in the fire. She was wandering the docks of Oakland when Lincoln spotted her. Lincoln's journal had burned up in the Palace Hotel, but he has graciously sent an account of both his travails and his grand journey with the great Caruso. Just yesterday, the third of his correspondence detailed his killing of Scarface with a derringer.

Ting Leo has been adopted by a Chinese doctor and his wife in Berkeley. Through a translator, I interviewed her about her frightening adventures. The twelve girls we rescued from Ah Toy's are safe and adapting to life with Donaldina Cameron.

I found much of the interchanges between Rolf and Schmitz in the barely literate scrawlings of Tommy Biggs, who probably planned to sell his notes and recollections to the highest bidder after Byron Fallon finished with him. I took license in recounting moments between Rolf and Tommy, Donen and Schmitz, Antoine and Tessie Wall, but as I stated at the beginning of this account, I believe the essence of what transpired as accurately as possible.

I have been informed by Fremont Older and the new prosecutor, Mr. William H. Langdon, that corruption charges against Eugene Schmitz, Adam Rolf, and their cohorts at City Hall will soon be presented to a Grand Jury. General Funston, it is rumored, may face a military tribunal.

Hence, I am ordered to change a name or two, to make composite some elements to avoid any conflict with judicial efforts. The law, Older and Langdon assure me, will render the ultimate truth. Another firestorm is brewing—perhaps even larger than the one we just witnessed—this one in a court room. I pray when it is finished that justice will finally have its day.

One hundred years from now, when the world looks back on our tragedy, I want them to see the human face of it. I pray they learn that Schmitz and Funston were not our heroes; that the feeble Mayor's sudden decisiveness and the little General's boldness merely hastened our demise. Hell will have a special place for Adam Rolf and Eugene Schmitz, Jessie Donen and John Kelly, Scarface and Ah Toy, who all thrived on the misery of others.

Fire Chief Dennis Sullivan lingered for four days, until the last embers of the fire died, as though his spirit were a part of it. In one hundred years, I would like people to remember him. I would like them to know of Hunter Fallon and his father and brother. Of a group of young men they called The Brotherhood, a fearless Chinese girl named Ting Leo, and Kaitlin Staley, a young runaway who came in search of Shangri-La and found more than she ever dreamed. Perhaps they will remember me as well, Annalisa Passarelli, a newspaper reporter and opera critic, and my friend, the great Caruso.

Most of all, I would like them to remember a fabled city that is no more. For this is the story of San Francisco, a place so unique we will never see her likes again.

But the story does not quite end yet.

Sometime after dawn this morning, Hunter entered the barren living room, where I was typewriting in a sea of ash.

"Are you ready?" he asked.

I nodded, looking up at him, a tinge of pink remaining in his once-ravaged face. The blue eyes, Byron's eyes, sparkled again.

"I am ready, Officer Fallon."

I held his arm as we descended the south side of Telegraph Hill, to Union Street, as a clanging trolley car approached. A golden light illuminated the scorched hills around us. *"La luce splendida,"* we whispered together, the spirits of Gioia and Giuseppe, Byron and Isabella and Christian palpable among us.

We climbed aboard the trolley where a tall man turned and doffed his slouch brim hat. "Officer Fallon. Miss Passarelli. I guess this is quite appropriate. The first passengers on the maiden voyage of the restored Union Street trolley line, a mechanical Phoenix rising toward our glorious future."

"Mayor Schmitz," Hunter nodded. "I hear things are getting lively down at City Hall." Schmitz was unaware that while Hunter recuperated, he had been aiding Prosecutor Langdon in the renewed graft hunt.

"Let us say they are always interesting, but I am confident that I will be exonerated." The Mayor handed us a newspaper, a joint effort by the city's publications, with his photo and a bold caption underneath.

> "Our fair city lies in ruins, but those are the damndest,
> finest ruins ever seen on the face of the Earth," said
> Mayor Eugene Schmitz.

Schmitz was grinning when I handed the newspaper back to him.

Hunter and I rode silently up Union Street, dressed in clothes we had borrowed from Francis and Eleanor Fagen, whose house in the Western Addition had been saved by the valiant effort on Van Ness Avenue. Hunter was dressed in brown herringbone English tweed, the sleeves an inch too long, and his father's bowler hat, which we found hanging near the wine barrels. I was in a lilac silk afternoon dress with white lace, crossover bodice and three-tier banded skirt, topped with a white, broad-brimmed bonnet with a plume of pheasant tail.

Not that it really matters.

Near the summit of Russian Hill, we stared down at the dusty ruins of Chinatown on our left. Beyond Chinatown, several square blocks of the Barbary Coast had miraculously survived. A song had already been composed in tribute.

"If God spanked San Francisco for being so frisky/Why did he burn the churches down/And spare Hotaling's Whiskey?"

We passed the aftermath of the firestorm on Russian Hill. Scarcely a structure stood and nothing remained unscathed.

At Van Ness, St. Mary's Cathedral stood by the inspired efforts of Father Ramm and a cadre of true believers.

Close by the cathedral was a row of newly burned buildings. Days after the fire had burned out, General Funston's dynamite teams tried to level a row of damaged structures. The flaming debris rained down over several blocks. Before irate firefighters could extinguish it, the blaze had added twenty-six buildings to the toll.

Everywhere, the usual sounds—honking horns, shouting merchants, squealing children, Caruso on the Victor—had been replaced by the churning of a paddy shovel, the clanging of steel hammers, and the bite of saws. The first building was raised four days after the fire died out. A new edifice was now rising every four minutes.

We asked the gripman to stop at Union and Webster Street, where we laid a rose near the spot where Christian and Carlo fell and read the Lord's Prayer for both of them. Hunter was calm and stoic, reading with a tiny streak of emotion in his voice, the pain seeping through the brave face just before he finished. I stammered through most of my part.

When we reached the end of the Union Street line, Hunter doffed his hat politely to Mayor Schmitz. We crossed Lyon Street and entered the Presidio, where a buckboard carried us to a hill above a cemetery

At the hill's crest, overlooking rows of fresh white crosses, we took our place behind three couples waiting patiently in line before Father Yorke.

"Do you, Rose Galante, take Neil Figurelli to be your lawful wedded husband?" asked Father Yorke.

"I do."

The good Father blessed them, they kissed and moved aside.

I gripped Hunter's arm, adjusted my hat to shield my eyes from the brightening sun, and stepped ahead.

"Do you, Thomas Cahal, take Donna Antonelli as your lawful wedded wife?"

"I do."

"Rosalind Rubenstein, do you take Randolph Johnson as your lawful wedded husband?"

"I do."

We stepped forward to face Father Yorke.

"Are you keeping busy, Father?" Hunter asked.

"I switched from wakes to weddings last week," he replied. "Just married a fireman and a woman he chopped out of a burning building. Married a hundred people this week. I think it's living in parks and tents that's doing it, cookin' and eatin' together' in the streets, like a big social gathering. Rich people, poor people, black and white, it's like the Devil brought out the saint in everyone. Never seen anything like it. More weddings than I've done in five years."

"That is a good thing," I said. "Hopeful."

"I hear the restoration committee promoted Francis to fill your father's vacancy on the detective squad," Father Yorke replied, opening his Bible.

"Francis wants to be Chief of Detectives someday. If I don't beat him to it. He and I are surrogate fathers to Christian's children."

"I expected no less. You're your father's son, which is the best I can say of any man. I can see him plain as day in you." Father Yorke had to take a breath and steady himself.

"And you, Annalisa, ain't a man alive who wouldn't love a gal that did what you did."

He recited some words I scarcely remember.

"Annalisa Passarelli, do you take Hunter Fallon as your lawful wedded husband?"

"I do."

"Hunter Fallon, do you take Annalisa Passarelli as your lawful wedded wife?"

"I sure do."

I reached up and kissed Hunter, my eyes wide open. Other than our fleeting encounters in adolescence, I had known him six weeks. In that brief time, I had seen more in him than I had dreamed possible in any man.

I do not know what will become of Hunter and me and of the great and terrible City as it begins anew. Those who God blessed with our very lives will be marked forever with "survivor" beside our names.

For now, that is enough. Whatever the future holds for the new San Francisco, it will be blessed with one thing.

It will have a Fallon looking over it.

In fact, it will have a few.

"Hunter and Annalisa Fallon, you are husband and wife. May God bless you for all your days."

Of one thing I am certain. Enrico Caruso will never again sing in San Francisco. "I prefer Vesuvio," he told a reporter as he was boarding the eastbound train.

I cannot say I blame him.

ACKNOWLEDGMENTS AND AFTERWORD

The writing of this novel was a six-year adventure that would never have succeeded without the help of the following people.

First and foremost, my most loyal friend and manager, Peter Miller, has stood by me when lesser men would have folded. Gladys and Richard Hansen of the San Francisco City Museum have devoted their lives to unraveling the distortions in the events of April 1906, and have provided their archives, insight, and support from the day of conception. The support of Steve Chicorel in all aspects of my career has been invaluable, as has that of my personal assistant, Lauren Gee.

Len Amato, President of Spring Creek Productions, was the first person outside of my personal enclave to hear this story and recognize its strength. His support, friendship, and counsel have been invaluable.

I had an army of dedicated researchers and personal editors. My wife Katie; Cy Bowers, Angelo Hazifotis, Lorraine Flett; the wonderful novelist Mary Wings; my sometime writing partner Lidia Fraser; "Citizen Jane" Alexander; Tim McDowell; Tony Mastrogiorgio, Barbara Brennan, my friend and ally Paul Aratow, Kenn Fong and Maitland Zane of the San Francisco Chronicle. A special thanks to Brooks Parsons for his constant needling for me to finish, and to his three sons, Anthony, Hunter, and Christian.

I would like to acknowledge Richie Corsello, Karl Dakin, Steve Haun, and my directing partner Ben Burtt, who are united in our efforts to expand awareness of this story via a documentary, *The Damndest Finest*

Ruins. The discoveries we made in that effort have helped dramatically in the writing of this novel.

Two great minds saved me when the *1906* effort seemed daunting and incomplete. The first was Otto Penzler, owner of New York's marvelous Mysterious Bookshop, who refused to let me produce anything less than my best work, and to one of the great freelance book editors in the business, Lou Aronica, who spotted the flaws that turned the corner in my effort.

To Nion McEvoy and Jay Schaefer of Chronicle Books, who care passionately about their work and have fun doing it: through them this book is now a reality.

And thanks to Lew Hunter, who made me think that a truck driver's son from Cleveland, Ohio, could actually do this.

Finally, with great joy and sadness, I acknowledge the inspiration and friendship of Ken Kesey. When I was twenty-three years old, a friend took me to Oregon to visit him at his farm. There began a friendship that lasted thirty years, until Ken's death. That first meeting led to the founding of the Santa Cruz, California, Poetry Festival with Lawrence Ferlinghetti, Allen Ginsberg, William Burroughs, Charles Bukowski, Ken Kesey, and where I came of age as the youngest writer on the bill.

Ken Kesey may have been the most civil and intelligent man I have ever known. I am still wounded at his loss: the world is a much less interesting place without him.

On April, 18, 1906, the city of San Francisco, wealthiest and most influential in the American West, was struck by an earthquake and subsequent fires that burned for three days. It was the worst natural disaster in American History, our most catastrophic event outside of war. Twenty-nine thousand buildings were destroyed. The death toll was fixed by city officials at 478 so as not to scare away investors: the death toll was easily 5,000, perhaps double that. The city's corrupt mayor, Eugene Schmitz, has long been heralded as a suddenly decisive leader who rallied a chaotic city when, in fact, his decisions contributed to the horror. These falsehoods have endured for a century.

On the day of the earthquake, the biggest corruption hunt in American history was underway in San Francisco, authorized by President Theodore

Roosevelt and aimed at prosecuting Mayor Schmitz and his entire regime. It was part of an attempt by Roosevelt to destroy Boss Rule in America and challenge the power of big business and broad "trusts" to corrupt every aspect of urban life. During and immediately after the chaos of the fire, the men under investigation struck back at their enemies.

Annalisa Passarelli, Kaitlin Staley, her father Lincoln Staley, and Ting Leo are all fictional. Also fictional are the Fallons (Hunter, Christian, father Byron), though the death of Byron is based on San Francisco's most celebrated unsolved mystery, the death of reformist Police Chief William Biggy, who in 1908 disappeared from the police launch on San Francisco Bay after a meeting with the Graft Hunters.

Mayor Eugene Schmitz is portrayed as accurately as possible, as are Fire Chief Dennis Sullivan and his wife, Margaret. Enrico Caruso is very accurate, with one uncertainty: no one knows for sure if he sang *Che Gelida Manina* from his window at the Palace during the fire/exodus.

Adam Rolf is a composite of several men, including Abe Reuf, the city's corrupt political boss at the time.

The prosecutor in the novel, Charles Feeney, is based on Francis Heney, who was gunned down in the courtroom during the corruption trials that followed, not blown up in his house during the fire. Abe Reuf's favorite method of eliminating people who stood against him was to dyamite their houses: he did it three times attempting to silence James Gallagher, President of the Board of Supervisors, who survived to become a key witness in the trials. The burning of the Spreckels mansion, many historians believe, was an attempt by Abe Ruef's goons to destroy evidence that Spreckels was hiding for the corruption investigation, which he was helping to finance in an attempt to break Abe Reuf's stranglehold on the city. Spreckels' wife Eleanor gave birth to a baby girl on the sidewalk as her house burned. The documents were actually in another Spreckels' mansion in the city.

The sequence of the fire is accurate hour by hour, neighborhood by neighborhood, including details of Mayor Schmitz having to move the command center three times in order to stay ahead of the blaze.

The original Emperor Norton and Shanghai Kelly had already died by 1906, but others periodically assumed their names and habits; I've kept the originals, and some other colorful characters alive as they were just too memorable to be left behind.

The events are real: this was San Francisco, and this is what happened. I deferred, at every juncture, to a simple notion: that no one named Rhett Butler fought in the Civil War, nor was he acquainted with a woman named Scarlett O'Hara and yet, where would our understanding of that turbulent moment in American history be without them?

—JD